Frost Publishing

To those souls who gave me love, love and more
love! Thank you for sharing.

Your Husband, My Lover
Your Husband, My Lover is published by
Frost Publishing.
Printed In The United States of America
Cover Design by Acropolis, Inc.

ISBN: 0-9614624-6-9

Copyrighted August 1985, TXU206-511

Frost Publishing
606 N. Wymore Road
Winter Park, Florida 32789
(407) 644-9611
E-mail FROSTWINN @aol.com

JENNIFER RAIN

YOUR HUSBAND
MY LOVER

Part One

*I*t all started out in Marksville, a small Tennessee town. On April 1, 1932 April Fool's Day and Easter Sunday, Aries Able entered the world kicking, screaming and searching for her Mama's nipple. Brown haired, brown eyed and beautiful, she was her Mama's pride and joy. Soon they nicknamed her "Little Brown Sugar."

She was reared on a farm three miles outside of town. It was the remains of what was once a Southern plantation. During the Civil War those Yankee soldiers came marching through burning down houses, tearing up everything and scaring the women and the slaves half to death. Aries remembered the tales her German Grandmother told about the war days and she knew for sure that no Southerner cared for the likes of any damn Yankee.

The war was over but the old timers still relived it time and time again. Parts of log slave cabins lay scattered about the farm. The slaves were gone now but there were lots of poor niggers nearby who bore the Able name. Their parents had been slaves on the Able land and their offspring, probably bastards or half breeds, were given the family name.

Niggers provided good cheap help and Mama Able always had several working about the house and yard. They were paid wages of about five dollars a piece a week which, in those days, was a lot of money.

Aries's recollections of early childhood were vague although several incidents were embedded in her memory. One in particular was that of her Mama leaving her at home. She remembered running down the driveway screaming after Mama as she drove away in her 1927 black Chevrolet When her car vanished from sight Aries lay face on the ground in the red clay driveway, sobbing and clinging to her brown milk bottle, a big brown beer bottle. Her sisters and the helper were standing on the front porch yelling, "Stop that crying and come on in the house." Having a mind of her own, she ignored them.

It wasn't easy being the fourth child of five, all girls, with older sisters always bossing her around. Pop was the only man in sight, most of the time, except for tenant farmers who stopped by occasionally.

Outsiders were rarely invited to the Able house. Mostly, Aries associations were strictly with family. Of course, there were plenty of relatives like both grandmothers who lived in big houses up the road about a mile apart, cousins, aunts and uncles. Her favorite was Pop's younger brother, Uncle Ross, who was a frequent visitor.

By age three, Aries was becoming bored playing with dolls and being left at home. She wanted to go to school so she could learn to read the funny paper. After much begging Mama sent her one day with her older sister, Angie. The day was a disaster and when Angie got home that afternoon she vowed that would never take her again. Aries had disrupted the class by flirting with Angie's boyfriend, Frank. The entire class was laughing and the teacher got real mad. After this complaint she was put back to pasture. Two years later, Mama took Aries to the schoolhouse, lied about her age and got her admitted to first grade.

For the next few years, Aries was content with the learning experience. After school there was homework and when tired of studying she would saunter to the slab pile in the barnyard. Climbing atop, she used it as a stage where she was the performer. There she sang, danced and pretended she was a movie star, like Shirley Temple. Sometimes, her younger sister, Betina, accompanied her but, of course, Aries was the star.

Aries was growing up and although studying was very important to her so were boys. She was developing physically and beginning to look more like a girl than the tom girl she actually was. Mama had given her a book about what happens at puberty but embarrassed, she certainly didn't intend to let anybody know when this happened to her.

In fifth grade, she had a crush on Tom Greer, a slender, dashing, green eyed, freckled blonde, the son of a country doctor. Tom was on the short side but he was mighty handsome and the sight of him set

2

her heart pounding. He was somewhat elusive but Aries was on the chase and her infatuation with him lasted until he went away from home to military school.

Soon after he left she developed an interest in a football player from Boonestown, thirty miles north of Marksville. As a cheerleader she attended a football game there. Surveying the lineup of the opposing team, her eyes fell upon a slender dark-haired player as he ran onto the field carrying his helmet. Standing beside her girlfriend, Donna, Aries jumped in excitement.

"That's the one I want," she squealed pointing to him.

"Look at him, look at him. I'm falling in love. I believe I'm falling in love," she exclaimed waving her arms. "Let's look in the program and find his name."

"What's his number?" asked Donna.

"His number is 40 and gosh, is he a dream!"

"His name's Bill Matson and he's a quarterback," Donna told her excitedly.

"Now, how are you going to arrange meeting him?"

"Don't worry about that, just leave it up to me."

"Well, going into the boy's locker room is off limits."

"I'm not about to do that, silly, but I could ask him for his autograph after the game. When I do, I'll introduce myself."

"What if he's got a girlfriend?"

"So what if he does. There's nothing wrong with my telling him I'm Aries Able."

"Well, while you're at it you might as well get the autograph of Number 24 , too. I like his looks, he's my type!"

"I'll try."

Boonestown won the game! Marksville was disappointed but still Aries had to accomplish her goal of meeting Number 40.

"Come with me, Donna. You don't have to say a word but please, come with me."

"Okay, if you insist."

The girls headed to the locker room entrance to wait for the players to make their exit. Soon they started filing out. Aries spied Bill Matson quickly and catching up to him she asked for his autograph.

His deep blue eyes twinkled as he looked her straight in the face. Like a hero he said, "Sure," smiling. "And what's your name?"

"I'm Aries Able."

"Well, Hello, Miss Able. You girls did a fine job of cheering your team along this afternoon. Too bad they lost."

"Hey, don't rub it in. I'm sorry, too. Maybe they'll win next time."

At that moment, the boy Donna wanted to meet came up.

"Hey, Matson, introduce me to your friends."

"Aries, meet Carl Warner."

"Hi."

"This is Aries. I can't introduce you to her friend because I haven't met her, yet."

"Oh, This is my friend, Donna," Aries chirped in.

"Hi, it's nice to meet you."

"We'd better hurry or the bus will leave us," Aries commented.

"Tell them to go without you. Let's go for a sundae. We'll drive you home later," Bill suggested.

"Drive us home," repeated Aries. "Do you realize how far that is?"

"Who cares, we'll take you home, anyway," Carl interjected.

Donna broke into the conversation.

"Well, we can't stay now."

"We would like to," Aries piped in but Donna's Mom is picking us up when the bus gets there. We'll have to take a rain check."

"What about our coming to Marksville, Saturday night? We could take in a movie," Carl remarked.

"That sounds good." Donna flashed her pearly white teeth, smiling.

Aries scribbled her telephone number down on a piece of paper and handed it to Bill. "Call me after school tomorrow and I'll tell you where we live. We'd better go now or we're going to be in trouble. Bye."

The girls ran toward the bus which had now cranked up and was pulling away.

"Wait for us, wait for us," they yelled. The bus driver stopped the bus and opened door for them to enter.

"Come on you two, shouted a player on the bus. Come on, get your tails in here or you'll be walking home."

4

Out of breath, they hopped in.

Johnny Simms and Doc Brown laid it all over them. "What were you all doing talking to those Boonestown players, anyway? Don't you know they're our enemies? First, they cheat in the game and then, they try to steal our women."

"Lay off you guys. We can talk to anybody we want to. It's just polite to congratulate the other team when they've won."

"Hey, Able stop rubbing it in. We nearly beat those bums."

"Alright, alright."

"Hey, pass me a soda pop, yelled Donna, I'm really thirsty."

As the bus made its way onto the narrow highway heading home the gang settled in and commenced singing Alma mater songs. Those bus rides home from the game were always fun.

The girls sat back in their seats talking about the new fellows they had just met.

"I wonder if they'll really call us," sighed Donna.

"They said they would. I guess we'll just have to wait and see. If they come can I spend the night at your house? Mama makes me come in so early when I have a date."

"Oh, yeah, when is your curfew?"

"Ten o'clock."

"My Mom lets me stay out until eleven.".

"I know. That's why I want to stay at your house."

"Okay, I'll ask my folks if you can stay the night."

Several days later, Bill Matson called Aries. Their Saturday night date was still on and Carl was calling Donna, too. Since Donna's Mom had given Aries permission to spend the night, she gave him directions to Donna's house, instead of hers. Aries had really flipped over Bill. Excited, she called Donna. She said Carl had phoned her, too. The guys would be there around six-thirty on Saturday evening.

"Now I have a real problem," complained Aries.

"What's that?"

"I don't have a thing decent to wear. You've got lots of nice clothes but my big sister gets all the new things and all I have to wear is hand-me-downs."

"Borrow something from your sister."

"I'll ask her but she's really funny about letting anybody wear her clothes. Besides most of her things are too tight in the waist on me. I'll beg Mother to take me shopping for a new dress."

"Hey, Aries, I've got to go now. My Mom's in the car honking the horn. I've got to see what she wants. Talk to you later."

Saturday arrived and after their first date there was no doubt that Bill Matson was her new love.

One Saturday, Aries borrowed Uncle Milton's brand new gray Plymouth on the pretense of visiting her girlfriend, Colleen, in town. Instead, she drove to Boonestown to take Bill for a ride. She had just gotten her driver's license. Bill was working that day at his father's funeral parlor and when she arrived he asked her if she wanted to take a tour of the place.

"Not really, I'm afraid of dead people."

"Oh, come on, they won't hurt you. They're all dead."

Taking her hand, he pulled her down the hall, laughing.

"I'm scared," complained Aries tugging him backwards.

With a plan in mind he led her down the hallway to a door on the right. Opening it, he told her to wait outside.

"I have to get something in there. Wait here for me."

"Hurry, this place gives me cold chills." She waited obediently in the hallway.

Several minutes passed but he didn't come out. Finally she opened the door and started calling him. She knew he had gone in that door but now he didn't answer. Aries looked around the room. Gracious, it was a room full of caskets.

What had happened to Bill?

Aries looked around to see if there was another exit but saw nothing but walls and rows and rows of caskets.

"Bill, where are you? I know you're in here, please answer me."

"Here I am."

She could hear his voice but she couldn't see him. Finally she realized he was playing a trick on her. He had climbed into one of the caskets. Some joke that was! What did he expect her to do, open all of them trying to find him?

"Get out of that casket, get out of that casket, Bill Matson, right

6

now! I don't think this is funny."

Aries waited but got no response. "Well, if you don't get out I'm leaving."

At that moment the lid of the casket beside her popped open and out he popped.

"Oh my God, you idiot," she screamed, "you scared me nearly to death." Aries face was as white as a sheet and she was angry but Bill was laughing his head off.

"There's nothing to be afraid of, honey, There aren't any dead people in here. These are display caskets. The corpses are at the other end of the building."

"How would I know that? Let's get out of here, I don't like being in funeral parlors." She tried to compose herself.

"Okay, let's go." He hugged her.

They went to the drugstore for ice cream sundaes. Nervous about being thirty miles away and feeling guilty for being untruthful about where she was going, soon, Aries high tailed it home.

Bill became her steady beau. They dated for a year and Aries was crazy about him. Their relationship was almost beyond the petting stage but going farther was a definite no, no. Aries was well indoctrinated against having sex before marriage. It was a sin and she would go to hell for committing one. The Bible told her so and Mama told her so, too.

Bill was determined to go further so their dates became more of a battle than just going out for fun. Hot and wild with passion, insistent upon going all the way, Aries would fight him off and make him stop. Disgruntled he would take her home.

Aside from morals, another reason for her refusing sex was the fear of becoming pregnant. What a disgrace that would be! Only those common white trash had bastard babies and dishonored the family name.

Aries wanted to marry Bill but there was high school to finish and college, after that. She rationalized that if he really loved her he would wait.

During the summer she was offered the option of completing high school at Marksville or going away to pre-college at Brenner where

Angie was enrolled. She was envious of Angie's being in college because she got all the new clothes. Now she had a chance to have new clothes and get away from that narrow-minded one-horse town.

With these things in mind she made the decision to enroll in Brenner Pre-College. She was slated to be Salutatorian at Marksville but maybe, she would be Valedictorian at Brenner. Second best never suited her anyway.

Going away to school and living on campus would be a new experience. Just the thoughts of it made her feel important. She had only been away from home once before, to Andrews to 4-H camp. She would miss Bill, her family and friends, too, but this was an opportunity to big to turn down. He would be graduating that year and leaving for college in the fall, anyway.

Breaking the news to him, they discussed plans for visiting at school and for holidays meetings. Their plans were well laid but time apart and the distance placed between them was the beginning of the end of their love affair.

Part Two

At Brenner, Aries was thoroughly involved in her studies and in adjusting to a new life in a dormitory with other girls and a housemother. Her roommate was Eva Collins from Carlton, Tennessee.

Eva had brown hair, freckles and she was about five feet four inches tall. She was sports minded and friendly with a good sense of humor. The girls hit it off instantly. It was apparent they were like "two peas in a pod."

Together, they were dare devils plotting and scheming to see just how many ridiculous rules they could break without getting caught. Miss Pilot, the housemother, had an eagle eye, though, and they got away with very little. Pilot's room was downstairs on the left side of the stairway and in order to get out of the dorm one had to walk right past it. If you didn't want her to hear you coming or going you had to remove your shoes and tip toe quietly. This was difficult because being quiet wasn't one of Aries best suits.

One night, the girls decided to sneak out after bed check to have a smoke. They had picked up this new habit by watching the older girls at Brenner. Neither really could to do it without gagging and choking but they were determined to learn. They dared not smoke in their room because it was against the rules. If caught they would be suspended or expelled. One never knew when old battle ax Pilot would bang on the door and barge in and heaven help them if she ever smelled smoke. Taking a chance just wasn't worth the hassle.

Eva tucked a package of Lucky Strike cigarettes safely beneath her pajama top ready for their escape outside. They had their alibi planned in case Pilot caught them. Eva would say that Aries was sleep walking and that she was following to bring her back to bed. Aries just hoped she could walk past Pilot's room without giggling her head off and peeing in her pants.

"All set, let's go," said Aries.

"I'm ready," replied Eva.

They made it out the front door alright but Eva lost her grip on the front door handle letting it slam shut behind them. They hoped Pilot was asleep and that she didn't hear the door bang.

"Let's hide over there behind that tree. Hurry, so no one will see us," Aries instructed.

"I'm coming, I'm coming," quipped Eva.

They were so afraid of being caught that they wondered if the smoke was really worth it.

Cigarettes finished, they headed back toward the dorm entrance. It was too bad the back door was bolted for they would have felt more comfortable going in that way.

As they reached the door it popped open in their faces. There stood Miss Pilot with her huge frame blocking the entire doorway. She was like a prison guard and Aries, at that moment, felt like an escaped prisoner who had been apprehended and sentenced to the guillotine.

"Well, Miss Able and Miss Collins, good evening, ladies. And where might you two have been in your night clothes?"

"No where, no where," replied Eva nervously. "We haven't been anywhere and we weren't going anywhere, honest, we haven't been anywhere."

"Then, for goodness sakes, explain what you are doing outside at this hour in your pajamas?"

"Aries was sleep walking and I followed her to bring her back. She got up out of bed, sound asleep, went down the stairs and straight out the door. I tried to wake her but I couldn't. Your light was out, Miss Pilot, and I didn't want to disturb you."

"Oh dear, a sleep walker."

"Yes, I was walking in my sleep."

"My, my, you poor thing. Have you ever done this before?"

"Yes, I walked in my sleep once before when I went to summer camp. I was sleeping in a cabin near the lake and I went out the door and walked to the lake. I didn't wake up until my feet hit the water."

"My heavens, dear, how frightening." Pilot's tone of voice was sympathetic.

"Yes, I was very frightened and my Mother was scared, too, when I came back home from camp and told her about it. She was afraid that I might have drowned."

"Well, girls, we'll talk about this more later but now you two had better get back upstairs and into bed."

"We will. Good night, Miss Pilot," said the girls in a chorus.

"Gosh, was that a narrow escape! Pilot really believed our story. It's a good thing our alibi was planned out." Aries giggled.

"Yeah! How did you ever come up with that camp story? I was scared shitless when she opened the door but when you told her that tale, I think she really believed us."

"It's a good thing. That woman is a battle ax and she would have thrown the book at us. Let's get to bed now, we've had enough excitement for one night."

"Good night, Eva."

"Good night."

The duo thought it was all over but Pilot wasn't through with them yet. The next day she sent a messenger to English class. They were to report to her office.

"I wonder what she wants," said Eva.

"I don't know but we'll find out."

Arriving at her office door, the girls poised themselves for ladylike entries.

"Good afternoon, Miss Pilot," they chimed in together.

Without responding to their greeting Pilot asked them to take a chair. She was seated behind a big oaken desk looking mighty stern and bossy. Her salt and pepper gray hair was neatly braided and piled on top of her head and her piercing blue eyes were covered by horn rimmed glasses. She wore a navy blue long- sleeved dress trimmed with crisp starched white collar and cuffs. A long gold chain support- ing an antique gold watch stately upon her large protruding chest. Pilot must have weighed two hundreds pounds. She was tall and big, everywhere, except for her legs. They seemed out of proportion to the rest of her body.

The girls seated themselves in two straight back chairs with faded black brocaded cushions.

Pilot commenced to speak.

"I have been thinking about Aries's problem with sleep walking and I've come to a decision. I have decided to change your room assign- ment from the second floor to the first. I wouldn't want to take the chance of Aries walking in her sleep again and, perhaps, falling down the stairs.

"But Miss Pilot, there aren't any vacant rooms on the first floor. All of the rooms are taken," Aries complained.

"Yes, I know but I have spoken with Polly and Emily and they have agreed to switch rooms with you. I want you and Eva to move your things this afternoon to room l04."

"Room l04," repeated Aries.

"Yes, that's the room next to mine."

The girls looked at each other, absolutely, in shock. The room next door to Pilot was all they needed. There was no way they could get out of the mess they had gotten themselves into this time.

"Miss Pilot, don't make us move, please don't make us move," begged Aries, "I hardly ever walk in my sleep. Instead of moving us, you could put an inside bolt on our door. We could lock it at night and then I couldn't get out."

11

"That's nonsense. I would feel better about it if you were next door to me. I've made up my mind and there's no need to discuss the matter further. You are excused, girls."

On the way back to class dorm, they bemoaned their fate. Nothing could be worse than having to room next door to Pilot. Now they would have to be quiet in their room and they'd never be able to get away with anything.

"I'm sorry, I'm sorry, I didn't mean for all of this to happen," said Aries.

"Don't worry about it. It's a rotten break but it was just as much my fault as it was yours. We'll just have to make the best of it somehow."

Soon after entering Brenner, Aries met, Jose Dominguez, a Spanish boy from Camoguay, Cuba. She was in the campus mail room one day trying to work the combination on her mailbox. She had read the instructions three times but unable to get it opened, she was becoming very frustrated. Suddenly she felt someone behind her and before she could turn away, a dark haired fellow with midnight black eyes grabbed her and popped a great big kiss on her lips. As she struggled to get away from him, he filled her ears with apologies and amorous ovations.

"Forgive me, forgive me, said the handsome young stranger, forgive me for surprising you but you are so beautiful I couldn't resist kissing you. You have such beautiful brown eyes. What's your name?"

Flustered and still in a state of shock, she replied, "Aries Able, what's yours?"

"Jose, Jose Dominguez." In broken English he repeated the words, "You are so beautiful. When I saw you, I fell in love with you. I love you and you are going to be my girlfriend."

Aries didn't know what to think. She had been approached by boys before but never quite like this. She imagined the Spanish must do it differently.

"Let me walk you back to your dorm. I will teach you some words in Spanish if you will help me with my English. I can't speak English so well."

Aries was dumbfounded at this sudden encounter but Joe really was terribly handsome. Maybe she would be his girlfriend. As he walked along side her to the dorm she asked him what his last name was, again.

"Jose Manilito Dominguez y Sanchez."

"Oh my, what a long name! What does Jose mean in English?"

"It's Joe, Jose means Joe."

"Well, that's easy enough. I'll call you Joe."

In the days that followed, Joe acquainted Aries with the customs of his country. He said his family owned sugar factories in Cuba.

"Someday, Aries, I am going to marry you and take you home to meet my family," he vowed.

"You don't waste any time, do you?"

"No, there's no time to waste. When you see a girl and you love her, you tell her and she belongs to you and to no other man. I love you and I am going to take you to Cuba."

"I'd like to go to Cuba. I've never been anywhere but I don't know if my parents would let me go."

As the days went by the two became constant companions. Joe made it clear that she was his girl and he would kill any guy who looked at her. Insanely jealous, he watched her every movement on campus. Aries felt suffocated by his constant surveillance. She warned him if he didn't stop being so jealous she was going to stop dating him. This admonition did little to change him. He was a very head-strong and emotional person.

Finally, graduation day came. They would be leaving Brenner and after the summer, heading for college. Joe had been accepted in Blue Ridge Military Academy and Aries had been accepted at both Dunam University and Wheeler College. The final decision was made by her father. Dunam was private while Wheeler was state supported and less expensive so she ended up a freshman there. Wheeler was an all girls college so her parents liked that better, too. "Keep her away from the boys so she will get an education," Pop advised.

Well, it almost worked. She studied her head off at Wheeler seeing very few boys, except on the weekends. Blue Ridge Military Academy was only sixty-five miles away. Joe came over to visit whenever he could get out on a Saturday pass. Military schools were stricter than regular schools and the restrictions placed upon him gave Aries, at last, some freedom away from him.

Joe's visits usually were only once a week. Aries was glad because his hormones were so active and he was determined to take her virginity. Studies were more important to her those days. They had to be because she had decided to become a woman doctor.

Part Three

Cramer University was located sixty miles away from Wheeler in the opposite direction. The Wheeler girls attended football games there on weekends. On other weekends, the Cramer guys cruised the Wheeler campus. That's how Aries became acquainted with Keith Kiser.

One Friday afternoon she and her roommate, Grace, were walking back to the dorm from the tennis courts when they spied a light blue Oldsmobile convertible coming down the street with two guys in it. As the car came upon them the driver beeped the horn and pulled up to the curb. He asked for directions to the gym.

"It's over there," pointed Grace.

"Thanks a lot. By the way, what are you two young ladies doing tomorrow night?"

"Studying. We have to study for a big Biology test on Monday," said Aries.

"You're studying on Saturday night?"

"Yes."

"Well, we go to Cramer U and nobody studies there on Saturday night. That's our free night. Hey, we're having a big fraternity party to celebrate our Notre Dame victory and we'd like to invite you to be our guests. It's really going to be a blast."

"We don't even know you," said Aries.

"Well, we can take care of that," said the driver laughing. "Let me make the introductions, ladies. My name is Keith Kiser and this is my friend, Huck Horner. And what are your names?"

"I'm Aries and this is my roommate, Grace Ward."

"So nice to meet you both," said Keith, "and now that we've met, will you say yes to our invitation? The party's really going to be a great. We'll have a ball!"

"Are you all football players?"

"Yes, Huck and I both play on the first string team."

"What positions do you play?"

"I'm a right tackle and Huck here is a left guard."

"Oh, I remember you," said Aries, "I saw you play in the Notre Dame game on television. You got hurt that day didn't you? I saw them carry you off the field."

"Yeah," laughed Keith. "I got hurt alright. I sprained my ankle and dislocated my hip."

"I'm sorry. Football must really be a rough game. I really feel bad when a player gets hurt. We'd really like to go to your party but I promised Grace I'd help her study for the test."

"That's okay," said Grace, "we can study tonight and Sunday."

"Okay, you guys have twisted our arms. We'll go."

"Where do you live?" asked Huck.

"Right over there in Jackson Hall," said Grace pointing toward the dorm.

"Great! We'll pick you up there tomorrow afternoon at four. We've got to get back now. Give me your phone number and we'll call tonight and fill you in on all the particulars. Plan to stay at Cramer overnight because it'll be too late to drive back to Wheeler after the party," said Keith, the planner.

Back in the dorm, the girls chatted about the new fellows they had met. "Can you believe we've just been invited to a fraternity party by two football stars? As bad as we looked, all worn out from tennis, they still invited us," said Aries.

"Speak for yourself. I don't think we looked so bad. We're the two best looking girls at Wheeler. If you don't believe me, just ask me," Grace said laughing.

The rest of the evening was spent in a frenzy preparing for the jaunt to Cramer U. Naturally, the plans for studying that evening were laid by the wayside.

The trip to Cramer was a memorable one. There were gobs and gobs of good looking guys there. There were eight boys to every girl on the Cramer campus. This was the kind of school Aries wanted to attend but a woman had to be a Junior to be eligible for admission.. She decided to transfer there as soon as she had enough credits.

Keith stood some six feet three inches tall. He had a muscular, strong, athletic looking body. His brown hair was in a short crew cut style and he had talking blue eyes and a smile that just wouldn't end. What she saw she liked!

They started going steady and so did Huck and Grace. Slowly, Aries was able to convince Jose she wasn't in love with him, that she wasn't going to Cuba to meet his family and he should start dating someone else. He took this news very hard but finally, he faded away in the woodwork.

Her feelings Keith were different than those she had had for anyone before. She wanted to marry him, to be his wife and have his babies. After meeting him Aries had eyes for no one else.

Since they had had the same religious and moral upbringing pre-marital sex was not an option. No matter what, they would wait until they had finished college and were married. They had their moments of wanting to let it all go, of wanting to make wild mad passionate love disavowing the beliefs that made them the moral characters they were. But restraining themselves, they maintained their purity.

It wasn't easy for Aries to keep her virginity in the midst of their passionate love affair. She wanted to be more intimate but always in the nick of time she would break away saying, "I love you, good night," leaving their fiery passion to be subsided only by the streams of water trickling upon them in a cold shower. Parting this way was driving them both insane but their will power controlled their desires. They would wait until they finished college and then, they would marry in the church.

Keith was her idol. Since freshman year she had collected and saved every memento of their relationship and put them in a scrap-book. Her bedroom wall displayed a Keith Kiser poster featuring his football write-ups and pictures taken on special occasions. Everything seemed rosy. Their future was planned but through a quirk of fate, suddenly their whole lives changed.

The sound of Keith's voice, his words the night he called, still resound in Aries memory. She was in her room pressing the dress she planned to wear the next day when the pay phone rang. Janie, the girl next door, ran to answer it.

"It's for Aries," she called.

Unplugging the iron, Aries ran down the long hallway to the phone. The caller was Keith and, as usual, she was glad to hear from him.

"Hi, I was in my room pressing my clothes," she said.

"That's good. I've been at the library studying. I wanted to call you, tonight, to tell you I'll only be able to take you to Fall German dances on Friday. Tommy Dorsey is playing both nights but I have a social obligation coming over from Winstock and I've promised to take her on Saturday.

Aries was beside herself. She didn't take this news lightly. "Social obligation hell," she stormed. "Well, you can just take her to both the dances because I am never going to speak to you again, Keith Kiser." With these words she slammed the telephone receiver on the hook and ran back to her room. Flinging herself upon the bed, she buried her head in the pillow and commenced sobbing, incessantly. Hearing her sobs, Janie came to comfort her.

"What's wrong?" she asked softly.

"Everything, just everything. I'm so furious with Keith Kiser. I've just told him to get lost that I never wanted to speak to him again."

"You didn't mean that! I know you're in love with him."

"In love with him, I can't stand the sight of him," wailed Aries.

Distraught, she bounced out of bed and began removing the pictures and write-ups of Keith, which were displayed on the poster above it. "I'm getting rid of everything that reminds me of Keith Kiser. I don't want to look at his face anymore. I'll show that two timing creep what I think about him and his social obligation."

Part Four

*T*he next day at the college book store Aries met a new friend, Greg Winston. He was a tall, striking blonde fellow, not athletic looking like Keith but quite handsome and definitely a ladies man type. They chatted on the steps of the G building for awhile and then, Greg suggested they take in an afternoon movie. Aries had been feeling rather down since Keith's phone call so she accepted thinking it might help to improve her mood.

After the movie he took her to the Sigma Chi house where she was introduced to some of his fraternity brothers. Greg seemed like a real nice fellow, clean cut with good manners and qualities that her Mama might like. Their meeting had been timely, since she was on the outs with Keith.

On the way home, Greg asked her to be his date for the Fall German dances that weekend. Since she was now without an escort, of course, she accepted his invitation. Keith would probably be furious when he saw her there with Greg but it would serve him right. He hadn't called back to say he was sorry about inviting his "social obligation" to the dance. It might make him realize he wasn't the only male at Cramer U.

After the dances Aries started going steady with Greg. Their dates were unlike the ones with Keith. Greg drank beer while Keith was a tee-toddler. Alcoholic beverages were strictly prohibited for football players. A party to Greg meant drinking. He must have taken up this habit when he was in the Marines. He was more worldly and experienced than she and Keith were. Greg introduced her to drinking. First, to beer and later, to gin with grape juice in a concoction called Purple Jesus. Aries hated the bitter, pungent taste of beer.

One afternoon at a Sigma Chi party, Greg handed her a glass of something that looked like grape juice.

"What's this?"

"Oh, it's like a punch. They call it PJ for short. Sip on it, you'll like it."

Aries tried it and it didn't taste bad. It tasted a lot better than the beer. After one glassful, she was feeling no pain. She accepted seconds. Pretty soon, the swimming pool looked like it was upside down.

"Gee Greg, I'm really beginning to feel funny. I believe the punch is making me inebriated. I can't go back to my dormitory like this. I don't think I could walk up the stairs."

"Don't worry about it, honey, you'll be alright in a little while. Let's get out of here and take a ride. Wait a minute, while I go ask Al if we can borrow his car."

Greg got the car and they left the party.

"Where are we going?" asked Aries

"Oh, we are going to a secret place I know about. What you need is a little nap before I take you back to the dorm."

"Nap," repeated Aries, "and just where do you think you are taking me? I'm not going to any motel."

"I'm not taking you to a motel, I'm taking you out to a castle, a secret castle, where our frat goes sometimes for parties. It's an old abandoned castle. There's nobody there and we can park the car and take a short nap. What we need to do is sober up."

Greg drove out of town to a road that led them, sure enough, to a real castle and he parked the car in back under a big oak tree.

"Let's get in the back seat so we can stretch out and be more comfortable," he suggested.

"Well, okay, if you think we're safe here." Aries head was swimming and she was beginning to feel silly.

Getting into the back seat, they squirmed around trying to get comfortable.

"There isn't room for both of us, you're about to fall off of the seat," she giggled.

"Wait a minute, let me take off these shoes," Greg said. He took off his shoes but he didn't stop with that. Bare from the waist down to his feet, he began smooching and petting her. He was aroused and she

19

found herself responding to his fondling.

"I want to make love to you, he whispered. I need some nookie. Please honey, give me some nookie. Just a little bit."

"I can't, I can't. I've never done it before and I don't know how."

"Relax honey. Just lay down and let me take your panties off. I promise not to hurt you. I'll be real gentle, I won't hurt you."

Not knowing really why she was doing it, Aries did as she was told.

"Now lay back in the seat and spread your legs. Relax, baby." Soon she could feel the head of Greg's penis touching the opening of her vagina. It felt really strange and she was certain that this act was going to be painful.

"Open your legs some more, baby and let me put him inside just a little bit." She opened them as wide as she could because she didn't want to be hurt. Greg withdrew his penis and stuck his finger part way up into her vagina. He began wiggling it and rubbing it across her clitoris. She had read about this in books.

"Now, now, you're beginning to juice up, baby."

Mounting her frame again, Greg spread her legs wide apart and told her to lock them together on his back. He put his hands under her ass and once more, she could feel the head of his hard pulsating penis probing its way inside her. It felt soft like velvet and yet, it felt so hard. It felt good and bad at the same time. Suddenly he thrust his entire penis deep inside her vagina.

Aries screamed, "Stop, you're killing me."

"Take it easy, take it easy, baby. It will only hurt for a little bit, then it's going to feel real good. Trust me."

Trust him, hell. This guy was like a bull and he was tearing her up.

"Wait, wait," wailed Aries.

By now, her pleas were in vain. Greg had plunged his big hard penis inside of her vagina and he wasn't about to stop. He had her where he wanted her and despite her groaning, he was going to finish what he had started. Soon he started to flood cum all over her.

My God, is this what it's like? she asked herself. Greg was hollering and groaning as if he was hurting. She wondered if he was in pain, too? This was quite an experience, an experience she would remember for the rest of her life.

On the way back to the dorm, Aries was sobering up and facing the harsh reality of what had happened. She'd had sexual intercourse for the first time. In a state of inebriation she had lost her virginity to Greg Winston, not Keith. Aries had never intended that he would be the one.

This spur of the moment act was to mold her destiny for years to come. She had sinned and would have to live with that sin. Her moral indoctrination was gone with the wind. She was in a state of shame and no longer fit for Keith Kiser. Now, she had no choice but to marry the boy who had ruined her.

A senior at Cramer U, her ambition was to become a woman doctor but her deep involvement with Greg led to a change of plans. Instead of being a career woman she decided to get married and have children. Pops would be so disappointed. He had agreed to send her to college because he wanted her to become somebody. It looked like everybody else at Cramer was getting engaged and making plans to be married after graduation so why shouldn't she? It seemed like the natural, sensible thing to do.

She had destroyed the opportunity of ever becoming Keith Kiser's bride. How could she? If she married Keith, on their wedding night he would discover that she wasn't a virgin. She had found blood on her panties when she came back to the dorm the night Greg violated her. She filled the tub, soaking her body in the water for a long time, hoping to wash away the fluid he had deposited inside her vagina.

A nervous wreck, Aries was worried that Greg may have gotten her pregnant. Someday, she wanted to have a baby but not now. What a disaster that would be!

Aries's first try at sexual intercourse was more traumatic than pleasing. Her fears of becoming pregnant and the shame of giving herself out of wedlock overpowered any pleasure that might have been created by the act itself. How could she possibly face Keith Kiser again?

That opportunity came a few days, later. She was in the University snack bar when Keith came up behind her. She was startled by his sudden appearance.

21

"Hi, Aries," he said smiling. "Where have you been hiding for goodness sakes? I've been wanting to talk to you, to explain things."

Trembling inside Aries looked at him. She felt like hugging him, burying her head on his strong shoulder and sobbing out her story but she knew she couldn't. Instead, she just stood there acting aloof.

"I've been busy and I don't have time to talk to you. Besides, I don't want to hear any of your explanations."

"Please. I need to talk to you. Please, give me just a few minutes. Let's go outside and sit on the steps in the sun."

"Well, alright but make it short because I need to study before my next class."

They found a quiet spot on top of the wide steps outside the Kenan building.

Keith said he was sorry about the dances. "I told you the truth. The girl who came up really was a social obligation. I've never told you before but I was one of twelve children. My mother died during my birth. My father tried to take care of us but we were very poor. Finally he placed my sister and I in an orphanage. A couple adopted my sister but nobody adopted me. I was raised there until I graduated from high school. I won a football scholarship to college and a kindly man from Wallace agreed to sponsor me. His granddaughter decided to come up to Wheeler for the foot-ball game and the dance. I didn't invite her. Mr. Burns called and asked if I would entertain her while she was here. After all he has done for me I had to say yes. Believe me, Aries, she was just a friend and nothing else."

After listening to his story Aries felt sorry for him. "I'm sorry, Keith, sorry about your Mother and sorry that you didn't get to grow up with your father and your brothers and sisters. I'm sorry I became angry the night you canceled me out for one of the dances, but you can imagine how I felt when I never even knew these people existed."

"Aries, I love you. I want to date you, again. Please don't be mad at me anymore."

"I'm not mad at you but I can't go out with you."

"Why not?"

"I can't date you because I'm going steady with someone else."

Keith was crushed hearing this news.

"Does that someone have a name? Who is the guy that's been cutting in on me."

"His name is Greg Winston. He's a Sigma Chi."

"Sigma Chi. That joker must be in the house across the street from ours. How long has this been going on?"

"Since the night of the dance. When you invited the other girl to the dance, I went to the dances with him."

The expression on Keith's face changed. He looked like he had lost his best friend.

"But Aries," he muttered, "I thought you were my girl. I thought you loved me and that someday, we would get married."

"I did love you and I did want to marry you but things have changed."

"Changed, changed how?"

"Things have changed because now I'm committed to someone else."

"You aren't engaged to him, are you?"

"No, but he's going to pin me, soon."

"Is that what you want?"

"No, yes," replied Aries nervously.

"No, yes, what do you mean? You aren't making a bit of sense."

"Maybe not but that's how it is. Go find yourself another girlfriend because I'm not available."

Keith looked at her in astonishment. Aries was certain that he didn't believe a word she was saying. "I can't talk anymore," she said, as she picked up her books. "The bell is ringing and I'm going to be late for class."

"I don't understand you, Aries," he called behind her. Walking briskly on, she pretended not to hear his words. She dare not look back for huge tears were pouring down her cheeks. She was still in love with him. If only she could tell him what happened and if only he could understand.

Their encounter had taken her by surprise and she hadn't rehearsed the performance she had made. If she had maybe she would have said something else or maybe she'd have said the same thing, differently. It was too late now. Someday she would tell Keith the truth about why she couldn't see him anymore, but not now.

Keith called that night begging her to change her mind about not going out with him. Aries gave him a flat, no. As the weeks went by she became more and more involved with Greg.

One day he received a phone call from his father in Florida, telling him that he needed him to work in his store during the season. Greg would have to take the winter quarter off from school. He broke the news to her that evening. "It's only for three months, then I'll be back in school," he said.

"Three month's," repeated Aries. "That's a long time. Do you expect me to sit at home and be true to you?"

"I wouldn't want you to go out with anyone else but no, I don't expect you to sit in the dorm for three months. If you want to go somewhere I'll get my buddy Woody to take you. He's my best friend and I know I can trust him."

"Well, that's a lot to ask of a girl who isn't even pinned to you."

"Is it important to you to be pinned?"

"Of course it's important. If you're going steady and you aren't going out with anyone else, being pinned is like a pre-engagement."

"Do you want to marry me, Aries?"

"Is this a proposal?"

"Yes, I'm proposing to you. Will you marry me?"

"No, no, not unless you get down on your hands and knees and beg me," she teased.

Greg got down on his hands and knees folding his hands in front of him. "Aries, I love you, will you marry me?"

"Yes, yes, I'll marry you. Now get up off your hands and knees." Aries smiled.

Greg took his fraternity pin off and pinned it on her sweater. It was all bordered with pearls and rubies with the Sigma Chi emblem in the center.

"It's beautiful, I will wear it always. I love you, Greg." She put her arms around him and kissed him.

"Now we are engaged," he said. Promise me you'll call Woody whenever you need anything while I'm gone. The time will pass quickly and I'll be back before you know it."

"I will. I promise to call Woody if I need help and I promise to be true to you.

"That's my girl." Greg was smiling.

That Saturday evening the Sigma Chis' all gathered outside Spencer Hall in a group below her bedroom window. At eleven o'clock, they began serenading her. This was customary for a new pinup. The sounds of their male voices in unison was breath-taking. All of the girls on the hall watched the affair as Aries stood by her window, listening. When it was over she waved to them and thanked them.

Greg took her to dinner the night before he left for Florida. After dinner, they drove again in Al's car to the scene of their first crime and repeated it. It was a little different now that they were pinned. Greg said it was alright for them to make love since they were engaged and after graduation, he promised to replace the fraternity pin with a diamond ring. "You're mine," he said.

That night Greg promised to be careful not to get her pregnant. Aries knew nothing about contraceptives. Greg had been unprepared the first time but this time he put on a rubber. This made her feel more secure until afterwards when he broke the news that the rubber had broken during intercourse.

"Be sure to take a douche when you get home," he warned.

"Douche, what's that?"

Greg looked at her and laughed.

"You really don't know much about these things, do you? A douche is something ladies take after having sex, to cleanse themselves."

"I don't have any," Aries replied.

"We'll go to the drugstore on the way home and get you all fixed up." Arriving at the drugstore, she told Greg she was too embarrassed to go in and ask for a douche.

"Don't worry, you wait in the car and I'll go in and get it. Just tell me what size you need."

"How would I know? I've never bought one before in my life."

"I'll ask the pharmacist what to buy."

Greg made the purchase and Aries tucked it safely away in her handbag. She wouldn't want any of the girls to know she had a douche because then they would know she'd had sex.

After Greg left for Florida Woody Fenton called. "Greg told me to take care of you so if there's anything you need just give ole' Woody a holler."

"Thanks, Woody. I really don't need a thing but if I do I'll call you."

About a week later Keith called and invited her to go with him to a Sigma Nu fraternity party.

"I can't go, Keith." Aries heart sank as she spoke those words because she was dying to see him.

"Why can't you go? Are your legs broken?"

"No, I'm fine but I am pinned to Greg Winston. He's not in school this quarter. He had to go to Florida to help his father during the winter tourist season. I couldn't be seen with someone else wearing his fraternity pin."

"Well, we can solve that problem. Take his pin off and I'll give you mine. "Come on, Aries, go to the party with me. It's a costume party and we can go in disguise and nobody will recognize us."

"Costume party? What are you going to be?"

"I don't know yet. Meet me in the park this afternoon and we'll try to figure something out."

Starving to be with him, Aries agreed to go. She decided to take the chance of not getting caught. The shindig was on the outskirts of town and no outsiders would be there. It was a closed party just for Sigma Nus" and their dates. None of them would squeal on them to the Sigma Chi 's.

They met in the park at two that afternoon and aside from having a happy reunion, they planned their costumes. After some deliberation they decided to symbolize the song, **A Penny A Kiss, A Penny A Hug.** Aries would put red kisses all over Keith's face and he would carry a little brown jug for the pennies. She'd would wear a blonde wig and go as Daisy Mae in Lil' Abner in the comics.

They had a ball at the party. Aries wore Greg's fraternity pin on her bra under her blouse so no one would see it. Keith didn't want her wearing it, at all. He begged her to give it back and to wear his, instead.

"I can't. It would break his heart."

"Well, what do you think wearing his pin is doing to mine?"

Aries just looked at Keith. She couldn't respond. She wanted to tell him why she had to refuse his pin and why she had to stay pinned to Greg. She wanted to tell him she loved him and about the great error she had made by having pre-marital sex. She wanted to beg his forgiveness but she was unable to speak the words.

Keith was puzzled but she didn't have the nerve to explain the situation. She couldn't blurt out the hard, cold facts. He would have to just keep wondering.

Several weeks later, Aries was faced with a new problem. Her menstrual period was late and she feared she was pregnant. The period never arrived. She couldn't tell her parents. They would kill her! She'd ask Greg what to do. After all, he was the one who had gotten her into this mess. She called him with the news that she might be pregnant. He was surprised but told her not to be upset. His words failed to calm her. Her intuition told her that she was in a predicament.

"Call the airlines and make reservations to Miami this weekend. If you can stay over on Monday I can take the day off and we'll visit a doctor here and get you a frog test.

"Frog test. What's that?"

"That's a test the doctor gives that tells if you're pregnant.

"I've never heard of that but I've got to know something. I'm scared to death of flying, too. I've never flown before."

Greg laughed and told her flying was really fun, that she would like it. "Don't worry about anything. Just get yourself down here. Plan on coming this Friday afternoon. I'll pick you up at the Miami airport and I'll show you beautiful Miami beach on the way home. You can stay in the guest room at my house."

Aries really hadn't planned a trip to Florida but right now, she needed Greg. She was going out of her mind wondering.

Checking with the airlines, she learned that the airfare round trip was one hundred dollars. That was about all she had in her expense account and part of that was for books next quarter. If she spent the money on a trip to Florida, Pops would be furious. Feeling that she had no choice, she would worry about the consequences with Pops later. She purchased the ticket and on the day of her departure, she mailed a postcard home saying she had gone to Florida. She wanted them to know in case the plane crashed and she got killed.

When she arrived in Miami Greg was waiting at the gate with open arms to greet her. After a stream of hugs and kisses they went to gather up her luggage. Greg picked up her suitcase. "What on earth do you have in here, rocks?"

"No, just the things that I thought I'd need."

He laughed. "You won't need anything but a bathing suit and a pair of shorts in Florida."

"Maybe you're right but this is my first trip and I didn't know what to bring."

Heading for the parking lot, they got the car and for the next two hours Greg became a tour guide.

Florida was really different from Tennessee. The white sandy beaches were dotted with rows of tall palm trees. She had seen them before in the picture postcards her sister had sent when she was there. What a beautiful place! It was so clean and the soil was so unlike the red mud of Tennessee.

That night Aries met Greg's parents and his little brother, Sammy. She felt awkward staying with his parents when she and Greg weren't married. She wanted to make a good impression on his family.

The weekend went by quickly and on Monday morning they went to a doctor. Aries was examined and given the frog test. She was told to call around four o'clock that afternoon for the results. During the interim they were on pins and needles. At four o'clock they called the doctor's office. The frog test was positive.

"Congratulations," the nurse told her. "You're going to have a baby."

Upon hearing the news Aries knees trembled. Her face was white as a sheet and for a moment, she felt like fainting. She dropped the receiver and turned to Greg .

"It's positive, Greg. I'm pregnant. What am I going to do? If I have a baby my parents will kill me."

Greg just stood there with his mouth hanging open and a worried

28

look on his face. Finally, he was able to speak.

"Come on. Let's take a ride and talk about this situation. We have to decide what to do."

Getting into the car, they drove down the beach road. Greg assured Aries that he loved her and wanted to marry her but he didn't want to begin married life with a baby. He wanted them to be married a couple of years before starting their family. They needed to finish college and he needed to make some money before they had kids.

"Your ideas are great but they don't solve my problem. I'm pregnant, Greg! We aren't married and I'm going to have a baby."

"There's a doctor over in Dawson who gives abortions," said Greg. "One of the fellows at the Sigma Chi house was telling me about him. We can call him and make an appointment for you. I want to marry you but I don't want to marry you just because you're pregnant. I don't want to start out marriage that way."

Aries looked at him in a state of shock. She couldn't believe he would suggest that she have an abortion. "I'm not going to have an abortion," she said adamantly. "That would be taking a life. It's a sin and I'm not going to do it." She was sobbing and tears were flowing, profusely, down her cheeks.

"Don't cry, honey." Greg begged. "I can't stand to see a woman cry." Pulling off to the side of the road he took his handkerchief out of his pocket and started wiping away her tears. "Please don't cry. You don't have to have an abortion if you don't want one. It was just an idea. We'll get married and you can have the baby if that's what you want."

"It's not what I want. It's what I have to do. I have no other choice."

"We'll get married. We'll get married in April when I come back to school," Greg was quick to suggest.

"In April", Aries repeated. I'll be showing by then. I can't get married in maternity clothes. I just won't eat anything for the next two month so I will stay skinny."

"We'll have to tell our folks we're getting married so it won't come as such a surprise to them," Greg advised. Let's go home and break the news to mine, right now, and you can tell yours when you get back home. We'll tell them we plan to be married in April."

"And what will we tell them when we have a baby six months later?"

"We'll tell them the birth was pre-mature."

"That's great! I hope the baby doesn't weigh ten pounds."

"Stop worrying. It will all work out."

As Greg drove them back to his parents house a thousand thoughts were floating through Aries head. What about school? If she went to class in maternity clothes everybody would know that she got pregnant before they were married. "Greg, if I have to wear maternity clothes, I can't go to class. I would be too embarrassed," she muttered.

"You can drop out of school for the rest of the year after we get married and you can go back and finish next year after the baby is born."

"My parents are going to kill me. My father expected me to become a woman doctor and to go on for my Master's Degree at Columbia University. None of what I am doing is in his plans."

"Well, Fathers don't always get what they want. My father would like for me to go into business with him but I want to go into marketing."

The two arrived at the Winston's house just minutes before they came home. It took awhile but, finally, Greg got up the nerve to tell them that they planned to be married in April at Cramer U during Spring Break.

Greg's father seemed to take the news, gracefully, but his mother was opposed to them marrying. She told them they should wait until they had finished college and had jobs so they could make a living, She related the hard times they had trying to raise a family during the depression. "You'll get married and start having babies and you'll never finish your education. You both are too young to get married," she said emphatically.

Aries hadn't felt too comfortable in this woman's house before and now she felt terribly ill at ease. How could Greg's Mother be so cold and display such a lack of feeling? She didn't even bother to congratulate them.

Greg sensed her uneasiness and he took control of the conversation. "Mother, our minds are made up. We're in love and we're going to be married and that's it."

After that, his Mother became silent and said no more. Aries was sorry she felt that way and she hoped she'd be more understanding after their marriage. She dreaded the day that his mother found out they were going to have a baby.

The next morning she flew back to Tennessee to Cramer U. Aside from being in trouble for cutting Archeology classes, there were no problems. She was glad to be back in school.

A week went by and she began to show signs of bleeding. She thought then, that the doctor in Florida had made a mistake. The frog test must have been wrong. She thought she was having her period. The bleeding became heavier and heavier, and she was going through box after box of sanitary napkins. Down to the last few dollars in her checking account, Aries was afraid to call home to ask for more money.

Aside from unusual bleeding, she was suffering from dizziness, nausea and weakness. Just walking up the dormitory stairs to her room tired her out. Something was wrong and she had to do something about it. Going to the college infirmary, she told the admitting nurse she'd been having trouble with her period and she'd been bleeding, heavily. The doctor examined her and admitted her as a patient.

"I'll come up to your room and talk to you a little later," he said.

Aries was put to bed and frankly, she was relieved to be there. She couldn't have survived much longer on campus, she was very sick.

When the doctor came up to her room he stood at the end of her bed. "Young lady, you are a very sick girl. You have suffered a miscarriage and you should have come to the infirmary sooner. Your hemoglobin count is dangerously low and you have pernicious anemia. We may get away by giving you iron and vitamin B12 shots but we are going to have to notify your parents for permission to give you blood transfusions, if necessary.

"Oh, oh, begged Aries, "please don't call my parents. I was pregnant, doctor but I don't want them to know."

"I promise you I won't tell them. I will tell them you are anemic but I must call them.

31

"If you must call them, okay. How long do you think I will have to stay in bed?"

"For a week or two, until we get your system built back up again.

"Please doctor, don't put in my records that I was pregnant."

"I won't. Your diagnosis will be pernicious anemia. You know you could have died, young lady, walking around in this condition. Didn't you know you were hemorrhaging?"

"No, I just thought my period had come and that I was bleeding a lot."

"Well, it's a good thing you came here when you did. You are lucky to be alive."

Aries was glad she had a warm and understanding doctor. She was thankful to be in the infirmary, too, for she was so weak and so tired. She had lost her baby and she was sorry, but it would be better for them not to have the baby, just now. When she was feeling up to it, she would call Greg and give him the news. Now, all she wanted to do was rest.

After two weeks of proper diet, shots and more shots, Aries was discharged from the infirmary. She would have to come back twice a week as an out-patient for Vitamin B12 and iron shots, but she had been given the green light to attend classes again.

Several days later she called Greg telling him that she had been in the infirmary, she had lost their baby and that she had almost died in the process.

"Why didn't you call me?"

"I didn't know what was happening and I didn't want to alarm you. Everything is alright now. The doctor says I'm going to be fine."

"Well, thank God for that." Greg breathed a sigh of relief. It won't long now until I'm back in school. Start planning our wedding. We'll get married in April, anyway."

"Yes, yes I will. I'll start working on the invitation list. Send me a list with names and addresses of people you want to invite." Saying Good bye, Aries was pleased at hearing that Greg still wanted to marry her despite the troubles they'd had. She would wait for his return to school before breaking the news of their upcoming marriage to her family. This would come as a real shock to them and she wanted Greg to be with her when she told them. She'd met his family and she needed to introduce him to hers.

When Greg came back at the end of winter quarter, they spent some time scouring the town looking for an apartment and discussing plans for their wedding. They decided to have a small wedding in the college chapel with the number of invited guests limited to their best friends. Their budget was small because neither of their families could afford the cost of a large church wedding.

The date was set for mid-April. Aries asked Nita to be her maid of honor and Janie to be the bridesmaid. Naturally, Woody Fenton would be Greg's best man.

They planned a trip to Marksville to introduce Greg to her parents and tell them about the wedding. Aries would never forget that day. Mama was standing at the front porch door to greet them. She was so happy to have her daughter come home. That's the way it was in the Able family. There was plenty of love there and they always kissed, hugged and cried whenever anyone came or went.

"Where's Pops?" Aries asked Mama.

"He's out in the backyard. He's been working on something down at the barn."

"Excuse me, Greg, I'll be right back. I want to go say hello to Pops and ask him to come in the house to meet you."

Leaving Greg sitting on the living room sofa, Aries made her way through the dining room, the kitchen, down the back porch stairs, out the door to the backyard.

The backyard view was a pleasing sight. The apple tree was standing securely on the left side of the porch. Aries looked to see if the pear tree was still there on the right and then, she turned her gaze to the slopping hills blanketed with baby purple violets. They made an ethereal covering of the boundary that divided the backyard from the woods beyond.

"Pops, Pops, where are you? It's me, it's me, it's Aries.

"I'm over here."

"Over here where?"

"Over here behind the woodpile."

Aries caught a glimpse of his shiny bald head and she ran down the hill, trampling some of the violets in her path, rushing to greet him. "Hi, Pops." Aries smiled and threw her arms around him hugging him as tightly as she could, plunking a big kiss on the top of his head on his most obvious bald spot.

"Well, young lady, It's about time you came home to see your Pappy. I was beginning to think with all of your high fangled education you had forgotten about me."

"No, no Pops, I didn't forget you, I have just been busy, busy studying.

"Well, if you're going to be a doctor, you need to be studying. It takes a lot of hard work and you don't have time for monkey business."

Changing the subject, Aries told him she had brought someone home with her, a fellow whom she wanted him to meet.

"Come on in the house and get your Sunday clothes on, Pops, because I want you to meet our guest."

"This sounds like monkey business to me. Who's this fellow you want me to meet?"

"His name's Greg Winston. He goes to school with me and he's from Florida. Please be nice to him because I'm going to marry him."

Hearing this, Pops put his hammer and nails down on the ground. Taking out a bandanner handkerchief, he wiped the sweat from his brow. "What's this? What's this about marrying? What kind of nonsense talk is that?"

"Pops, I've brought Greg home with me to meet you because we're going to get married in two weeks, at Cramer U and I want you to be there to give me away." Aries had blurted it out and she wasn't surprised at his reaction. Now, she would just have to wait for him to calm down.

Pops picked up his hammer and nails and started pounding away on the bench he was making. Soon he lifted his head and started talking. "I'm not coming in to meet him and I'm not going to any wedding, either."

"Pops, please, please come on in the house and meet him. He's real nice and he's from a decent family, too."

"I don't care where he's from. Can't I have one daughter to finish

34

college without getting married? I don't want to meet him and I don't want my daughter getting married either. Go on in the house so I can get my work done." He was very irritated.

Aries went back into the house where she found Greg still sitting on the living room sofa. Mama had served him iced tea garnished with mint leaves. She told Greg that her father was busy on some project and he couldn't come in, right now. "He's not too happy with the news about us getting married but he'll get over it," she added.

Awhile later, her sister, Angie, stopped by. Aries told her about their plans to marry at Cramer in two weeks. Angie was excited because planning weddings was right up her alley.

"I'll help you, offered Angie. I'm good at planning weddings. What have you done so far?"

"Well, nothing except we've made out an invitation list, selected the chapel, the preacher and picked the time and date. That's all we've done."

"What about your dress?"

"I don't have one, yet."

"Well, I'll come over there next week and we'll go shopping," Angie continued.

"We can visit the florist to pick out the flowers and order the cake for the reception, too. Don't worry about anything, just leave the arrangements up to me. We've got to get busy, though. You really aren't giving us much time."

"I've got the invitation list with me,"said Aries.

"Let's take a look at it."

Going over the list, Angie started mentioning people who should be invited that she hadn't included.

"We can't invite everybody. We want to keep it a small wedding, fifty people and that's all," Aries reminded her.

Angie made plans to spend a couple days at Cramer the next week. What a relief it was that big sis had taken over! Aries was getting pretty nervous about the wedding, anyway.

"Pops says he won't come to my wedding," she told Angie when they had excused themselves from Greg.

"Well, I'll take care of him," Angie assured her. "He's stubborn, sometimes but he'll change his mind when he's had time to think it over. Don't fret about it, he'll be there if I have to drag him."

Angie liked Greg. "He's good looking and he seems terribly nice," but I want to ask you something," she said.

"What?" Aries interrupted her before she could ask the question.

"I wanted to ask you what happened to Keith. The last time I saw you, you told me you were in love with him."

"Oh, Keith Kiser, we broke up and I met Greg and started going steady with him."

"How long have you known, Greg?"

"For six months."

"Well, "I guess that's long enough. I just didn't want you to make a mistake and marry somebody you weren't sure of."

Pops never did come in to meet Greg and as it was getting dark, they decided they had better head back to Cramer. Aries apologized for his rudeness. Greg told her no apologies were necessary because he understood her father's feelings at losing a daughter.

"The news had to be a big shock to him. Remember how my Mother acted when we told her?" Greg reminded her.

Back at school, time flew by and their wedding day was just around the corner. Aries was nervous but terribly excited. It was hard to believe that in a very short time she would be Mrs. Gregory Thomas Winston.

Angie had helped her pick out an expensive but beautiful white organdy, ankle length wedding dress. It was trimmed in lace with white embroidered roses. All of the arrangements were made. Greg's family would be unable to attend but Aries's family planned to arrive on Thursday night for the wedding rehearsal.

The wedding was scheduled for two o'clock on April 20th. Aries had picked that hour knowing that Keith would be at football practice, then. She was afraid if he knew about the wedding he would come to the church, interrupt the ceremony and tell the preacher that he objected. Could it have been a coincidence that the date she picked was Keith's birthday, too? In her heart she still had very deep feelings for him. Those feelings must put away in her treasure chest for she was about to become the wife of another man.

The hour arrived. Everything was perfect, except for one thing. Pops still had not shown up at the church. He never attended the rehearsal the night before so Uncle Ross offered to do the honors in the event he didn't make it the next day. Aries was saddened at the thoughts of him not attending.

It was almost time for the ceremony to begin. It looked like Uncle Ross was going to have to do the honors. He was dressed in a tuxedo, standing by, just in case. The music was playing and the guests were all seated waiting for her to walk down the aisle. She couldn't wait any longer, it was time to start to the altar.

"Let's go honey, it's time," said Uncle Ross preparing to escort her down the aisle.

"Maybe Pops will be here in a minute. Let's wait a minute." Angie tugged at Aries wedding dress and motioned for her to start. Taking Uncle Ross's arm, they commenced the walk to the alter.

Aries was sickened and disappointed at Pops failure to appear.

They were almost to the altar when Pops came bursting in through the chapel door. He rushed down the aisle to Uncle Ross's side. Tapping him on the shoulder, Uncle Ross stepped aside and took a seat at the end of the pew. Pops took over and escorted her the rest of the way. Aries was so happy it was all she could do to hold back the tears. It didn't even matter that he wore a dark brown suit when the rest had on black tuxedos. Her Pops loved her and he had arrived, despite his feelings, to give her away. Aries would never forget that.

After the wedding there was a lot of handshaking and congratulations. Finally, the newlyweds bid everybody farewell and prepared to leave for their honeymoon. The car was parked outside all decorated up with tin cans, streamers, a painted Just Married sign and a few practical jokes that Woody had drummed up. Nita caught her wedding bouquet. Dashing into the car amidst the rains of rice pouring down on them, they made their getaway.

The extent of their honeymoon was driving eight miles over to Dawson for dinner. They couldn't afford one now so they'd spend the weekend in their new apartment getting better acquainted and getting organized in their new home. They had deliberately withheld their address from everybody, except Will and Nita, so they could have some privacy.

Being married and living together was a new experience. They would be sleeping in the same bed every night. Sex between them was now, legal.

Sleeping in a bed with a man would be something new for Aries. She had never done that before. She'd had sex with Greg twice in the back seat of a car. Each time she had all of her clothes on, except her under panties and each time, she'd been afraid. She wondered what it would be like now that they were married.

Would he expect to see her naked? She wasn't used to undressing in front of a man. She had never seen a naked man either, except for a glimpse of her father's back in the shower, once.

In the excitement of making plans for the wedding, Aries hadn't given any thought to the things that were popping up in her head. She and Greg would have a lot of adjustments to make. She was sure she'd be very shy about all of this intimacy and she hoped he'd understand that she had come from a family where nobody ever saw anybody naked.

After dinner they went directly home and prepared for bed. Aries went into the bathroom, locking the door behind her so she could get into her gown without Greg seeing her. When she came back out she found Greg lying in the bed without a stitch of clothes on. His penis was standing straight up and he had hair on him, just like girls did. Aries was shocked. She didn't know boys had hair there. Turning her back, she told him to get his pajamas on. "I've never seen a man naked before and I'm embarrassed," she explained.

"Honey, we're married. It's alright to be naked," Greg assured her.

"I know, I know but I'm just not used to it, yet. Please be patient with me."

Complying with her request, Greg got up and finding a pair of pajama bottoms, slipped them on. "Now, honey, does this make you feel better?"

"Yes, yes it does."

They talked awhile and then Greg suggested that they go to bed. Taking his pajamas off, he climbed in. Aries lay down beside him, keeping her night gown on.

"Take it off, honey, take your gown off."

"No, I can't take it off. Tennessee girls don't take their gowns off in front of men."

"Oh, they don't. Well, leave it on then if you'd like."

Leaving her gown on she asked Greg to turn off the light. He turned off the bedside lamp but he left the light on in the hall explaining that he liked to see what he was doing.

Aries wondered what was going to happen, next. She felt really strange. Greg was her husband and she had to submit to him whether she wanted to or not. This was their wedding night. He expected to make love to her. Complaining that she wasn't too well versed in this, Greg assured her that he would be gentle and teach her.

It took awhile for him to convince her to spread her legs and cooperate. When she did, he was ready to cum and as soon as his penis touched the opening of her vagina, he did just that. "I'm sorry, honey. I was so excited I couldn't wait," he explained.

"That's alright," she said relieved. She thought it was over but this was just the beginning. She was in for a long weekend of sex, sex, and more sex. Greg fucked her over and over again. Finally on Sunday Greg went to the drugstore to purchase some vaseline. Her pussy was tight and it was hurting him, too. By Monday morning, Aries was so sore that she could hardly walk.

Greg enjoyed sex from the beginning but she never had an orgasm during the first weeks of her marriage. She didn't know how. Greg expected her to have one so she pretended she was when she wasn't. She talked to Nita, about it and she advised her her to see a doctor. "You won't be happy with him if you can't reach a climax," she warned.

"How do you know? You're not married."

"I've read about it. Maybe Greg's not being considerate of you, sexually. Maybe he's too eager and he doesn't wait until you are ready."

"That's true. He starts and he goes like a fire engine rushing to a fire until he's had an orgasm. I'm just lying there and nothing is happening to me, except it hurts."

"Take my advice and discuss this with a doctor. I'm no expert but the book says you're both supposed to reach climaxes."

"I will, I'll go home and call the doctor and make an appointment. Please don't tell anybody that I talked to you about this problem."

"I won't."

Aries was really worried especially since Nita told her that she wouldn't be happy in her marriage if she didn't have orgasms. She called the doctor and made an appointment to see him. She wouldn't mention this to Greg.

The doctor gave her an internal examination and found nothing wrong with her. "You have nothing to be concerned about, Mrs. Winston. Your husband just needs to be a little more patient with you, to give you more foreplay before sex and to exercise more control during intercourse. You are newlyweds, it takes time to adjust. It is very normal to have this happen in the beginning of a marriage. Just give it more time and stop worrying about it."

The weeks whirled by quickly and when they weren't in the sack "getting nookie" as Greg called it, they were hitting the books trying to make the grades to graduate from college. They were finishing up their Senior year and soon, they'd be out in the hard, cold world of working people. In June, it would all be over and they'd be moving to Florida to work in Greg's parents business. The store was closed for the summer so they would look for jobs elsewhere until the season started.

Their plans were made. After finishing exams the last week of school, they would drive to Marksville visit Aries's folks before they left for to Florida.

Aries didn't have an exam on the last day but Greg did. When he got back from his exam she had tidied up the apartment and everything was all packed up and ready to go. "All you have to do, Greg, is to put these things in the car and we'll be ready to leave."

Greg looked at the last pile stacked by the doorway. "I hope there's enough room left in the car. I don't know how we have accumulated so much stuff," he commented laughing.

"Wait until we get to Mama's. She'll probably have another load for us," Aries jested.

Greg gathered his arms full and went to the car. Aries took a last minute check to see if they were leaving anything behind. The telephone rang and she ran to answer it. To her surprise, the caller was Keith.

"How did you get this number?"

"I got it from a friend of yours."

"Well, why are you calling me? I'm married now."

"Yes, I heard you got married on my birthday."

"Yes, I did."

"That was a pretty rotten thing for you to do. Why did you marry him in the first place? You know I'm in love with you."

"That's none of your business. The fact is that I am married now."

"Divorce him. Divorce him and marry me. I love you."

"Forget me. Forget me and go find yourself a nice girl to marry. I've got to hang up now. My husband is in the car waiting for me."

"Where are you going?"

"We're leaving. We're going to South Carolina. I've got to go now. Goodbye."

Hanging up the phone, Aries rushed to get in the car. The temperature outside must have been 105 degrees and she knew Greg was in a hurry to get on the road.

"I'm sorry," she said as she got into the car. "I had to answer the telephone."

"Who was calling?"

"Nobody, it was just a wrong number."

"I was beginning to wonder what was taking you so long, It's as hot as hell out here and I'm ready to get on the road. Is the house locked?"

"Yes, I locked the door behind me. Aries was silent as Greg backed out of the driveway. She was thinking about Keith's surprise phone call. He had told her to divorce Greg and marry him. She stilled loved him but she couldn't just divorce Greg out of the clear blue. They were getting along fine, together. She didn't love him like she loved Keith but maybe in time, she would. Why had she lied to Keith when he asked her where she was going? She told him she was going to South Carolina, instead of Florida. Was she afraid he would find her and cause problems? Now he would never be able to find her.

Aries had to try to forget Keith Kiser. She would never be content in her marriage unless she did. As Greg drove she closed her eyes pretending she was resting but all the while she was consumed with thoughts of Keith. When she finally opened them, they were almost they were almost at their destination.

"Well, you got a good rest," said Greg as he leaned back and lit up a cigarette.

"I was tired," she responded drowsily.

"When we get to your Mother's, let's don't stay long. We have a long drive to Florida and we got a late start today as it was," Greg advised.

"We won't stay long. I've already told Mama we'd just be dropping by for a little while. She wanted us to spend the night but I explained that we had borrowed your Uncle's car and we had to hurry up and get it back to him."

Mama and Pops were sitting on the front porch when they arrived. After the usual warm family greetings Aries told them they had just stopped by to tell them goodbye. They had to get on the road, soon, because they had gotten a late start and Greg had a long drive.

Mama said, "Well, at least you can have some milk and cake before you leave."

"We're not hungry, Mama, we ate a big breakfast this morning."

"I've packed a picnic lunch for you to take on the trip. Let me go to the kitchen to get it." Following her to the kitchen, Aries found a picnic basket full of food.

"Mama, you shouldn't have done this. We could have stopped at a restaurant on the way."

"It's better when it's a picnic. It was no trouble and I wanted you to have it."

Thanking her, Aries hugged and kissed her.

Mama could hardly hold back the tears. "I don't like you going to live so far away from us."

"Mama, it's not so far, I can be back home in two days of driving."

"You're liable to get bitten by a shark in that ocean. You're liable to go out in the water too deep and drown. I am going to be worried to death about you."

42

"Mama, stop imagining that horrible things will happen to me. I'll be fine. Greg will take good care of me. I want to live in Florida. The beaches are beautiful there and the weather is nice. You and Pops can come to see us. You'll like it."

Taking the basket out to the porch where Greg and Pops were sitting, Aries told Greg to put it in the car.

"Do you have enough pillows and quilts?" asked Mama.

"We've got enough of everything," answered Greg. "We don't have room for another thing in the car. If we get much more, we'll have to leave Aries here."

"I wish you would leave her," Pops replied. "I need her here to help me on the farm."

"No, I have to go with my husband," she was quick to respond.

"Speaking of going, Aries, we'd better get going.

"I'm coming. Let me go to the bathroom, first."

"Go ahead, I'll get the car started."

As she ran through the house to the bathroom, Aries suddenly began to feel a tinge of loneliness. She was leaving Tennessee and she was leaving her parents. She would miss them and she would miss this house. At only nineteen years old, she had finished college and she was a bride. She was excited about her new venture and about making her home in Florida but Mama was right, it was a long way from Tennessee.

She would be far away from her family but she'd be getting a new family in Florida. Greg's family would be her family, too, but it would be different being around boys all the time, instead of sisters. It would be new for the Winston's having a girl around when all they had was sons.

Finishing in the bathroom, she went out into the driveway where Greg was waiting with her folks. The old green chevrolet that Greg's Uncle had loaned them was packed to the hilt with college books, wedding presents and clothing.

It was exciting to have a new husband, a new home, a new life! Although Aries would miss her parents, at last, she was getting away from those Tennessee country hicks, from the red mud and those cold, damp winters.

43

Goodbyes were said in the driveway. Aries got a big lump in her throat when she hugged and kissed Mama and Pops. Mama had tears in her eyes and Pops was trying to be brave and hold them back.

As Greg backed the car out of the driveway she opened the car window and told them again not to worry about her. "I'll write to you and you all can come to visit us in Florida."

"I'll take good care of her," said Greg.

"Be careful," called Mama, "be careful and don't drive fast and stop along the road to rest when you're tired."

"We will, we will." They waved good bye. Aries was crying now herself and Greg put his arm around her to comfort her.

As the old green chevie eased over the miles of highway, Aries was filled with a multitude of emotions. Greg was content to be going home but for her it had been a traumatic day. First, with Keith's call and then, saying good bye to those she loved so much. She was going to be living far away from home and it would be a long time before she'd see Tennessee again.

Before long, they could see the mountains coming up in the distance. Mountains meant one thing to her, "car sickness." Just try not to think of it, she told herself. She tried but it didn't work. Pretty soon, she was begging Greg to stop the car and let her out so she could throw up. Luckily, there was a cool mountain spring by the roadside and the coolness of the water slapped on her face after vomiting made her feel better.

Back in the car, Aries laid her head down in Greg's lap and went to sleep. When she awoke they were somewhere in Georgia. They had passed the mountains and were getting into the flat lands. Greg was getting hungry so they decided to stop at a wayside park and have a picnic with the food Mama Able had prepared. The sugar cured Tennessee country ham, fried chicken and brown sugar pies surely did smell good. They made pigs of themselves sampling all of the goodies in the basket and with tummies full, they scrambled back to the car.

On the road, they amused themselves with fondling and gentleness and as dusk set in, Greg was ready for some "nookie."
"I'm horny, honey, he said slowing the car down. Let's stop and get some nookie."

44

"Sounds like a good idea to me but where can we find a safe place?"

"Look over there, there's a nice country road in a cluster of oak trees, "said Greg pointing. "Let's pull in there."

"I don't know. I'm afraid, some farmer is liable to come out after us with his shotgun for trespassing on his land. The highway patrol might surprise us, too, and I don't to be caught with my undies down."

"Come on, honey." It will only take a few minutes. I want to screw you right now." Greg pulled into the narrow dirt road parking the car beneath the branches of an old oak tree.

"Oh, my goodness," murmured Aries, I am scared to death."

"Relax, baby, we're safe here. Nobody will see us."

As she slipped her sandals off she could see that Greg was dead serious about fucking her under that tree. Unzipping his trousers, he let them drop to his ankles.

"Slip down in the seat under me," he instructed.

"Wait a minute," she giggled, "wait until I get these undies off."

Suddenly, all conversation was silenced as Aries could feel the thrust of Greg's mighty penis in her tight vagina. The scorching heat of July was no comparison to the fire that was beginning to swell to it's peak within their bodies pressed firmly together. The giggles of foreplay were now exuding in the form of moans and groans. It was delicious, refreshingly delicious. They were screwing furiously, breathing harder and faster, suffocating in the confines of the car. For awhile, they were oblivious to time and place, possessing no more than the desire to become a part of one another.

"Screw me deeper," wailed Aries.

"Oh, hold on a minute," Greg cautioned. "Don't move, one more move and I'm going to pop."

"Wait for me," sighed Aries.

"Oh my Lord, I'm coming, we're coming together," she cried. Their sighs of ecstacy could not be contained. Twas' as if a volcano had erupted and lava was pouring into every open cavity. Aries pulled Greg's hair in excitement as he kept pressing his fingers deep into her buttocks. Then all was calm.

Grappling for her undies in the floor of the car, Aries bent over as the wet tresses of her hair gently touched her shoulders. She noticed Greg, still with his socks on, sitting there panting like a worn out pup.

"Honey, that was beautiful," she sighed. She didn't tell him but for the first time in her life she had had a genuine real orgasm. Now she knew what Nita was talking about.

Part Five

On the road again the old green chevy kept putting along. Greg finally stopped in a rest area and they slept for a few hours during the night. When they awoke it was daylight and they were just a few miles from the Florida state line.

"We're almost in Florida, honey," Greg said. The soil was light colored and very flat compared to the hills of Tennessee.

As they traveled over the miles Aries watched the signs and billboards. Through Georgia, the signs had advertised fireworks, pecans and peaches but the signs in Florida were different. Most of them were for tourist attractions like fish aquariums, shell factories, alligator farms, snake milking places and old Spanish forts.

For awhile they drove past rows and rows of orange trees as far as they could see but as they got closer to the East coast, the orange trees thinned out and were replaced by coconut, palm and pine trees.

Aries couldn't believe she was actually in the land of real orange trees. There weren't any in Tennessee. The only oranges she'd seen there were those on sale in the grocery store. Mama didn't buy them, except for their stockings at Christmas and on special occasions, she'd purchase a half of dozen for a salad. Oranges were too expensive. Bananas were costly, too. There was no shortage of apples, pears, plums, cherries, grapes and berries though. Aries always got her belly full of those fruits.

She asked Greg about the alligators and snakes in Florida and he said there were lots of them but they were out in the Everglades.

"I'm afraid of alligators and snakes. Florida must be a dangerous place to live. I'll be scared to go outside."

Greg laughed and told her that very few people had been bitten by snakes or eaten up by alligators.

"They won't bother you if you leave them alone," he assured her.

None of this was of any consolation to Aries. Her Mama had been worried about her getting drowned in the ocean or being attacked by a shark in Florida. She would have heart failure if she told her there were alligators and snakes, big boa constrictors, too.

"What are all those bushy things growing with stickers on them?"

"Those are palmetto bushes. They are natures natural barriers to keep the soil from washing away."

"They sure are ugly. Those trees over there with the big thick leaves, they're nice. What do they call them?"

"Oh, those are sea grape trees. They have grapes on them. Aunt Rhoda makes sea grape jelly with them every year."

"And those funny looking red things hanging on those trees, what are those?"

"Those are mangoes," laughed Greg.

"Mangoes. Do they eat them?"

"Yes, some folks love them. Mangoes are very plentiful in Florida."

Aries was beginning to realize she knew nothing about the stuff that grew in Florida.

"Don't they have any apple trees here?"

"No, it's too hot in Florida for apples. We have to buy them here like you have to buy oranges in Tennessee. Let's stop at the next fruit stand and get some orange juice. I need to get out of this car and stretch my legs a bit."

"I'm sorry you've had to do all the driving. I would help you if you'd let me."

"Never mind, I'll do the driving. I get nervous with a woman behind the wheel. I want to get there in one piece."

"Greg, I know how to drive. I don't know how to drive as well as you do because I haven't had enough practice but I do know how to drive."

"You can practice driving later but on this trip let me keep the wheel," he responded.

Aries ceased the conversation because she knew his mind was made up.

They stopped the car at the next fruit stand. Greg pulled up to the gas pump and told the attendant to fill her up. Aries was glad for the break because she was dying to go to the rest room. While there, the fruit stand attendant gave them a cup of orange juice, free. This was their way of getting them to buy a bag of oranges after seeing how delicious it tasted.

"Let's buy a bag, Greg".

"No. Mother's got plenty of oranges at home. My uncle has a fruit stand and we get all the oranges we want for nothing."

"Oh, in that case, that's fine. I didn't know." Settling for a pecan log candy, she got back in the car.

"How much longer will it be until we get there?"

"It won't be long, we're coming up on Fort Pierce now. We only have about one hundred miles left to go."

"I sure hope your Mother doesn't mind storing our things at her house until we get an apartment."

"It'll be alright. We'll stay with my folks for a couple of weeks and after that, Aunt Rhoda and Uncle Frank will be boarding up their fruit stand and heading to the mountains for the summer. I thought I'd ask them, if we could stay in their place until they returned. That way we would have free rent, for awhile, and we could save some of the money we earn during the summer."

"That would be great if we can stay at your Uncle's, free."

"We're here," Greg announced as they reached the Pompano Beach road sign. "This is it, Pompano Beach, Florida."

It was almost dinner time when Greg pulled the faithful green chevie in the driveway of his Mother's house. She was in the kitchen fixing supper. "You all are just in time. Supper is almost ready. You two must be worn out from that long hard trip," said his Mother.

"We are," answered Greg. "After supper we're going to hit the sack. Dad came home about that time and after washing up he came to the table."

48

"Can I do anything to help?" Aries asked.

"No, everything's done. You and Greg just sit down at the table."

Aries had only asked to be polite. She was too exhausted to help. She was glad she wasn't needed after that long drive.

Greg really pigged out at supper. He loved his Mother's cooking and, jokingly, he told Aries she would have to let her teach her how to cook. Then, he blabbed out that she didn't even know to boil water. This may have been a joke but Aries didn't think it was funny. How did he expect her to be a cook when the only times she'd been in the kitchen was to snitch something that Mama had made before she brought it to the table?

During the next couple weeks Greg went out everyday looking for a summer job, while she stayed home and helped his Mother with the cooking and cleaning.

When Aries asked Greg's mother what she wanted her to call her, she said "Call me Bridie, Maree, the cashier at our store, calls me Bridie so you can call me Bridie, too." This comment made no sense since Maree was hired help and she was her daughter-in-law. Mother Winston would have been more appropriate.

Aries tried but somehow she felt very awkward calling her Bridie. In Tennessee you didn't call your elders by their first names. Finally, she decided to just call her Mrs. Winston. This was a bit formal but so was she. At least, this was showing her some respect.

In a way, she was relieved at not having to call her, Mother. That would have been awkward because she was a very cold person, not warm and loving like Mama was. There was little display of affection in the Winston house. The only sign of caring came from Greg's Dad. His personality was gentle, warm and friendly but Mrs. Winston was such an over-bearing, controlling woman. She bossed everybody around, including Greg. Aries hated her dominating ways, her coldness and the doom she was always predicting.

She was uncomfortable in Bridie's hospital sterile house. It was so immaculately clean, you couldn't breathe in it. Aries wondered how could families be so different? Was it because she had all boys instead of girls? She could hardly wait until Uncle Frank and Aunt Rhoda left for the mountains so she and Greg could get out away from there.

They had only been there for two weeks and already, Bridie was ruining their marriage with her dominating and over-bearing ways. Maybe things would be better when they got into Greg's Aunt's place.

When Uncle Frank and Aunt Rhoda left for vacation they moved into their apartment. The move would be temporary, only for two months, but they would have a place of their own even if it was just a loaner.

Greg got a job at a lumber company and his take home pay was sixty dollars a week. Aries needed to work, too, to supplement his income. They had graduated from college only to come to Florida and find that jobs were scarce and the pay was poor.

Aries was qualified to be a school teacher so she applied for a position not realizing that the legal age for teaching in the State of Florida was twenty-one. She would have to look for a job elsewhere because she was only nineteen with two years to wait. Refusing to be beaten, she went from business to business for interviews. Finally she was hired clerk at a department store. Her take home pay was only thirty dollars a week but anything was better than nothing.

Having no rent to pay, they hoped to save up enough money to rent an apartment of their own. Aries had decided she would starve before she would let Greg take her back to live with Mrs. Winston.

They had a good summer. Aside from working they spent their time off going to the beach. This was a new and wonderful experience for Aries. There were no beaches in Tennessee and she had been to the beach only once before at Myrtle Beach, South Carolina.

The beach road was long and narrow with the Atlantic Ocean on the east stretching to infinity. West of the road, there were dozens of wooden beach cottages nestled among coconut palms and sea grape trees. The sight was virgin, quaint and beautiful. There wasn't a lot of traffic. Everybody had vacated the area for the summer and there were no big buildings to block the magnificent ocean view.

Beaching was such fun! Aries loved going into the water and then, basking her body in the sun on the beach. Greg, was fair-skinned so he had to be careful to keep from burning, but Aries's olive skin just got darker and darker. She was getting a beautiful Florida suntan. Her sisters would be so envious!

50

Aries wrote home about her life in Florida. "You'd love it down here, except for the heat. It's been awfully hot this summer. What's more, you can't go outside after dark because monstrous black mosquitoes as big as flies are swarming. They are so thick one can hardly see. They don't bother Greg too much. He must be immune to them but they bite me all over. The fog trucks come along every few days and spray insecticide to kill them. It keeps them away for a little while but they always come back. The mosquitoes are the worst thing I've seen in Florida. At least they don't have chiggers here. Greg says the mosquitoes will go away in the fall when the weather cools off. I surely hope so.

Write to me and try to come down and see us this winter. We should be settled in an apartment of our own, by then. Everything is fine, so don't worry about me."

Summer went by quickly and by the first of September, they had found a small apartment not too far from Greg's mother's house. She pitched a fit when they rented it. She said they should live with them, that it would be cheaper for them all to live under one roof. Greg was about to believe her but Aries won out in the end by bawling her head off for a week.

The season started and Dad needed both of them in his store so they quit their jobs and went to work there. This proved to be a mistake because that put them back under Bridie's thumb. It was really awful. She told them what to do and when to do it. Even when they had a day off, she told them whether they should go to the beach or take in a movie. Aries wanted to get away from this woman.

A few months later, Aries discovered that she was pregnant. That night they visited the Winstons' to give them the news.

"We're going to have a baby," she told them excitedly.

Greg was pleased about the baby but not so with Mrs. Winston. After hearing the news she informed them that they had ruined their lives by having a baby. She went on and on about the terrible mistake they'd made. Finally, Aries fled in tears from the house. At that moment she didn't want her to be the baby's grandparent.

Several weeks later, she began to miscarry. Greg was at work when she discovered she was bleeding. He couldn't get away from the store so he called his Mother to take her to the doctor. She arrived several hours later with the excuse that she was in the middle of washing her hair. It was too late. Aries lost the baby and Bridie Winston was happy about it.

"So this doesn't happen to you again you two had better start using contraceptives," she told them.

"But we want to have a family," argued Aries. "My sister has six children and Greg and I intend to have an even dozen." The look on Bridie's face changed and she was quick to retort.

"You might want a dozen children but I can guarantee you that Greg doesn't."

Greg just listened and kept his mouth shut. He knew better than to get into a discussion with two women, particularly when they were his wife and his Mother.

They were never going to be able to lead lives of their own with Mrs. Winston lording over them. She was a thorn in Aries side.

Bridie stood big and tall, and she was somewhat like Mrs. Pilot, the housemother at Brenner. Her spindly toothpick legs didn't quite match the rest of her torso. Greg was six feet two and he must have gotten his height from her because his Dad was much shorter.

It was evident that Greg was a Mama's boy. Bridie prided herself in telling everyone that he never got dirty and never did anything wrong as a child. "Daniel, his younger brother, was mischievous but Greg was a perfect child," she bragged.

That didn't even sound normal. With all of her perfection she never allowed Greg to be a child. He was a grown man and still, he was trying to please his domineering Mother.

When the season was over they decided to go back to the University of Tennessee to take a couple more courses. Aries was looking forward to going back home for a visit. It had been a long time since she had seen her folks and she was homesick. They packed up the things that they would need during summer school and headed for the hills.

Upon their arrival in Tennessee, they rented a cheap furnished apartment upstairs in a private residence. There was no sink in the kitchen so she had to carry the dishes to the bathroom to wash them after eating. Otherwise, they were comfortable.

In July, the thermometer hit 105 degrees. Aries thought it had been hot in Florida but, at least, there had been the ocean breezes to cool them. The apartment had no air conditioning. It was stifling, scorching hot, and they felt like they were in an attic without a wisp of cool air to relieve them. It was almost unbearable.

Several weeks before summer school ended, Greg got a job offer in marketing at a mill in Georgia. Aries was thrilled when she heard the news. As much as she liked living in Florida, she would live anywhere else, just to get away from Greg's Mother.

"Take it, take it," she begged.

"Well, I told them I would go there and look the plant over after we finished summer school. If I like the set up and they are willing to pay me enough, I will consider it," he responded.

Aries kept her fingers crossed.

When school was over they went to Georgia as planned. Greg was interviewed and they offered him a job. He had a chance for advancement in salary and he would get to use his college training there. He accepted the position and Aries was pleased.

They would have to go back to Florida and get the rest of their things. Greg had to report back in two weeks so they decided to stay in Georgia for a couple of days to look for a place to live near the plant.

"Let's check into a hotel and take a ride back out that way to see what there is. They told me we might be able to get a house in the Briarwood subdivision for around two hundred and fifty dollars a month. With my salary we'll be able to afford that," said Greg.

Driving to the Briarwood development they drove up and down the streets looking for For Rent signs. Finally they spied one in front of a small brick house sitting up on a hill.

"Let's stop and look at that house," said Aries.

"Okay, it looks like it's vacant. I guess we'll have to go to a telephone and call the number on the sign."

"Alright, but let's pull in and walk around the house and look in the windows to see what it's like, first. There aren't any curtains up so we ought to be able to get a pretty good look."

Greg pulled the car into the driveway and they got out.

"I love brick houses," declared Aries. Going ahead of him she looked in every window. She counted two bedrooms, a bathroom, living room, separate dining room, kitchen and a big back porch.

Greg was still making his way around the house when she ran back. "It's perfect, Greg, it has everything we need." Aries was gleeful. "The trees in the yard are great, too. I like it! Let's get to a telephone, call the owner and find how much the rent is."

Greg made the call and luckily, the owner was at home.

"We were riding down Clover Street and we took your telephone number off of a sign in front of a little brick house. My wife and I were wondering how much you were asking for the rent?" He said.

"We want two hundred seventy-five dollars a month for the house. Would you like to see inside?"

"Well, yes, yes, we would."

"I live just down the street. If you'll go back to the house I can be over there in fifteen minutes."

"Fine, we'll be there."

 Back in the car, Greg announced that the owner was on the way over to show them the house. "The rent is twenty-five dollars more a month than we can afford to pay but let's look at it and make her an offer."

They both really wanted that house. It would be their first real home. They were weary and tired of moving and eager to get settled. With Greg's new job, a new town and a new home, they'd be on their own, at last. Maybe then, Greg could get weaned from his Mother's coattails.

The owner of the house came over and after hearing they were newlyweds just starting out in a new job, she agreed to let them have the house for a year for two hundred fifty dollars a month.

"We'll take very good care of the house and yard, " Aries promised

Greg gave her a hundred dollar deposit and signed the lease. "We're going back to Florida to get the rest of our things but we'll be back in a week. We'll pay you the rest of the rent the day we move in," he explained.

The lady agreed to hold the house for them because they seemed like a nice, honest couple.

The next day Greg stopped by the plant to tell his new boss that they'd found a house and they were going back to Florida for their belongings. They planned to return to Georgia in about a week.

Aries was glad he had taken the job. Now they could go back and tell his folks they were moving. Greg had gone to college to get his degree in Marketing. Surely they would understand why he couldn't turn down this offer.

Back in Pompano Beach, Greg broke the news to his parents. They said they were sorry to see them go to Georgia but this time, they acted like they understood his decision. Greg had an opportunity to go to work with a real big company. He was starting out on a good salary and he could have a good future with them. What could Bridie say to that one?

They spent the next few days beaching and preparing for the return trip to Georgia.

They had supper with his folks the night before leaving. "We'll keep in touch with you," Greg told them, "and you can visit us when you take your vacation next year."

Soon after they moved to Georgia, Aries learned she was pregnant again. She had miscarried twice before but she was determined to carry this baby to term. Greg was working every day and adjusting to his new job. Aries was nauseated and "sick as a dog." For the most part, she spent her mornings in bed taking it easy and resting.

The months went by. She was in her seventh month and was looking "very pregnant." I'm going to make it this time, she told herself. This time, I'm going to make it.

The doctor thought the baby would be a boy. Greg was excited about that because a boy was what he wanted. Time was getting short and still, they hadn't decided on a name for the baby. Aries didn't mind naming him, Gregory, after Greg but she resisted the idea of giving their child his middle name. It was Mrs.Winston's maiden name and definitely Bridie wasn't one of her favorites. Finally they settled on another middle name that they both liked.

Aries was just getting out of nausea and into heartburn in her pregnancy when, one evening, Greg received a phone call from Dad in

55

Florida. They talked a few minutes and when Greg hung up the phone he seemed very upset. The news must have been bad.

"What's wrong?" She inquired.

"Mother's very ill. She's been sick for weeks and we'd better make plans to go to Florida, right away. Dad sounded like he was mighty concerned about her."

"What's wrong with her?"

"Dad said she'd had been fighting off a bad cold for a long time. She didn't get any better so the doctor gave her some tests. She has contracted tuberculosis and she will have to go to a sanitarium."

"Tuberculosis! What on earth is that?"

"I don't know much about it but the Doctor says it's very contagious, and she won't be able to stay at home. Dad has depended on her so much that he is about to go out of his mind. We'll have to go, Aries, we'll have to go to Florida and see what we can do to help."

"Alright, we'll go. If your Mother is ill, of course, we'll go."

Aries tried to comfort Greg.

"I'll have to tell my boss that I have an emergency in Florida. I'm not due for a vacation so I'll have to take the time off without pay."

Aries wasn't so worried about that, but she was worried about tuberculosis being contagious. She was seven months pregnant and didn't want anything to happen to hurt her baby. This matter would have to be handled ,tactfully, to avoid alarming Greg. She would call her obstetrician and ask him about the dangers involved.

The next day Greg got a leave of absence from work and they prepared to leave for Florida. That morning, Aries called her doctor. He warned her about traveling this late in her pregnancy and cautioned her to avoid contact with Greg's mother until she was in the inactive stages of tuberculosis. Aries didn't know how the Winston family was going to take this but was taking no chances of contracting the disease and jeopardizing herself and her unborn child. She would stay away from Bridie.

They returned to Florida and things were as bad as Dad had said they were. Mrs. Winston was very ill and she had to be placed in a private sanatarium fifty miles from Pompano.

This was the end of Greg's marketing job in Georgia. Since his mother was no longer there to help his Dad, he felt obligated to work in the store. This was bad, bad news. Through illness, Bridie Winston had won control of her son, again.

Greg made all of the major decisions so they would stay in Pompano Beach. They rented a small apartment close to the Winston's house. It was there that Aries went into labor and there that she brought her firstborn child, Gregory Samuel, home. Little Gregory was a healthy baby and he was their pride and joy.

A year later, Aries became pregnant again and this time she gave birth to a beautiful baby girl. They named her Mia. Aries was very happy. Being a mother was just what she had always wanted to be.

With two children the apartment was becoming crowded so they rented a bigger one a couple miles away. It was newer and nicer than the dump they had lived in before.

A year after Mia was born, Greg made the decision to split from his dad's business and to open a place of his own. A two thousand dollar loan from Uncle Ross made this possible. Although they had no experience in the restaurant business, they opened a barbeque restaurant. Prior to opening, they spent days at home in the kitchen trying to come up with the perfect homemade barbecue sauce. Finally, they concocted one that was pleasing to their taste.

Greg's first business venture required long hours and hard work but, financially, it was a success. Thank goodness, Uncle Ross was kind enough to loan them the money when he did because they were finding out that raising two children was not inexpensive. The new business gave them a substantial increase in income.

The next year, Aries received bad news from Tennessee. Uncle Ross had dropped dead from a heart attack. She flew home for the funeral. Although it was a sad occasion, she got to see her folks. She hadn't seen them often since marrying, Greg. Pops didn't take to traveling too well so he hadn't been to Florida, yet. Mama and Gwen, her youngest sister, came down for a short visit, once.

While in Tennessee Aries learned that she and her sisters were to receive an inheritance from Uncle Ross's estate. It turned out to be a goodly sum of money. Greg would be surprised when he heard the news. At last, they would be able to afford a dishwasher and a television set. When she got back home she told Greg about the inheritance. He was pleased with the news but he said she still couldn't have a dishwasher. "That's a luxury, a luxury that you don't need."

Aries heard his words but she didn't like what she was hearing. What did he mean by saying a dishwasher was a luxury? If he had to wash all the dishes she did he wouldn't think so. It was her money, anyway. What right did he have to tell her what she could do with it?

Greg operated on the theory "what's mine is yours and what's yours is mine." He planned to take the money when she received it and invest it for the future. He had this crazy idea that he was going to be rich and retire when he was forty and if Aries would stop having babies for him to support, he would be able to retire.

In her mind, Greg Winston was getting just like his Mother. They had two children and that was all he wanted. What was happening to her dream of getting married, having twelve children and living happily ever after?

Greg had seen just enough money and just enough good living to prefer it over the things that really counted in life. Aries was opposed to this way of thinking. His attitude made her wonder where Keith Kiser was these days. She had walked away from him in college to make a life with Greg. Now, he was beginning to show signs of wrecking her dream.

If she had divorced Greg when Keith asked her to marry him maybe things would have been different. Keith had come from a large family. They had planned to have lots of children before Greg came into the picture. Perhaps she'd made the wrong choice in a husband.

The next year Greg sold the restaurant. He make a good profit on the sale. They used the proceeds along with thousands more that were coming in from Aries inheritance to purchase two drug stores.

The businesses were prosperous. Greg invested their savings in the stock market. With his insatiable desire to get rich and get rich fast, he wasn't a conservative investor. He played the stock market like betting on long shot horses at the race track.

Greg had a real gambling streak in him. Aries didn't want him to lose everything they had so she decided to try to curb some of his spending. He had control of all of the money. She was allotted only enough to pay the monthly bills.

One evening she took him aside for a serious talk. "It's time we stopped renting and started thinking about buying a house, she told him. "We have enough money on reserve that we can afford a home of our own."

Greg looked at her in surprise. This was the first time, aside from asking for the dishwasher and the television set, that Aries had suggested what should be done with their money.

"We don't need to buy a house. If we leave the money in the stock market it will multiply and by the time I'm forty, I'll be able to retire."

"That's my inheritance you're talking about. My Uncle left that money to me and I would like for us to have a house of our own."

"Don't you know, you idiot," said Greg interrupting, "that what I'm doing is for you and the children? You don't know anything about investing so you have to leave the money decisions up to me."

"That's just what I've been doing. That's why we are still crammed up in an apartment with two children. How much money did you lose in those wild investments in diamond mines in Virginia and uranium mines in Costa Rica?"

"Enough, but I'll be able to recover my losses on some of the other stocks that I have bought."

Aries was annoyed.

"I'm telling you one thing, Greg Winston. I don't want another penny of my money invested in that stock market. If we can't have a house with all my family's money that's been entrusted to you, then we have a problem."

"I don't want to talk about it anymore tonight, my stomach is beginning to hurt. We'll talk about it, tomorrow," he said.

"Well, we'd better because I am very serious about this matter."

They talked again the next day, the next day and the next. Aries talked until she was blue in the face trying to convince him that now was the time for them to buy a house. Finally, she won the argument and Greg agreed to contact a builder.

A few weeks later they found a lot and they signed a contract with the builder for the construction of a new house.

Six months later, they moved out of the apartment into their brand new home. It was a beautiful house, big enough for all of them. Now, they had a nice big side yard, all fenced with room for a swing set and a sandbox for the children.

Not long after moving Aries became pregnant again. As usual, she was delighted with the news. She wanted a boy this time so Gregory would have a brother.

Greg didn't want another baby. In fact, he hated her being pregnant so much that he denied being the father. He had been so careful and this baby couldn't be his. This remark was astounding! Aries was livid at his making such an accusation. Perhaps, she had taken the diaphragm too soon after intercourse. This pregnancy wasn't planned but she knew the child she was carrying was Greg Winston's and nobody else's. What nerve! How could he expect her not to become pregnant when he fucked her three times a day?

Aries was so hurt by his accusations that she seriously considered leaving him but having two small children and another on the way stopped her.

Her family was totally against divorce. Aries was very unhappy about the way Greg felt about their having a family. She hoped he would change his mind about the baby when it arrived.

Her pregnancy was a difficult one. By the sixth month she was threatening to abort so the doctor ordered her to bed for the remainder of the time. At seven and a half months she delivered a five pound boy. Being premature, the baby had to stay in the hospital incubator for two weeks before coming home.

They named him Mark and now, their children numbered three.

A year later Aries found herself with child, again. She went into premature labor at five and one half months. This time it was twins. One of them died at birth and the other one died shortly thereafter. She took this loss very hard.

After the twins Aries gave birth to a fourth child. The doctor predicted that the baby would be a girl but he was mistaken. It was a beautiful little boy, Ralph. Now, they had three boys and a girl.

Greg had stopped denying being the father of his children after number two. He merely told people that two of the children were his and the other two, meaning Mark and Ralph, belonged to his wife.

Greg's Mother was discharged from the sanitarium shortly after Mia's birth and she was back in town giving Greg advice. She told Greg to stop having babies. They didn't need Bridie interfering in their marriage. Aries wished that "bitch" would mind her own business and leave them alone.

While she was in the hospital having Mark, Bridie replaced the double bed in their bedroom with two twin beds. What a shock to arrive home with her new baby and find her bedroom re-arranged. Aries didn't want twin beds. Did Greg's mother think twin beds would keep them from getting pregnant? She had no right to do this.

Bridie came over one morning for a visit. In a shrill voice she gave Aries a stern warning, "You've had all of those children and Greg did not want them. He's going to have an operation to get his cords cut . He's on the verge of a nervous breakdown."

Well, this was news! Maybe she knew something about her son that Aries didn't.

"He can't stand being around all of these kids. He needs peace and quiet," his mother said.

Aries didn't know what to do. She had come home from the hospital with a new baby, she wasn't recovered yet, and she was hearing that Greg was getting ready to crack up. This was all she needed.

Mrs. Winston said she was worried about him.

"If you are worried about him, please help me by taking the two older children home with you for a couple days so I can have more time to take care of him," Aries pleaded.

"Help you. If you want me to help you I'll tell you what I will do, I'll take Greg back." The venomous words of Bridie Winston resounded in Aries head. Over my dead body, she thought. She'll take my husband over my dead body. She ordered her out of her house.

Bridie left slamming the door behind her. "You haven't heard all you are going to hear from me, yet," she said angrily as she left.

In tears and beside herself Aries went to the phone and called Dr. Beaty, the pediatrician. "It's an emergency," she told the nurse." Dr. Beaty came to phone. Aries told him that her husband was having a nervous breakdown and she didn't know what to do.

"Do you have any relatives who can help you?"

"No, all of my family is in Tennessee. I have no family here. Greg's Mother won't help me with the children but she said she'd take her son back."

Dr. Beaty advised her to call her sisters in Tennessee and ask them to fly down and take the two older children home with them for awhile until things got straightened out.

Aries thanked him for talking to her. She'd call her sister right away. Aries called Angie, and Angie promised that she and Jamie would be there as soon as they could. "We'll call you when we find out what time our flight will be arriving in Miami."

"Thank you, Angie, I really appreciate your help."

Greg came home a little later. He was acting strange. All of this must have happened to him while she was in the hospital. He took one short look at the baby and then he climbed into bed.

Aries asked him what was wrong. He said he was depressed.

"I'll call the doctor. I'll call him and make you an appointment."

On the way to the phone Aries wondered what kind of doctor to call for depression. She'd call Dr. Beaty's office back again and ask them. The nurse recommended Dr. Wallace, a psychiatrist.

The next day she took Greg to see Dr. Wallace. After talking to Greg at length, he told him to wait outside while he spoke with Aries.

"What's wrong with him, Doctor?"

"He's going through some type of depression. I've prescribed some mood elevator pills that should bring him out of it."

"What caused this depression?"

"Many things can bring on depression but in your husband's case, I believe his problem stems from emotional immaturity. Right now, he's displaying the emotional maturity of a twelve year old."

"Oh, my God! That's all I need to hear. We have four babies and you're telling me that my husband has the emotional maturity of a twelve year old. I don't need a child for a husband."

"I'm sorry to have to tell you this, Mrs. Winston, but your husband has a lot of growing up to do. I have told him I want to see him once a week. Perhaps my sessions with him will make him realize his problem and he will begin to correct it."

"Well, I hope so, doctor."

Outside the door, Aries was patient with Greg but she was beginning to realize she had a big problem on her hands.

The next day her sisters came to Florida and took baby Ralph and Mark back to Tennessee with them. After that, when she wasn't taking care of little Mia and Gregory, she was babying Greg, trying to get him to feel better. Finally, he was up out of bed and back to work.

It had been six weeks since her sisters had taken the children. It was time to bring them home. Angie and her husband had become so attached to baby Ralph that they wanted to adopt him. Naturally, adoption was not an option. They went to Tennessee to bring the children home. Aries was joyous at re-uniting with her babies.

Several months later Greg decided he was tired of the drug store business. He wanted to become a stock broker. They discussed selling the stores and Aries had no objections so both businesses went on the market for sale.

The stores sold quickly and with the profit they made from the sales, they were "nigger rich." On top of that, Aries received a large sum of money from the sale of some land she owned in Tennessee.

With four children their first house was becoming inadequate to meet the needs of their growing family. Once more Aries approached Greg about selling the house and building a larger one. This time they wouldn't have to cut corners so much. She had inherited enough money to build their "dream home."

Greg wasn't so hard to convince. They found a nice lot on deep water in Lighthouse Point, just north of Pompano Beach. The subdivision was definitely upper class, inhabited mostly by doctors, lawyers and professionals. The development also had a private Yacht and Racquet Club that they could join. They already had friends who lived in the area, and they had heard it was a great neighborhood.

Aries had only one reservation. She had been unhappy with Greg in the old house and she didn't see how building a new house would make their marriage any happier. The source of her unhappiness with him was his attitude toward the children. He didn't treat them right. If he couldn't love them Aries would never love him right. In spite of her admonitions, they went ahead with the plans for the construction of the new house.

63

The businesses were sold and Greg was going to New York for three months training in stock broker's school. She'd stay home, watch the construction of the house and take care of the children. That was a big responsibility. Greg agreed to come home several weekends during his training but he couldn't come often because the airfare would cost too much.

Not long after he left Aries learned that she was pregnant. They would be having another baby at Christmas. Maybe this one would be the little girl she wanted so badly. Greg wasn't going to be very happy when she gave him the news. He always blamed her when their sex life led to conception. He had sworn that Ralph was the last baby he was going to father.

Greg called and upon hearing the news he threatened to go for a vasectomy. Aries begged him not to.

"We'll talk about it later," he said, but that talk never came. When he came home from New York, his mother accompanied him to the doctor's office where he had a vasectomy without her knowing.

After the vasectomy things weren't the same between them in bed. Aries was turned off psychologically and sex with Greg was no longer pleasurable.

Time passed and Aries began to fantasize during sex. With this new game she was having orgasms and enjoying them. She kept her eyes closed during intercourse because she felt guilty for pretending she was someone else's lover, although she was still physically faithful to Greg. She hoped he couldn't tell she was directing her passion toward someone else.

At first, her fantasy was Paul Newman but later, her fantasy was replaced by a real idol. They had become good friends of a Delta airline pilot, Dick Frazer and his wife, Judy. They took weekend boating trips together, exchanged mates as dance partners at social affairs and visited each other's homes, frequently.

Aries had an instant chemistry with Dick. When they danced she could feel his big hard cock rubbing against her legs on the dance floor. She wanted to put her hand on it and touch it. She had fallen for Dick. They loved the excitement of the chase but their desires had to be shielded carefully from their unsuspecting mates.

Aries was hot with passion and Dick wanted her, too. They tried to resist their feelings as the passion mounted amid the constant tease and anticipation. She arranged parties and accepted invitations to social events that Judy and Dick would be attending. When she could find an excuse to get out of the house, she'd meet him at the airport on his return flights from Chicago. They had stolen moments together but there was little time. Greg would wonder where she'd been and Judy would be concerned about Dick's getting home late from a flight.

When she was screwing Greg she was mentally fucking Dick. With her eyes closed she could see him, smell him and feel him. Her orgasms became more frequent, sometimes three or four in a session. Sex was good as long as she visualized she was with Dick but when she came back to the reality that her sex partner was Greg, she was as discontent as ever. Fantasizing only made her want Dick more but in real life she hadn't slept with him.

To outsiders, the Winstons gave the appearance of having a solid marriage. They had lots of children and lots of money. What could be missing? A lot.

Aries was becoming more and more discontent with Greg. It appeared that he was more interested in martini's for lunch and fishing trips with the "boys" than in making her and the children happy.

Their new house was almost complete and the certificate of occupancy was soon forthcoming. Greg had a new stockbroker job. Maybe things would be better when they moved into the five thousand square foot mansion. Maybe then, they might get back to "happy ever after."

Part Six

"*I*t would take, I know, a Michael Angelo to try to paint a portrait of my love."

Aries and Greg had married for "better or worse" and it looked like Greg was dwelling on more of the worse than the better. They had everything that comes with a long term relationship. Along with the babies, Aries had her hands full of soiled diapers, dirty dishes, tons of housework and toys, toys scattered everywhere. None of this bothered her much because she had always wanted to be a mother.

It had been two years since the birth of their final child, Sara. The children were now like stair steps in ages ranging from two to ten. Aries loved her family. Things had been much better since Mama had come for a visit and straightened things out.

The night Mama arrived, Aries was down on her hands and knees scrubbing the kitchen floor. She was rushing to finish the job before the company came but she was caught in the act. When Mama saw her on her knees in the floor she let Greg have it in no uncertain terms.

"I didn't raise my daughter to be a scullery maid. If you want a maid you hire one. My daughter is not going to be your slave. She has enough to do just taking care of five children. She needs help and you had better get her some."

After Mama's chewing him out Greg agreed to hire a live in Nanny to help with the children. This was a big victory for Aries because before Mama came he had refused to hire help. According to him, Aries had had all of these children and she could take care of them. He wouldn't even change a diaper or dry a dish.

Mama certainly straightened his ass out. He was careful to be on his good behavior while she was visiting because he knew she could cut the money off. With his style of living, heaven forbid!

Mama didn't stay long and after she left, Greg started right back giving Aries and the children a rash of shit. He chastised her daily upon his arrival home from work. "You've got help now, why haven't you taken care of all these kids problems before I got home?" He yelled angrily.

 Aries could predict his behavior. No matter how hard she worked, Greg would have something to gripe about when he came home from work. What did he think she'd been doing all day, twiddling her thumbs? Didn't he realize how many times a day she had to solve problems between the children? Didn't he realize that she ran her legs off, all day, just meeting their needs and helping the Nannie with the housework? Did he think she was some miracle woman? What did he expect her to do with the children, send them back?

She wished Greg would be more understanding of her problems and that he'd be nicer to the children. He was so dammed mean to them. One night, he lined those poor babies up like they were in the army and made them salute him like he was an army sergeant.

When Sara was about two Aries decided to give up the morning "coffee klatches" she'd had with her friends while their children played together. Gossiping and drinking coffee with women was becoming a bore. How many people can you talk about and how many times can you tear someone apart when they aren't there to defend themselves? She needed to get her body in shape. She had enjoyed playing tennis in college so she would take that sport up again..

That week, she signed up for lessons with the pro at Pompano Beach Recreation Center. This was an ideal situation. The Nannie could watch the children at the playground next to the courts and she could exercise her body rather than her mouth. Her decision to go back to tennis was a good one. She loved the game and Gregory and Mia were beginning to bat that ball back and forth with the racket. This new regime was slated to continue for a long time.

Aries became a proficient player. Ultimately, she set about to convince Greg to join the Yacht and Racquet club. "It would be a good place for you to pick up prospects for the stock market and the children can become good swimmers and tennis players if we join. We can use the money we would spend on sending them away to summer camp. They have all kinds of activities at the club. They even have swimming teams and tennis teams that the kids can participate in."

Greg finally agreed. They joined the club and from then on, Aries and the children spent most of their their free time there. Aries was invited to play on the A tennis team.The children concentrated, mostly, on swimming and they all ended up on the team. They brought home lots of blue and red ribbons from the swim meets.

Aries and her brood enjoyed the activities at the club but Greg was jealous of the time she spent there. He complained about her playing too much tennis and his resentment showed when anyone called the house inviting her to play. Her love for the game of tennis was causing problems in their marriage. Perhaps, it was because she had defeated him once in a game of singles and his male vanity couldn't handle it.

Aries had a conversation about this with a psychiatrist friend, Jim Duncan, one evening at a dance. She told Jim she loved playing tennis but her husband was jealous of her playing. "My husband treats my tennis like another man and if he keeps this up I am going to give up tennis and take up men," she threatened jokingly.

Jim laughed.

The final blow came one evening in early fall. Greg came home from the office and announced that he was going to Alaska. "Jack Sanders, Warren Rittle and I are making plans to go to Alaska bear hunting. After the hunt, the other guys wives are meeting them there and they will go on to Hawaii for another week of vacation," he said.

"That sounds great! Hawaii! When are we leaving?"

"You can't go. You get your vacation all year long, playing tennis. Now, I am going to have mine."

Aries was disappointed to learn that Greg intended to take a vacation without her. In all of their marriage they had never been apart, except when she had a baby or when she went to Uncle Ross's funeral or when he went to New York to stock broker's school.

In spite of all her pleading, Greg was determined to make this trip without her. "We can't afford a vacation in Hawaii and the trip to Alaska is just for the guys, so you can't go. This trip will cost me three thousand dollars, alone. I deserve this trip. Your whole life is a damned vacation." Aries was given no choice. Greg would leave for Alaska the next weekend, and she had to stay home and hold the fort. He would be gone for three weeks.

Several days later Greg started packing for his trip. Aries offered to help. As they were putting his things in his suitcase she told him, "You'd better come home from Alaska with a bear rug."

When he came home, three weeks later, he didn't bring a bear rug or anything else, except a few tokens for the kids. As she helped him unpack his suitcase, she found lipstick on his handkerchiefs and black hairs on his tee-shirts. This bothered her some but she had other things to think about, now.

Aries life had changed in Greg's absence and none of what had happened had she consciously planned. It just struck her like a bolt of lightening out of the clear blue.

Aries conducted her life as usual in Greg's absence. Her days were filled with tennis, household chores and the children. Nights were different. She was used to sitting with him after the kids were bedded down. Now, she was alone.

During the second week of Greg's absence, Aries received a phone call from Clara at the club. Clara asked her to play in the club tournament on Saturday. This was a mixed doubles tournament and Aries hadn't signed up because she didn't have a partner.

"I don't know. My husband's out of town and we usually play together if it's a mixed doubles social."

"Don't worry. We have you a partner."

"Oh you do. Who might that be?"

"His name's Bob Benton. His wife doesn't play and he needs a partner. He's fat and ugly and he can hardly hit a ball," Clara went on, "but we know you can carry him as well as you play. Come on, help us out."

"Okay, okay, I'll play. Stop the teasing. I'll be there but if this guy can't play I'm walking right off of the court."

On Saturday afternoon, Aries arrived at the court having no idea of what her partner really looked like or how he played. She was somewhat apprehensive.

Entering the pro shop, she asked the pro if her partner had arrived.

"No, he isn't here yet but I'm sure he'll will be along shortly. You know, you two will probably win this thing," he volunteered.

"I don't know. I don't even know my partner."

"Well, he's an excellent player. I think he was number one at the University of Georgia."

"If he was number one at University of Georgia, he's probably too good for me."

"Don't worry about it, you two will have no problems. Here comes your partner now. Wait here a minute and I'll introduce you."

Aries glanced toward the door as Bob Benton entered the pro shop.

"Hello, Tom," he said wearing a million dollar smile on his face. "Thanks a lot for getting me a partner. I really wanted to play in this tournament, today. You know, my wife, Lana, doesn't play tennis, at all.

"Well," said the pro, "we've found you a gal who does. I'd like you to meet Aries Winston. Aries, this is your partner, Bob Benton."

"Hi." Aries returned his smile. As she looked at him his blue eyes were talking to her in a language that only the two of them could understand. Embarrassed, she sensed the strongest vibrations going back and forth between them. How could this be? She was a married woman, he was a married man. They were strangers and yet when he looked at her, she felt he was her long lost love returned.

"Come on, Aries, let's go out on the court and hit a few balls before the match starts," he suggested.

"Good idea. I haven't played in several days and it takes me awhile to warm up."

"You'll do fine."

"I don't know. I hear you were a number one in college and I may let you down."

"That was awhile ago," he answered smiling. "I'm really out of practice now. Don't fret, you'll do just fine."

Aries picked up her racquet and followed him out of the pro shop. Her heart was pounding and she just hoped she could hit a ball. What was happening to her? She'd had good chemistry with Dick but this was very different. This guy had ignited her like a stick of dynamite and he was dissolving her right there in front of his wife and all of those spectators.

Bob Benton was absolutely reeking with charm and politeness. He exuded sex and masculinity. His body was perfectly gorgeous! Aries liked what she saw and as they say in Tennessee, "That man looked "licking good." Aries tried to pull herself together. Straighten out, she told herself. Straighten out and get out there and hit that ball. Don't let them see your knees shaking!

Bob was just as personable on the court as he was off the court. His manners were impeccable and he stroked the ball with style, grace and ease. He must have been number one in college. This fellow played a spectacular game of tennis.

Before the match was over, it was obvious to both of them that something was happening other than their just being partners. The chemistry between them was flying all over the court and their exchanges of glances were ones of tenderness.

The love bug has struck us, thought Aries. It can't happen, I'll just go home and lock myself in the house until my husband gets home from Alaska. Bob Benton can mean nothing but trouble. She'd never violated Greg Winston in her life. She had warned Greg that any man who stayed out of her bed for three weeks was out of her life but she really hadn't meant what she said.

Bob and Aries were great tennis partners. They took first place in the tournament. They were the winners! What a perfect match they were in more ways than one! The twosome shook hands amid the sparks of the fire that had been innocently created between them. Then, they went to the sidelines where Bob received a hug from his wife and they received congratulations from the others.

Clara presented them each the a large trophy. "Leave them here until next week," she said, "and we'll have your names engraved on them."

Bob hugged Aries and told her, "Job well done."

"You were the good one," she replied, "you could have won the whole match without me."

"No such thing, young lady, I needed you." He was smiling.

About that time Bob's wife came up and started talking to him. She was a pretty thing, tall, slender with black hair, light skin and very blue eyes. Somehow, she didn't seem like his type. Lana told him she was going to the pool to round up the kids.

"Okay," he replied, "I'll meet you at the car."

Aries gathered up her tennis gear in preparation for leaving. She didn't intend to hang around the club, today. She had enough excitement for one day and she needed to get home and sort out her thoughts. Meeting Bob Benton had left her in a state of shock.

As she turned to leave, Bob stepped up and offered to carry her bag to her car.

"You don't need too. I can make it."

"I'm going that way anyway, let me help you," he insisted. On the way to the car, he told her that he wanted to see her and talk to her. "I have to go out of town Monday but I'd like to meet you somewhere in the morning for coffee before I go," he suggested.

"I don't know about that."

"Please, I need to talk to you. Those dreamy eyes of his were so convincing she couldn't turn him down. He was begging her from the depth of his soul.

"Instead of meeting you somewhere, why don't you come to my house after the children go to school? I'll make coffee. Around eight-thirty will be fine."

"What's your address?"

"It's 3000 S.E. 30th Place. Can you remember that? If not, look it up under Greg Winston in the telephone book. I've got to go now. See you, Monday."

Aries was a nervous wreck with Bob walking her to her car and standing there talking to her. That bunch at the club gossiped enough without her giving them something juicy to gab about.

On the way home she wondered what she had gotten herself into by inviting Bob Benton over for coffee. Greg would kill her if he knew about this. All kind of thoughts were going through her head. What if the neighbors saw him come into the house? If they saw him they'd think she was having an affair while her husband was out of town. What if his wife drove by and saw Ben's car parked at her house? He'd never be able to explain that and she'd kill both of them. Why did she tell him he could come? Aries was as nervous as a cat but there was no getting out of it. She couldn't call him at his house. Besides, she really wanted to see him.

She spent the evening in Greg's private study thinking about the situation. She was playing a dangerous game but the love bug had struck her and she hadn't thought of the inevitable consequences.

On Sunday, Aries devoted the entire day to the children. After Sunday school they went out to lunch and to a movie. Afterwards they went to Burger Castle for burgers and milk shakes. It was a good day! That night she tucked the children in at nine and exhausted, she went to bed herself.

The next morning she got up early and went through the clothing in her closet trying to select something to wear for Bob.

After getting the kids dressed, fed and off to school Aries hurried into the kitchen to get the dishes in the dishwasher before he arrived.

Luckily, it wasn't her week to drive car pool. She was in a nervous frenzy and feeling a terribly guilt when she hadn't done anything. It was her thoughts about what she would like to do that were causing her a problem.

Coffee on brewing, hair combed and all dressed, she sat down to relax a few minutes before Bob arrived. She'd been rushing like a house on fire ever since she had gotten out of bed. As she pulled the chair out to sit down she was startled by a soft tapping on the door. Bob Benton was there. The fact that his car was parked in the driveway made her feel uncomfortable. She'd get him to move it before the neighbors noticed. At the door she gave him a friendly greeting and told him that perhaps he should pull his car into the garage. Getting back in his car, he started the engine and waited for Aries to press the garage door opener so he could enter. Aries felt like a real criminal. Her and her big ideas. This time Bob entered the house through the side door. Aries closed the garage door behind him.

"Come on in," she said smiling.

"I'm sorry I had to ask you to move your car but with the nosey neighbors I thought it might be better. I was just about to pour myself a cup of coffee. Will you join me?"

"That sounds good."

Aries poured two cups of coffee.

Over coffee, Bob flashed that nice smile of his and told her again what a great game of tennis she had played on Saturday.

"We make a good team. We'll have to play more doubles together."

"I'd like that. I don't think anybody out there can beat us."

"I play doubles every Wednesday night at Holden Park," he said. "Do you think you could go with me this Wednesday?"

"I'd love to go."

After talking about tennis they talked about his job. Bob worked for a pharmaceutical company and the job necessitated him being out of town three or four days a week.

Aries told him her husband was a stock broker and that he kept bankers hours.

"He's on vacation in Alaska but when he's at home I never get out

at night unless we go together to some social function or once a
month, I go to bridge club. Occasionally, there's a meeting like P.T.A.
or Junior Women's Club but I have almost stopped going to women's
club meetings. I'll work it out for tennis on Wednesday night because
I would really enjoy that. My husband's just a social player and he
hardly ever plays."

Finally, the chit chat subsided and they sat there gazing at each
other. He was such a handsome stranger. After moments of silence
Bob blushed as if he was embarrassed to say the words he was about
to speak.

"Aries, you know I am tremendously attracted to you. From the
first moment I laid eyes on you, I have had this funny feeling in the
pit of my stomach. I think I'm falling in love with you."

He got up from his chair and went around to the other side of the
table where she was sitting.

"Please don't say that," she responded in surprise.

"Oh, "just let me put my arms around you and hold you close to
me for a moment," he begged.

With this request Aries was apprehensive about his motives. She
placed her hands firmly on his shoulders and shoved him away gently.

"Bob, I have feelings for you, too, but we're married and we are
not allowed to feel this way about each other." She was talking fast
but the heat of their two bodies was increasing. Placing her hands on
his shoulders probably had been a mistake. When she touched him she
wanted to touch him again in a more tender manner.

Bob laid his head upon her shoulder. She raised her hands up to lift
it away but the chemistry between them was all consuming. Suddenly,
they were just where Aries had wanted to be since meeting him. They
were locked tightly in each other's arms. They kissed. Bob made
squeaking and painful sounds as his body was pressed firmly against
hers.

"I love you," he murmured. I love you and I want you. I want to
make love to you."

"I think I love you, too, but there is nothing we can do about it.
You can't make love to me in Greg Winston's house." As Aries was
saying these words, mentally, they were already in the bedroom lying

in Greg's bed making mad, passionate love.

Bob's excitement was getting the best of him. "Aries, please", he pleaded, "I can't take this, I need you."

"I know but we can't make love in this house. My conscience wouldn't allow it."

"I understand."

Bob backed away. With tears, almost, in his soft blue eyes and with a huge bulge in the front of his pants, he promised not to press her. "You mean too much to me," he said. "Let me use your bathroom and I'll get on to my ten o'clock appointment."

Relieved but sad Aries pointed the way to the powder room which was situated to the right of the foyer. While he was in there, she rushed to her own bathroom to tidy her hair and to freshen up her mussed lipstick.

What a close call! She wanted to make love to him but certainly, she didn't want it to happen in Greg's bed.

Moments later, they were back in the kitchen.

"I must go now. I have a meeting downtown and then I have to drive to St. Petersburg. I'll be back in town tomorrow evening. Will you meet me then?"

"Yes, I'll meet you. Just tell me when and where."

"I'll call you on my way back across the state. I should get here around seven or so but I'll call you about an hour away and let you know exactly the time and place for us to meet." Hugging her, he emphasized "I love you. I can hardly bear to leave you."

Kissing her again, he pulled himself away because he was getting excited again all over. "You do such wonderful things to me. I'd better get out of here before I beg you to let me stay. See you tomorrow night."

Aries stood by the side door until Bob's car was out of her garage. She wanted to close it behind him. She hoped nobody had noticed the strange vehicle entering or leaving. Although she had a king-sized guilty conscience, she was floating on cloud nine and she couldn't tell anyone why.

Aries had fallen hook, line and sinker for Bob Benton. Their mates would kill them if they knew. She didn't mean to be having an affair but Cupid seemed to be running this show and she was defenseless against his arrows. Thank goodness Greg was in Alaska. If he came home tonight, he would know there was something wrong because she would be unable to hide her excitement. Maybe by the time he arrived home, next week, she'd be adjusted and she could handle it better.

Looking at the clock, she realized that the children would be home from school in a short time. It was teachers' conference day and they were letting them out early. There was just enough time to get the house picked up before lunchtime.

This afternoon, she'd ask Dolly, her neighbor, to watch the three little ones while she took Gregory and Mia shopping. The nannie was off duty today, so Aries had to do the housework, attend the kids and be ready to meet Bob without help.

The next day all she could think of was meeting Bob. She called Jackie, the baby sitter, and arranged to pick her up at five-thirty. The children liked her so they wouldn't complain about Mom going out.

Plans all made, Aries waited to hear from Bob. He called at six o'clock saying he would be back in town by six forty-five. She was to meet him at the entrance of Brownlake Hospital.

"Do you know where that is?" He asked.

"Yes, I know how to get there."

"I can hardly wait to see you, honey. I've really thought a lot about you today," he said.

"Me too. I'll see you, then. Bye now."

Hanging up the phone, she went into her bedroom to get her purse and to take a last minute look at herself in the mirror.

As she was leaving Gregory came into the house. "Where are you going, Mom? Will you take me to the movies, tonight?"

"No, Gregory, you can't go to the movies. I have to go to a club meeting and I'm late now. Jackie will be here and she can help you with your homework. Afterwards, you can watch television until bedtime. I won't be out late. Be a good boy and help Jackie with the kids." Aries hugged him as she ran her hands through his curly blonde hair. He looked so much like his Father. She hoped when he grew up he would take more after her side of the family. They were made of much stronger stock than the Winstons.

On the way out the door, Aries kissed and hugged each child in her path. She cautioned Jackie to lock the doors and to make sure she did not let them stay up too late. "I should be home by ten," she said waving goodbye.

In the car, she began to ponder about her rendezvous with Bob. Where would they go and where would she park her car so nobody would see it? Everybody in town knew it. She'd worry about that later. Right now, her main objective was to get to the spot where they were supposed to meet.

She headed down Romer Road to the entrance of Brownlake Hospital. Bob's car was there when she arrived so she pulled up beside him. Waving, he motioned for her to follow him. He pulled into the parking lot of the pharmacy across the street from the hospital, parked his car and got out.

"I need to go in the pharmacy for a minute. I'll be right out," he said.

Aries waited. When he came out, they left her car parked at the pharmacy and she went with Bob in his car.

As he drove they talked. "I've got a good place where we can go. Honey, I have missed you so much, Aries."

"Me too."

He stopped the car on a dark street behind the hospital. Putting his arms around her, he said, "Aries, I've thought a lot about us while I was in Tampa. I have fallen in love with you and I want to be with you."

Barely able to resist his charm, Aries shared his warm and passionate feelings. He was such a romanticist. She loved it but this game of playing hide and seek was a bit too daring.

Bob began to caress her. Instinctively, she responded.

"Darling, I need to make love to you, tonight. My heart was hurting the whole time I was in Tampa. I wanted to hold you in my arms and whisper words of love to you."

"Oh," exclaimed Aries. "I can't believe the chemistry that's going one between us."

"Yes, it's wonderful, isn't it? Honey, slip your panties off. I have something I want to give you. I want to let you know how very much I love you."

Bob was panting and Aries, scared to death, was blabbing out her peck full of worries. "What if the police sees us? What if we get caught together in your car and get arrested?"

"Don't worry honey. This is a safe place. No one will find us."

Unzipping his trousers, he allowed his big throbbing penis to escape from the fly in his undershorts. There it was hot, hard and beautiful!

"Oh," exclaimed Aries! "I'm afraid. I want to do it but I'm afraid."

"Don't be afraid, I love you. I will be very gentle with you, I won't hurt you. I need you so much."

"But what if you get me pregnant?"

"I took care of that." He pulled out a condom. "I got these at the drugstore."

"But I don't like to use contraceptives."

"I don't like them either but, tonight, we'd better use them. I don't want to get you pregnant before we are married."

"Married?"

"Yes, married. I love you and I want to marry you." Bob was thinking out of his mind. Had he forgotten that they both were very married?

His throbbing penis was sitting on go. "Let's see if it fits," he said as he was scrambling out of his pants. Moments later, he laid his gorgeous athletic frame over her now quivering body. "Raise your legs up some, honey, and let me put him in just a little bit."

"I am so scared."

"There is nothing to be afraid of, darling. He tried to reassure her. "Feel the head of my penis. It feels so good against the lips of your pussy. I don't want to hurt you but I am so excited I can hardly wait."

Momentarily, Aries could feel the thrust of his pulsating throbbing penis plunging deeper inside of her moist vagina.

"Oh," she moaned, "this is beautiful."

"Oh, Aries, "I knew it would feel like this. I knew it would be wonderful. It's so good that I want to feel you without the rubber. Let me take it off and I will hold back and try not to cum in you. I love you so much."

Partially withdrawing, he reached down and removed the rubber. Re-inserting his penis, he teased her with a few quick motions at the mouth of the vagina and then, a deep plunge took it as deep as it would go. "Oh, darling, this is wonderful. It is all I can do to keep from cumming inside you right now."

"Please don't cum in me. Hold back and let me cum. Then you can withdraw."

"I'll try, I'll try but I had better try to think about something else or I'm going to explode inside of you."

Aries tightened her pelvic muscles locking them tight around his penis. She sucked her stomach in and contracted the muscles of her vagina. This was an old Chinese method she had read about and it worked really well.

"You're driving me crazy. This is heavenly. Honey, I am going to cum, I can't wait. It's about to pop," he groaned.

"Cum, cum, darling" moaned Aries. "Cum for I am coming, too. Oh, oh, oh, darling, we are cumming together. It's so beautiful."

"Oh, Aries, you are woman of magic. I love you. I love making love to you." The raging fire between them was temporarily tamed.

"I'd better get my pants back on now. I can see the lights going on in the house down the street," Bob said.

"Hurry, let's get our clothes on and get out of here before someone catches us," exclaimed Aries.

"Next time, I am going to make love to you in a proper bed," he declared. "We'll to go to a motel. Tomorrow night, when we go to Holden Park for tennis we'll talk about it. I've arranged for us to play doubles with some friends of mine."

"We'd better get home. I told Lana that I'd be in around nine and it's nine-thirty, now."

"Yes, we had better go. I told the baby sitter I would be at home by ten. She has school tomorrow and I don't want to keep her out too late. What time do we leave for tennis, tomorrow?"

"I'll pick you up at you house at six. Lana will think we're just tennis partners. She knows how much I love the game and she doesn't play. She'll never suspect a thing."

The next day, Aries got a baby sitter and went with Bob to Holden Park. She was somewhat self-conscious during the match fearing that the couple (who knew both Bob and Lana) would notice they were fond of each other. Fond wasn't the word for it. They were head over heels in love.

On the way back home, Bob told her that he would be out of town for the rest of the week. He promised to call and they arranged to meet at the Post Office on Saturday afternoon when he took his wife to the grocery store.

"We can bump into each other by accident there and we can see each other and talk for a few minutes," he said. Lana's mother's coming this weekend and I guess I'm stuck with them. Next week, when I'm in town we can meet somewhere and go to a motel. Making love to you in the car was wonderful but I want you in a bed, young lady."

Pulling his car in her driveway, he leaned over to kiss her. Aries wanted to get inside before the neighbors or the children saw them. The kiss turned Bob on. His voice was trembling and his big, hard, throbbing penis was protruding inside his trousers.

"I am so much in love with you," he uttered. "I can hardly stand to leave you now. I think I want to marry you."

"Please, honey, I'm in love with you, too, but you'd better go home and I'd better get inside before somebody finds out about us and kills us. Call me tomorrow. Bye now."

Safely inside the door, Aries greeted Jackie and asked how the children had been. "Mark and Ralph got into a big fight. Mark threw Ralph's crayons in the john and tore up the picture he was coloring. I had to punish them both by not letting them watch TV and sending them to their rooms. They cut up so bad I wasn't able to get much home work done."

"I'm sorry. I'll talk to them about this tomorrow."

"Don't punish them. My two brothers fight all the time."

"Well, come on I'll give you a ride home. I guess the kids will be okay alone for a few minutes."

Back at the house, Aries was needed time to think. She needed to sort out her feelings about Greg and Bob. Her whole life had been turned upside down, topsy turvey. Greg was still on vacation but he would be coming home soon. How could she be faithful to him any-more when all she wanted was to be with Bob? Things had happened so suddenly. Aries didn't know how to handle this situation. She had a husband and five children. How could she have fallen in love with another man? A married one at that!

What a terrible but beautiful mess! Aries had no answers to this dilemma but she had no intentions of giving up her relationship with Bob Benton. He was talking about marriage and he wanted to have a baby with her. Greg had had a vasectomy after their last child was conceived. If she got pregnant there would be only one way to explain it. Just the idea of this made her a wreck.

Just the thoughts of Greg discovering their affair terrified her. She knew he would do something drastic if he ever found out. He was coming home and she would have to act like she did before he left. How could she? She didn't feel the same. Things had changed and she would never be the same.

She met Bob on Saturday as planned. He had his little girl with him and they had only several minutes to talk. Greg was due to return home on Friday and Aries warned Bob to be careful about making phone calls to the house.

"Meet me Tuesday morning," Aries, "at the Seafarer Motor Lodge. I'll meet you in front at ten o'clock. I've got to go now," Bob said, "There goes Lana to the car. We can make our plans, then."

She agreed to meet him.

Aries went home and looked up the address in the phone book. The motor lodge was fifteen miles south of Pompano Beach but, of course, she would meet him. Suddenly she remembered that she had a date for doubles in tennis on Tuesday. She called Sadie to cancel.

"What are you doing that day?" asked Sadie. "We always play on Tuesday and you wouldn't miss it for anything. You must be having a daytime affair or something."

"Affair! You must be crazy. Who would I be having an affair with?"

"Well, what about the guy you played tennis with at the club last week? We all noticed that you two seemed to be getting pretty cozy together."

"That's ridiculous. He was just nice. He's polite and friendly with everybody, that's just his way."

"Come on Aries, you can't kid me. Remember, I'm your partner. I know that Benton guy was struck on you."

"Forget it, Sadie. You're imagining things. I can't play Tuesday because I'm going to the dentist. I forgot about the match when I made the appointment. My tooth hurts so I'd better not cancel it."

"Oh, in that case, I'll call Beatrice and ask her to fill in,"Sadie replied reluctantly.

"Thanks a lot, Sadie. Talk to you later."

Tennis settled, Aries called Effie to make sure she would be there on Tuesday. Effie promised, faithfully, that she'd show. That left one last thing to do-- arrange for the private bus to bring Mark and Ralph home from school that day.

Aries spent the weekend at home with the children, mainly guarding them at the pool. The boys got up on the roof and they dove into the pool from there. Aries was afraid they would fall off the house or miss the pool and land on the concrete so she went for the switches. What would they think of next?

On Tuesday morning, she drove to the Seafarer Motel Inn. Bob was parked there, waiting. Coming over, he told her to park her car and wait for him while be checked in.

Afraid of being recognized by someone who knew her, she said, "I can't, I can't. Someone may see me get out of the car. I can't go into a motel in this town. It's too close to home."

"Very well, I understand your feelings. I love you, Aries and I want you."

"I want you, too, but it can't be here."

"Follow me, he said. I know another place, private and secluded twenty miles north. Nobody will see us there."

"Okay."

Getting back into his car and cranking up the engine Bob headed north. Aries followed him. When they pulled up at the hotel it was raining very hard. There was no escaping now. The poor fellow had driven for miles just to satisfy her fancy but she was facing another problem! Her period had started. She was embarrassed to tell him she was bleeding and not in condition. She would blurt this news out to him at the right moment. She felt bad about him paying for a room when he wouldn't be able to use it.

They checked in as man and wife.

"Now, you can relax. honey," he said. "We are perfectly safe here."

The room was very nice and there was a beautiful ocean view looking out of the window.

Aries turned from her gazing to find Bob undressing. "Don't take you clothes off," she cautioned.

He looked at her in surprise. He had a puzzled expression on his face. "What do you mean?"

"Wait, honey, I need to talk to you, first. There's something I need to tell you."

"What is it?"

"It's hard to say. I'm embarrassed but we can't make love today."

Bob's face was flushed and his eyes opened wide just waiting for her to explain.

"I love you, I want you but we can't make love, today, because I have my period."

Relieved, he laughed.

"Come here, darling. You don't need to worry about that. It doesn't matter. We can make love, anyway. Don't you know I love you?"

"But we might get you and the sheets messed up."

"I'll get some towels to put over the sheets and everything will be fine." Case closed! Bob didn't intend to let her period stop him. He pulled the bedspread back and going into the bathroom he came back with a stack of fresh white towels.

Aries excused herself and went to the bathroom, too. There she removed and disposed of the tampon she was wearing. She hoped she wouldn't get blood on his penis. It would be embarrassing if he ended up with a bloody cock.

At least his understanding about her condition helped. Greg would never have said that. He wouldn't touch her during her period for fear of getting his jewel of a cock messed up. Bob was cut from a different mold. He was warm, tender and he made her feel comfortable.

Their love making was filled with passion and excitement. It was

83

wonderful. Love made their sex together, "the best." In between the moans of orgasms, they whispered words of affection. This time, they were in the raw with no protection, hopefully safe since Aries was wearing the rag. The sensations was great and Aries never wanted him to use a rubber again. It didn't feel that good with Greg.

After sex Bob got up and went to the bathroom. Aries stayed in bed. After dressing, he went to his car to get a phone number out of his briefcase. "Take your time, honey. There's no hurry. I've just go to call this guy before one o'clock," he said as he left closing the door behind him.

With Bob out of the room, Aries bounced out of bed looking back to see how bad the battle scene was. There was blood all over the sheet. It looked like someone had been murdered there. Quickly, she ripped off the sheet and bed pad and took them into the bathroom. She was terribly embarrassed. She wondered what the hotel maid would think had happened in there? She hoped Bob hadn't seen it. She showered and put a fresh tampon in. Then she ran cold water and tried to wash the blood stains out of the bedding.

Bob came back. She could hear him on the telephone. Still embarrassed, she emerged from the bathroom and commenced getting dressed. She left the wet sheet and pad rolled up in the bathroom. She knew if there had been that much blood on the bed, Bob's cock had gotten pretty bloody, too.

"Honey, I'm sorry, I'm sorry about all the mess."

Sweetheart, don't worry about it, I'm in love with you."

His words made her feel so relieved. He was so wonderful!

As they parted, Bob invited her to play in a doubles match at the club on Friday afternoon.

"You know Greg will be home, Friday evening. His plane gets in at eight p.m. and I'll have to be finished in time to pick him up."

"No problem, I'll get off early and we'll start at three thirty."

"Okay, it's a date," said Aries as she started her car. See you then."

Back home, she reminded herself that she had only two days to get everything organized before Greg returned home. He was so particular about the house being clean and in perfect order. He was such a damned perfectionist. Without a full time maid she'd never make it.

Greg could always find things to complain about. She recalled a particular incident. One evening he was hanging his suit in the bedroom closet. He ran his fingers across the top closet shelf and yelled out. "You haven't dusted this shelf."

"Hell no, I haven't. I'm so short and the shelf is so tall. I haven't seen any dust on it," Aries quickly retorted.

Greg was such a prick. In two days he would be home. He'd been gone a long time and Aries was becoming accustomed to life without him. Soon all of her new found freedom would cease. Greg would be home cracking the whip and things would be back to normal. But things weren't normal because while he was away, she had fallen in love. She had violated their marriage vows and consequently, she was worried shitless about the situation.

Friday came and after her tennis date with Bob, Aries came home, bathed, dressed in a tee-shirt and slacks and headed for the airport to pick Greg up. His plane was on time and she met him at the arriving passengers terminal. After friendly greetings they chatted about the children on the way home.

Greg had taken her place at the wheel because he was always the driver when they rode together. He jokingly told their friends he was trying to teach her to how to drive but she was a slow learner. "She just loves to ride the brake petal," he would say.

"How was your trip?" Aries hoped friendly chatting would cover her guilt.

"We had a good trip. Hunting was really great!"

"Did you catch anything?"

"No, a couple of the guys shot deer but I didn't get anything."

"You mean you didn't even kill a bear? I thought you were going to bring me a bear rug."

"Sorry, but I didn't get anything."

When they arrived at the house all of the children were still up waiting for Daddy. "Daddy, Daddy, they cried as they all ran to meet him. Daddy, what did you bring us?"

"Oh, I brought you some nice things but go to bed now and I'll give them to you, tomorrow, when I unpack my suitcase. I'm too tired to get that stuff out now."

"Greg, please don't make them wait. Give them their presents now. They're just children and they're too excited to wait until tomorrow. Please, take your suitcase in the bedroom and get their presents out."

"Okay, kids. Go watch TV for a few minutes and I'll unpack the stuff after I've mixed myself a drink and talked to Mommie for awhile. Were you all good while I was gone?"

"Yes, yes, we were good," said Ralph. Everybody was good, except Mark. Mark was a bad boy. Ralph was such a tattle tale.

"Bad boy. What did he do?"

"He got on the roof when Mommie told him not to."

"Mark did you get on the roof?" Greg asked him sternly.

"Yes, Daddy, we all did. Ralph did it, too, but he got down before Mommie saw him."

"You kids had better stay off that roof and I mean it or I'll take my belt to your hineys. Now go watch TV until I get unpacked."

Greg took his drink and headed for the bedroom. Aries followed. He threw his luggage on their king sized bed. She loved their bedroom. It was decorated in blending colors to match the moss green carpet. The spread was elegant, all brocaded with avocado green and gold. The room was softened by a sheer gold ruffle dust ruffle and matching gold sheers on the windows.

Greg put his drink down and opened his luggage. He was throwing the dirty clothes out as he scrambled through them trying to find the bag that contained the children's presents. Picking up one of his undershirts off the floor, she noticed something pink on it. She took into the bathroom where the light was better.

"What's this?"

"I don't know."

"Well, it looks like lipstick to me."

"Well, it isn't. I haven't turned queer."

"Nobody said you had. It looks like you have lipstick on your under shirt."

"Don't be ridiculous."

"Let's see what else you have in here." Aries started removing his clothes from the bag. As she lifted his wrinkled shirts from the suitcase she noticed several long black hairs on one of his shirts.

86

"Where did you get these black hairs on your shirt?" Aries held one of the strands up in her hand. "How did these long hairs get into your suitcase?"

"Who knows? They're probably bear hairs."

"Likely story. You didn't even get near a bear! They look more like Eskimos hairs to me."

"What's with you tonight, Aries? First, you see lipstick and now, you see Eskimo hairs. One might think you didn't trust me."

"Should I?"

"Well, all I did was go hunting with the boys. There's nothing for you to be upset about. Now, let's close the subject."

"What did you bring the kids?"

"Oh, just some trinkets that I picked up at the gift shop at the lodge where we stayed. I didn't get a chance to do much shopping."

"Well, what did you do in Alaska for three weeks? Surely you couldn't hunt and fish all the time. What did you do in the evenings?"

"What is this, forty questions night? That's a stupid question. I went to bed at night. I was tired."

"To bed, alone?"

She was letting him have it from both barrels. It must have been her own guilty conscience that made her suspicious of him.

"What did you do while I was gone?"

"Now that is a stupid question. What do you think I did? I stayed home and took care of your children. I am worn out from tending them and I need a vacation."

"You're really on your high horse, Aries. What's wrong with you?"

"Nothing," she answered in a short tone of voice. I'm going in to check on the children. Please give them their presents, now, so I can get them into bed."

The children were pleased with the eskimo dolls and stuffed seals that Greg brought them. Afterwards, Aries gave them milk, cookies, kissed them good night and ushered them off to bed.

The weekend was filled with grocery shopping and cooking. Greg supervised Gregory and Mark while they mowed the yard and picked up the trash. The rest of the time was spent sitting by the pool watching the children show off their dives and counting the number of laps they could swim.

Greg was exhausted from his long vacation and he had stomach pains so he spent most of Sunday afternoon in bed, sleeping. Thank goodness, he hadn't bugged her for sex this weekend like he usually did. But she had told him she had her period knowing he wouldn't bother her when she was indisposed.

Aries didn't suggest going to the club that weekend. She was afraid Bob might be there and she didn't want Greg to see him.

On Monday evening, she and Greg were sitting in the den watching television when Ralph came in. "Daddy, did you see the trophy Mommie won playing tennis while you were gone?"

"No, I didn't."

"Look at it, look at it, daddy. It's that great big one up there on the shelf. Mommy won a great big trophy at the club. She played real good. Mark and I were ball boys."

"Well let's take a look at it," Greg said as he lifted the king-sized trophy down. "Aries, you didn't tell me about winning a tournament."

"I forgot. We've had so many other things to talk about."

Greg read the inscription, First Place," Mixed Doubles. "Well, congratulations. You must have had a real good partner."

"Yeah, he wasn't bad."

"Who was he? A guy named Bob Benton."

"Bob Benton? Do I know him?"

"Probably not. He doesn't come to the club much. I didn't intend to play but they called at the last minute and said they needed me."

"So that's what you've been doing. Playing tennis while I was away, huh?"

"Oh, I've played some, the usual matches with the girls but not that much. I've been home most of the time."

"Bring my newspaper, Ralph, and go fix me a coke, Aries. I'm tired tonight and I want some peace and quiet. Why don't you get those kids in bed?" How she despised Greg's commanding ways!

"It's early yet. It isn't their bedtime."

"Well, go to in the family room with them so they won't keep coming in here. I want to read the newspaper." Getting up from her chair and leaving the room, Aries thought, grouch, as she headed for the kitchen. She wished he could be nicer to her and the children.

Greg spent the rest of the evening sitting in his chair, feet propped up on his ottoman like a king, reading the paper and watching TV. Aries joined him long enough to watch the eleven o'clock news and then, giving him the usual peck on the cheek, she told him she was going to bed.

"I'll be in later," he said.

It was nice in bed without Greg. Aries needed to be alone with her silent thoughts. She hadn't seen or heard from Bob since Friday and she was beginning to miss him. They'd arranged a telephone signal for communicating. When his wife was out of the house and he could talk he would call, let it ring once and hang up. Upon receiving the signal she'd call him right back if she could.

Aries fell asleep thinking about Bob and wondering what would happen to them. They had to continue their relationship for love like theirs was rare. They were going to have to be very careful because Greg Winston was more clever than Lana was.

Aries was awakened around two a.m. by the feel of Greg's stiff prick in her vagina, fucking her. He had a habit of having intercourse with her without asking after she was in bed asleep. Greg was on top of her going at it, complaining that she wasn't moving her ass. How could she when she was barely awake?

She just hoped he couldn't tell she'd had intercourse with someone else. She had heard that men can tell if you've had relations with another man. They could sense another male's odor. She had douched after sex with Bob and surely by now, his odor would be gone. But maybe her pussy was stretched bigger and he could tell that way. Bob was bigger than Greg. She certainly wasn't relaxed about things. Maybe the affair with Bob hadn't been such a good idea. There was little she could do about it now, except break off the relationship. That would hurt both of them too much, she imagined.

Greg fucked her until he got his kicks. He came a bucketful. Aries didn't cum at all but she pretended to enjoy it.

The next morning, he slept in and went in to work, late. "Take the kids to school," he said, "then come on back to bed. We've got some catching up to do."

"Are you sure? Don't you have to be at work?"

"No, my first appointment isn't until ten thirty."

"Okay, I'll be back in a half hour."

Kids in the car, Aries headed north to the Mrs.Tinsley's private school where Mark and Ralph were enrolled. Bob lived up that way. As she drove she watched the passing cars hoping to catch a glimpse of him. On the way home, she would ride down his street to see if his car was parked in the driveway. It was Wednesday and she really was missing him.

Dropping the children off, she cautioned Mark to bring his home-work home. Then she headed down the road in the direction of Bob's house. As she approached the end of his street she saw him backing his blue car out of the driveway. Turning around, she waited for him to make his turn. He saw her and pulled up beside her car.

"Hi darling, "What brings to up this way?"

"That darn major highway is so congested. I took the back road."

"I'm glad you did. I've wanted to call you but I was afraid your husband would answer and get wise. I need to talk to you. We've got to do something, I can't stand being away from you. My wife doesn't know what's wrong with me. I don't want to have anything to do with her in bed anymore."

"Well, call me this morning and we'll talk. Greg's home but he'll be leaving at ten-fifteen. Call me around ten-thirty." Aries threw him a kiss. The look of adoration on Bob's face penetrated her being. Her heart was fluttering. He had an innocent way of turning her on. He was a Leo and she was was so physically attracted to him.

Arriving back home, Aries went into the kitchen and poured her-self a cup of black coffee. Greg never drank coffee in the morning. He had ulcers and he had to pamper them with milder things. At lunch, frequently he had two dry martini's. Just perfect for his so-called ulcers! Aries thought they were in his head. There was always some-thing wrong with his Mother and there was always something wrong with him.

Going into the bathroom, she sat the coffee cup down on the Grecian marble counter top that spanned the full six feet of the vanity, carefully placing a wash cloth under the cup to avoid leaving an unsightly ring on the marble.

Greg was stirring now in bed and he called out. "Back already, what time is it?"

"It's eight-thirty. I had to stop at the store on the way home."

"Get your clothes off and come back to bed. I'm still sleepy but I'll let you screw me this morning."

"I'm coming. I need to brush my teeth, first."

"Hurry up. This thing isn't going to stay this way, forever."

In bed, Aries climbed on top of him. His spry penis was sticking straight up like a lightening rod. Sex should be good this morning for her pussy was already wet from her brief encounter with Bob. Closing her eyes, she remembered the look of love he had on his face. Her body was fucking Greg but her mind was fucking him. She imagined they were in bed together, terribly excited and passionate. These thoughts made her pussy hot and juicy.

"You had better hurry," she told Greg without looking at him. "Hurry because I'm getting ready to cum. I can't hold on much longer."

Aries had worked herself up into a high level sexual state and she was on the verge of exploding in powerful orgasm. This morning, Greg had no trouble joining her.

When it was over Greg commented. "You nearly screwed me to death. Maybe I should go to Alaska more often."

Not answering, she lay back exhausted. Little did he know that mentally she wasn't screwing him at all.

"I've got to get bathed, shaved and dressed, Greg announced. Molly Mitchell is coming to the office today to invest all of her money in stocks."

"I'll fix your breakfast now," offered Aries. Donning her blue tee-shirt and white short shorts, she went bare-footed into the kitchen. Effie was off today, so she would have to clean up the house. Looking at the dirty dishes in the sink, she wished she didn't have to prepare Greg a separate breakfast and dinner every day. If he'd eat with the children it would be good for them and less work for her. She took the bacon out of the refrigerator and put it in a clean frying pan. Bacon and eggs, eggs over light, that's what he wanted with one slice of wheat toast, no butter.

The telephone rang. It was Sadie inviting her her to play tennis that morning at the club.

"I can't. The maid is off and I have to stay home and clean house."

"What's with you, Aries? Last week you couldn't play. Have you given up tennis? I didn't see you at the club this weekend, either. Is there something wrong?"

"No, nothing. I'm just busy. We'll play soon, I'll call you. I have to hang up now because Greg's still here and I'm fixing his breakfast."

When his plate was ready, Aries went into the bedroom. Greg was still there primping. He always looked like a million dollars and smelled to the high heavens with cologne when he went to work. Maybe he was trying to entice one of the secretary's at the office. Aries never knew what went on there. If she called him at work after eleven thirty he was out to lunch and sometimes, lunch lasted until two p.m. If questioned, he was out to lunch on business. Monkey-business, she guessed. She never got a satisfactory answer.

Aries told him she didn't care how many time he screwed those gals during the day as long as he could do it three more times when he came home. He couldn't do that but generally, he was good for two.

Telling Greg that breakfast was ready, she went back into the kitchen. Another five minutes passed. Watching the hands of the clock, it was ten a.m. She called him again. "Greg, your breakfast is getting cold. I'm going to stop cooking it if you don't eat when its ready."

With this admonition he came to the table.

"Gee, I'm a good looking devil," he remarked. From this comment, Aries knew he'd been standing in front of the bathroom mirror admiring himself. He was famous for that but he never told her how great she looked. Men are so vain, she thought.

Greg finished his breakfast, picked up his car keys and prepared to leave for the office. "Tell Mark to get those skates out of the drive-way before I get home," he commanded as he opened the garage door.

"I will."

Aries waved him goodbye and closed the door. Looking at the kitchen clock, it was ten-nineteen. Bob would be calling soon. In the meantime, she needed to pee and load the dishwasher. The phone rang promptly at ten thirty. As expected, it was Bob.

How are things?

"Same as usual."

"Same here and its driving me crazy. I need to talk to you about what we're going to do."

"What do you mean about what we're going to do?"

"I can't go on this way, Aries. I am so much in love with you, I can't work or sleep anymore. Lana said I was talking in my sleep last night. I hope I didn't mention your name. I'm playing racquetball with Tom tonight, and I can leave early and meet you if you can get out. Can't you tell Greg you're going to visit a girlfriend?"

"Well, I can't usually get out at night unless it's bridge club night but I'll call Judy and see if her husband's out of town. If he is I'll ask her if I can come over. Then, I'll leave her house and meet you.".

"Where can we meet?"

Bob thought a few seconds and then, he told her to meet him at John's Pier at the beach at nine o'clock.

"I'll park by the beach road and wait for you."

"Okay. Call me back in thirty minutes. Give me time to call Judy and see if she's going to be at home tonight."

"Fine, I'll call you back at eleven."

Hanging up Aries dialed Judy's number. "Hi Aries," Judy said in a laughing voice. She was always laughing and she was cute as a bottom's button although she was somewhat heavy for her petite frame.

"Long time no hear. I'm glad you called."

"I called because I was wondering if you were going to be home this evening?"

As a matter of fact I am. Dick's been out of town on a run to and from Chicago for two days. He's due home late this evening. I never go out when he's expected in. Besides, I don't like to leave Tracy with a sitter. She's just too young for that."

Aries knew that wasn't the problem. Judy had tried for many years to have a baby and she couldn't so finally they adopted a baby, a little girl. Since then, she'd been an over protective mother.

Aries told Judy she needed to get out of the house, that taking care of kids all the time was getting to her.

"Well come on over. I'd love to chat with you. We can crack open a bottle of wine and have a merry old time." Judy had been an airline stewardess and having a good time was old hat to her.

"Okay. I've got to hang up now but I'll see you around eight."

When Bob called back she told him everything was all set. She would meet him at John's Pier at nine.

Greg came home, as usual, at five and shortly thereafter, Aries gathered up the nerve at ask him if she could go over to Judy's for awhile that evening. "Dick's out of town and Judy gets lonesome. I get tired of kids all the time, too." He agreed to baby sit if she would get them fed, bathed and ready for bed.

Tonight would be a breeze because she had already made planned the meal. Hot dogs, tater tots, and applesauce. The children liked them and they were easy to fix. She had fresh oysters so Greg could fix his own oyster stew, later.

At dinner Aries told the children she was going over to Judy's. Daddy was going to keep them. "Now be good," she warned. "You know how Daddy likes his peace and quiet."

"Mommy, can we play outside if we don't get dirty?" Mark whined.

"I don't know. Ask Daddy."

Cleaning off the table, she loaded the dishwasher and began ushering the children to their respective bathrooms, girls in one and boys in the other.

"Mia, please help Sara with her bath."

"Mommy, she's big enough to do it herself."

"Yes, but she plays too much and gets water all over the floor when nobody's watching her."

"Well, I'm getting tired of cleaning up after her messes," Mia grumbled.

Please don't argue with me tonight, Mia. Mommy's in a hurry. Please help me."

"Alright, but she'd better not yell when I put shampoo in her hair."

"Be careful and try not to get shampoo in her eyes."

Sara was the baby, six years old, and Mia was big sister at the ripe old age of twelve. She had her own interests and taking care of Sara wasn't one of them. They shared a room and argued all the time over who messed it up. Already, Mia had dibs on the next room that came available. Gregory had his own room but Mark, Ralph, Mia and Sara had to share. The rule in the Winston house was that the oldest always got the first choice. Mia would be next in line but she would have to wait for Gregory to leave home and go to college.

After the children were bathed and dressed in their pajamas, Aries kissed them goodbye and she went out into the front yard where Greg was fooling around with his car.

"I'm leaving now. I don't know what time I'll be home but it will be before midnight."

"Take your time. We'll be here."

Aries was relieved to be out of the house. She felt guilty about playing tricks in order to meet Bob but now, she had to make plans for the rest of the evening.

Judy lived in one direction and John's Pier was in another. She would only be able to visit with Judy for a little while because it would take thirty minutes to get from there to the beach. What if Greg called and Judy told him she wasn't there? She would have hell to pay. She couldn't explain leaving Judy's and not coming home. She would call Greg before she left and tell him she'd be home in a little bit. Then he wouldn't have any reason to call back.

Arriving at Judy's, Aries looked at the new baby and then, baby settled, they sat down to chat.

"I won't be able to stay long."

"What? I thought you were out for the evening."

"No, no, not tonight. I'll have to be on my way by eight-thirty."

"My goodness, that's not long. It's seven forty- five already. You'll be leaving almost as soon as you got here. It was hardly worth the trip. Anyway, let's have some wine and you can brief me up on the latest happenings. I feel ostracized from society since we got little Tracy. I hardly ever leave the house but I love it. I love her and I love taking care of her. She's so precious."

"I know, I know. Babies are so wonderful. I wanted twelve but we compromised on six. Greg stopped me by having a vasectomy after I got pregnant with our fifth child, Sara. I hate him for doing it. If something had happened and I had lost her I wouldn't have been able to have another baby."

"I didn't know he'd had an operation."

"We don't go around telling everybody but that's exactly what he did and the way he went about it really hurt me."

"How's that?"

"Well, he mentioned having the operation but I told him I didn't believe in it and I didn't want him to do it. Then he came home one day with stitches in his balls and told me he'd been to the doctor with his Mother and had it done. I was furious. The nerve of him to make a decision like this without me. I will never forgive him. It has almost ruined our sex life as well as our marriage."

"I'm sorry, I'm sorry to hear that, Aries. Life's funny, like us for instance, we wanted children so badly and I couldn't have any. Then there are folks who can have as many as they want and they don't want them."

"I always wanted to have a large family," confided Aries. "I had the dream of getting married, having a lot of children and living 'happy ever after.' I would end up marrying a man who didn't want children. He only claims the first two, he says the other three belong to me. That burns me up when he knows damned well that all of those children are ours. He didn't mind screwing me but when I ended up pregnant, it was my fault."

"Well, I heard that you punched holes in his rubbers.".

"That's a lie. The truth is that he either took the rubber off before he came or he came first and put the rubber on after."

Judy roared in laughter.

"Come on Aries, you've got to be shitin me! Is this true?"

"It sure is. Besides that, my Uncle sent him a gross of rubbers two years ago and he's only used three of them since."

Judy kept pouring the wine and they kept drinking. Aries wished she didn't have to leave so soon because she was enjoying Judy's company. She was going to have to bust out of there, shortly. She was dying to tell Judy about her problem, about Bob, but she wondered if she could trust her to keep a secret.

Judy was beginning to sense that something was up.

"What's that silly look on your face, Aries?"

"Well, I've got a problem and I was wondering whether or not I could confide in you."

"Sure you can."

"If I tell you something will you promise not to tell anybody, not even your husband."

Judy laughed.

"Aries, I'm the world's best in keeping a secret. Tell me."

Aries withdrew her thoughts, temporarily, from her friend. "Okay, okay, I'll tell you. Judy, what I'm going to tell you is very serious. It's a very serious matter. I met this fellow at the tennis court at the club. We played together in a tournament and won. After that, I made the mistake of seeing him again and now he's in love with me."

Judy looked at her in surprise.

"Go on, go on."

"And I'm in love with him, too. We don't know what do to about it. That's why I'm here tonight. I had to get out of the house to meet him to talk about what we're going to do about our situation."

"My word! You really do have a problem. Are you sure you're in love with him?"

"Yes, yes. I've loved him from the first moment I saw him. We're in love and Greg and his wife don't know a thing about it. He wants me to marry him."

"What are you two going to do? Are you going to get a divorce?"

"I don't know what we're going to do. That's what we're going to talk about, tonight. If Greg finds out about this the whole problem will be solved because he'll kill me. Please don't say anything to anybody. I've got to go now but I'll keep you posted. I need to call Greg before I leave so he won't call back and discover that I'm not here."

Judy told Aries she was playing with fire. "You'd better get this problem resolved and be careful."

"I will, I will. Now, let me call Greg." On the phone she told Greg that she and Judy were there just talking "girl talk. "Is everything okay with the kids?"

"Yes, they're in bed. Well, if everything is okay I'd like to stay awhile longer."

"Stay as long as you like. I'm busy working on the checkbook. We're going to have to cut down on some of these expenses."

"We'll talk about that later. See you in awhile."

Aries bid Judy goodnight and told her she would call tomorrow. Leaving, she headed for the appointment with Bob. She was a guilty, nervous wreck with Greg at home watching the children while she was bound for a rendezvous with her lover.

Bob was sitting in his car at the appointed spot when she arrived. She pulled up beside him.

"Hi, Aries. Lock your car and let's go sit on the beach." Bob said smiling.

"I'm afraid. I might get sand on me and Greg will notice it when I get home."

"Well, what about me? Lana thinks I'm playing racquetball so sand wouldn't look so well on me, either. Can you imagine us both back home in bed, tonight, with sand all over our asses? We'd be in trouble then for sure," he laughed.

"That's right and there's no way we could explain that."

"Well let's just sit here on the car. We can catch some fresh ocean air. Smells good, doesn't it?"

"Yes, I love it."

"I love you, Aries, and I want to marry you."

"But what about Lana and Greg and all of our children?"

"Well maybe we could just change partners. Let Greg come and live with Lana and I'll come live with you."

"Don't be ridiculous. I don't think that would work out."

"Well, why don't we ask them for a divorce?"

"That wouldn't work, either," Aries was quick to respond. Greg doesn't believe in divorce. He thinks we are married forever."

"We can make them divorce us. We can make them so miserable that they'll want to divorce us and they'll think it's their idea. Maybe that's the way we should work it," Bob declared.

"But if they decide to divorce us what will happen to our homes and to our children?" asked Aries concerned.

"You'll get to keep your children. No court would take your children away from you and Lana will probably get custody of ours. I'll ask the court to give me rights to have my kids stay with me in the summer."

"Would you mind not being with your children?"

"Well, I wouldn't like it but both of us can't have them and I think a child belongs with its mother until he's older. Don't worry about anything. It will all work out.

As he was talking, Aries noticed there was a man in a car parked nearby. "What's that guy doing over there?"

"Oh, he's probably just stopped by to look at the ocean. Lots of people park at the beach at night."

"Well, I don't like it. He seems to be staring at us."

"Honey, don't worry about it."

"I'm getting cold out here. It's becoming windy," said Aries.

Bob put his arm around her and pulled her close to him.

"Here let me keep you warm." He lifted the sides of his jacket wrapping them around her as he hugged her. Her breasts nestled against his chest. His voice began to quiver and as he spoke softly to her, he was almost crying. "Aries, I love you. I want you. I want to be with you and sleep with you like your husband does."

"I want you, too," darling, "but that man over there is too close to us. He's watching us kiss. Let's get out of here. Where can we go?"

"Follow me, Bob said. "Leave your car here, let's go in mine. We'll drive down and park for awhile under the bridge. No one can see us there."

Aries felt safer under the bridge. It seemed like a good place to hide. Bob had romance in mind. "Honey, I can't stand it when I get close to you. You turn me on and I want to make love to you."

"Not in the car again."

"Why not? No one can see us here."

Aries was turned on, too, she could feel her pussy quivering. His penis was bulging in his trousers and she laid her hand there giving it a tight squeeze.

"Don't honey, don't," he begged. "I'm so excited I might cum all over my britches."

"Well take it out, darling, and let me kiss it. I love your sweet cock." Pulling his zipper down, he gave her the room she needed to reach in and expose his beautiful cock. Already cum was oozing so she licked it off with her tongue. She touched the opening with her finger, wetting it with the cum that still was leaking out. Rubbing his cum around the head of his penis, she placed her mouth gently upon its velvety head.

"Darling, darling, you're so beautiful," he exclaimed. "Stop, don't do that or I'll pop now. Take your panties off and let me love you. I want to feel my cock inside your warm, wet pussy."

"Oh yes, I want you now, too, but what about contraceptives? What about a rubber? Put one on or you'll get me pregnant."

"I can't. I forgot to get one. We'll just be careful and I'll pull out before I cum."

Although Aries feared pregnancy, her passion overrode the fear. Making love was better without a condom but what would she do if she became pregnant with him when they were married to other spouses? She didn't mean to make love to him tonight, not with Greg at home, not when she had to sleep in the same bed with him.

It was too late, now. Overcome with passion and desire, they were going ahead in spite of everything. She removed her panties, put them in her purse and lay back with legs raised. Bob positioned himself and inserted his throbbing penis in her vagina.

"Oh my, this is unbelievable with you, Darling, you possess me."

"Please, please make love to me, put it in deeper, darling, but please don't cum and get me pregnant, she murmured.

"My God, I'm about to cum," he wailed. "I can't stop it."

"Jerk out, jerk out. What are those lights shining in our window?"

"What lights?" Bob lifted his head but it was too late. A police officer was standing there tapping on the car window.

"He shined his flashlight in their faces. "Hey, you two. Don't you know its against the law to park here? Don't you know its against the law to have sexual intercourse on public property? Why don't you two lovers go somewhere and get in bed together where you belong? You are liable to get arrested for indecent conduct out here."

At that moment Aries was dying. She couldn't get her panties on with the policeman standing there shining his light on them. She pulled her shirt down as far as she could hoping to hide her privates. Bob was caught in the same unfortunate condition. He sat there bare-assed talking to the officer. Luckily the cop let them go and they scrambled into their clothes. What a circus this night had turned out to be! They had been interrupted right when they were beginning to climax. This making love in the car was too nerve wracking.

Embarrassed and feeling lucky to have gotten away, Bob drove back to the beach so Aries could retrieve her car. It was getting late, almost eleven, and they needed to get home before they had further explaining to do.

"I'll call you when I can. Remember, let's try to make our mates miserable so they will divorce us as soon as possible."

"Okay, its a deal." Aries knew it wouldn't be hard to make Greg miserable because he stayed that way most of the time, anyway. She could, however, pretend to have headaches and be too tired for sex. She could say no all the time. That should get the best of him, sooner or later.

Arriving home, Aries dashed into the powder room to wash up before facing Greg. Afterward, she found him still sitting behind his big desk in the den.

"Working late?" she asked as she greeted him.

"Sit down," Greg ordered. "I want to talk to you."

"Here I am," she answered reaching for her cigarettes.

"Where have you been tonight?"

"Where have I been?" She repeated.

"Don't answer a question with a question," he snapped angrily.

"You heard the question, tell me where you've been."

"You know where I have been. I've been at Judy's. You knew I was going there. What's wrong with you? Have you lost your memory or something?" Greg was angry. He also had been drinking.

"What's the matter? Are you drunk?"

"Sit down and shut up. I'm asking the questions and you'd better give me some straight answers. Now, I'll ask you again. Where have you been and who were you with tonight?"

"I went to Judy's and I've been drinking wine and talking to her. You left her house at eight thirty-five. Do you want to tell me where you've been and who you've been with for the last two hours?"

"I told you where I've been."

Greg shouted, "I'm about to lose my patience with you. Are you going to stick to that story or are you going to tell me the truth?"

"Hey, if you know the truth why are you asking me questions? You tell me where I've been."

Suddenly, Greg jumped up out of his chair screaming. "You were at the beach, leaning up against his car rubbing yourself all over this guy, petting and smooching."

"Really."

"Yes, and then you were laying down in the front seat of his car with him parked under a bridge near John's Pier."

Shit, now it was all becoming clear. The man she had noticed at the beach must have been a private detective. There was no other way that Greg could know this. Aries was caught but she prayed to God that he didn't know who she was with.

"Now do you want to tell me his name?"

"No, I don't want to tell you anything."

"Well, I'm going to tell you something. You've been out with that tennis player, Bob Benton, and I'm going to call his wife, right now."

"Please, please, don't do that."

"Why not?" stormed Greg as he went to the liquor cabinet to pour himself a straight Scotch. Now, he was drinking it straight and he was wild. He sat down at his desk in front of Aries who was still frozen in her chair.

"Please, please, don't make a fool of yourself," she pleaded. "Oh, please don't call his house at this hour of night."

Greg paid no attention to her. Picking up the phone, he dialed Bob Benton's number.

"Hello, is this Lana Benton?" Apparently it was because the next thing Aries heard was Greg's question.

"Do you know where you husband was tonight?" She must have told him that he was out playing racquetball with the guys. Then, Greg told her, "your husband was out with my wife." She must have been dumb founded.

Greg inquired if Bob was home, yet?

"No, no he isn't." Lana answered.

"Well, when he gets there you ask him to call me back."

Hanging up the phone, Greg jumped up from his seat shouting, "I'm going to kill that son of a bitch." Aries was terrified.

He went to the gun rack and took out the shot gun she had given to him for Christmas. It had belonged to a neighbor across the street. Greg had admired it so she traded her new golf clubs for the gun. Now, she wished she hadn't.

Aries got up from her chair. The situation was worsening. Greg was out of his mind. "Please, please," she begged. "Put the gun away and let's talk this thing over."

"There's nothing to talk about. Bob Benton, that son of a bitch, is a dead man."

Greg loaded the gun, picked his car keys up off the desk and said he was going to Benton's house to wait for him to come home. "I'm going to blow his brains out. I'll teach that bastard to mess around with my wife. I'm going to take care of him and then, I'll be back to take care of you."

Aries couldn't stop him. He was about to cause a tragedy. The car tires squealed as he sped out of the driveway and down the street. Thinking quickly, she picked up the phone and called Lana.

"Hello," said Lana.

"Hi, this is Aries Winston. Is Bob home, yet?"

"Yes, he just walked in the door."

"Well, my husband's on the way to your house with a loaded shot gun. He says he's going to kill him. If you ever want to see your husband alive again, I suggest that you get him out of the house, fast."

"What's going on?" asked Lana. I don't have time to talk about it now but you'd better tell Bob to get out, fast."

Lana yelled to Bob. "Aries Winston's on phone and she says her husband's on the way up here with a shotgun. She says he's going to kill you and that you'd better get out, fast. Bob, have you been out with Aries?" Aries heard that much of the conversation before Lana came back to the phone telling her that Bob had grabbed some clothes and he left

"Now what's this all about? Have you been out with Bob?"

103

"I don't want to talk about it now but I warn you to talk to my husband and see if you can calm him down when he gets there. Somebody's got to talk some sense into his head because he's crazy. I'll call his Father and see if I can get him to come to your house and take the gun away from him."

"What has Bob done now? I can't believe this nightmare."

"Well I'm sorry but it's true. I've got to go. Don't let Bob come home. It's not safe."

Aries hung up the phone and went into the kitchen. It was after midnight. She was shaking like a leaf in fear. She hated to call Greg's Dad but she needed help. Picking up the phone, she dialed his number. Bridie answered and she could tell by the sound of Aries's voice that something was wrong.

"What's the matter?" she asked.

"Nothing. Let me speak to Dad, please."

"He's asleep, said Bridie.

"Well, wake him up. I have to talk to him, right now.

"Ned, Ned." Aries could hear her calling him. "Wake up," Aries is on the phone and she acts like something is wrong. She wants to talk to you." Dad took the phone and Aries blurted it out.

"Come over here, quickly. I need you to go get Greg. He's gone up to the Benton's house to kill Bob Benton. He's got a loaded shot gun and somebody's got to take it away from him.

"I'll be right there."

Thank goodness, he didn't ask what had caused Greg's violent behavior. Aries turned on the porch light and waited for him to arrive. Luckily, they lived only a couple streets away.

She wrote Bob's address down in big letters on a piece of paper so Dad could read it. Minutes later, he pulled up in the driveway. Aries told him briefly what had happened and sent him on his way. Dad was shocked but there was no need to talk about what she had done now. Later, would be soon enough. First things first. He had to rescue Bob Benton and prevent his son from doing something awful.

Back in the house, Aries went to the phone and called Lana.

"What's happening? she asked. "Is Greg still there?"

"Yes, he's here. He's waiting for Bob to come home. He says he isn't leaving until he does."

"Well, give him lots of black coffee to sober him up. Don't tell him but his father is on the way up there to take his gun away."

"I'll do the best I can. I'd better get back in there."

Bob was safely out of the house. Aries wondered where he went. Greg, hopefully, was being calmed. Now, she had another urgency. She had to worry about her own ass. If Greg would shoot Bob, he probably would shoot her, too. She certainly wasn't going to wait around to see. What if his father was unsuccessful in getting the gun? She had to get out of the house before he got back. Where would she go in the middle of the night? She didn't want the children to know anything about this dreadful matter. She decided not to disturb them but to leave them sleeping. The maid would be there at eight a.m. Surely he wouldn't do anything to harm his own children. It was she and Bob Benton that he was after, not his kids.

Aries took her purse, went to the car and drove away. She felt like a fool out on the streets at this hour with no where to go. It definitely wasn't her style. She hadn't called the police when all of this happened. She didn't even think of calling them. The Winston's were proud people. They wouldn't want to be disgraced in the community. This was a family matter.

Aries drove south in the opposite direction from her house. What a calamity this had turned out to be! It looked like their affair had been blown straight to hell. They had been discovered and she wondered what the repercussions would be. Death? Divorce? Whatever Greg decided to do, she knew he would get even. If she stayed with him he would punish her and make her miserable.

She looked at her gas gauge. The car was getting low on fuel. She was getting sleepy, too, so she drove to the park to sleep there until dawn. She'd call Dad Winston early in the morning and get him to go home with her before the children woke up. She dared not go to his house because Bridie would chastise and blast her for her disgraceful wrong doing. Dad was understanding but she would give her no mercy. There would be no point in even trying to explain things to her. She wouldn't be sympathetic. Greg was her favorite fair haired son and the only side of the question she would see would be his.

What a mess this was! It wouldn't have been so bad if they had been childless but they had the matter of eight children to consider. Breaking up with Greg wouldn't be so bad. What mattered was what would happen to her children? There was no room for discussion on this. She was in love with Bob, she was married to Greg but her real love was those babies that she had brought into the world.

Aries pulled her car up under a tree in the park where she had taken the children to play so often. She turned the motor off, the lights out and curled up in the seat to get a little shut eye. Her head was beginning to pound and she was exhausted.

She wondered what had happened with Greg but she was too tired to worry about it. She would find out in the morning. There were many unsettled matters between them and the Benton family. Their plan to make Greg and Lana miserable so they would ask for a divorce was no longer necessary. Either divorce was inevitable or the other choice would be for them to abandon their relationship, stay with their mates and suffer the consequences of their untimely affair.

Aries dozed intermittently during the wee morning hours. She awakened at six forty-five a.m. and drove to a service station for fuel and to use the rest room. Afterward, she stopped by Dunkin Donuts to get a cup of coffee and call Dad. She knew he would be up early although he had been up half the night. He had a business to open.

Dialing his number she waited for an answer. Again, Bridie answered.

"I'm sorry to call so early but I have to talk to Dad," said Aries nervously.

"I want to talk to you," said Bridie.

"Yes, yes, I know you do but let me talk to Dad, first."

"Okay, but I want you to know, young lady, that you've got a lot of explaining to do. What are you trying to do, she continued, ruin my son's life and drive him crazy?"

"Mrs. Winston, I'll explain things to you, later. Please, put Dad Winston on the phone. When Dad got on the phone Aries asked him if he had taken the gun away from Greg..

"Yes, he gave it to me but things aren't right, yet. Where did you stay last night?"

you'd be playing. How are you, Aries?"

"Not too well. How are you?"

"I'm okay. I've moved out of the house and I'm staying with a guy who's a friend of mine."

"What's going on at your house?"

"Well, Greg's gone, too. He's staying with his parents, now. I'm really sorry he's caused you so much trouble. I had to get you out of the house that night because I didn't want you hurt. You know when we were parked at the beach, he had a detective following me. That's how he found out about us."

"Aries, I need to see you. I need to talk to you about our plans."

"The match is about ready to begin. I have to go now but I can meet you at the library after the match. I should be out of here by noon."

"Fine, I'll meet you inside in the first reading room. I love you, Aries."

"Me too, I love you. See you later."

Aries didn't play well in the match that day. She had unnecessary interferences from the outside. Some guy was there peering through a hole in the wind breaker, watching every move she made. Maybe she was becoming paranoid or maybe this was another detective following her. She had noticed a strange car parked down the street from her house that morning. Greg must have been at it again. She wondered why he was wasting his money. He had all the evidence he needed against her. Why look for more?

She finished the match and on her way off the court she went over to the peeper and commented, "Come on, let's go. I'm going to the bathroom and after that, I'm going to the grocery store so you won't have much fun. You should have picked a better day!" The man walked away, saying nothing.

Aries paged Bob at the library. She was damned sure she was being followed so she told him that it might not be a good idea for them to meet there, after all.

Hearing the change of plans, Bob said, "Honey, he was probably just looking at your pretty legs but if you'd feel more comfortable, we'll do it another time. I'm afraid to call you at home. Your husband might have your phone tapped, too. Take my number and call me at four o'clock and we'll decide what to do."

"Okay, okay. That's a good idea. I really want to see you but we've got to be very careful. We can't let Greg or Lana know we're in contact. We'd better to "lay low" until the smoke clears. I'll call you at four. By the way, while you're at the library you might as well check out a good book," she laughed. Something had to be funny about this damned mess.

Aries told Sadie she had to get on home, that she didn't have time to go out to lunch. Apologizing for playing lousy tennis, she said, "Sorry, I played so badly. That guy standing outside the fence made me nervous and I couldn't concentrate."

"What's going on with you, Aries? Are you keeping secrets from me? You've been so quiet, lately."

"I can't tell you now. I'll call you later this afternoon and tell you all about it."

"I hope so," said Sadie. "We have a lot of catching up to do."

Aries gathered up her gear and headed for home. Everything was fine there. At least, the house and the children were still in one piece. Things had been a little hectic with them since Greg left.

At three forty five, Aries made the pretense of going to the store. She told the maid she would be right back. She went to the pay phone outside the laundromat at a nearby shopping center to call Bob. On the line, they renewed the conversation they had started earlier that day. Bob said Lana wanted him to come back home but he thought would probably stay out of the house since he was out.

"Let's go ahead and get divorced from them, he said. We can get married and have babies, together. I want to marry you."

"I want to marry you, too, but it's not quite that easy. Greg would give me a divorce but he would leave me with nothing but the shirt on my back. He says I can't have the house or the children."

"Why don't you see a lawyer? I'm calling mine. Let him have the house and the children if that's what he wants. I'll give Lana our house and the kids, too."

"What will happen to us? We would have no home, no nothing."

"We will have each other and I could sleep in a tent with you."

"Greg not only would keep the house and take the children but he would take my inheritance, too. It's in the stock market and in the bank in our joint names and I'm sure he wouldn't let me have a penny of my own money."

"Who cares? We could get married and leave the country. We could go to Australia and sweep tennis court lines. Why don't we arrange a meeting with Greg and Lana. All four of us together can sit down and see if we can't work this thing out. The way things are now, it's driving me crazy."

"I don't know. I don't think Greg would be very cooperative."

"Well, what have we got to lose? I'll call Lana, tell her my idea and let her call Greg to ask him if he would sit down like an adult and try to resolve things."

"Okay, I certainly am not going to ask him. I haven't talked to him since he went to his Mothers to stay. His father came by the other day to pick up more of his clothes but otherwise I have no idea about what's going on with him."

"Don't worry honey, I'm sure that once they see us face to face we can come to some agreement."

Two days later, Greg called. Lana had called him saying that she and her husband wanted to meet with us.

"I have agreed," he said. "They'll be at our house tomorrow evening at eight so I'll come by and visit the kids for awhile before they get there."

"I wish you hadn't told them to come to the house. Enough has gone on in front of the children, already."

"Well, meeting there will save you a baby sitter. Lana says we can sit down and attack this thing between you two, intelligently. I'm willing to try if you are."

"Okay, but I'm not so sure this is a good idea."

"I've got to go now, said Greg. "I'll see you tomorrow."

The next day Aries was an absolute wreck knowing that her lover was coming face to face with her husband. Then, he would have them together in the same room and he could shoot them both. She wondered if his father had given him the gun back. Bob Benton was a brave, brave soul to have the nerve to walk into Greg Winston's

111

house. Aries dreaded facing his wife. This idea of a meeting between them was crazy. She wanted to chicken out. She and Bob were guilty. They were bringing them to trial and the hangmen would be there ready to hang them.

Greg showed up early in time to greet the kids. They all hugged and kissed him. They missed their Daddy and they didn't understand why he didn't come home from work anymore. Greg wasn't much for displaying affection, He quickly extricated the children from tugging at him. He had brought a quart of scotch in with him from the car. "Now go outside and play," he said. "I have something to talk to your Mother about."

Aries asked Greg how he was doing.

"Not bad. How are the kids?"

"They're okay, they miss you but they're fine."

"Well, you caused the whole thing," he snapped.

"Greg, I thought this was going to be a peaceful meeting. What you think is not true, anyway. You think I slept with Bob Benton and I didn't."

"Don't lie to me. That detective saw you under the bridge laying down in the front seat of his car."

"I don't care what that mad man said," she replied curtly. "I wasn't doing anything. Can he prove that I was?"

"Shut up, stupid. You must think I'm a damn dummy."

The the doorbell rang. Aries peered out the window and saw Bob's car parked outside in the driveway..

"They're here."

"Bring them in. Bring them into the den," ordered Greg.

When Aries answered the door, she got a cool look from Lana. Her deep blue eyes were flashing with madness. Bob appeared to be very nervous. She was sure his knees were wobbling just as hers were.

Ushering them into the den, Greg greeted Lana and she introduced Bob to him. What a way to meet someone for the first time! Lana's expression said, "Here he is, here's that jack ass who's been running around on me and courting your wife." It was just like Aries thought. They were bringing them to the slaughter. Before it was over, Aries felt like she was being placed on the auction block.

What a meeting! Lana and Greg took turns admonishing them and accusing them. Then, they began to interrogate them. They asked questions Aries didn't want to answer. First, they started in on Bob.

"Have you slept with Aries?" Lana asked.

"No, I haven't."

Greg asked Aries the same question. Again, the answer was no. "Well, if you haven't been sleeping together what is it with you two?

"We've been playing tennis. We like to play tennis as partners. We make a good team," Bob said.

"What else do you like about each other, playing footsies in the car? Do you love her? Do you love my wife or do you just want to screw her?"

This went on for awhile with Greg and Lana directing the show. Bob had been silent but the expression on his face showed that he was getting more and more frustrated. Finally, he jumped up out of his chair and there was no doubt that he had taken the floor.

"I've listened to you, Lana," he said pointing to his wife "and I've listened to you," turning to Greg. "Now, I've got something to tell both of you. Yes, I love Aries." Standing face to face with Greg he spoke in a resounding voice. "Yes, I love your wife. I want your wife but I want her like you've got her. I want to marry her."

Greg slumped back in a state of shock. Lana jumped up and started yelling in a shrill voice, "Did you hear that? Did you hear that, Greg? He loves Aries and he wants her to be his wife. Can you imagine that? He's married and he's got three children, she's married and she has five and he wants to marry her. Now isn't that cute! He hasn't even considered the consequences of breaking up two homes and ruining the lives of eight children."

Then she started in on Aries. "Do you love Bob? Do you want to marry him?" There was silence in the room. Aries looked at Bob, then turned her face toward Greg, "My answer is yes, yes, I'm in love with Bob and I want to marry him, too."

"Well, this beats all I've ever heard in my life," Lana said. Those two are both insane. Why don't we excuse ourselves and go to the kitchen and let these two love birds be alone together. Greg got up and left the room with Lana. Aries felt like a fool. She couldn't believe that Bob stood up and told her husband that he loved her and wanted to marry her. Now Greg would really kill her when they left.

When they were alone, Bob put his arms around her saying it was all out in the open. All they had to do now was file for divorce and get this ordeal over with.

"I suppose you're right but I can't believe you had the nerve to tell him," Aries responded still trembling.

"I had no choice. I had heard enough from both of them accusing us, trying to make us feel like criminals when we couldn't help being human and falling in love. Now, maybe they will stop badgering us and leave us alone."

Aries whispered, "Hush, be quiet, they're probably in the kitchen listening to us over the intercom. Those two are out to get us. Let's open the door and tell them to come on back in." Aries opened the door, invited them in and the meeting was on again.

This time the subject was about who would get custody of the children and what to do about their respective homes.

"Aries will get nothing," said Greg adamantly. " She'll get nothing, not the kids, not the house and no money. Any woman who screws around on me gets nothing from me but a kick in the ass."

"Bob's getting nothing either," said Lana.

"Well, I think this is a useless conversation," Bob interjected. "We'll call our attorneys and put the matter into their hands. Lana, Let's go. I'll take you home."

Aries saw them out and she told Greg it would better if he left, too.

"So you're in love with that yellow bellied son-of-a-bitch," he jeered as he walked toward the door.

Aries was afraid to say, yes. Bob had gone home and she had no protection. "No, no, I'm not in love with him. I don't want to marry him, either. I just said that because you all were badgering us to death. If you think I'm marrying anybody and leaving my children, you've got another thought coming. All we had was an innocent relationship, and you and Lana have blown it all out of proportion."

Greg looked at her. He was really confused. "What are you going to do, Aries?"

"I don't know. I know you'll never forgive me. I haven't decided what to do yet. When I know what I'm going to do, I'll let you know."

The phone rang. It was Greg's mother wanting him to come home to dinner. She relayed the message and saw him to the door. On the way, she reminded him that they had five children and they should try to be civil to each other in their presence. "They don't understand what's wrong and they love us both," she continued.

"Well you're going to have to make up your mind, fast, Aries. Either go with him or tell him to get lost. You can't have your cake and eat it, too."

"I'll make a decision. Goodbye."

The next day, she called a lawyer and made an appointment to talk about getting divorced.

Bob called from St. Petersburg that evening and they discussed divorce and marriage. This fairy tale of theirs could now become a reality but Aries didn't like the conditions. She was frightened at Greg's threats of taking her children. If her choice was Bob without her children she would tell him goodbye. She refused to give them up. Greg said the children had to stay with him. If this was the deal, then there was no deal. She would stay with him the rest of her life to be with her kids.

Bob was eager to know her decision.

"I don't know yet. I'm going to see a lawyer. Greg says he will give me a divorce but he gets to keep the kids."

"Well, let him keep them."

"I couldn't I couldn't. I couldn't bear leaving them."

"Aries, it looks like our only choice."

"Oh, no, oh no, that's not my only choice. The other choice I have is to tell you, goodbye."

"If that's what you want, darling, I'll do it." She could feel the pain and hurt in his reply. "I'll get out of your life and never see you again if that's the way you want it."

"It's not the way I want it but it may be the only answer. I love you but if it means the loss of my children, I will have to stay where I am."

Bob was out of town all week. Aries went to a lawyer and told him she wanted a divorce. He took the pertinent information and agreed to draw up the papers.

Bridie called to advise her that Greg had checked into the hospital. His nerves were bad and she thought he was having a nervous break-down. Aries told her that she had filed for divorce and she could have her son back.

"If you divorce him with him sick, I'll never speak to you again," Bridie warned.

It was becoming evident there was no easy way out of this thing. The relationship with Bob had caused many problems in both of their marriages. Taking assessment of the matter, Aries made the decision to give Bob up and try to salvage whatever she could of her marriage with Greg. She couldn't just walk out on him for another man. He was the father of their children and their marriage had been a long one. She didn't love him the way she did Bob but the stakes were too great.

When she visited Greg at the hospital he was cool and had little to say to her. He acted very strange. She was very worried about him. What would happened if he didn't get well? Greg's doctor told her that he'd had another nervous breakdown. It would take time for him to recover.

Calling called her lawyer, she canceled the divorce. She told Greg she loved him and she was sorry that Bob Benton ever happened. "Please forgive me. I love you and I love our children. Let's try to start over again," she begged.

Greg came home and he promised to give her another chance but he didn't let the subject drop. He still hounded her about her relation-ship with Bob Benton. When questioned, Aries declared that he was just a fling. She'd never slept with him and she wasn't in love with him. As she said this she knew she was being untruthful.

Bob was devastated when she told him she had decided to go back with Greg and that she could never see him again. He said he would just vanish if that was what she wanted.

She told Greg that Bob was now out of the picture.

"I'll make sure of that," he said. "I'll make that rotten bastard sell his house and get out of this town."

Not long afterwards Aries heard at the club one day that the Bentons had sold their house and they had moved away.

"Where did they go?" she asked.

"Nobody knows," said the pro. Bob called a couple days ago telling us to take his name off the ladder. He said they were leaving town but he didn't say where they went going."

Months passed and Aries heard nothing from him. Why hadn't he, at least, called to say goodbye? Why had he just vanished like this? Aries suspected Greg knew where he was but he would never tell.

Bob Benton was gone but things were no longer the same between them. Greg was over-bearing and frequently, he became angry with her. These times, he would accuse her over and over of having slept with Bob Benton. His violent outbursts were frightening. She began to wish she'd gone through with the divorce. Greg's drinking increased and his behavior toward her was so different she feared he was having an affair. It was as if he was hell bent on getting even with her. Their life together was a living nightmare.

Aries missed Bob and she wondered where he had gone. On his birthday, she sent him a card marked please forward, return receipt requested. The slip came back signed by Bob. The address was Clearwater, Florida. She would have never thought of looking for him there. She felt better knowing where he was.

Greg never let up on her. For days, he kept accusing her and telling her she was still in love with Benton. He didn't believe their affair was over. Maybe it was the look on her face.

"You still haven't gotten this man out of your system."

"Oh yes, I have. The problem is yours, not mine. Stop badgering me."

"Prove it to me. Prove to me that you're over him," he shouted.

"How can I? You won't believe me."

"See him again and if you can come back and tell me you don't love him, I'll believe you."

"That's ridiculous. You've got to be crazy. I don't want to see him in the first place and in the second place, I don't know where he lives."

"Well, I do. He lives in Clearwater and I want you to set up a meeting with him. I can't live with you until I am sure its over between you two. I'm going to call them right now."

Going to the phone, he dialed Bob's number. Lana answered and Greg proposed that they let their spouses meet to make sure this thing was over between them. Lana agreed. She invited them to come over to Clearwater. She and Greg would stay in the house and they could sit out in the backyard and talk. How did Greg get Bob Benton's phone number and how did he know where they had moved? Greg and Lana must have had this whole thing planned.

Aries didn't like this idea, at all, but she was dying to see him. Her life had been so miserable and she wondered if his had been the same.

Later, Greg decided she should fly to Clearwater without him. Lana would be there to watch them. Aries sensed this meeting at Bob's house was another one of Greg's traps. Instinct told her to alter the plan. When her plane arrived at the Clearwater airport she rented a car. Instead of going directly to Bob's house, she waited at the end of his street. It was early morning and surely, he would be going out for a newspaper or something. Maybe she could catch him alone and they could foul up Greg and Lana's plot.

Her plan was successful. Around eight, she spied his car approaching. He had a child in the car with him. Aries beeped her horn as he passed hoping he would recognize her. Bob's head turned in her direction. Recognizing her, he stuck his hand out of the car window and motioned for her to follow him. He stopped at the 7-11 nearby. Leaving his child in the car, he went in and so did Aries.

"Hi!"

"Hello," smiled Bob.

"You know I'm here for a meeting with you that Greg and Lana have planned. I don't want to go to your house, though."

"Stay here, Aries. I have to drive Jewel to school but I'll meet you back here in a few minutes and we'll go to the park. We can sit and talk there."

"Okay."

She watched Bob leave the store and get into his car. How wonderful it was to see him again! Greg was right. She was still in love with him.

Soon he came back and leaving her car at the 7-11, they went in his to the park. They found a nice secluded spot where they could sit down and talk. At last they were alone. Embracing and crying, they were so happy to be together. This was the first time that they had really had a chance to talk since their mates had abruptly discovered them.

Most of their meeting was spent in tears of regret. Aries explained how Greg had cracked up and how she felt obligated to stay with him because he was ill. She told him how miserable her life was with him, now. Bob was so sorry and he was so hurt. It had cost him, too. He had to sell his house at a loss, move and take a new job. Things hadn't been rosey for him, either.

"Why did you decide to leave Pompano Beach so suddenly?"

"Lana bugged the shit out me until I finally gave in and did what she wanted me to do."

"Well, Greg was the instigator behind that. He told me he was going to force you to sell and get out of town. It looks like Greg and Lana won all around. Losing you has been one of the greatest tragedies in my life but my decision was made for the sake of my children."

Aries was in tears. Bob couldn't stand to see her cry. He cried, too. In a warm embrace they kissed and professed their undying love for each other.

"Stay with your wife. I have to stay with my children. I love you, Bob and I'll marry you when I'm eighty. Maybe no one will object to us being together, then."

Parting that day was almost unbearable. They made plans to meet again in a month. They would meet halfway and spend some time together during the day at Lake Placid. Aries was somewhat consoled knowing that Bob wasn't lost forever, that she would see him again. They wanted to make love but painfully, they decided to save it for the next time. Greg knew where she was and she had to be careful.

Arriving home that afternoon, Aries went into the den where Greg waited. She had dreaded this moment with him.

"Well, you're back. How was your lover?"

"I didn't go there. After getting to Clearwater, I decided your idea wasn't such a good one so I waited for another plane and came back home. I didn't want to disturb those people just because of our problems. We should leave them in peace. After all, you caused him to sell his house and get out of town. What else do you want?"

"You're still in love with him. You're lieing to me. You went to Clearwater and you saw him. You two were sitting on a bench in a park there, necking and petting. You were crying because you aren't with him. I had a detective on you from the time you arrived at the Clearwater airport. You two thought you were smart sneaking away from his wife."

"That was rotten of you, Greg."

"Tell me you don't love him," he shouted. "Tell me you don't want him."

Aries stood back and looked at Greg. I can't tell you that because I do love him. As she spoke her face was flushed and she could feel her adrenaline start to flow.

"And when did this happen?" he screeched.

"It happened the first time I saw him. It happened that day at the tennis tournament."

"You bitch, you whore." Greg was very angry. Aries was terrified.

Going to the shelf, he reached for the trophy she had won with Bob in th tournament. "I'll tell you what I think of this." Shoving the sliding glass doors to the bedroom open, he went outside to the pool deck and flung the trophy out into the dark waters of the canal behind their house. Ralph must have been watching from his window because soon, he came into the den and told her that Daddy had thrown her trophy in the canal.

"Daddy, you shouldn't ought to have done that," Ralph told his father.

"Get out of here and keep quiet," Greg shouted. He was on a real rampage and he intended to create a major ruckus.

Aries told him she couldn't live this way, that she wanted a divorce. "I dropped it last time because you were ill and needed me but this time, I'm going through with it. You don't ever intend to forgive me. You just want to punish me the rest of my life and I've had it," she screamed. "I'm going back to my attorney, tomorrow."

"Wait! I'm willing to try one more time if you are. Greg put out this challenge. "Let's take a vacation to Mexico before we make a decision to end things. Maybe we can put Humpty Dumpty together again, there."

What a new twist! What was Greg's plan now? Did he intend to take her sailing and throw her overboard in the Gulf. He knew she couldn't swim well. Wanting the fight to end and to pacify him, with apprehension, she agreed to make the trip. "Okay, okay, if you promise me you'll be nice to me and not be ugly, I'll go.".

Plans were made and they flew to Mexico. What a waste of time and money that turned out to be! Greg argued most of the time and the rest of the time, he was in bed sick with dysentery. Breaking his promise to be nice, two days before going home, he got on the Bob Benton kick again. Enraged, he got Aries down on the bed and was choking her. Finally extricating herself from his clutches, she ran out the hotel room door with purse in hand. As she fled she informed him she was leaving him and if he laid another hand on her she would have every Mexican in that hotel on him. Aries got help to get her bags out of the room. Catching a taxi to the airport, she flew home leaving Greg in Mexico.

The next day she was at her lawyers seeking a divorce and a restraining order against her him. Enough was enough. The divorce papers were filed. Greg moved out as the court directed and the big court battle ensued. A year later and thousands of dollars poorer (the attorneys tried to take it all) the nightmare ended.

The breakup had been traumatic for both Aries and the children. She got custody of all of them. The years ahead, raising them alone, would undoubtedly be difficult but at least she was free of Greg. Battle worn, she set about to pick up the pieces and start a new life. Nothing lasts forever.

Part Seven

*I*n the years that followed the divorce, Aries was terrified with the responsibility of raising five young children as a single parent. Greg hadn't been the ideal father but, at least, the children had had the security of having two parents at home.

The events that had led up to the divorce had literally devastated her emotionally and Greg had devastated them financially by robbing their savings account, forging her name and selling her out of the stock market.

He hired an unscrupulous attorney to represent him in the divorce and under his auspices, he stole every cent she had inherited along with the profit they had made on their investments. Greg pleaded mental illness in court when they were finally successful in getting him there. His doctor verified it by telling the judge that he suffered from undifferentiated schizophrenia.

Greg said he had lost the money he had taken in a gambling casino in the islands. A fellow stock broker testified that he was with him and he had seen him gambling, heavily. All of the money was gone and Greg was temporarily unable to work due to his illness.

Her attorney said that under the circumstances she would have to settle for whatever support he was willing to pay. "The guy's not working, he has blown your money, and now he's broke. You could put him in jail for forging your name but what good would that do. If he goes back to work, he thinks he can pay five hundred dollars a month child support. I know that's not enough but you can't get blood out of a turnip. Take it and get rid of the jerk."

Aries was awarded the mansion that had been built with money from her inheritance and there was no contest over the children. They would remain with her. Greg would have visitation rights, naturally.

The house payment was three hundred sixty-four dollars a month so with a total income of five hundred dollars monthly, she was going to have to beg, borrow and steal to survive herself and her children. She didn't intend to sell the house. She would get a job, take in roomers, sell Avon cosmetics, Amway soap or something. Somehow, they would make it. Greg Winston was not going to put them down the tubes.

After thinking of all the ways she could supplement the meager donation that Greg was court ordered to make, Aries decided to start teaching school. She had been qualified in college to teach. The hours would coincide with the children's school and she could be with them afternoons and on weekends. Teachers had summers off, too, so that would be good.

Explaining their financial dilemma to the kids, the oldest ones said they would help. Together, the Winston bunch turned out to be a real good team. They had to make a lot of sacrifices and sometimes, they weren't happy about them.

In Greg's endeavors to hurt her, he was hurting his kids. Aries hated him for this. The only consolation she had was the fact that, once, a psychiatrist told her he had the emotional maturity of a twelve year old. He was selfish and his God was money. Her hatred for him, eventually, turned into pity.

Aside from finances there was another adjustment Aries had to make, that of going from a long term marriage into single life. Having been a housewife, she knew very little about what was going on outside of her own little bailiwick. Her circle of friends had been other married couples whom she and Greg had associated with socially. After the divorce, her friends dropped her like a hot potato, excluding her from their parties.

After pondering, she realized her girl friends had cast her out of their social circle because she was single and available. Not having have a man of her own, they were afraid she might go after theirs. Aries was not interested in their husbands. If she had been she could have had them when she was married.

For three weeks after the divorce, Aries stayed home alone with the children. Her nights were lonely, and she wasn't sure how to break out of her syndrome. She'd no sex in days and with no lover in sight she was in a sexual predicament. She needed sex for her general well being and to keep the zits from popping out on her face. Simply speaking, she was still in her prime and she needed to be fucked.

Bob Benton was gone. Dick was out of the country on a flight. Aries would have to think of someone else. She put her thinking cap on and suddenly, she remembered Carl, a tall, handsome mutual funds man who she'd met at one of the stockbroker functions. His manner had been quite appealing. He was a Senior officer in the Eaton Fund. He had come to the party alone because his wife and mother of their four children had succumbed to leukemia, recently. Maybe she would give him a call and ask him if there's any way she could assist him with the children. With the five she already had what trouble could four more be? Aries was a glutton for punishment.

Flipping the pages of the telephone book, she remembered that Carl lived in Pompano but momentarily, she had forgotten his last name. Finally, the name flashed before her. Carl Hahn. Going to the H's, she quickly found him in the directory.

Lighting up a cigarette, she mixed a nightcap. She needed time to muster up courage before making the call. With drink in hand, she returned to the softly lit study where she had been sitting for the last two hours. How she loved that room!

The cabinetry was Austrian style and tastefully accentuated by the soft lighting that reflected through the cranberry stained glass inserts on the cabinet doors. The beamed ceilings and the brown leather desk top was complimented by blending shades of cool green velvet on the chairs. The carpet was plush moss, eye appealing green. A real rich and elegant looking layout! Greg spent a lot of time in that room. Surely, he must miss it. Momentarily, Aries was reminiscing.

Back in the chair behind the desk, she glanced at the clock on the wall. It was ten-fifteen p.m. She wondered if it was too late to call Carl. Would he think she was being forward by calling him? He had only met her, once. He probably didn't even remember her.

Nothing ventured, nothing gained.

Lifting the heavier than usual receiver off the hook, Aries decided to take her chances. She dialed his number. After three rings a young girl answered.

"Hello, this is Gay speaking."

"Hello, Is your father at home?"

"No, he's not here. He's been racing the boat today and he's not home, yet. May I give him a message?"

"Yes. Ask him to call Aries Winston at 688-4567."

"Okay, I'll tell him but he probably won't call until tomorrow because he may be getting home late tonight."

"That's fine. Thank you." Hanging up the phone, Aries assumed she had just talked to one of his daughters. She wondered if she would give him the message.

Turning off the light at the desk, she turned the television on and then plopped down in Greg's easy chair to watch the evening news. Soon drowsiness overtook her and she went into her bedroom for another night of sleep in the giant-sized bed she had shared for so long with Greg. It was damned lonely there now but there would always be the dawn of tomorrow. Saying her prayers, Aries hugged her pillow and started counting sheep. Shortly thereafter, she fell into a deep slumber.

Part Eight

*T*he next day was filled with the usual routine, teaching school and meeting the needs of the children. Around five-thirty as she was preparing dinner the telephone rang. Mia ran to answer it.

"Mom, Mom, the phone is for you. It's some man calling." Placing the lid back on the bean pot, Aries told Mia she would take the call in the study. "Hang up the kitchen phone when I pick the other one up," she called. Racing from the kitchen to the study, Aries grabbed the phone and held it to her ear.

"Hello, hello," this is Carl Kahn returning your call.

"Oh," said Aries, almost forgetting that she'd called him. "Thank you for returning my call. Do you remember me?"

"Yes, you're Greg Winston's wife."

"Wrong, I'm Greg Winston's ex-wife. I'm not married to him anymore."

"Well," laughed Carl, "this is news. So you've joined the ranks of the swinging singles."

"I'm sorry but I don't know what swinging singles means."

"Well baby, you'll find out soon enough. You must have led a real sheltered life when you were married to Winston. I can't blame him, though, for keeping you under wraps as pretty a thing as you are."

During the conversation he asked her if she liked to sail.

"Yes," she responded, "we used to have a sail boat and I went sailing a few times. I liked it."

"I'm going to take the boat out Saturday. How would you like to come along?"

"That sounds good. Where shall I meet you?"

"At the boat. I'll meet you at the boat at nine o'clock Saturday morning. I keep it docked at Howard's Marina on Raven Road. The exact address is 1700 Raven Road. Bring your bathing suit and some shorts and a shirt. That's all you'll need but be sure to wear tennis shoes so you won't slip and fall on the deck."

"How big is your boat?"

"It's a 48 footer, sailboat. I spend most of my weekends racing."

"That sounds like fun. I have to go now and serve dinner to my children but I'll see you Saturday."

"Hot damned," said Aries snapping her fingers as she hung up the phone. "I've got my first date and here I go sailing, sailing."

They went sailing that Saturday and every other Saturday for months to come. Carl was her steady beau. He was a very interesting person and Aries quickly grew fond of both him and his children. He filled a void in her life by giving her good companionship and good sex.

Carl soon realize she knew virtually nothing about sailing. He tried to make a sailor out of her but she became seasick every time she went to the galley. She tried Dramamine and other seasick stuff but none of it worked. Flat on her back was the most comfortable position she could find on that boat. Carl tolerated this but sometimes he really needed her help. He finally told her if she was going to be his first mate she would have to learn how to stand up on the boat. Aries knew he meant it. He was very serious about sailing.

Determined to overcome sea sickness and to prove to him that she could be an asset rather than just a piece of ass on his boat, she asked him to give her a job. "Let me handle the mainsail or something. I need to be kept busy so I won't have time to think about being sick."

Carl was protective over his boat and impatient with novices but he reluctantly he agreed to teach her how to sail. Too boot, she signed up for classes in sailing and bought a book that familiarized her with boating terminology. Eventually, Carl began to trust her as his first mate. He even loaned her the boat for an all ladies sailboat ocean race off Fort Lauderdale beach, one Sunday, and her ship won first place.

After that, she begged him to take her on as a crew member for the annual sailboat race from Florida to the islands. He said that going over it would be too rough for her but she could fly over and sail back with them after the race.

What an experience that turned out to be! The guys placed well in the race over. They had some trouble with the wind but they finally made it to the Bahamas. They would stay the night there and set sail for the return trip home, the next day. Aries convinced Carl to get off the boat and spend the night with her in a hotel. He had been on that damned boat for twenty-four hours and if they stayed aboard they would have, absolutely, no privacy with a five man crew. She wanted him all to herself for deep down inside she felt the urge for sex.

They feasted that night on all the lobster and stone crabs they could eat. The sounds of the calypso band resounded throughout the native island atmosphere. It was nice dancing music but after dinner Carl wanted to turn in for the night. He was all tuckered out. The sun and the wine coolers had gotten the best of him. No sooner than he hit the bed, he was a goner.

The next morning, a surprise awaited them when they arrived at the boat. During the night there was a grease fire in the galley and it was a burned out mess. Luckily, the ship was still sea worthy.

The crew was making preparations to set sail home. When Aries saw them she wondered if she should be sailing back with them. They were still drunk from their night in port. A couple of the guys were still missing and unaccounted for. Carl was the captain and perfectly capable of handling his own ship so would keep her mouth shut and trust herself in his hands.

The trip back was a real disaster. They had failed to replenish the food supplies in the galley so all they had to survive them on the crossing was wine and bloody Mary's. There was very little wind so it took them twice as long to get home as they had anticipated.

The guys had no real need of her help but as night fell upon them she was soothing to the Captain. Carl took a break accompanying Aries to the lower deck. Once below, away from the gazing eyes of his crewman, he proceeded to fuck the hell out of her. It had been three days now and they were ready. The trip would have been more fun if he had taken more "breaks" but he was so proud of that damned boat that it was difficult for him to let some one else take over.

On the trip back to Fort Lauderdale, the scorching sun was beating down on Aries's scantily clad body. It nearly burned her alive. The crew occasionally poured a bucket of sea water over her to cool her off. Those five guys were tantalized watching her move about the boat, but she was Carl Kahn's woman and they all knew it.

The trip lasted much longer than she wanted it to and to make things worse, they missed the port and had to motor the boat for thirty miles.

They arrived back at the dock sun burned from head to toe and famished. Carl promised to buy her a great big steak when they got back on shore but that was a promise he couldn't keep. Almost everything was closed. "Too late for a steak now, baby. Would you settle for a hamburger? I'll take you home with me and cook you one."

"No, no, thanks. I really need to get on home." She had had her fill of boating and sailors for awhile. Glad to be on solid ground again, she yearned to return to her air conditioned home. Frankly, after that trip, Aries didn't care if she ever saw a sailboat again.

Suddenly, she remembered she had taken a limousine to the airport and had left her car at Carl's house. Damnit! She would have to go home with him, after all, to pick up her vehicle. On the way, they stopped at an all night joint and got hamburgers to go. It was late so Aries left as soon as they arrived back at Carl's house. She was tired and the sun burn was beginning to bother her.

Almost home, she stopped for a stop light. While waiting for the light to turn green, a friendly fellow in the light blue convertible stopped next to her and tooted his horn.

"Hi," he said. "Where are you headed?"

"I'm on my way home."

"Do you live around here?"

"Yeah, I live just a few streets down." This good looking stranger was being so friendly.

"How about having a nightcap with me?" he said.

"No way, I'm too tired."

"Awe come on," he coaxed. "The Boone House is open and it's right up the road. Let's go for just one."

Giving his invitation second thoughts, Aries said, "Okay, just one, I'll meet you there."

By now, cars were coming up behind them and they were holding up traffic. She had to be nuts stopping for a drink with a stranger but she couldn't resist his shy blue eyes.

Over the drink she learned that he was John Clemson, a big politician from Kentucky. He had run for some high up office and came close to winning the election, but being separated from his wife hadn't helped him much in his campaign. He seemed like a very nice person.

One drink led to another and they were talking like old friends when Aries got up to leave. "If I don't go now I'll be bringing in the milk and the newspaper when I get there," she said.

"Let me go with you," he begged.

"Oh, no, not tonight, I'm exhausted and I've got to get some sleep."

"What about tomorrow night? I'm going to be in town for several days."

"I don't know."

"Well, I'm staying at the Gardner Hotel in Room 206. If you change your mind, call me tomorrow after lunch. I'll be playing golf in the morning but I should be back in the room by two."

"Very well. I'll call you tomorrow."

The next day Carl called. He wouldn't be available that evening so Aries decided to call John Clemson, after all. The good thing about being single was variety, although some fared better on a bland diet.

John was in his room at the hotel.

"How about dinner tonight?" he asked. "I'll take you to Monty's in Hollywood."

"That sounds super. I've eaten at Monty's before and the food is really good there." She gave him directions to her house and he said he'd pick her up at six thirty.

Dinner was great and afterwards, they went back to the Gardner Hotel to meet some of John's politician friends. The rest of the evening was spent chatting and socializing with them.

Around eleven, he took her home. Aries invited him in and what a surprise he had in store for her. His company had been nice but the real fun was about to start! John Clemson ended up in her bed. His pants were off as he lay beside her. Instinctively, she reached over and touched what must have been the biggest cock in the world. Taking a glance, it was gigantic. He was an absolute horse. She was so shocked that she couldn't believe her eyes. She told him it would never work.

"It's too big," she said laughing. "It's too big and I'm too little. You'd kill me. I'm sure you'd kill me."

"Relax baby. Just relax and I'll take it easy. You'll see, it'll work fine."

Oh my, thought Aries as he parted her legs. This guy has a lethal weapon. At first, he was very gentle. He let the head of his cock play around at the opening of her vagina.

"So you're from Kentucky," she teased. "My, my, I knew they raised good horses there but I didn't know they grew guys like this. So you're from Ken, Ken, oh my goodness, Kentucky," screamed Aries. John had made a major move. He had lunged his big cock deep inside of her. What a thrill! John Clemson's cock was every woman's dream! This fellow made the organ of every other man she had slept with seem like a peanut. He was fucking her hard. He was killing her just like she thought he would, but what a sweet, sweet way to die.

John spent the night. They arose early the next morning before the kids were awake. Aries sent him outside after he was dressed and told him to ring the front doorbell. "I'll let you back in for breakfast. That way the children will think you have just arrived."

John laughed but he did as he was told.

The children enjoyed him at the breakfast table. He played games with them and gave them all silver dollars before he left.

"It's been great," he said as he was leaving. "I'll be going back to Kentucky this afternoon but I'll be sure to give you a jungle the next time I'm in town." He was smiling.

After he left, the kids asked who that nice man was?

"Oh, he's a friend of mine from Kentucky who just stopped by to visit for awhile." Aries sighed quietly. Last evening had been great.

She wondered why his wife hadn't appreciated him.

Carl never knew about her interlude with John. There was no reason to tell him. After all, she was free, white and twenty-one with no one but herself to account to.

A few weeks later Carl proposed marriage. "Let's get married and merge our families. There's no need for you to live there and me to live here," he said Aries thought it over. His proposal had come to her, suddenly, and by surprise. Her children needed a father but was she really ready for marriage so soon? She promised Carl to give him her answer very soon. That weekend she told him, "yes."

The date was set and plans were made for their engagement party. The invitation list included about fifty of their friends. The affair was scheduled for October but fate took charge and their plans were canceled. It happened like this. Carl was going sailing one Saturday. Aries had things to do at home that day so she didn't accompany him. Since Carl had come into the picture she hadn't spent enough time with her children.

"I'll come to your house around six o'clock and hem Cindy's brownie uniform while I wait for you," she told him.

"Fine, I'll see you at home at eight o'clock."

Aries arrived at Carl's early and hemmed Cindy's uniform. Cindy stood in front of the mirror admiring herself in the finished job. "Let's go and show Daddy how good I look in my new uniform," she begged. Cindy was Carl's youngest, six years old and about the size of a minute. She was such a sweet thing!

"Your Father told me to wait here for him," Aries announced.

"Come on, he won't care. He's at the boat now. Let's go show him."

"Very well, let's go." They drove down to the marina where the boat was docked in its slip. Aries assumed that Carl was zipping it up before coming home. Leaving Cindy in the car, she ran to the boat calling for Carl. Although he didn't answer, she knew he must be on board. He wouldn't go off and leave things unsecured. In the galley, she spied a pair of ladies panties and a bra on the floor. Carl's shorts and underwear were draped over the sink. Aries smelled a rat and that rat had to be in the lower cabin with her fiancee. She picked up their under garments and carried them below.

Busting through the door, she found Carl with an an ugly pig of a woman. The two were stark naked. Surprised, embarrassed and intoxicated, they fumbled for their underwear. Finders, keepers. If these two wanted to show their asses she'd let them. Turning from the doorway, Aries flung their garments overboard. Then she opened the cabin door again and said to the pair, "Oh, pardon me, don't let me interrupt you. Cindy's out in the car. I'm going to take her home and fix her dinner. Don't rush home because of me, Carl. Take your time." The look on his face was priceless. He appeared dumb founded.

Devastated by the startling events of the evening, Aries was barely able to hold back the tears. Making excuses for Carl, she took Cindy back home. It was seven-thirty. If she had arrived at eight as planned, if she had stayed away from the boat she would have known nothing. Everything would have still been "peaches and cream" between them. It was too late now.

Nothing Carl could say would change things. It was over. The engagement was off and there would be no wedding. He was a lousy scoundrel. As quickly as it had started, it had ended. Maybe fate planned it that way.

Part Nine

*A*fter the breakup with Carl, Aries vowed to think twice next time before becoming romantically involved. But fresh out of male companionship, she needed a friend.

One day she was having problems with the commode in the master bathroom so she contacted, Gary Winn, the Kohler representative, and he agreed to come by and take a look at it. Aries had met him on the job site during the construction of their home. He was cute with strawberry blonde hair, blue eyes and a freckled blushing face.

As promised, Gary stopped by one evening after work to check the john. It was defective so he agreed to replace it. Appreciative, Aries offered him a drink. One drink led to another and before the evening was over, they were becoming pretty friendly.

Gary was separated from his wife and available. Before leaving, he invited her to have dinner with him the next evening. "I know a place that's great for steaks," he said grinning. Aries welcomed the chance to get out of the house so she said, "yes."

Promptly at seven the next night, Gary arrived neatly dressed in grey trousers, navy blue blazer and white shirt with a paisley cranberry colored necktie. The children were all at the door to greet him. The baby sitter had come early so soon, they left for the restaurant. Gary was a real Southern gentleman. It was apparent that he had been brought up well. Dinner was pleasant and the conversation was refreshing. By the end of the evening, Aries knew they were going to be good friends.

Afterwards, one date led to another and she and the children were becoming very fond of him. Gary had three kids of his own but unlike Greg, he appeared to be a devoted father. Their friendly relationship was quickly turning into a romantic one, at least, on Gary's side. He was constantly professing his love for her. Aries liked him but love him, no. Maybe someday she would but not now. Gary was overly amorous and deep inside, Aries knew she would never be truly in love with him. She was itchy to escape and to date someone else.

Part Ten

*O*ne day Holly her sailing friend suggested fixing her up on a blind date with Alden Austin from Clearwater. He was living aboard his sixty-eight foot yacht at Bahia Mar Marina so he had to be a rich guy.

"What does he look like?" Aries asked.

"He isn't the best looking guy I've seen but he is one of the nicest." Holly confessed.

"Describe him."

"Well, he's tall and lanky and he wears thick horn rimmed glasses.

Go out with him one time and see if you like him. His wife's a good friend of mine. I like them both a lot."

"His wife? If he has a wife why are you fixing him up with a date?"

"He's separated from her. She lives in the house in Clearwater and he lives here. They've been apart for several years and they both date."

"Well, give him him my number," Aries replied.

Several days later Alden Austin called.

"Our mutual friend, Holly, told me to give you a jingle," he said in a jovial tone of voice.

"Really! Holly's such a matchmaker."

"Well," laughed Austin, "I thought you might just like to go out with me for an early-bird dinner, tonight."

"I don't know. I've never had a blind date before. I'd have to get a baby sitter and it is rather late to get one."

"Had you rather make it tomorrow night?"

"Yes, that would be much better."

"Fine, tell me how to get to your place and I will pick you up there between seven and seven-thirty." After receiving the directions, he said he was sure he could find it.

Hanging up the phone, Aries was nervous. She dreaded going out with a stranger and she wondered what Gary would say if he found out. She started to call Alden back and cancel their date.

The next day she was den Mother at the cub scout meeting at four o'clock so she picked up the baby sitter at on her way home. At seven-fifteen Alden arrived. The sitter let him in and he was just like Holly had described him, tall, skinny and wearing horned rimmed glasses. He certainly didn't look like the football hero type.

Aries invited him in for a drink before they left. Feeling ill at ease and awkward, she considered feigning sudden illness and sending him home. She didn't think she was going to like him, at first impression. He could take his yacht, his money and go somewhere else. Lacking the nerve to bow out, she'd endure the evening but it would be the last time she'd go out on a blind date.

"Well, we'd better take off. We have reservations at the Rainbow for dinner at eight," Alden reminded.

"I'm ready. Just let me say goodbye to the children and give the sitter her instructions."

Aries gathered up her evening bag and Alden hustled her into the old faded blue Lincoln town car he had parked outside. His old car further diminished her impression of him because she drove a shiny Mark 111.

In the driveway, she remarked, "I see you have a Lincoln, too."

"Yes, I've been driving this car for almost twelve years."

"My, my, why don't you trade it in?"

"Why should I? It's a good car. It gets me where I want to go," he chuckled.

All the way to the restaurant Aries thought and Holly said this guy was rich. As he drove Alden puffed on a cigar. Aries was nauseated by smelling the aroma from his nasty cigar. From what she had seen, so far, she definitely didn't want to date this man.

After dinner he suggested they continue their evening aboard his yacht. Aries wanted to see the boat so she agreed. They drove to Bahia Mar where they went aboard "The "Aldeberon." She was a real beauty!

After a couple more glasses of wine Alden coaxed Aries into the sack. Once there, she thought she was losing her mind. What was she doing in bed with this strange fellow? They were in his sack with all their clothes off and before she knew it, he had his big long hard cock inside of her. He was fucking her.

"Stop, stop," cried Aries. "I can't have sex with you." I hardly know you. Please stop." She insisted so vehemently and pushed him so strongly that he got the message. Removing his cock, he rolled over in the bunk.

Aries jumped up out of bed and began retrieving her clothing. "Please take me home. I am sorry about tonight but I just couldn't do it. I'm just not used to having sex with someone I've just met."

"No problem. Before this is over, honey, you'll be begging me not to stop." Alden was laughing. "You're one young woman that I intend to get to know better."

Things were pretty quiet on the ride back home. Walking her to the door, he said he would call in a few days. Aries was embarrassed at making him quit in the middle of sex.

The next morning, Gary called inviting her to have breakfast with him at Friar's."

"No, come on over here," she said. I'll fix your breakfast today."

"That sounds like a real winner to me. I'll be right over." Aries hurriedly threw a pair of shorts and a pink tee-shirt on. Heading for the kitchen, she began cleaning up the mess left from the children's breakfast. Soon, Gary came bringing fresh orange juice and sugar roll with him.

"You'll get fat eating that stuff," she quipped."

"Fat," he laughed. "You mean fatter. I already have a spare tire around my middle."

"I love your spare tire. It feels soft and warm in bed. With those tender words Gary melted and began to shower juicy kisses all over her.

"Hey, don't you want breakfast now, Gary?"

"Not now, honey, that can wait." Gary was blushing. "Right now, all I want is you, sweet thing." He led her by the hand to her big bed. Undressing, she lay there waiting for him as he neatly piled his clothes in a stack. As she looked at his big round pulsating cock, her pussy started oozing warm juice.

"Hurry, Gary," she purred. "Please come make love to me. Diving into bed, he nestled his hot body close to hers and pressed his pulsating hard penis up against her stomach."

"Do you want this, honey?" He was teasing.

"Yes, yes, I want your cock," she moaned. "Please put it in just a little to see if we like it."

" I know I'll like it," said Gary smiling. "I love to fuck you but you're not going to get it, yet. First, I'm going to eat your sweet cunt. It really turns me on to suck your cunt and to lick your pussy." Gary called her cunt "Suzanne." "How is Suzanne, today?" he asked gently.

"She's fine."

By now, Gary was on his knees with his ass in the air and his mouth buried deep in her cunt. His tongue was licking its velvety lips and occasionally, he would thrust it deep inside of her.

"Fuck me, fuck me," she wailed. "Fuck me with your tongue or anything."

Gary was sighing as he sucked and licked her beautiful brown pussy. Moaning and groaning, Aries hunched her cunt up against his mouth. She could feel her clitoris throbbing as it swelled.

"Oh, Oh, I'm coming, I'm coming," she panted. "Please, fuck me hard, now."

Gary mounted her and began to solidly penetrate her dripping juicy pussy with his hard cock. After a couple hard punches he bore his cock deep inside of her vagina and held it there. Aries twisted her ass holding it, firmly, against his steel cock. Moving her hips and buttocks in a slow motion, she caressed his immobile penis until she burst in violent orgasm.

Gary was coming, too. His penis was jerking and he was shooting hot cum into her vagina. "Oh, Aries, I love you, he murmured. "I love you and I love your tight pussy! You drive me crazy!" Satisfied for awhile, they lay in each others arms and fell into tender sleep.

Aries woke up around ten-thirty and went to the bathroom. Her movement about the room caused Gary to commence stirring. His eyes opened and he motioned for her to come back to bed and snuggle with him.

"Want a cigarette?" she asked.

"Yes, hand me one, please. What time is it? I didn't mean to fall asleep. I have an appointment with a man in Hollywood at eleven-thirty so I'd better get rolling. By the way, I called you last night and one of your children, I believe it was Mark who answered, said you were out."

"Oh, I was visiting a girlfriend."

"Well, if I could have found you I was going to invite you to take a boat ride."

"I'm sorry. I would have enjoyed that. Maybe next time."

Gary left for his appointment. With him out of the house, she was able to commence some serious cleaning and serious thinking, as well. She really liked Gary. Being with him was comforting but being with Alden was more exciting. She wondered if he would call her, again. If he ever did she was going to let him fuck her. No sooner than that thought came to mind, the telephone rang. Speak of the devil, it was Alden Austin.

"Well, hello. This may be a little early to ask but are you free this Saturday? My wife's having a cocktail party and I wondered if you'd like to go with me?"

"To your wife's cocktail party? Are you sure you want to take me there?"

"Sure, she knows I date. She dates, too. She doesn't mind me having a girlfriend. She has a boyfriend, in fact, he was my best friend until I found out he was going out with my wife."

"If you're sure it will be alright, I'll go."

"We won't stay long," Alden continued. "We'll just stop by for a drink and then, we'll meet Holly and Ray for dinner. I'll pick you up at six o'clock."

They went to the party as planned. Aries met Alden's wife, Hazel. She was an attractive woman, courteous and friendly, but before they left she pulled Aries aside in another room and probed her about her relationship with Alden. Aries assured her there was no relationship between them. "I barely know him. We met on a blind date and I have only been out with him once. He talks about you a lot. He's very fond of you, Hazel."

About that time Alden came up and said it was time to leave. It sure was! Aries was glad to get out of that tense situation.

In the car, she told him that she didn't think Hazel was as happy about his dating as he thought she was.

"I don't want to talk about her tonight," he replied. "I want to talk about our plans for the evening. Ray mentioned that Holly might want to go dancing somewhere after dinner but if it's alright with you, I'd rather split from them and spend the rest of the evening alone with you."

"Oh, no, you're just wanting to make love to me," Aries kidded.

"That's right! Tonight, I intend to screw your eyeballs out. Sweets, you should call the baby sitter and ask her to stay overnight because it will probably be dawn before I take you back home. I'm going to teach you the art of love making and you aren't going to learn it in just one session. You might as well plan on spending lots of nights with me because I intend to make love to you a lot. What do you say to all that? Do I frighten you, Aries?"

"No, oh no, I love to make love. I just wanted to get to know you better, first."

"After tonight you'll think you have known me all of your young life. I went for two years without having sex when Hazel and I were having problems but I'm over that now. I'm in good shape and ready for some real good fucking. You're a sexy little bitch and I figure you are just the kind of girl who needs to be loved a lot."

"Well, you're right about that but this is all so sudden."

"How much time do you need to accept a good offer like that?"

Alden was secure and self-confident. Aries liked a man like that. If she could get adjusted to his looks she just might go for him. He was a unique fellow and certainly very interesting. Tonight, she would make love to him and who knows she might end up liking it.

After dinner Alden took her back to his yacht. Inside, he offered her a nightcap.

"How about a margarita?" she said laughing. She really didn't expect him to have that on board.

"One margarita coming up," he replied smiling. "My captain keeps this rig stocked with everything."

"Your captain? I've never seen a captain on this boat."

"Young lady, a eighty-two foot yacht is not a boat."

"Oh, excuse me. Ships and boats are all the same to me." Alden brushed his brown curly hair back and started laughing. "Well, I guess you'd call my Harley Davidson a motor scooter."

"What's a Harley Davidson?"

"It's a motorcycle, dummy."

"Oh my, are you a motorcycle driver? If you are, I sure hope you don't ride around with one of those Devil's Dragon signs on your jacket." Aries sipped on the margarita.

"Now about the captain," said Alden. "I have a full time captain on this ship. He's off tonight but stick around awhile and you'll get to meet him. He's a real nice fellow," he went on. "I pay him two thousand dollars a month to take care of this baby."

"Two thousand dollars a month! My gracious, that's a lot to pay someone to watch a boat. Oh, excuse me, I mean ship."

"He's worth every penny of it and more. There's a lot of work to do around here." Alden poured himself a glass of wine and sat down beside her on the sofa. "Let's drink up, sweetie. It's getting late and ole Alden needs to call it a day."

Aries put her drink down. "I don't have to finish it. I've had enough to drink tonight, anyway. I've got to call the baby sitter. I guess she'll stay overnight. She's done it before but I should have given her notice."

"Tell her my old Lincoln konked out and you're stuck in Fort Lauderdale. Tell her you'll be home bright and early in the morning."

Aries made the call and it worked. Jackie agreed to stay over. She'd call her Mom and tell her not to wait up.

"Okay, baby," said Alden. "Let's hit the rack so we can get down to some serious fucking." Aries followed him below to the master suite. Undressing and climbing into bed she knew what was in store.

In bed, Alden wasted no time in covering her like a blanket with his lanky body. "Want to get fucked? Ole Alden's going to fuck you like you have never been fucked before."

She lay there purring like a kitten. He was ready. Shyly, she placed her hand on his stiff cock.

"Squeeze it, honey, squeeze my cock and rub your fingers up and down the shaft."

As she fondled it, she could feel it getting harder and harder.

"Open your legs, baby, and let me taste the juices of your sweet pussy." She obeyed and his wet tongue touched her quivering lips. Instinctively, she tightened her legs but Alden pushed them open again.

"Relax, baby, you're suffocating me."

"What are you going to do to me?" Aries squealed.

"What do you think I'm doing? I'm licking your pussy. Now lay back and enjoy it." Alden was sucking and licking her cunt. It felt strange but she began to enjoy it. Thrusting his tongue in her vagina, he commenced fucking her with it and then, he started flicking it back and forth across her clitoris. This was really getting to her.

"Let's go, baby, let's go. cum."

"I can't, I can't, I've never done it that way."

"Relax, let it come, baby," he chanted.

"Stop, stop now." Alden had a tight hold on her clitoris. She was sighing, moaning and groaning. She felt like a tiny beetle being stomped by Alden's big foot. Helpless under his spell of torture, she pleaded, "Stop! Stop."

"Okay, baby, now I'm going to fuck you." Mounting her again, he plunged his hard cock into her vagina. It felt wonderful. Alden Austin was a master at fucking. His stroking was down pat and he knew just what it took to please a woman.

Aries had one tumultuous orgasm after the other. "I love this, I love this," she murmured. Alden commenced fucking her in rapid motions. She was satisfied and it was his turn. "I'm getting ready baby, I'm getting ready to cum. Lift your ass up here, baby. Ole Alden's going to fill your cunt full of hot juicy love juice. Here I go, Oh God, I'm coming." Aries got almost as much excitement out of his powerful orgasm as she did her own. This night had been truly wonderful and to think she had made him wait.

After that evening they became good friends as well as lovers. Aries wanted to be with Alden. He treated her the way a woman likes to be treated. Except for his still being married to Hazel, she could find nothing wrong with him. She loved everything about him, except his cigar smoking. Alden was a Libra, perhaps that was why. Libra, according to astrology, was her most compatible sign. Whatever the reason they got along great.

They had a routine of making love every morning, playing tennis in the afternoon and in the evening they dined at the Down Under, the most fashionable restaurant in town. Usually, they ended the evening by making love again. Alden Austin kept her fucked and fucked well.

That year, Aries rented out the mansion to an attorney who was willing to pay her an exorbitant price for a two year lease. She rented a smaller house for a much less money in Coral Ridge Country Club. This put her closer to work and closer to Alden. His boat was moored half way between the house in Coral Ridge and Hollywood where she taught school.

Alden drove her to the tennis courts on his big Harley Davidson motorcycle. But at night, Aries insisted that they go to dinner in the car. He didn't consider that an unreasonable request so he complied. As for as he was concerned he would have been perfectly happy going every where on that bike.

Alden was well healed and he didn't have to impress anybody. His father had been the founder of one of the major drug store chains. When he died Alden became the major stock holder in the company. He would never have to work a day in his life.

Aries kidded him about loafing.

"What do you mean? I don't loaf. I'm busy while you're working everyday. I'm at home counting my gold and keeping close watch on my investments." Alden's money meant very little to her. She was happy with him and that was what was important.

Alden decided to move his ship back to Clearwater for repairs and refurbishing. During that time he would reside in the house he had lived in with Hazel. She had moved to Fort Lauderdale when she and Alden were separated.

The thoughts of Alden's leaving saddened Aries. She had become very attached to him and was accustomed to his being there. He woke her up every morning at five-thirty, like an alarm clock. He would say, "Wake up honey, it's fucking time." Those words meant sweet pleasure. Making love to Alden was so good! He had such beautiful control and he satisfied her so completely.

After the loving he served her orange juice in bed. He prepared breakfast and did the dishes, often. His behavior was so different from Greg's. Greg was demanding and bossy. He expected Aries and the kids to wait on him hand and foot, like he was a king. Appreciative of Alden's kindnesses, Aries felt a little guilty for letting him do things. Whenever she tried to take over the job, he would smile and say "What's wrong with my doing it? I've got two hands." Alden wanted to help and after awhile, she learned to sit back and enjoy it.

On the tennis courts, Alden wasn't much competition, at first, but with their frequency in playing his game improved drastically.

After moving back to Clearwater, Alden rode his bike to Fort Lauderdale on Thursdays for long weekends. In his absence Aries kept busy taking care of the children and teaching school. She hadn't seen much of Gary Winn, lately, but the children apparently were still in touch with him. He talked to them on the phone, occasionally, when she and Alden were out wining and dinning.

With Alden out of town Gary came back into the picture. Aries called him one day and he was tickled to hear from her. She invited him over for breakfast. "I'll bring the orange juice and donuts," he said.

He arrived at her door at seven a.m., all smiles.

"What have you been doing these days, Gary?"

"What have I been doing? I think that's a question I should be asking you."

"Not much, just working some and playing some."

"Well, some of the time while you've been out playing, I've been taking care of your children."

"What do you mean by that? I know you must have called here because Mia told me but you haven't seen my kids."

"Oh, I've seen them a few times. I've stopped by to see you and visited with them for awhile." Gary was red faced and grinning.

"You creep! You know they like you but what were are you doing over here spying on me?"

"I wasn't spying on you, I was just visiting the kids." He grinned sheepishly. "I love you."

"You love me. I don't want to hear you say that again. That's why I'm dating someone else because you kept chasing me around telling me you loved me."

Gary turned red in the face. He looked like he was about to burst into tears. "Go ahead, date someone if you want to. When you get finished playing around with that guy remember I'll still be here. I love you, Aries, and I love your children."

"We'll talk about it later. I've got to go teach school now, she exclaimed as she looked at the clock. "Why don't you come over for dinner tomorrow night and we'll finish this discussion?"

"I thought you'd never ask me. I accept your invitation."

On the way to work, Aries wondered if she'd be clever enough to handle two men at the same time. She could date Gary, on Monday, Tuesday and Wednesday but he'd have to vanish on the days Alden was in town. Could she successfully keep the two apart? She'd only date Gary if she could do it without Alden knowing it.

The next evening Gary came for dinner as planned. They enjoyed chatting with each other. She even let him fuck her but the feeling of love for him definitely wasn't there. He was warm and soft like a teddy bear you held in your arms for comfort but Gary could be no more to her than a very good friend. Alden was her guy.

Aries confessed to Gary that she was dating Alden. She explained how he lived out of town and came to stay Thursday through Sunday. "If you want to see me it will have to be Monday, Tuesday or Wednesday. Otherwise, I'm tied up and I don't want you calling or coming by, then."

"Well, I don't like it. I can't stand the thoughts of you dating another man and I don't like being told what days I can come or call but if that's the way you want it, I'll play your game. You won't mind though if I date Grace Simpson on Thursday, Friday, Saturday and Sunday?"

Aries was surprised. She had no idea that Gary was seeing someone else. "You know, what's good for the goose is good for the gander," Gary said.

"You're dating Grace Simpson? How did you meet her? She used to play on the B-team at the tennis club. I was her captain. That girl's a real scatter brain. She was married then. What happened? Did she get a divorce?"

"I met her playing tennis one day at the club. She's separated from her husband and, incidentally, she's a very nice girl.

"Well, from what I saw she has the intelligence of a dart! I don't even like her but you can date her if you want to. I told you what my situation was."

"Yes, you told me that my nights are Monday, Tuesday and Wednesday. Tonight is Wednesday so I'll see you at seven."

"Fine." Gary had gotten Aries goat. That was one for him!

Alden called that evening while Gary was there. Aries left him in the den and went into her bedroom so she could talk in private.

"I miss you, Alden."

"I miss you too, sweetheart. I'm calling to tell you I won't be able to come to Fort Lauderdale this weekend. I have to take the ship out and give it a trial run at sea."

This news was disturbing.

"Don't get your feathers ruffled, honey," he laughed. "You little idiot, I called to invite you over to spend the weekend with me in Clearwater. You can come after school on Friday. We'll take the ship out all day Saturday, spend the night at sea and we'll bring her back into port Sunday morning."

"Oh, that sounds great! I'll get a sitter for the children and I'll leave for Clearwater straight from school."

"I'm not staying on the boat, you know. Let me give you directions to my house. It's a little confusing."

"Wait a minute, let me get a pencil and write them down or I'll get lost for sure." Putting the phone down, she went into the den to get a pencil. Gary started to speak but she silenced him quickly by putting her index finger over his mouth. "Shush, he's still on the phone," she told him softly. Grabbing the pencil, Aries left Gary standing there looking like a fool. When she got back on the phone Alden asked what all that commotion was about?

"Have you got company?" he asked laughing. "Don't tell me you've got some fellow over there sleeping in my bed," he teased.

"Don't be funny. What you heard was the television blaring. The children have it on too loud, and no, I haven't got any fellow sleeping in your bed. I love you, you fool, don't you know it?"

"I love you too, honey. Hurry up and get your sweet ass over here. I need some good fucking. Now let's hang up this phone and stop wasting nickels. See you Friday. Bye, Bye."

Alden's call ruined Gary's evening. Aries face was aglow after he called. "You're grinning like you swallowed a gold fish. That guy must have really turned you on. I'll bet your conversation burned the wires off the telephone."

"Stop it! Alden's a nice guy. He's a perfect gentleman."

"So am I, but tell him not to call here on Wednesday because that's my night."

"He asked me if I had some fellow sleeping in his bed. Do you think he's psychic?"

"I don't know if he's psychic or not but he's crazy to leave a sexy thing like you for half a week."

Aries was glad when her date with Gary was over for all she had on her mind was Alden and getting ready for her trip. Thank goodness, she'd have tomorrow night alone to wash her hair and pack her things.

On Friday afternoon she made her way across Alligator Alley to Clearwater. What a long desolate stretch it was with miles and miles of nothing but swamp and Everglades. It was almost dark when she arrived and although she had the directions, she couldn't read the signs too well. She wished she had left school earlier so she would have been there sooner.

Alden lived on the outskirts of town. She stopped twice asking directions before she finally found the place tucked neatly away in an oak treed, paradise setting. It was private and secluded.

Upon entering his home, Aries was in another world. The world of Alden Austin. He gave her a big kiss and hug. Then, handing her a much needed refresher, he took her on a cook's tour of the house. It was lovely. Hazel had done a fine job of decorating it. She could see touches of her hands everywhere.

It was too bad those two couldn't make it. They'd been married for almost thirty-five years. They must have developed some sort of attachment to each other. Alden had insisted he had no romantic feeling for Hazel. The only thing that had held them in marriage, he swore, was two children and the fact that he would have to give her too much money if he divorced her. That's why they stayed married and lived apart. "She's a nice woman and we're good friends but that's it," he vowed.

Perhaps Alden wasn't telling her everything. She wondered why their marriage broke up and she suspected their being content with going their separate ways wasn't exactly so. Aries had an intuition that they still loved each other but stubbornness and vanity on Alden's part prevented them getting together. Aries never mentioned this to him because she was his lover, not his counselor. Deep down inside, she secretly wished he could forget Hazel and marry her.

Alden prepared steaks on the grill that night and to compliment the meal he had chilled one of the finest bottles of wine.

After dinner he showed her though his work shop. Aries was amazed at the works of art in there. Alden was was a talented metal sculptor. His work was excellent and she was impressed with his craftsmanship.

"You say I loaf, huh," he laughed as he displayed his work. "I forgot to tell you that this is another way I spend my idle hours. It takes a long time to create one of these gems."

"They're wonderful, just wonderful," Aries exclaimed in delight. "Why have you been keeping your talent a secret from me? I knew you were "King of Sex" and a great tennis player but this really is a pleasant surprise."

Alden hugged her and told her if she hung around there would be lots of surprises in store. "It's dark outside but remind me in the morning to show you the garden I'm growing. I'm a farmer, too."

How nice it was to see Alden's other side. She knew he was a boatsman and he was becoming a proficient tennis player but she didn't know he had all these other worthwhile hobbies. Aries was multifaceted herself and she appreciated knowing someone with a brilliant mind.

The weekend was fantastic! Their outing in the ship was a real thrill. Alden stayed at the helm a lot watching the captain man the ship. That night, he took the first watch on the radar so they could hit the hay early and get down to some serious fucking. The other guests aboard tucked in early, too, so Alden didn't have to spend the evening entertaining them.

Making love to him was an out of this world experience and the more he gave her the more she wanted. He claimed to be an old man and he declared she was going to fuck him to death. Aries knew that was a lie. Fucking, good hard fucking was right up Alden Austin's alley.

They brought the ship back into port Sunday right after lunch. The guests left and they were sitting on the aft deck having bloody Mary's when, all of a sudden, Hazel stormed aboard. She had on a wide brim hat. That brim was flopping everywhere as she stomped her feet and yelled at Alden. She was as mad as an old wet hen. She really tore into him. Aries had met her once before and she was nice but today, she was like a different person.

"How dare you bring women on this yacht?" she screamed. "How dare you bring your women into our house? I'm going to divorce you."

Alden was embarrassed and Aries didn't know what to think. He took Hazel aside and talked to her. A couple minutes later he escorted her down the ramp. Coming back, he apologized for Hazel's outburst saying that she had come to Clearwater, unexpectedly. He didn't know what had caused her to act that way.

"I can tell you what's wrong. She's jealous of me. I thought you said it was all over between you two."

"It is."

"Well, it sure doesn't look like it."

"She knows I date. She didn't mind when I was with you in Fort Lauderdale but she got her dander up because she found out that I had invited you to the house and to go out on the ship. She doesn't like me bringing other women into her territory."

"Oh, that doesn't make much sense to me. Either it's over between you two or it isn't. The way she acted, I wouldn't be surprised if you two had been sleeping together."

"Now you're imagining things," laughed Alden. "I haven't had sex with her in over two years and I have no desire to." The subject was dropped. Aries left the boat around seven so she could get back to Fort Lauderdale at a decent hour.

The next week Alden came over as usual and he came back again the week after. They were in bed on Thursday night when the phone rang. It was Hazel asking to speak to Alden. He was asleep but Aries woke him up. He talked to her briefly. Aries looked at the clock and noticed that it was after midnight.

"Why was she calling here? Is something wrong?"

"No, she just wanted to talk to me about something."

"At this hour?"

"I'm sorry she called so late but we still have two children and there are things we need to discuss."

"Fine, but I wish she didn't have to wait until after midnight night to do it. I think you're more attached to her than you admit and furthermore, I'm beginning to think you all should get back together."

"It'll never happen," replied Alden.

All in all, their weekend was filled with sunshine, tennis, good company and absolutely divine pleasure in the sack. Alden was a guy who really aimed to please a gal. Aries hated to see him leave on Monday morning.

With Alden out of town it was back to her solid friend, Gary.

Alden called Wednesday before Gary arrived. He sounded depressed and down in the dumps, not like his usual self at all.

"What's wrong, Alden? You don't sound like yourself."

"Well it's me, Alden Austin, in person but I don't feel so good."

"I'm sorry. Are you sick?"

"Yes, you might say I feel a bit sick. Hazel called today and said she was filing for divorce. I'm sick because she's trying to take all of my money. When she gets through with me, I'll have to fire my captain, sell the ship and maybe even get a job. She wants me to pay her three thousand dollars a month alimony and that's more than I pay my captain. She's out to ruin me financially."

Alden's news was shocking. She had heard Hazel threaten to divorce him but she didn't think she meant it.

"Don't let her have everything. Try to work out a fair settlement with her."

"Hazel doesn't intend to be fair. She wants everything, except my balls."

"I'm so sorry. I hope that my coming to Clearwater didn't cause this to happen."

"It's not your fault. She's been talking about divorce for years. I guess now she's found some guy she likes well enough to marry and she's decided to get rid of me. Don't worry about it, it's my problem and I'll solve it."

The conversation continued.

"Incidentally, I won't be able to come over this week until Saturday because I've got an appointment here with my lawyer on Friday. We'll stay in a motel Saturday if it's alright with you because I need some time away from your little monsters to be alone with you."

Aries thought his suggestion was rather unusual but she told him she would make arrangements for Effie to stay with the kids.

Alden didn't come straight to the house when he arrived. Instead, he checked into a nearby hotel and called her to come over. This was a different twist.

They had dinner at their favorite restaurant by the Intercostal waterway. It was a romantic spot with candlelight, wine and the sounds of the strumming violinist. Balmy breezes were blowing and the rippling waters were accentuated by the moonlight shining over them. That night, at dinner Alden talked about the divorce. He told Aries that Hazel probably had a detective on him and she would bring her into the divorce court as the other woman and accuse him of adultery. "That's why I didn't want to come to your house. I don't want you involved in this mess."

"Is she blaming me for your divorce? When I started dating you you told me you were separated and you even took me to her house to a party. She knew we were dating. What is this all about?"

"I don't know, I think she's going through the change of life. All of a sudden she's trying to tell me what to do and what she's going to do. She's flipped out."

"Well, if she thinks I'm going to be the cause of your divorce, I'm not. Go back to her, Alden. You've been married for thirty-five years and she's the mother of your children. I'll bow out of the whole picture."

"Well, that's a gallant speech you've just made, young lady, but I'm afraid that none of your suggestions are possible. Hazel wants a divorce and I'm going to give her one."

"Fine, but until you two get this thing straightened out, I'm staying out of the picture. I don't need an irate wife after me." Before they left the table Aries was in tears. She didn't want to give Alden up but she didn't want to be the reason for his divorce, either.

"Don't cry, honey." Alden tried to comfort her.

"I can't help it, I'm in love with you and I didn't want it to work out this way."

"Hey, I beg your pardon. I didn't promise you a rose garden. Now, let me dry those tears. I can't stand to see a woman cry."

They went back to the hotel.

The next day after tennis, Alden wanted to stop by the book store to pick up a book. Aries browsed around while he asked the clerk where Rod McCuen's poetry books were located. He found the book he wanted but he wouldn't show it to her. When he left that night he gave her the book as a gift. It was titled **Stanyon Street and Other Sorrows**. Inside the cover he had scribbled, "to Aries, for the good times, love Alden." Was this his going away present? Aries sensed that this was his way of saying goodbye.

She was right! She didn't see Alden for weeks after that. He called her occasionally, just to find out how she and the children were. Alden was at home in Clearwater. Hazel had moved back there, too. They were trying to put Humpty Dumpty back together again while Aries spent her evenings pouring a flood of tears over **Stanyon Street and Other Sorrows**.

Eventually, Alden stopped calling. How long can one cry over spilled milk?

Part Eleven

*T*he lawyer who had rented her mansion moved out and Aries took her children home. Losing Alden had been a tremendous jolt to her emotions. She really was in love with him.

Gary had gotten pretty thick with Grace Simpson but it didn't take long for Aries to thin the pudding. Losing Alden hurt and Gary's re-appearance was like holding a warm, soft teddy bear. Gary, on the other hand, was delighted that "that son of a bitch was gone."

Shortly after the breakup with Alden, mama died. Several months later Uncle Ross succumbed to a heart attack and not long after, Pops passed away. After all that losing, Aries, emotionally devastated, was easy prey for Gary.

Convinced there was no love left for her, he would do fine. Soon, Gary moved his houseboat from Grace's dock to hers. He had been living on the boat there with two of his children. After docking they didn't stay on the boat, long. In no time, his kids were out of the boat and they had taken over her mansion.

That worked okay for awhile but Aries became weary of coming home from teaching to seven children, a guinea pig which she had inherited from Gary's kids and ashtrays filled with his cigarette butts.

Aries let the maid, the yardman and the pool boy go because they couldn't afford them. Letting the help go was the second mistake she made. Allowing Gary Winn and his children to move into her house was the first.

While she taught school Gary stayed at home. Many times she would come home and find him still in his blue velvet house robe at three o'clock in the afternoon. The yard grew up in weeds, the pool turned green, the house was a disaster with dirty dishes and laundry and there were problems with the children. Mia didn't get along with Gary's daughter, Gwen, because she was always borrowing her clothes and messing them up.

One afternoon the girls got in a hair pulling, name calling fight. It was over Mia's clothing. "It's not that she can't wear my things but she's a slob," declared, Mia. "She takes my best things without asking me and brings them back torn or dirty. Tell her to stop wearing my clothes. She's ruining all of my best things."

Aries suggested that Mia go through her clothes and give some of them to Gwen.

"No," said Mia. "Just tell her to stay out of my closet. I don't want to give any of my things away. I wear everything I've got. She ruined the new blouse that Aunt Angie sent me. She spilled grape juice all over it."

Realizing that this issue was not going to be peaceably resolved, Aries told Gwen not to touch anymore of Mia's things. "I'll take you shopping tomorrow and buy you some new clothes," she offered. Aggravated, Mia went into her room and slammed the door behind her.

The next evening Gary was scolding Mark for playing instead of doing his homework. That episode ended up in a real ruckus. The arrangement just wasn't working out. Gary would have to take his boat, his children and the guinea pig and go.

The next day she told him to find another place to dock his boat and move out of her house. "The children aren't getting along and it's too hectic this way," she said.

She expected Gary to honor her wishes and move but instead he suggested that he let, Nora, his ex-wife take Gwen and Karen back. Aries was surprised to hear him say this because he had fought so hard in court to gain custody of them. The court let Nora keep Gary, Jr. and now he was willing to send the girls home. This was a switch! Aries didn't fight the issue.

Gary called Nora who was happy to hear his decision. Returning the children meant he'd have to pay more child support but Aries thought it would be well worth it.

After his kids left Gary spent most of his time bemoaning the fact that Nora had them. According to him, she was drinking all the time, having men in the house and not taking care of them. Gary's loafing around the house, complaining about his lack of money and his ex-wife was getting old. Things had been better before when he just came for breakfast, gave her a good morning fuck and went on his way.

Aries discontentment grew and they were arguing a lot but Gary wasn't about to leave on his own. He was enjoying his luxury too much. Free boat dockage, free rent and free pussy with little or no obligations.

Aries could have married him if she had wanted to but for what reason? What she really wanted to do was to throw him out.

One afternoon when he was off on an appointment she packed all his belongings and put them on his boat. When he returned he realized that his clothes were gone. Aries was quick to tell him she had moved his things into the boat.

"What's going on here? Is that a hint?"

"Yes, I'm trying to tell you that you're moving out."

Gary became angry. "Oh, oh, now I see, first, it's my children and then it's me. You're trying to get rid of me."

"I'm not trying, I'm doing it."

"Well, I'm not leaving. I'm bringing my things back in the house, right now."

"If you bring your things back in this house, I'll throw them into the canal."

"If you do, I'll turn you over my knee and spank you right in front of your children."

About that time Ralph and Mark came in from playing. "What's going on Mom?" Mark asked.

"Nothing, honey, I was just saying goodbye to Gary. He's getting ready to move his boat."

"Oh, can we go for boat ride with you, Gary?"

"No children, not this time. I'll take you for a boat ride, later. Taking some cookies out of the refrigerator, the boys went back outside.

"Gary, please go before the children get back in the house."

"I'm not going anywhere." Gary was getting red in the face. He went out the patio door and boarded the boat. He began taking his things back out of the boat and stacking them on the dock. "You took this stuff out, now be a good girl and help me carry them back in."

Aries would have to show him that she meant what she said. Going to the dock, she started flinging his junk into the canal. Gary stopped unloading and started retrieving his belongings. He was really mad so she went back in the house.

"Now take your things and leave," she yelled. She watched from the kitchen window long enough to see him loading his stuff off the boat and into his station wagon. After awhile, he came back in to tell her she'd had her way but he wasn't leaving, she was driving him away. He left saying he would be back later to get the boat.

"Call Grace, maybe she'll let you bring the boat back there," Aries suggested. Apparently, he did call Grace because that weekend, she dropped him off to pick up his boat. Maybe they were meant for each other.

Part Twelve

*T*he year was 1972. Aries was in her second year of full time teaching. After moving back to the mansion in Light house Point, she managed to get transferred to a school closer to home. She would still be teaching mentally retarded children. Integration was in full swing so Aries found herself teaching both black and white students. She liked the job but the pay was poor and insufficient to feed and clothe five children. She also disliked the constancy of a schedule. Her life was was rather dull with nothing but work at home, at school and too little association with adults.

One day she overheard some teachers discussing real estate in the teacher's lounge. This was a subject she knew nothing about. In her nineteen years of marriage, her husband took care of all of the important transactions, like real estate.

Their conversation interested her. Perhaps she would look into the profession of real estate. She checked around and found out that everybody was doing it, everybody was in real estate. Some of the real estate people made money but some were just in it for a hobby. Aries didn't need a hobby but she did need a job where her time would be more her own.

She decided to take a correspondence course in real estate while she was teaching school. Finally, when school was out she had completed the course and she was ready to take the state test. This was ideal! She could try her hand at real estate during summer, still keeping her teaching contract for the fall. This would give her a chance to see if she liked it or not.

Aries took the test in June and passed. She was then licensed to sell real estate. Not knowing exactly where to hang her tag, she decided to hang it with a small office in Fort Lauderdale on East Oakland Park Boulevard. Placing her license there turned out to be a bad move.

They offered no training there. The sales people were experienced and none of them were interested in taking on a green horn to train. Instead, they advised her to refer her prospects to them because she didn't know how to handle her deals. All summer long her only deal was a rental on which she made eighty dollars. It looked like she was going to have to keep her teaching job.

Then a stroke of luck came. One day on the tennis court, Aries gave her real estate card to Troy King. "If you ever want to buy or sell anything, please call me," she said.

"Thank you, but I don't want to buy anything or sell anything," Troy answered.

Aries's tennis partner, Henry, told her that she had just wasted one of her cards on that flake. The weeks went by and she kept on playing tennis and talking to Troy who wasn't interested in buying or selling any real estate.

One day the telephone rang at her office. The caller was Troy. "Hi, Aries. How's about taking Nancy, my fiancee, out and showing her some houses tomorrow in Adam's Ridge. We're getting married and we might like to buy a house."

"Sure, I'll be glad to show her houses."

Aries set up the appointments and spent the next afternoon escorting Nancy through house after house in the area they had selected. She really liked one of the homes but Troy wouldn't buy it. Maybe, she was wasting her time on that flake.

One day Troy called again.

"Hi, Aries how are you?"

"Just fine, but I wish I could sell some real estate."

"Well, maybe you can sell me some. I've decided what I want to do. I want to build a condominium. Find me a site. I want to build a luxury condominium on the water. I realize there are only a few sites left but go to work on it for me, Aries."

"Oh yes, I certainly will. I'll start researching it and I'll be back in touch with you, soon."

Hanging up the phone, Aries was ecstatic. She ran into Mrs. Modlin's office, one of the few associates who she had become friendly with, and gleefully told her that she had a client who wanted to build a condominium. He wanted her to find a waterfront site and she didn't know where to begin.

"Perhaps, you should turn your client over to me for a referral fee since you are new and inexperienced in the business," Mrs. Modlin replied. Aries heard what she had to say but she wasn't going to give away her one and only decent prospect. She would find him a condo site, herself.

Going back to her desk, she began to scan the multiple listing book for hi-rise sites. She could find only one. Excited, she called Troy to inform him that she had found a high-rise site on the water for only $150,000. He ended the conversation by telling her to go take a look at it.

"Remember, Aries, I want to build eighty units and you will have to find out about set-backs, parking requirements, etc. Get all of the details, look at the site and get back to me."

What the hell was he talking about? How was she supposed to gather all of the information he was requesting? Why couldn't he just buy the site "as is"and do all that investigating later? Aries drove over to the northeast location where the site was situated. It was on the water alright but the area left much to be desired. There were "black folks" fishing from the creek bank. This site would not be suitable for building a luxury condominium. She had made a dead run and what was worse, she had to call him and advise him that the site she'd found was unsuitable.

In the meantime, the men at the planning and zoning department assisted her in determining the setbacks, height restrictions, requirements for parking, etc. She had found no site but she was acquiring a lot of valuable information. She kept looking, asking, watching the newspapers and the MLS book in search of the perfect high-rise site. At last, she found another site on Lake Fate across from the Grand Plaza hotel in the southeast section of town.

That afternoon she saw Troy and Nancy at the club. She told Troy about the new site. This one was priced at $375,000.00. He told her, again, to go look at it. After tennis she did just that. The site was beautiful. The next day she called Troy and told him she had seen the site and the location was great. Troy promised to ride by the site and

and take a look at it.

Several days went by and Aries hear nothing from him. She invited Nancy to play doubles on Sunday at the club. After tennis as they were sitting at the bar for a cooler, the conversation finally got to the condo site.

"Hey Aries, said Troy. I took a ride by that site you found and you're right, its beautiful. I believe that we'll have to acquire the adjacent property to the north, also, because I don't believe the site will accommodate eighty units. Find out what are chances are of acquiring that piece.

Troy had given her another assignment. She hadn't even noticed the adjacent property. Aries got into her car and drove down to Lake Fate. Beside the vacant lot there was a quaint small Spanish style house. What would she say to those people? The house wasn't listed for sale. There were cars in the drive way so, nervously, she rang the doorbell. She'd never done anything like this before. Soon, a little grey-haired short man came to the door.

"Yes."

Aries hesitatingly said, "Hello, I have some people who have indicated an interested in buying a house in this area. I was wondering if your house could be for sale."

"Young lady, this house is in R-3 zoning for high-rise and it certainly could be for sale at a firm price of $195,000.00 and not a penny less." He knew. There was no fooling him. This old man knew exactly what was going on. Aries got the dimensions of the property, his name, telephone number and told him he would hear from her again.

She was on the brink of putting a real estate deal together for six hundred thousand dollars. The commission, if paid in full, could amount to about three years school teacher pay. Aries was elated but she had no money, yet.

She had a difficult decision to make. Troy was going to put an offer in on the site but he hadn't done it, and school was about to start. Should she stay in real estate or should she go back to teaching? She liked real estate but she wasn't content at this real estate office because she was getting no training and no prospect referrals. Time was running out. After giving it much thought, she decided to quit teaching and to transfer to another real estate office. She resigned from teaching and from her company on the same day. A day later, she was interviewed by one of the largest real estate firms in town. She got the job. This started another chapter in her life.

Aries had gone from a company of about ten people to one boasting more than one hundred employees in two offices. After signing the independent contractor agreement with the company, she was turned over to the manager who led her into a huge room filled with sales people situated in little cubbyholes. She was assigned a desk in the left hand isle across from the manager. She placed her name tag on the desk and as she sat down she was thinking, "I'm new here alright but how many new people do they get with a $600,000.00 deal coming in with them?" She was right. It wasn't often that a beginning salesman brought a good customer and a good deal like that.

Aries was successful in real estate and when the first year had ended, she knew she would never return to the teaching profession. She'd found her niche in the business world and her earnings far exceeded her former schoolteacher pay. The new job had its amenities, also. Those amenities were men, men and more men. She got to deal with lots of rich, professional, sexy men. It was great!

Aries had made the final break with Gary. She had no new companion but her life was filled with business and the friendship of company employees.

She started team working with Jed Ricco, a dark-haired, black eyed wiry Italian fellow, who sat directly down the isle from her. Nathan had introduced them and soon she found herself going to Jed's desk for help. He usually knew the answers to her questions and if he didn't he was always willing to help her find them.

They began going on listing calls together. They were constant companions at work but their dealings were strictly business. Aries knew Jed was married and she wasn't interested in him. He was thin, mannerly, quiet and as Aries was to learn later, very cunning.

A few weeks after she had been working at B.K. Stein's she decided to have a champagne party to celebrate a successful closing that Jerry, a lawyer friend of hers, had negotiated. She had sent out the invitations, bought the food and champagne. Everything was all set!

This party would give her a chance to become better acquainted with the other salesmen.

Aries went home from work early that afternoon to make sure that Mrs. Key, the live in housekeeper she hired after Gary left, had everything just right for the party. After bathing she put on a robe and went into the kitchen for final check on things before her guests arrived. A few minutes later, the doorbell rang. It was Jed.

"Hi, am I the first to arrive?"

"You certainly are. I'm not quite ready yet but come on in the kitchen and meet, Luella Key, my friend and housekeeper. Mrs. Key, who was always glad to see visitors and who enjoyed her afternoon cocktail, came waddling into the kitchen.

"Hello, I'm Luella."

"My name is Jed. I've heard a lot about you from Aries. It's nice to meet you."

Aries pointed to the bar and asked Jed if he would mind mixing cocktails for the three of them. "I've got to finish getting dressed," she said as she headed to the bedroom. "I'll be right back."

She returned a few minutes later in her most provocative dress to find Jed making himself at home and talking to Luella.

Forty-five minutes passed and not a single guest arrived. "I wonder why everybody is late," Aries commented. "I'm sure that I mailed the invitations in time for everybody to get them. "You got yours didn't you, Jed?"

"No, I didn't. You told me you forgot to send me one, remember?"

"Oh, that's right. Well, I'll just call Nathan and Sheryl and see why they aren't here. I'm sure Ruby would have been here by now, too, if she had received hers. Come to think of it, not a single sole mentioned the party at the office, today." Aries hadn't mentioned it, either, for she had left quite a few out at the office and she didn't want them to know she was entertaining.

She dialed Nathan's number. Sheryl answered. "Hello."

"Are you and Nathan coming to my party?"

"Sure we are but the party is not until Thursday. We are getting ready to go to the Pollocks' for dinner, tonight."

"Oh, my God. What day is this?" Aries whined.

"It's Wednesday, you pea brain. What have you done, gotten your days mixed up?"

"I guess so." Aries was embarrassed. "Jed is here all dressed up but no one else has arrived. I told him the party was today."

"Well, you two have a good time! We'll see you, tomorrow evening."

"Have I made an error," Aries told Jed. "The party is tomorrow and not tonight."

"Don't worry," comforted Jed. "We'll have our own party. Let's crack a bottle of champagne and then, we'll go out to dinner." Aries felt a little odd because up until now, her dealings with Jed had been strictly on a business level He was married and she felt funny going out to dinner with him, alone, when he had a wife sitting home and when he, apparently, was unavailable.

One glass of champagne led to another.

Afterwards they went out for dinner and dancing. Aries couldn't remember how it happened but after their arrival back home, she found herself on the foyer floor with Jed on top of her screwing the hell out of her. My God, it was great! She had never, absolutely never, had sex as good as this was. After the session in the foyer they ended up in her bed where Jed repeated his prize winning performance. He certainly was a wolf in sheep's clothing.

It was almost five a.m. when Jed bounced out her bed holding his hand to his head. Aries aroused from slumbering long enough to ask him if he wanted an aspirin.

"Yes, I'll have one," he replied.

"Well, they're in the medicine cabinet in the bathroom. I'd get it for you but I can't move.

"Don't worry. Stay in bed. I can find it and then, I'd better go home. My wife thought I was out on an evening real estate appointment. I don't know how I am going to get out of this one."

"Maybe you can sneak in without her awakening."

"That will be the day. She wakes up at the drop of a pin. I'll call you when I get a chance."

"Just lock the door on your way out."

Jed left quietly.

By afternoon, Aries's headache subsided and she prepared for her dinner date with Howard Kuhn, a friend of hers. They went to the Wren Club. After cocktails, dinner, dancing and a lot conversation he delivered her back home around midnight.

After saying goodnight to Howard and locking the front door, the phone rang. It was Jed and he sounded upset.

"Where have you been?" He asked. "I've been calling and calling you, all night."

"I went out to dinner. I really didn't expect to hear from you this evening. I thought you'd be home with your wife."

"Well, I'm not. I have been out all evening, waiting for you. Can I come over?"

Aries looked at the clock on the kitchen wall. It was quarter past twelve. "It's getting late but I guess you can come over for a little while," she said. Hanging up the phone, she went into the bathroom to pee.

Moments later, Jed was tapping on the front door.

Letting him in, she noticed that Jed looked a sight. "What's wrong? You look like something the cat just dragged in."

"What's wrong is that I haven't had a wink of sleep since I saw you last. My wife woke up when I pulled in the driveway last night and she started screaming, yelling, throwing things at me and accusing me of having been out with another woman."

"Really, what did you say?"

"Well, of course, I denied it. I told her I went out with the boys and we ended up in a card game but she didn't believe me.

"Really, why not? It sounds like a good story to me."

"She didn't believe me because my shirt smelled like perfume and there was lipstick on my collar."

"Not mine, I hope."

"Of course it was yours! Who else was I out with last night?"

"Nobody. May I fix you a nightcap? Aries smiled.

"I'll take two."

"What brings you out so late, tonight?"

"I'm out because my wife didn't believe my story and I have had it. I've had enough of her badgering so I packed my things and left."

"What are you going to do now?"

"I was hoping I could borrow your couch for the night."

"Well, I guess I can accommodate you. It's just for tonight, though."

The next day at breakfast Jed asked about the possibility of renting a room from her for awhile. Aries was reluctant, at first, because of her children. Finally, she agreed telling him that she would move her clothes out of the master bedroom closet into the hall closet. She would tell the children she had rented out the master bedroom to a co-worker from the office. She warned Jed not to tell anyone at the office of this arrangement

As the weeks passed it became obvious that Jed had come to a parting of the ways with his wife and he had ended up on Aries doorstep. Although she was fond of him, Aries hadn't planned on this. She felt somewhat responsible for the breakup with his wife but she didn't expect to be living with him on a steady basis.

After Jed moved into her house he got his own telephone number. At the office they pretended he lived somewhere else but soon, everybody suspected that they were occupying the same bed.

That part of it she liked! Jed was her first experience with an Italian lover. Now she knew why they called Italians, "lovers." They made love three times a day and Aries had never loved nor been loved better. His sensitivity and tenderness captured her completely. His adeptness in the sack left her moaning, groaning and glowing with pleasure. They stayed "flat on their backs" when they weren't working in real estate.

Aries worked hard to become established in real estate and she was getting the reputation among the associates as being "on the ball." Jed was in the commercial department, upstairs, and she wanted to be there, too, but commercial was a no, no for women at B.K. Stein, Inc.

She disliked renting stuff and selling houses and she wasn't too thrilled at working with women prospects. One day she spent eight hours driving an indecisive little old lady around looking at duplexes, only to find out later that she was just lonesome and wanted a free tour of the city.

It was pouring down rain when Aries dropped her off. Fifteen miles from town, weary and in a hurry to get back to civilization, she got a speeding ticket. The lady called a week later to tell her she had decided not to buy. She had gone to live with a relative. Aries tried to keep this incident in close recall in order not to waste her time and gas in the future. B.K. Stein was always preaching, "Qualify your prospects, your time is valuable. This was a perfect example of what he meant.

In some respects, selling real estate was like fishing. She had to bait her hook a lot. She got lots of bites and lost lots of bait but Aries was sure if she baited her hook enough and kept casting her line in the water, sooner or later a fish would bite and she would catch it. They couldn't all get away. By the law of averages, if she was persistent enough, eventually, she would win.

Aries made a concentrated effort to gain entry to the commercial division. One incentive was the fact that the boss had moved all of the commercial guys up to the fourth floor leaving her downstairs with the residential and condo salesmen, who were mostly women.

About this time she received a phone call from a rancher friend who had offices across the street. He wanted to buy two thousand acres of land to put a show ranch for his Charlois cattle. It needed to be near a major airport because ranchers from all over the country would be flying in to inspect the cows and bulls.

"I'll find you one," she told him.

At that moment Aries decided to become "an acreage specialist." She told her Broker that she had a qualified prospect who wanted her to find 2,000 acres of land for a ranch. She didn't know where to begin. He gave her a book listing all the Brokers in Florida and he told her to look in the National Multiple Listing sheets on acreage. After making many long distance phone calls and writing letters she began to get feedback on available acreage.

Soon, she had gathered parcels of land to show Mr. Korn. One site, 8,000 acres in Lake City, Florida interested him He made arrange-ments to take her with him in his Commache airplane to fly over it. Proudly, Aries told Jed and the other associates that she would be out of town the next day showing land, by air, in Lake County.

The following morning, she dressed up in her cowgirl outfit.

Making arrangements with Jed to check on the children, she stopped by the office on her way to the airport to meet Mr. Korn for takeoff. The girls at the office were in awe of her daringness. Ruby, a tall German blond with a harsh nature, sat poised upon the couch in the reception area of the office. Ruby gave her a skeptical look and said, "Where are you going all dressed up lake dat? You look like a clod hopper or a farmer in doz boots."

"I am going in an airplane to fly over and show some land."

"You sure have a lot of nerve. I wouldn't take off in any private plane and risk my life to show land. You're a fool," she uttered in her broken German accent. "I'll take care of Jed until you get back, if you get back,"she laughed.

Realizing it was time to go, Aries gathered up her briefcase and took off for the local airport. She, too, was secretly a little scared of flying but she had a job to do and she was going to do it.

The flight to Lake City was smooth. They were met at the airport by Tad Road and Ben Block, two Brokers up there. Ben wasn't much to look at but Tad Road was another Rock Hudson.

After the introductions Tad Road made his apologies and told them he had to go to Jacksonville that day. He assured Aries that Ben Block was quite knowledgeable and he would show them the land and provide them with any information they needed. They decided to drive to the site, first. Afterwards, they'd fly over it for further visualization.

The property was located about eight miles from the airport. Ben asked them to load up in the jeep so they could get on their way.

Upon arrival at the site, Aries noticed a lot of cattle on the land. Ben said someone was leasing part of it. Mr. Korn asked him a thousand questions about the soil, the grass, the fencing, the water supply, the price, etc. It was mostly cow talk and since Aries knew nothing about cattle she kept her mouth shut.

They drove round and round and up and back. Occasionally, they stopped, got out of the jeep and walked for a distance. Mr. Korn showed her how to walk in a pasture without stepping in cow manure. "You just spread your legs and straddle the pile," he said. They spent a lot of time opening and closing gates. Some of the cattle became frightened and ran in the other direction. Aries was afraid when they got close to the bulls.

Finally, they headed back to the airport to pick up the plane. Mr. Korn told Ben Block that he could find the land without his assistance. He thanked him for his time telling him we would contact him later.

Aries had flown before but she had never flown low and sideways trying to look down at anything. She knew the pilot was experienced but frankly, she didn't enjoy the flight Both Mr. Korn and the pilot were so busy talking and looking for landmarks that she wondered if enough attention was paid to controlling the plane. She was scared shitless a couple of times. They made it, however, and she had a story to tell at the office.

As the days went by Aries gathered a wealth of material on large parcels of land from Florida to Kentucky. Mr. Korn continued to show an interest in buying but she never did see his cash.

Jed had been living at her house for almost six months and divorce from his wife seemed eminent. Aries and Jed were inseparable most of the time. She had become sexually very attached to him. In May, after his divorce Jed asked her to marry him. Aries was enamored with his charm, his sweetness and his tender touch so his proposal was tempting. However, her children were violently opposed to the idea of her marrying him.

"He's a phony," said Mia. "He's too poor and you wouldn't like being married to him. The secretary at the office out her two cents in, too. "He's a gopher, Aries, he's only using you to get where he wants to be." Margie, her best friend, wasn't any help either. "Don't you dare marry him. He's a jerk! He's just out after all of your money. Get rid of him. You're so turned on with his big cock that you're blinded to reality. Get rid of him before he takes everything you've got."

Aries didn't enjoy hearing all of these admonitions about Jed. How could she give him up when the warmth of their bodies together put her soul afire? She ignored the advice she had been given and told him she would marry him.

Jed was so persuasive and such a dynamo in bed that Aries was allowing him to lead her down the primrose path. When talking with Margie, she would gather the courage to protect herself. Then night would fall and after a two hour fucking session and another super fuck the next morning all of her defenses were destroyed. Through sex Jed had gained complete control. She detested herself for being such a slave to sex.

One morning after the loving they dressed and checked into the office. Jed went out to lunch that day and didn't come back. He left a message in her box asking her to join him at Stinson's after work. Stinson's was a fancy place so if he was paying, sure she'd go. When she arrived Jed was sitting at a table alone.

"Would you like a drink?" He asked as she sat down at the table.

"Yes, please order me a scotch and water. After a day like this I could use one."

"What happened?"

"Oh, nothing. Just the usual problems with prospects. Mrs. Cohen cancelled her appointment to look at condos this afternoon and the deal on the Smith house fell through. The Johnson contract was about to blow up, too, but fortunately I was able to hold it together. Where were you this afternoon? Out taking a listing?"

"No, I went somewhere else." Jed smiled and then there was utter silence.

"Don't play games with me. Is it a secret or do you want to tell me where you went?"

"No, it's not a secret, it's a surprise. I've got a surprise for you but you will have to wait until later."

Aries had suspected that something was up when he had left a note in her box asking her to meet him at Stinson's. People only went there on special occasions. At dinner Jed ordered a bottle of champagne. It was quite a setting, soft music, candlelight and everything to set the mood for romance.

As they were dining Jed began to dig in his coat pocket for something. Finally, he pulled out a velvet covered box and handed it to her.

"This is for you, Aries."

"For me," she exclaimed in surprise!

"Open it," he said smiling. "Open it and see if you like it."

She opened it. The box contained a diamond ring. "It's beautiful," she said leaning over to give him a kiss.

167

"Try it on to see if it fits. It belongs on your second left finger, you know." Handing him the ring, Jed slipped it on her finger. The fit was perfect. It was a beautiful ring.

"Now, Miss Winston, we are officially engaged."

"Yes, we are." Aries wondered if she had done the right thing by accepting it.

The next morning, she showed her ring off to the girls at the office. "Jed and I are engaged. He gave me a diamond ring, last night," she told the girls in the coffee room. Congratulations were in order for Aries that day, that is, until Margie got there.

"You're a fool. Take that ring off and give it back to him before it turns your finger green. It's a phony, it's not even real. He's just trying to con you and get all your money."

Why, why, Aries thought, would Margie talk this way? Why would she want to mar her joy?

"How do you know it's a phony?"

"Look, look at my diamonds and then look at yours." They went into the restroom and under the light Aries examined the rings on Margie's fingers. They were so brilliant they could knock your eyes out.

"You're right, your diamonds shine more than mine does."

"That's because yours isn't the real thing."

"But he told me he paid a lot for it."

"The creep probably got that piece of junk for fifty dollars. Ask him where he bought it. Tell him it's the wrong size and you want to exchange it, and at lunchtime, we will go check the price."

"That's a good idea. I'll go back to my desk and call him now."

Aries called Jed and told him she needed to know where he bought the ring.

"Why?" Jed sounded puzzled at her question.

"I have decided I need a half size smaller."

"Oh, it came from Brattons. I was short on cash and I bought it there so I could put it on my charge I will go with you later today."

"Never mind, I have already told Margie that I'd have lunch with the girls to celebrate our engagement so I'll do it in my way back."

"Can you take a coffee break now?" Jed asked.

"I guess so," she replied. "There isn't much going on here, right now."

"Okay, I'll meet you in the front lobby in five minutes."

She met Jed in the lobby and they went down the street for coffee at Deliah's. Jed had something on his mind and he told Aries that there were some things they had to get settled between them.

"Well, what are they? Let's have it."

"It's money. Now that we're planning to be married, soon, we need to get our bank accounts in joint names. It's the only way I'll have it. In Italian families the man must have complete control of the purse strings."

"I can understand your having control of the money we make together in the marriage but I can't understand why you should control the money I had before I met you or why I should control yours," Aries argued.

"Until you are ready to go with me to the bank and transfer everything into our joint names I won't feel right about our marriage. I want us to start out right and that's the way it has to be." Aries listened to what he had to say and finally, she promised to go with him to the bank the next day.

"Fine," smiled Jed. We'll go in the morning on the way to work."

Back at the office, Aries head was spinning. Maybe Margie was right. Maybe he was after all her money. He certainly didn't have much left after his wife got through with him. How could she trust him with her life's savings?

Aries had lunch with Margie and told her of the conversation she had that morning with Jed.

"You'd better dump him and dump him fast," Margie warned. "That guy's just a common crook."

Gee, thought Aries, Margie's probably right. What had she gotten herself into? She had tried to convince Jed that her money was hers and his money was his, that neither of them had a right to the others but he had refused to listen.

"If we take that ring back and it's a phony, will you listen to me and get rid of that creep? Margie asked.

"Yes, yes, that's a deal. If the diamond is a phony I'll believe you."

"Well, let's go down to Bratton's and get this thing over with," said Margie getting up from her seat. "You pay the check, Aries, you owe it to me for getting you out of this mess. I don't know why I am always taking care of you."

In Bratton's the clerk verified that the ring had been purchased there. She showed them some others just like it. "It's a zircon," she said. "The price was seventy dollars. Do you have a problem with the ring?"

"No, no problem. I just wanted to know how much it costs."

"Now, do you believe me?" stormed Margie. "That bum wouldn't even buy you a decent engagement ring. Seventy dollars would have been a small price for him to pay to talk you out of sixty thousand dollars of your money after you put his name on the bank signature cards. Boy, have I saved your life!"

Aries hated to admit it but Margie had been correct in her assessment of Jed Ricco.

"You just can't trust those Italians. They think they're God's gift to women, yeah, one rich woman after the other," exclaimed Margie. "You ought to ask Renee Lovitt what her Italian lover did to her. He wiped her out of almost every cent she had."

"Margie, how could I have been so blind?"

"You weren't blind. You were, temporarily, insane. It's what they call losing your head over a piece of ass. There are plenty of guys around as good in bed as he is and they've got lots more on the ball, too. Get that cheap ring off your finger."

"What will I tell Jed about the ring? Won't it hurt his feelings if I don't have it on? Shall I give it back to him?"

"No. There is a garbage can over there," pointed Margie. "Throw that piece of junk away and tell him you did it."

Taking the ring off her finger, Aries opened the lid of the garbage can and dropped it in. "Heavens, when he finds out what I did with the ring, he'll die," she confided.

"Who cares? Who needs guys around who are trying to steal from innocent women? Do you realize that since you have met him you've paying him about $500.00 a piece for ass?"

"You're probably right." Just recently he had borrowed thirteen thousand dollars from her. He paid back five but he still owed her eight and didn't know when he'd be able to repay it. She had better not tell Margie about that!

That evening Aries made Margie come to her house after work. "You've got to be there. I'll throw him out. I'll tell him I threw his ring away, that the engagement is off but I need you there to protect me. He's going to be really furious."

After work, Margie followed her home. "You wait in the den. When he comes home I'll tell him," she instructed Margie.

When Jed arrived Aries lit into him like she was firing him out of a cannon. "I went to Brattons today. The diamond ring you gave me was a phony. It was a cheap seventy dollar zircon. If you can't afford anymore than that for an engagement ring I don't need to be marrying you." As Aries looked at Jed she knew her desire for his body was still there, burning feverishly, but that passion would have to subside. She'd be dammed if she was going to pay any man for sex.

"The engagement is off. The marriage is cancelled," Aries yelled. "Get your things and get out of my house. I am tired of supporting you. You may be Italian, but I'm a Southerner from Tennessee and I've never seen a man treat a woman like this before. I don't know where you came from or what your upbringing has been but in Tennessee men support their women and give them real diamond rings. They don't have to pay their men to make love to them, either. Buddy, you are looking at one woman who doesn't have to pay for sex. Now get out of my house and don't come back," she wailed. She was really letting him have it and Jed didn't get a word in edgewise.

On the way out, he called back. You know I'm not leaving you, you're driving me away. It seemed like Aries had heard these words before on the day Gary moved out.

Jed Ricco had just found out he couldn't do everything with his golden cock. Aries had been and was still addicted to it but with time and determination, she would overcome that craving. Sometimes, the things you like best aren't really good for you and time heals everything.

Part Thirteen

It took Aries a long time to get over the breakup with Jed. She knew she was better off without him but still she was faced with one big problem, an insatiable sexual craving for his body. She had become sexually addicted to him and it wasn't easy kicking this habit. The only way they had really ever gotten along was flat on their backs in surrendering prone positions. This part of their relationship, she missed. How could she have given up the pleasure of feeling his big hard, pulsating cock deep inside of her?

Jed had taken advantage of her. He tried to take her money but he sure made her feel good while he was doing it. It was over between them and those memories were going to have to cease.

Aries felt somewhat uneasy after he left. Not knowing his where-abouts disturbed her. Though she didn't want him she certainly didn't want him sharing that powerful cock with any other woman. She began to wish she hadn't made him take his clothes. Then, he would have come back to get them. While there, he would have ripped her undies off right at the front door, pushed her down on the cold slate floor, and he would have fucked her, over and over. Jed had loved fucking her.

After three days, Jed was back banging on her door wanting to come in and make love to her. It was midnight when he arrived and Aries had gone to bed. Letting him in, he was silent. He took her by the hand and led her into the bedroom closing the door behind them. He wasn't there for conversation. Pulling her gown off her shoulders, he motioned for her to get back into bed. What was wrong with him? Did the cat have his tongue? His behavior was weird. Removing his clothes, Jed lay his bean pole frame on top of her and with little adieu proceeded to fuck her, wildly. He never uttered a sound, not even when he exploded in orgasm. The chemistry was still there but he was strangely silent. Aries wondered what would happen next.

Afterwards, he moved over to the edge of the bed and just sat there, saying nothing. When she spoke he didn't answer but she could feel him simmering inside. Something was really bothering him.

"Maybe you'd better go now, Jed. It's very late and I need some sleep." Jed put on his clothes and left without a word.

Aries pondered about his new behavior. Their relationship wasn't a healthy one. There was no communication between them, except sex. Perhaps, this was all they had ever had together. Aries sought the counseling of her friend, Sal, a trained psychologist. She told him about her relationship with Jed and why she was trying to end it but she admitted that sex had held her in bondage to him.

Sal declared that sex was a most powerful retainer. "I'll work with you if you want me to. You have been operating below the waist instead of using your head. I can help you learn to rise above your animalistic desires for this man. If you want this man out of your system you have to stop letting him come to your house. You have to learn to stay away from things and people who are bad for you whatever the reason might be. In your case, there are number of reasons why you should end this relationship."

"I want to, I really want to but I don't know how."

"If you are willing to spend the time I will counsel you in the evenings after work."

"I'll do it. When do you want me to start?"

"We can start at seven o'clock, tomorrow night. I do my counseling work at home so I will give you my address." Taking his card Aries left promising to be there the next night.

For several months, Sal tried to teach her to think with her head, instead of her lower torso. His task wasn't easy. She stopped Jed from coming over but he had rented an apartment five miles away and many nights after her sessions with Sal, she went straight there. This was strictly against the rules. Sal would have dropped her if he had known what she was doing.

The counseling hadn't helped. She still wanted Jed. She wanted to feel that powerful orgasm that he was so expert in making her have.

Each time she went to his place they argued but each time, they ended up making love. Her conscience told her to break off with him but her burning desire for sex told her to run back for more of the same.

Having a guilty conscience about meeting Jed behind Sal's back, she finally mustered the courage to tell him she'd been running to Jed for sex.

"You've got to stop this."

"But I love to sleep with him," Aries argued. "It's like a disease that I can't get rid of."

"He will destroy you. You've got to start thinking above your waist. A person shouldn't be controlled by sex but should be controlled by his mind. There's nothing wrong with sex but you are paying for it. When you need sex, for God's sakes, go out and find yourself a clean man, get satisfied and then go back to your business and forget it. Don't let sex be your God."

Aries tried to heed Sal's advice but she had no will power. She was locked in Jed's sexual prison. Suddenly out of seemingly nowhere, her escape finally came.

Jed made plans to go to Indiana for ten days to visit his parents. Aries had been there once with him when they were dating. She was sexually frustrated on the whole trip because they were staying at his parents house and Jed was embarrassed to have sex with his mother sleeping down the hall.

Aries slept in the guest room. She got damned horny on that trip, and she pleaded with Jed to either fuck her there or move into a hotel away from his folks. Her pleas were to no avail. "It wouldn't hurt her to do without sex for a few days," he said. She disagreed. It always hurt her when she had to go without sex.

Jed's taking a trip would give her some free time. He had left B.K. Stein's and was working with another company. Everyone thought he was out of the picture. Frankly, she didn't want her friends to know she was still playing around with him. Margie accused her of having a secret lover but she never imagined it could be Jed. She would kill her if she knew. With him out of town maybe she'd go out with Margie, one evening, or maybe she could sell some real estate.

Part Fourteen

*I*t was Friday morning and Aries was at the office. She needed to schedule the closing on the house she was buying. She had reluctantly sold the mansion and had moved her family to Fort Lauderdale. The children were unhappy about the move but the house was more than she could afford.

She purchased a smaller home, Spanish style, on deep water close to her office and across the canal from Mickey Rooney. Being in the real estate business she listed the house to get prospects. Very soon, she got a an offer too good to refuse so she sold the new house.

She rented a smaller house near her office and a few months later, she made a deal with the owner to purchase it. Mia and Gregory were away in college and Ralph and Sara were in boarding school. Only Mark was left at home on a full time basis so a smaller house would do just fine.

Aries needed to call the Sellers to discuss a closing date. After speaking with them she would coordinate things with the closing agent. Going back to the coffee room, she poured herself a cup of steaming black coffee. On her way back to the to her desk Hattie stopped her. Hattie was a super salesperson but, perhaps, the most insecure woman Aries had ever met.

Short and fat, Hattie must have weighed two hundred pounds. It was a shame because she had such nice hair, face and eyes. Her husband looked like a wimp beside her. He was about half her size. Everybody in the office talked about Hattie's being so roly-poly fat. They wondered why she didn't do something about it. Hattie tried to diet but if she ever lost a pound it wasn't noticeable.

"Hey, Aries, I hear you bought another house," Hattie said grinning and breaking into a chuckle. That was one of her habits.

"How much did you pay for it?"

"Who needs to know?"

"I'd like to know. If I could have gotten that house at a right price I would have bought it myself."

"Well, I got it at a right price."

"Do you want to sell it?" asked Hattie teasingly.

"No, I don't want to sell it. I haven't even closed on it yet. Find yourself another house, this one is mine, all mine."

"Who was the Seller?"

"My, my, but you're nosy. You have to know everything, don't you?"

"Well, I was just curious."

"For your information, Hattie, the Sellers are from out of town. They're from Madison, Wisconsin. I haven't met them yet but I'm getting ready to go call them and schedule the closing, right now."

"Why are they selling?"

Aries laughed. That woman just wouldn't stop.

"They're selling because the wife likes San Diego better than she does Fort Lauderdale. The house is really not much of a house but the location is good and it puts me only five minutes way from the office."

Hattie's dark brown eyes twinkled as she laughed.

"You get all the breaks. If you decide to sell I'll give you five thousand more than you paid for it."

"Forget it, Hattie, I don't want to sell."

Back at her desk Aries looked up John Roberts telephone number in Madison. It was ten o'clock a.m. there and she hoped to find him at his place of business.

Dialing his number, the phone started ringing and a pleasant sounding male voice answered.

"Hello, hello is this John Roberts?"

"Speaking, yes it is."

"Oh, hello Mr. Roberts, this is Aries Winston calling from Fort Lauderdale. I got your letter and I appreciate the things you have agreed to do to put the house in sales condition."

"No problem. I know the house was in bad shape and as long as you are willing to make the arrangements for me, I'll be glad to change the carpets and have the inside painted. I'll leave it up to you to select the colors. Just let me know how much it is and I'll send you a check. Incidentally, when do you think we can close?"

"That's what I'm calling you about. When would you and your wife like for me to schedule the closing?"

"Anytime is agreeable with us. What about next Friday? I believe I can work it out in my schedule to fly down next Thursday evening and be there for the closing on Friday morning."

"Friday sounds fine."

"Is it really necessary for my wife to come?"

"If the title to the house is in both of your names, both signatures will be required on the deed. However, I could Federal Express the deed up there and she can sign it and get her signature notarized and witnessed in Wisconsin. If your wife isn't coming, I'll ask the attorney to send the necessary documents to her for signing."

"Great, you take care of those details, please, and I'll see you next week. By the way, would you do me a favor and make a reservation for me at a hotel down there not too far from the house?"

"Sure! I'll also give you a ride from the airport to your hotel when you arrive if you don't want to get a rent a car. There's a nice hotel just a few streets down from the house. I'll make your a reservation there."

"Good girl. I'll call you back in half an hour and tell you what flight I'll be coming in on. May I have your telephone number?"

Giving him the office number, Aries said she would await his call.

Hanging up the phone, she whirled around in her chair. She felt good inside after talking to him and she wondered what he looked like. He sounded so pleasant. Enough day dreaming! He'd be calling back in a few minutes so she called Attorney McLean's office to get a time set for the closing. His secretary answered.

"Hey, Mary, May I speak to Mike McLean?"

"Just a minute," she said putting her on hold.

As she waited Aries looked at her calendar to see what date next Friday would be. It was June 6th, one day before Jed was due to arrive back from Indiana. Still waiting, she scribbled the Roberts closing on the calendar for June 6th.

Finally, Mike McLean came on the line. "Hello Miss Aries," he said in a friendly voice. "What can I do for you?"

"Oh, Hi, Mike. I'm calling to see if we can close on that property I'm buying next Friday morning. I sent you a copy of the contract."

"Friday morning, just a minute, I'll let you talk to my secretary. I believe we have the abstract in on that. Who's handling the closing for the Sellers? They're from out of town, aren't they?"

"Yes, they live in Wisconsin and we want you to do the whole thing. The husband is coming but the wife won't be here so we want you send the necessary papers to Wisconsin, right away, so she can sign them. Her husband will bring them back when he comes down for the closing."

"Well, that's probably rushing us a little but I believe we can get the job done. You've told the Seller, I hope, that I won't be able to represent both of you. I can only represent one of you. I can prepare the documents for both sides but if you both want to be represented then one of you will have to hire another attorney."

"Well, represent him then and just prepare my documents. I don't need an attorney for this deal."

"Very well. It was nice talking to you. Now let me give you back to Mary so she can get this on her calendar."

Back on the line, Mary refreshed her memory about the contract, etc. Aries stressed that they needed to close early on Friday morning as the Seller planned to catch a plane back to Wisconsin on the same day.

"How about ten o'clock?"

"Ten o'clock sounds good. I'll let him know. Be sure to send the documents out, right away, Mary. Time is of the essence. It's only a week away."

"Hey, Aries, you've got a call on line three," Robin yelled.

"Okay, okay, tell them to hold a minute. See you next Friday, Mary. Call me if you need anything. Goodbye."

The other line was still flashing so she picked it up.

"Hello, Aries Winston speaking."

"Hello again," the caller said. "This is John Roberts."

"Oh, hi, Sorry you had to wait but I was tied up with the attorney's office on the other line."

"That's okay. I've got my flight schedule now. Would you like to write it down?"

"Sure!"

"I'll be arriving in Fort Lauderdale at ten p.m.on Delta airlines Flight 608."

"Great! I'll pick you up at the airport."

"How will I know you, what do you look like?" he asked.

"I'm beautiful," Aries replied, without thinking about the words that were pouring from her mouth."

"He laughed and said, I'm sure you are. Then I'll just look for a beautiful woman."

"I was just kidding. How will I recognize you?"

"To make it easy for you I'll be wearing a navy and white checked blazer."

"Okay, I'll wear a navy and white polka dotted jersey pants suit." Aries wasn't to good at planning what she was going to wear on such short notice but when he said blue and white that was the first thing she could think of saying.

"By the way, I've called the attorney and they will be sending the deed for your wife's signature. Be sure to bring it back with you or we won't be able to close," Aries cautioned. The closing is tentatively scheduled for ten o'clock on Friday morning so you should be able to catch a flight back to Wisconsin sometime after lunch."

"Thanks a lot! I really would like to spend some time in sunny Florida while I'm down there but I have prior commitments that will necessitate my making this trip a short one."

"That's too bad! It's so nice down here. I'll meet you Thursday evening at the Delta arrivals."

Saying goodbye, Aries hung up the phone wondering why she had opened her big mouth and told him that she was beautiful. Why had she volunteered to pick him up at the airport? He could have taken a taxi to his hotel. What would John Roberts look like? She assumed he'd be short and fat but very nice. What difference did it make? All she was doing was buying his house and it didn't matter what he looked like.

As the week went by Aries was getting horny and anxious for Jed to return home. The season was over and nothing exciting was happening in Fort Lauderdale. Thursday evening arrived and as she had promised, she dressed in her navy and white polka dotted jersey pants suit so the Midwestern arrival would be able to recognize her.

Arriving at the airport she parked her car and went in to wait for the arrival of Delta Fight 608. She was a few minutes early and the flight hadn't come in yet. This was a first because she was usually late everywhere she went. Tonight, she had made it a point to be early so Mr. Roberts would feel more comfortable upon his arrival into the city. When she got to the gate the plane had just landed and the passengers were deplaning. As Aries waited she told the man who was standing beside her that she was there to pick up a man she had never met before. "He'll be wearing a navy blue and white checked blazer but I have no idea of what he looks like."

At that moment, the man pointed to a tall dark haired man standing in the doorway of the airplane ramp. "There he is," he said.

The passenger headed straight toward her. His physical appearance was striking. Walking up to her he said, "Hi, you must be Aries Winston and you're right, you are beautiful."

So this was John Roberts in the flesh. He had sounded so nice over the telephone but she had no idea that he would be such a gorgeous creature. In a state of shock, she was beginning to feel all kinds of feelings. Her stomach was fluttering and her heart was pounding. What an impact the sight of John Roberts had on her! The chemistry between them was instant.

They chatted as they made their way out of the terminal and into the parking lot. Aries was responding to his statements but at the same time she was talking to her self a mile a minute. John Roberts was the best looking man she'd ever seen. He was about six feet three, his dark blue eyes were filled with expression and his facial bone structure was perfect. The way he walked, the way he talked, he was absolutely handsome!

Aries was so flustered she remembered little of the conversation that they had on the way to her car. In fact, it was all that she could do to find the car. Finally, she found it and they headed north on A1A toward his hotel.

"Have you had dinner? He asked.

"No, I haven't."

"Well, then, I'd like to take you out to dinner, tonight. By the way, please call me John."

"Okay, and you may call me, Aries. I know a real nice restaurant on the way back. They call it "The First Time." The food is great and the atmosphere is good, too. Would you like to go, there?"

"You're the driver, it's your choice."

"Let's go there, then. It's open until midnight so we won't have to hurry so."

Arriving at the restaurant, John gave his name to the hostess and Aries piped in and asked to be seated in Albert's section. She had been there many times before with Alden Austin. Albert was her favorite waiter. He was German and he had mastered the art of waiting on tables.

Getting to know one another was an enjoyable experience. They seemed to hit it off together perfectly. They were served a gourmet meal amid wine, candlelight and strumming violins. As they conversed about various subjects, they were further entertained by a parade of yachts moving up and down the Intracoastal Waterway. By the time they left the restaurant they had become friends, good friends, who liked what they saw in one another.

Looking at her watch, Aries realized they had stayed there thirty minutes past midnight and nobody had asked them to leave. The restaurant had closed without them even noticing.

"It's late, said Aries. I'd better drop you off at your hotel. I have reserved a a real nice place for you not far from the house."

Soon they approached the hotel.

"There it is, it's that big hotel on our left," she said pointing to the sign. Pulling up into a parking space in front, she waited for John to get out of the car.

"Let me get checked in and I'll buy you a nightcap before you go. I hear the sounds of music and maybe, we can catch a few dances," he suggested.

"Are you sure? It's awfully late."

"Lady, I'm very sure. I'm not going to say good night to you until I have to. Please wait for me, I'll be right out."

Aries waited because she didn't want to leave him either. Sparks had been flying back and forth between them ever since he had gotten off the plane. John Roberts didn't know it but unless she had to she was never going to leave him.

After he checked in they went into the pool side lounge and sat down at a table. John ordered their drinks and then, taking her hand, he said, "Young lady, May I have the pleasure of this dance?" How could she refuse a gentlemen who had invited her with such politeness and such charm?

"Of course, I'd be delighted." Aries slid out of her chair and John led her onto the dance floor. The trio was playing a slow one as he wrapped her in his sturdy arms. There was such a warmth as their bodies touched. The blend was perfect. The chemistry between them was overpowering.

"Come on, let's get out of here," he murmured, "let's take our drinks to the room. I want to make sweet love to you."

Aries knew she should say no, that she should tell him that she had to go home but the pull between them was too strong.

"John," she said softly, "I really shouldn't. We know we shouldn't. I shouldn't be here with you," Aries told him unconvincingly.

"Stay with me," he pleaded. "Stay tonight with me. I want to feel your warm soft body next to mine."

"But I've just met you."

John took her hand squeezing it with his firm grip. "What difference does that make? Don't you believe in love at first sight?"

Good gracious! He had hit the nail on the head. That's exactly how she felt about him. From the moment she saw him it was love at first sight. Did he feel that way about her, too? John Roberts had found the right words, "love." Aries took no more persuading. She willingly accompanied him to Room 205. Undressing, they lay down together caressing, making love and whispering sweet nothings to each other.

"I knew it would be like this, he uttered. "I knew it would feel wonderful with you."

As the hours of the early morn clicked on, the passion between

them grew deeper and deeper. It was truly an interlude in paradise.
Aries had one orgasm after the other and they had simultaneous climaxes, too.

"Your body is so soft and beautiful," he said tenderly.

"Your body is beautiful, too. Where did you ever get such fantastic
muscles?" she asked.

John lay there soaking up every compliment she made. He was
loving every moment of it. Aries must have made his ego ten feet tall
but she truly meant every word she voiced.

John said he kept his body in shape by playing tennis, racquetball
and working out a lot.

"You're in good shape, too," he commented.

"That comes from being a tennis player," She smiled proudly.

They made love that night until their bodies were saturated with
total contentment. Then they slumbered quietly in each others arms.
Aries would never forget the first night they loved as long as she
lived.

The next morning, they made love again and she knew she had
fallen in love with John Roberts. In the heat of their passion she had
forgotten that he was married, that he had a wife. When they were
making love nothing else seemed to matter but when daylight came
Aries remembered.

Getting out of bed, she asked, "What about your wife?"

"My wife and I aren't getting along too well."

"Oh, I'm sorry to hear that. What happened?"

John's face seemed uncomfortably pained when she popped that
question. He hesitated a moment and then he began his story.

"It all started when I allowed her to go to work. She met some
interior decorator and really flipped over him. She came home and
told me she was in love with him."

Aries's big brown eyes opened wide in astonishment "I can't
believe that! How on earth could a woman with a wonderful husband
like you even look at another man?"

"Well it happened and I stayed with her. I'm Catholic and
Catholics don't believe in divorce. I stayed with her because we have
children." As he talked Aries could see the deep hurt in his warm blue

Irish eyes. She felt sorry for him because already she was in love with him and she couldn't bear for him to hurt.

They had breakfast sent to the room and afterwards, Aries told him she had to go home and get dressed for the closing. "I can't wear this jersey pants suit. I'll be back to pick you up after I change clothes. Maybe you'd like to take a swim in the pool or walk across the street to the beach while I'm gone."

"Honey, go do what you have to do but hurry back because I'm going to miss you while you're gone."

"I won't be long." Aries gave him a warm hug and kiss.

Outside she started looking for her car. She didn't see it and for a moment she thought it might have been stolen. Then she remembered she had parked in front of the hotel. She hoped she wouldn't see anybody she knew when she was leaving. She knew a lot of people in that town and she wouldn't want them to know she'd spent the night there with a man. Her Tennessee upbringing wouldn't permit this.

Aries detested leaving hotels at the crack of dawn in the same clothes she had worn the night before. It always made her feel like a prostitute although she had never been paid for a piece of ass in her life. In fact, it was the other way around. Aries had money from her inheritance and every man who knew it tried to take advantage of her, financially. It had become a common joke among her friends. How much did he take you for, they would ask? Jed had been the last one and she was determined not to be made a fool of again.

Thinking of John, Aries wondered if last night was just a beautiful one night stand or if he really had fallen for her. No matter what she wasn't sorry. She was in love, really in love and the feeling was wonderful. Finding her car, she hurried home to get dressed for the closing.

As she pulled into the driveway her son, Mark, was standing by the front door. "Hi, Mom," he said with a twinkle in his eye. "Where were you last night?"

"I was home. I came home very late and I went out very early this morning."

"In that outfit, come on, Mom," he teased laughing. "That fellow you went out with must have been good."

"Stop that kind of talk, Mark," Aries remarked sharply. "I've got to get ready. We're closing on this house, today. By this afternoon, we won't be renting it anymore, we'll own it," she said gleefully. "I won't be home for lunch but I'll leave you five dollars and you can eat at Mcdonald's."

"I'm going to the beach today with Tad," Mark announced. "Is that alright?"

"Sure, but be careful and don't swim out too far. Have a nice day, honey. I'll see you at supper."

Luckily, she had already planned her dress for the day so dressing didn't take long. She had to pick up her messages at the office and get a cashier's check at the bank for the closing.

At the office Aries was greeted in the reception room by Patsy, the receptionist, a tall attractive blonde with a set of knockers that would knock your eyes out. Aries wondered how it would feel to walk down the street with a pair of boobies sticking out like that. Patsy was such a showcase. She must have driven guys wild when they saw her. Aries felt completely flat chested and somewhat of a runt when this tall hunk of woman stood beside her.

"What have you been up to?" Patsy chuckled.

"What do you mean?"

"You know what I mean." Patsy stretched her shoulders further back displaying her mountains of breasts.

"Look at you, your face is lit up like a glowworm and you've got a smile on your face that looks like you've just closed a million dollar deal."

"No such luck." Aries laughed. "No sales at all but I did find a million dollar man and I'm in love."

"Who is he? Where did you meet him? Surely not in this town."

"Yes, I met him right in this town."

"Well, he must have been just passing through because there aren't any million dollar men around here. Where is he from and what's his name?"

"His name's a secret but he's absolutely gorgeous. Everything he's got is in the right place," said Aries as she clinched her hands and raised them up in a hurrah stance.

"You beat all," exclaimed Patsy, blushing. "I'm going to have to start taking lessons from you."

"I can't teach you anything. With your looks and those boobies, you don't need lessons from me."

"But guys don't pay any attention to me. What do you do to these men to have them all falling in love with you?"

Aries shrugged her shoulders and tightened her lips, momentarily. "Who knows, Patsy, maybe it's just my irresistible charm."

"I wish you would show me how you do it. I lead such a dull life."

As they were chatting, Margie entered the room arms laden with files and papers. She'd overheard some of their conversation and she couldn't resist putting her two cents in. "I can tell you what she does to them. She's a big flirt and she woes them with that innocent Tennessee, back on the farm, accent. When she meets a guy she becomes the sweet, innocent but sexy girl that every man would like to know. She's a real ham! I've been out with her and when she's along the rest of us can forget it. She hogs up all the men and has them flocking around her like flies. They always pick her over me," Margie went on. "Half the time her hair looks terrible and she wears no makeup but the guys still love her. Me, I spend three hours getting dressed and getting beautiful but with Aries along they don't even notice me."

Margie was saying her piece. Nobody could stop her when she had the floor. When she took a pause Aries grabbed the conversation and started handing the shit back to her. "I've told you that guys like them natural. As she spoke she surveyed Margie's bird nest of teased and stiff sprayed hair. "Take that teasing out of your hair, take that eye shadow and makeup off and you'll see what I'm talking about. Men like natural women."

Changing the conversation, Aries turned back to ask Patsy where her messages were.

"In your box, the same place they always are. Mrs. Carson has called you twice and she wants you to get that extra set of keys over to her house, right away."

"Well, Mrs. Carson will just have to wait. Today I have something else to do. Patsy, please hand me the Roberts file. I'm going to Mike

McLean's office for the Roberts closing. I'll be out of touch for the rest of the day. You can just tell my public that they'll have to wait."

"Hum, going out with that million dollar man again," chuckled Patsy. "It's a good thing Jed's not around anymore or he'd be jealous."

"Jed, who? I don't even know anybody by that name."

"Great," Margie interjected still listening to the conversation. Margie plunked her things down on the conference room table. "At last, you're getting some sense in your head. That guy was a loser! All he wanted was your money and to think you considered marrying him. I get furious every time I think about how much money and misery that rotten jerk has cost you."

Aries didn't want to hear anymore so she excused herself and sat down at her desk to read her messages. One of the calls was from Mike McLean's office. She returned the call and Mary, his secretary, informed her that the attorney had been called into court, suddenly. He wouldn't be able to do the closing at ten. "We'll have to re-schedule it for one o'clock this afternoon. I hope that doesn't foul up Mr. Roberts return flight plans. It's the best we can do. Is that okay?"

"I guess so but I'd better get over to his hotel and tell him because he's waiting to be picked up. We'll be there at one. Bye, Bye."

Aries gathered up her things and left the office. She was so eager to get back to John that she almost forgot to stop at the bank for the cashier's check. No money, no closing.

Arriving back at his hotel, she stopped by the pool but saw no signs of him. He wasn't in the bar either so she went up to his room. Tapping lightly upon his door, he quickly responded.

"Well, you're back and don't you look sharp." Taking her in his arms again, John gave her a kiss and a warm hug. "Honey, I'm so glad you're back, I really missed you. You made such beautiful love to me last night. You've got my head spinning!"

"You made beautiful love to me, too, and I'm beginning to miss you even before you're gone. Our closing plans have been changed. The lawyer was called into court, unexpectedly and they have re-scheduled us for one o'clock. I thought I'd better let you know, right away, in case you needed to change your flight back."

"You're right, I'd better give them a call because a one o'clock appointment is calling it too tight. I'll cancel and take the five o'clock flight, instead."

"Can't you stay another day? Please stay another day."

"I wish I could, I really would like to but I've got to get back to my business."

"Can't someone else run it?"

"Not really. I have to open up and go to the bank and I've got a radio show to do."

"What kind of radio show? Are you on the radio?"

"Yes, I'm a sports announcer on Station WIOZ in Madison. It comes on, early, at six- thirty in the morning."

"Gee! I'd like to hear your sweet voice on the radio. How do I get that station?"

It's just a local station and I don't think you can get it down here. Don't worry, honey, you'll hear my voice because when I get back I'll call you every morning at eight o'clock, your time. I'll call you and wake you up and pretend we're in bed together making love. I'll make love to you over the phone. Is that alright ? When I call you will you rub your clitoris and put your finger in your pussy and pretend it's my cock? I'll play with my cock and think of your pretty breasts and imagine my cock is in your sweet pussy and we'll cum together. It will be wonderful making love to you."

"Stop it, you're turning me on. "Yes, yes, I'll make love to you when you call. Promise me you won't make love to anyone else, except your wife, and promise me you'll think of me when you're making love to her."

" I promise. When I make love to her I'll always be making love to you, mentally."

"That's good. That way I won't be jealous of her."

Looking at his watch, John suggested that they have an early lunch before going to the attorney's office. "If we have time I'd like to ride by the house and take a look at it, too. We'd better get out of this room before I take my clothes off and make love to you again, he threatened."

"Don't tempt me. I'd love to make love to you, right now, in fact, I'd like nothing better but you'd mess up my hair."

"Well, Miss Aries, we'll just have to settle for lunch but after the closing you'd better watch out because God willing, I'm going to hold your warm and tender body close to mine just one more time before I fly away. John was smiling.

Aries looked at him. He was so gorgeous! "After the closing you're on," she said nodding her head positively.

At lunch they chatted about their respective families, familiarizing each other with names and ages of their children etc. They planned and discussed how, when and where they would meet again.

"You live so far away from me and you're married." Aries bemoaned the fact.

"I know but there will be times we can get together," John said. "When I get home, I'll check the Snobird football schedule. I travel with the team and do the announcing at the games. Maybe you can fly to meet me at some of the out of town games."

"That would be great! I really love football."

The minutes flicked on and soon, it was time to go Mike McLean's office. The closing went smoothly with abundant credits to the Buyer. Money didn't seem to be the big thing with this Seller and when the matter of the air conditioning came up he offered credit, not for repair but for replacement of the system. They were finished by two forty-five. That left two hours and fifteen minutes before John's plane would be leaving. There would be time only to go back to the hotel, pick up his things and head for the airport.

Traffic would be hectic at that time of day. Aries dreaded that journey, not because of the traffic, but because she didn't want those "magic moments" to come to such an abrupt halt.

"I'm really going to miss you."

"I'm going to miss you, too. I really hate to see you go. You know, don't you, that this is ridiculous? I shouldn't feel this way. I've only known you since last night."

I know you shouldn't, I shouldn't but we both do. That's fate, I suppose and I'm very happy fate has brought us together."

"Together is fine with me but it's that being apart that bothers me."

"Don't worry about it, honey. Football season will be starting in September and we can meet at some of the games. I believe the first one is in New Orleans or Chicago and we can spend two whole nights together, then."

"Promise."

"I promise. I'll write to you as soon as I get back and send you the schedule so we can make our plans."

Arriving at the airport, Aries swung the car into the third lane for departing passengers. "You're flying Delta home, aren't you?"

Checking his ticket, John confirmed that Delta was the airline.

"Delta's right in front of us so I'll drop you off right here. I can't stand long goodbyes."

"We are never going to say goodbye," John said putting both arms around her, hugging her firmly. "You're quite a lady and I have very deep feelings for you. Be my good girl. I'll write to you. Send me a picture of yourself in a bathing suit or something so I can look at you when I get home."

Aries was about to become tearful. She could feel tears swelling up in he eyes. Turning her head, she wished John a good trip and told him he'd better go before he missed his plane. Walking away, he waved, threw kisses and called back, "I'll see you."

"See you," repeated Aries as she waved to him, her heart sinking.

She was in deep thought as she drove her yellow mercedes down the highway toward home. Was it really possible that all of this could have happened to her? Only day before yesterday her life had been so bleak and dull. Maybe she was just dreaming, maybe she would never see John again.

The surroundings were oblivious on the journey home. Finally, she pulled up in the front driveway without having noticed the path that had brought her there. She was back from her dream world and back to a house that had been lately, left unattended. The kitchen a sink was full of dirty dishes that had been left from the day. The place was a mess. Mark must have had all of his friends in there.

Changing clothes, she dug in to put the place back in order. As she cleaned she thought, "This house is mine and it's very special to me because it used to be John's house." Maybe someday, she would give it back to him. For now, it made her feel better just knowing that he'd been here.

From the first day they met, John was always with her in spirit. She could feel his presence throughout the house but it didn't stop there. His presence was everywhere in the atmosphere that surrounded her. It was a strange but beautiful feeling. She spent many hours enjoying their togetherness, even though he was physically more than a thousand miles away.

Aries had an ability to mind travel and sometimes, she would find herself beside him in Madison. This mental transplanting of heart and soul made her feel even closer to him. Since meeting John her life had changed completely. It had taken on a new and beautiful meaning.

The day after he left, Jed called her at the office. He had arrived home from Indiana. It was Saturday and she was there trying to catch up on the work she had neglected when John was in town.

"Hi there," he said.

"Who's calling?"

"It's me, it's Jed, don't you remember me?"

Aries was glad Margie wasn't at the office then. If she had answered the phone she would have hung up on him.

"Certainly, I remember you. I just didn't recognize your voice. How was your trip?"

"Not bad. How about having dinner at my place, tonight?"

"Well, I don't know." Aries hesitated. "I've really got a lot of work to do and I was planning on wall papering the bathroom."

"Well, you have to eat, sometime."

"Eat, but I'm not hungry."

"Well, you will be later. Come on over to my apartment. I'll get some food and we'll have dinner about seven."

"Okay, you've twisted my arm. I'll see you around six-thirty."

Aries really didn't want to see Jed. If he thought their relationship was going to continue like it had been he was in for a surprise. Certainly she couldn't tell him about John. He would be very upset. She would have to come up with another excuse to make the break with him. Finishing her work, she went home to pick up a pair of shorts and a tee-shirt before going to Jed's.

He wasn't at home when she arrived so she would wait fifteen minutes before leaving. Wanting to avoid the evening, she hoped Jed wouldn't show up in the time she had allotted him. Watching the car clock, Aries commenced the countdown. Suddenly, she was startled by a tapping on the car window. Jed was standing there with a big bag of groceries in his hands.

"Hi, sorry I'm late. I got held up at the office and couldn't make it any sooner."

"That's okay. I was going to wait a few more minutes. Well, get out of the car and come on in."

"Is it alright to park the car here?"

"It would be better, if you parked in the lot across the street. These spaces are for tenants, only."

"Okay, I'll move the car."

Inside, Aries changed from her office attire into shorts and a tee-shirt. Kicking off her shoes she went barefoot into the kitchen where she found Jed preparing spaghetti sauce. His homemade sauce was really delicious. Naturally, with his Italian up-bringing he knew how to make it.

"Can I help?" she offered positioning herself on a stool at the kitchen counter.

"No thanks, I have everything under control. Would you like a glass of wine?"

"Sure, I'll get the glasses."

Wine poured, Aries sat on the stool swinging her legs as she watched Jed's expertise as an Italian chef. Mainly, their conversation was confined to talk about his trip and events in her real estate office while he was gone. She carefully avoided any mention of John Roberts other than to say that the Seller flew down from up north for the closing and all went well.

The meal was delicious. Aries helped with the dishes and after-ward, they turned the television on to watch the eleven o'clock news. They didn't have far to go from the table to the television because Jed's dining room, living room and bedroom were the same.

After the news Jed said it was bedtime. Pulling the sheets down from the top shelf of the closet, he flipped the sofa open to make up the bed. As Aries watched his preparations she shrugged within her-self. How could she sleep with Jed when she was in love with another man? What would he think if she refused when before she had such a sexual attraction for him? She couldn't tell him she'd found someone else. One more time really wouldn't matter. Undressing in silence, Aries lay down in the bed beside him. She had a terrible feeling deep inside her gut. "I don't want this man anymore," she told herself. "How can I be intimate with him when I'm in love with John Roberts?"

"Penny for your thoughts," said Jed as he rolled over close to her.

"My thoughts. Oh, I'm thinking nothing, really my mind is a complete blank."

"Nothing, huh, well, put your hand on my hard cock and I'll give you something to think about. Touch it and see what I've got waiting for you."

With reluctance Aries moved her hand slowly across the sheets to find Jed's erected penis. Placing her hand around the shaft she found it hard, pulsating and warm.

"Heavens, you're really ready tonight, aren't you?"

"Yes, I'm really ready. Spread your nice legs and get your ass up here so I can fuck you."

Go ahead and fuck me, thought Aries. You'd better fuck me good tonight because I don't need you anymore and this will be your last time. Jed climbed her awaiting frame and plunged his iron rod deep into her vagina.

"Stop you're hurting me," she complained. "Don't be so rough, that hurts me."

"Baby, I'm going to hurt you good, tonight. It hurts you good doesn't it?"

"Oh, oh, you're killing me."

" I'm going to drive you crazy. Tonight, I'm going to fuck you until you beg me to stop." Aries knew there was no point in resisting. She had opened her legs, she was in the midst of this thing and the only compatible way out was to stop complaining and finish it.

With this thought in mind she tightened up her pelvic muscles converting the walls of her vagina into a suction cup. She grasped his big cock, sucked it in and held it tightly. The squeezing of her muscles and her movements as she threw her cunt up to meet his cock drove him wild.

"Slow down baby, you're going to make me cum if you don't. Please, I'm going to cum if you don't stop."

Suddenly, he withdrew leaving Aries panting.

"Please, please put it back in." Complying, Jed slid his cock into the her pussy. Aries lifted her ass up high and tightened her pelvic muscles tantalizing him so much that he couldn't hold off any longer. He tried to withdraw, to hold off, but it was too late. He was shooting cum everywhere. Exhausted he lay back, limpless.

Aries waited for Jed to fall asleep before she eased quietly out of bed, took her things and headed for the door to make her exit. As she turned the doorknob Jed stirred and called out drowsily, "Hey, what's happening?"

"I'm going home. I have an early morning appointment. I'll lock the door on my way out. I'll call you tomorrow." She made her escape scurrying past the brightly lit streetlight outside.

Home again, Aries climbed into bed, said her prayers and exhausted went soundly to sleep. She never called Jed the next day as she had promised and the next time he called her, she gave him a flat NO!

"We're broken up," she told him, "I don't know why I've even been seeing you." Jed was angry but Aries stuck to her guns. She never went to him again.

The ensuing weeks were spent in selling real estate and telephone calls and correspondence with John Roberts. Often he called early in the morning and they made love, long distance. Their love making sessions were torrid and exciting but nothing could have been more exciting than to have John's body next to hers in the "flesh." John whispered sweet nothings and wooed her with his sexy voice until she was actually having orgasms over the phone. He was climaxing, too, and it was wonderful.

At night when she went to bed Aries could hear John's voice, feel him touching her and making love to her. She'd masturbate pretending that although he was in Wisconsin, he was in bed with her making love. Over and over, she read the contents of his cards and letters that had arrived special delivery. One was signed, "Nobody loves you like I do."

John sent the game schedule and in a separate letter he had mapped out the plans for their meeting at the New Orleans game on September 5th. Aries was bursting with excitement with the anticipation of seeing him. About a week before the 5th, he called revising their plans. She should fly to Chicago on September 12th, instead. His wife was going out of town so after the game, she could can fly back to Madison and they'd be able to spend a longer time together.

Aries was unhappy about the week's postponement but she was elated to learn they would have a longer togetherness. She changed her flight reservations and from New Orleans to Chicago. With the anticipation of seeing John she was floating on Cloud Nine.

The arrangements were made. Margie would handle her real estate affairs in her absence for fifty percent of her commission. That was a lot but it was better than nothing. Mark would stay at Tad's house while she was away.

The day of departure arrived and there was nothing left to do but to get to the airport and catch that plane.

The flight was a long one. When the plane finally landed Aries gathered up her baggage and caught a taxi to the hotel where John had made reservations.

Chicago was a a huge city. The cab driver made his way through a maze of crowded streets. Aries hoped John would be at the hotel when she arrived. He had instructed her to ask for the key to his room if she got there, first.

As the cab pulled up in front of the Seron Hotel several black porters with black and red caps were waiting to greet her.

"Good evening ma'am," said one.

"May I take your baggage?"

"Yes, thank you."

Paying the cabbie, she followed the porter to the registration desk in the lobby. Seeing no signs of John she got in line at the desk. When it was her turn she asked the clerk if John Roberts had arrived yet?

"No ma'am," said the clerk.

"Well, he told me if I arrived first I was to ask for the key."

"Mr. Roberts has a reservation. He hasn't arrived yet but his room is pre-paid so that's no problem. I will tell him when he arrives that I gave you a key."

A handsome fellow standing there overheard her conversation with the desk clerk and as she took the key and started to walk away, he asked, "Are you sure you want to wait in Robert's room? Maybe you'd like to wait in mine."

Aries looked at him wondering who he was and how he knew John. She gave him a blank stare and responded, "Certainly not."

She was embarrassed. She wished John would hurry up and get there. Once in the room, she felt more comfortable. It was a beautiful room all decorated in satin and gold like a Queen's suite. There was a vase of red roses on the south wall desk and there were two wine glasses and a bottle of wine on the table. There were roses, wine and everything. Roses were her favorite flower. She wondered if they put them in all of the rooms. John Roberts must have paid a pretty penny for this outlay.

Unpacking her bag, she sat down at the desk and bent over to smell the sweet fragrance of the roses. She loved the smell of roses and the velvet softness of their dress. She spied a card tucked in the vase of roses. She had overlooked it before. Carefully lifting the card from its resting place, she discovered that the roses were for her. "To Aries, I love your magic, Your Snobird." How thoughtful and how sweet of him! She would save this card and cherish it always. She would press a rosebud and keep it, too.

Aries went into the bathroom to freshen up. As she was putting the final touches on her hair she heard a light tapping on the door. Hurrying to open it, she expected to see John. Instead, the stranger who had spoken to her in the lobby was standing there, smiling.

"Oh, excuse me, I'm sorry to bother you but I forgot to introduce myself in the lobby." Aries just listened.

"My name's Marvin Stokes, I'm the public relations director of the Snobird team. I have just received a message that their plane took off late and the team won't be here until eight o'clock. I figured you were John's girl and you would be wondering why he was late. They always send me ahead of the team to get things set up. Can I buy you a drink in the lounge? No sense staying up here in the room by your lonesome. Come on down to the lounge and we'll await their arrival together."

Aries was surprised at his concern for her. He knew John, though, so perhaps he was just being a good will ambassador. Thanking him for the invite she said she might come down to the lounge, later, after she rested awhile.

After Marvin Stokes left she looked at her watch and realized that she had another hour to wait for John. Kicking her heels off she lay down on the bed and closed her eyes. She'd stay right there. John wouldn't appreciate finding her in the company of another man when he arrived.

Aries rested until she heard another soft tap, tap, tap at the door. She got up to answer.

"Who's there?"

"It's me honey, open this door, you beautiful thing."

Aries flung the door open and fell into John Roberts awaiting arms.

"My, how great it is to see you, Aries. My, what a feast for sore eyes you are!"

They were so happy to be reunited. They spent their second night together consumed in love and passion. Making love with John was delightful. He melted and dissolved her to the point that she wished she could be a "grain of sand" in his pocket and be with him always. He warned her that if she was a grain of sand in his pocket he might lose her. Spending the night in tender love making, finally their bodies were exhausted and limp from pleasure and they fell into sweet, sweet slumber.

During the night the hotel across the street was bombed but they heard nothing. They were told about the incident at breakfast. When they were alone they looked at each other and commented that if they had died last night, they were so happy they wouldn't have cared.

John was busy in pre-game meetings that day so Aries went down the street to browse in the department store. She didn't need anything but it was be a way to pass the time.

After the meetings John had to plan his announcing at the game that evening. He had to be certain his information on the players was accurate. He also gave her instructions. He would be leaving for the stadium early, at six, because traffic through Chicago wouldn't be easy at that time of day. Aries was to come there later to watch part of the game before flying on to Madison to rejoin him. He would return on the team plane. Her plane would arrive an hour before his and she was to wait for him at the baggage department. Then, he would check her into a hotel before going home.

Ava, his wife, would never know that his trip had been any more than just a routine trip to cover the game.

Aries planned to stay in Madison all week. John had made reservations for her in a hotel just minutes away from his place of business.

After John left with the players Aries packed her things up and caught a cab to the game. Leaving her luggage in the taxi, she instructed the driver to come back to take her to the airport at ten.

Finding her seat in the stands, she looked for John in the press box. He was there working and enjoying the game. Aries had a perfect view of him. How she loved to look at him and how she loved to hear his sweet voice!

From the way things were going it looked like Snobird team would win the game. They were making the Chicago Bears look pretty sick. Chicago seemed to be headed for disaster. Finally, Aries looked at her watch and realized it was time to leave for the airport. Luckily, the cabbie was waiting at the gate as planned.

The plane was on time and Aries was on the way to her final destination, John's hometown. The flight from Chicago was a blast. Everybody was wild, either celebrating the Snobird victory or drinking their sorrows away if they were Chicago fans. Aries chatted with a several male passengers. Her accent was immediately recognizable as being Southern and they asked her what brought her to the Mid-west. She dared not tell them she was there because she was having an affair with the announcer on the Snobird team. Someone might know him or his wife.

The flight to Madison was a short one and pretty soon the plane was on the ground. Aries headed to the rest room. She wanted to look nice for John so another make-up check and hair combing seemed to be in order. Organized again, she went to find out what gate he would be coming through when his plane arrived.

198

"We don't know yet," said the agent, "but you'll have no trouble finding your party. When that plane lands a cheering squad will be here to greet them."

Thirty minutes later, Aries was standing by the window when she heard the agent say in a loud voice, "They're here." With this announcement the crowd began to gather. She headed to baggage pickup trying to avoid being seen but she was too late. The door behind her swung open and in paraded a happy but weary group of players. Amidst them was John.

The crowd was congratulating and cheering them and there was all sorts of excitement and commotion. Aries hastened her paces in an effort to walk ahead of them but the players began to catch up with her and she was walking down the ramp with the team. She saw John and wanted to wave at him but intuition told her to act like she didn't know him.

When he met her at baggage he was like a different person. He seemed agitated and nervous. She had never seen him act like that.

"Don't talk to me and don't touch me either," he cautioned. "Everybody in this town knows me and if they see us together it'll get back to my wife."

So that was what was wrong with him. Aries was so crushed at his curtness she could have cried.

"Go on outside. I'll get the car and pick you up," he commanded.

"Yes, sir."

In the car, the argument continued.

"I told you to meet me at the baggage department," he snapped angrily, "Why didn't you didn't listen to me? You stayed upstairs where everybody could see us together. What if my wife had been there?"

"I'm sorry, I'm really sorry but it was an accident. I didn't realize the plane was in and I couldn't get out of sight in time."

Aries was beginning to realize that it wasn't what she had done that annoyed him. It was his guilty conscience and fear of being caught that bothered him. John's attitude upset her. She was in love with him and he had never uttered a harsh word to her before.

"What do you want me to do? Do you want me to go home?"

"No, I want you to stay but we are going to have to be careful. Everybody knows me in this town. It's getting very late and my wife will be wondering where I am. I don't have time to take you to the hotel downtown, tonight, so I'll take you to a motel near my house. In the morning, I'll pick you up and take you to another hotel near my work."

"Fine." Aries became silent.

John drove to a hotel, checked her in, unlocked the room door and sat her luggage inside. "I'll call you early in the morning. Get some sleep." He gave her a hug, hustled to his car and drove away.

The room was cheaply furnished and dismal in appearance. She would have never picked that place but at two o'clock in the morning she was tired and weary and glad to have a place to sleep.

Undressing, she climbed into bed and lay there thinking. Last night, John was making love to her and tonight, she was left alone while he rushed home to his wife. Of course, he had to go home. He was a married man with a family. She knew this when she fell in love with him and now, she was getting a taste of what it was like being "the other woman." This time there was one consolation about his going home. He was exhausted and he would sack right out.

John called the next morning at nine a.m. Aries was still sleeping when the call came in. "Good morning, sunshine. How about some breakfast?" He said in a sexy tone of voice.

"Fine."

"I'll be over in a half hour. Will that give you enough time?"

"Sure, I'll hurry."

"No hurry, I just wanted to call you and let you know that I was on my way. Stay in bed until I get there, I want to feel your warm soft body next to mine. See you soon."

Hanging up, Aries wondered if this was the same John Roberts who had been so irritable the night before. He was on his way. She took a quick bath, sprinkled bath cologne all over her body and slipped into a fresh slinky nightgown. All clean, she slid her refreshed body back between the sheets to wait for him.

Aries loved morning sex and the thoughts of making love to John made her pussy moist and wet. She began rubbing her finger gently back and forth across her protruding clitoris in a circular motion. As she massaged herself, her hips and buttocks joined in moving upward in a rhythmic sway. John wasn't there, yet, but she was imagining his big smoldering penis inside of her. She was getting very hot. Her pussy was becoming moister and moister. She'd better stop masturbating and wait for her love. She didn't want to finish the act without him.

Flipping over on her stomach, Aries moved her hand away from her pussy and closing her eyes, she began to doze lightly. Soon she heard a light tapping at the door. It was John. Letting him in, she gave him a friendly morning greeting.

"Get back in bed, young lady, I've got something for you." Still standing at the door, he dropped his trousers.

"Hurry," she purred, "come here. I want to love you a little bit."

Wasting no time, John crawled beneath the warm covers and lay down beside her.

"I love you," she said, as she curled her body close to his. "I love you and I love your body all over." Running her fingers through his shiny thick dark brown hair, she rested her fingertips upon his face and proceeded to trace it's curves. "Let me lick your eyebrows," she teased as she placed her tongue upon his closed eyelids.

"You're just too much, honey. You love me all over and you're so beautiful." As he spoke his hands slid down her hips grasping her tight buttocks. His mighty cock was standing erect and throbbing, begging for her pussy.

Aries parted his legs, turned over and began to lick his scrotum with her warm, wet tongue. Her saliva was pouring now and she was purring like a kitten. "I want to suck your nice balls."

"Ah, yes," he exclaimed in excitement.

"I love your sweet lips on my balls." Licking his sack all around, she gently took his left ball slowly until she had the whole thing in her mouth."

"Oh, oh," he moaned. "You're driving me crazy."

As she sucked on his ball, her pussy was getting wetter and she was consumed by the desire to make love. She wanted to make love to him but not until she had teased him further by placing her mouth, firmly, around his now cum oozing cock.

"Oh my God, darling, that feels so good. Watch out, watch out, you'll make me cum," he murmured. Flipping her over John grabbed her ass in his hands. He was going to fuck her. Now, he was going to fuck her. He plunged his excited hard cock in her vagina and they began to make wild, mad, passionate love.

John was ready to cum but he was trying to hold back until she commenced to orgasm. "Honey, hurry, I'm not going to last much longer."

"Think of something else."

"I'm trying to but it isn't working."

Suddenly, the talk between them ceased and they were consumed by tumultuous climactic explosions.

"What a way to begin the day," John sighed as he nestled his head back upon the pillow! They lay there motionless, exhausted and drained. Peacefully content, they fell into a restful sleep.

Around ten-fifteen they began to stir.

"What time is it?", John asked.

"It's ten-fifteen."

"Ten-fifteen. Oh my goodness, we've got to get going. I'm late. I've got to get to the bank and get some cash for the register."

"I'm ready. Let me comb my hair, first."

In the car they headed for the city.

"I'll just have time to drop you off at the hotel. You can get settled in and I'll call you this afternoon after I've finished working out."

"What time is that?"

"I should be finished around four. Maybe I can stop by your hotel and have a drink with you around five-thirty."

"That's sounds good."

As the car pulled up at the Seron Hotel a uniformed bellhop, black as the ace of spades and all smiles, stepped off the curb to greet them all smiles. John got out of the car and opened the trunk for the bell-boy. Handing the fellow a sizable tip, John told him to take good care of his lady.

"Oh, I will, Sir, I will, Sir."

John gave Aries a friendly, "I'll see you" and drove away leaving her on the sidewalk with the bellboy.

"Mr. John said to take care of you and you'll be in very good hands with us, ma'am. Let me take your luggage and you go right on up to the reservation desk."

Going to the desk, Aries gave them her name. "Your room number is l007," the clerk told her. "Riley will show you up to your room. How long will you be staying, Miss Winston?"

"I believe I'll be here until Saturday."

Surveying her surroundings, Aries could tell that this was a first class hotel like the one in Chicago.

Following Riley, she entered the elevator on the left side of the wide marbled floored lobby. In the elevator she told the bellboy she had noticed that he had called her friend by his first name.

"Do you know him?"

"Yes, ma'am I knows him," he replied with a grin on his face. "All the folks around here knows Mr. John. He's been in this town for a long time."

The tenth floor light flashed and they got off. Aries was anxious to get in her room and to get settled. With so much moving around she was beginning to feel like a traveling saleswoman.

"Room l007 is to the right, ma'am, on the garden side."

The hallway leading to the room was furnished lavishly with plush carpet and Victorian style gold inlaid mirrored credenzas. Each table was adorned with a vase of real yellow roses.

Riley swung her room door open. What a lovely room it was! The furniture was gold inlaid and there was a big king-sized bed with a beautiful quilted lace spread. On the secretary, there was another vase of roses and a bottle of champagne in the ice bucket with the usual two glasses sitting on the side. The telephone was ornate, too. It was neatly bound in leather with a gold trim. By the window, Aries spied two french blue velvet tufted chairs on either side of a round white marble topped table. Looking out the window, she could view the gardens in the patio below. It was fall and the trees were beautiful with their multi-colored autumn toned brown, red and yellow falling leaves. She could see the shoppers scurrying back and forth, carrying their parcels and paraphernalia, all of them on their way to somewhere.

Opening her purse, she handed Riley a two dollar tip and thanked him. Home at last, she unpacked her bag so her clothes wouldn't get anymore wrinkled than they already were.

A little later, she decided to go outside to view the surroundings and browse in the nearby shops. After working so hard in real estate in Florida this week off was a real treat. Down the elevator and down the escalator, Aries arrived at the street level of the hotel. There was a restaurant, a news stand and a gift shop specializing in Irish goods on this level. Looking in the window and reminded that John was Irish, she hoped to find a gift for him there. Stepping into the shop, she contemplated over half a dozen items. Finally, she bought him a plaque that said, "May God Keep You In The Palm Of His Hands." Her selection was appropriate because that was just the way she felt about him.

On the streets in Madison, Aries had to pinch herself to see if it was real. She was so far away from home. She had studied geography in elementary school but all she knew about Wisconsin was that they made cheese there. Fate had led her from the sandy beaches of Florida to a strange new city but she was where she wanted to be, near John Roberts.

Walking alongside the mid-westerners, Aries breathed in the cool, crisp air as she sauntered leisurely from store to store. She could develop an affinity for this city. She had been drowning in humidity in Florida and didn't know it.

Madison, Wisconsin was a wonderful place. The people were polite and nice, quite different from the way people were in New York City when she had visited Greg there. She felt secure and comfortable on the streets of Madison. Those Mid-westerners were decent, hard-working down to earth, friendly folks. On a scale of one to ten, she would give them a eight or nine and she would give John Roberts a ten+.

The week went by quickly and day by day, Aries fell more in love with John. While there, she was up at six in the morning so she could hear him on the radio. Thirty minutes after he got off the air, he was at the hotel tapping lightly upon her door and minutes later, they were in bed making love. John usually stayed until mid morning when he had to rush to open his other business. Around five, he stopped by on his way home.

Her evenings were spent alone at the hotel. On occasion, she'd go up to the rooftop lounge and gaze at the lights of the city. The lounge scene wasn't easy. There were lots of men there, traveling on business and most of them looking for a bed mate for the night. Aries was a target for them but she always said no, explaining that she was taken. But if such was so where was her man? How could tell them her guy was right there in Madison but unavailable nights because he had to go home to his wife?

John never called in the evening. He couldn't. Aries couldn't call him either. They had their signals straight. They tried to be discreet in their relationship because they cared about each other and wanted it to continue. John dared not vary his schedule with her in town or his wife might become suspicious. She expected him to come home by seven, except on Wednesday nights when he worked at the lounge until ten. Aries assured him that she wouldn't rock the boat. She'd see him when she could.

The week was almost over. Aries had shopped all her pocketbook could afford. She'd made love with her lover at least twice a day and she had felt every emotion a woman could feel. She was happy and sad at the same time. Soon her time with John would be coming to an abrupt halt, soon they would be tearfully separated.

Over a cup of coffee in her room on the morning before she left, John told her that his wife was angry with him.

"Why?" asked Aries in surprise.

"She must sense that you're here," he said laughing.

"She couldn't know that."

"Well, maybe she's just upset because I don't make love to her when you're in town."

"You can solve that problem. Make love to her."

"I don't want to make love to her and when I do it's just to shut her up."

"I know, but you do have to keep her happy," prompted Aries.

"I try, but when I make love to her I close my eyes and pretend I'm making love to you, I'm always making love to you."

Taking another sip of coffee John straightened up in his chair.

"Aries, before you go this time, I've been wanting to ask you something," he said nervously. "Would you like to marry me?"

"No, no, I don't want to marry you. I love you and I wouldn't want to ruin a beautiful relationship. I don't want to marry you but I'll be your girlfriend for fifty years."

John seemed relieved at her answer. "That's my girl."

"Just stay home with your wife and raise your children."

"But I don't get along so well with my wife, she's always fussing at the children. She's always fussing, particularly with Jodi, and because of it, we've had some real problems with her."

Looking at John sympathetically, she wanted to put her arms around him and comfort him. Aries asked him to tell her about Jodi. Maybe she could help him.

"Well, my wife puts Jodi down all the time. She makes her so upset and nervous that she eats too much and she's getting too fat."

"What about the other children?"

"Oh, the other two are fine. They're like me and they don't react to her like Jodi does."

"Have you talked to your wife about this?"

"Sure, but she doesn't want to hear it."

"Well, you'll just have to give Jodi more positive attention to make up for the wrong that your wife is doing."

"I try, but I think Ava's jealous of her own daughter. She's a pretty discontented woman."

"Are you happy, John?"

"I'm happy with you but I'm not always happy with my wife."

"Then, why don't you divorce her?"

"I'm Catholic and we don't believe in divorce, I'll never divorce her."

"I really don't want you to divorce her. I'd be very uneasy if you were single. You'd have all of the women running around after you and I couldn't stand it. I don't mind sharing you with your wife but I'm not going to be just another one of your girl friends."

"You're my only girlfriend, honey."

"Well, I hope so. Stay home and raise little Johnny to be a nice person like you were."

"I'm trying, I'm trying."

Finishing his coffee, he said he had to get over to the lounge. "Why don't you come over to my place this afternoon? I'll have a drink with you after workout."

This was the first time he had invited her to his place of business. "Are you sure it's alright? What will your help think?"

"It's okay. I talk to customers all the time. They'll just think that you're some good looking chick who stopped in for a drink. Take a taxi over and I'll give you a ride back to the hotel."

"But what about your wife? What if she comes in when I am there? I would die."

"Don't worry, she's at a meeting twenty miles away and she won't be coming into town, today. I've got to get going now," he said as he donned his brown leather jacket.

"What a gorgeous specimen of man you are," remarked Aries! "I love you in that coat. I love the way you move. I just love you in every way."

"You say the nicest things to me," he said smiling. "See you later, sweetheart."

Aries spent the afternoon napping. She awoke just in time to get dressed and call a cab. Inside the cab, she asked the driver to take her to O'Reilly's Pub at the corner of 5th and Maxwell.

"Yes ma'am, I know where exactly where it is," said the driver.

"Is it far from here?"

"No, it's only about ten blocks away, just on the other side of the river." Aries paid attention to the direction the cab driver took and it was close enough that had she known the way, she could have walked.

Soon, the driver pulled up by the side of the building. "That will be two dollars and fifty cents." Handing him the fare, Aries looked up at the sign on the building. Yes, this was John's place. It was just like he had described it. She guessed everybody in Madison knew this place for the sign was so catching.

Inside, there were football schedules and pictures of famous football players were hanging all over the walls. This was definitely a sports pub. The most interesting thing Aries saw there was John, the star himself, standing behind the counter waiting on customers smiling and making small talk with them in his friendly manner.

She lifted her fanny up onto an empty bar stool. Now this was going to be good. She was supposed to act like a stranger to him. She hoped she could pull it off. She hoped nobody could tell by the look on their faces that they not only knew each other but they were in love. The look of love was hard to conceal and she wondered if John had made the right decision by inviting her to come.

Opening her purse, Aries took her cigarettes out and put them on the counter. John had spied her entering and he came over.

"Hi, can I get you a drink, young lady?"

"Yes, I'll have a vodka and orange juice."

"Oh, you want a screwdriver," he said laughing. "Coming up."

Aries stuck her hand in her purse for the money to pay for the drink. She laid her money on the counter but he handed it back to her.

"This one's on the house."

"Oh, thank you."

They didn't get to talk much after that. The place started filling up with people and John had to help the bartender wait on them. Most of the customers seemed to be locals and most of them called him by name.

The fellow sitting next to her attempted to start up a conversation. "You're not from Wisconsin," he said.

"No, no I'm not but how can you tell?"

He laughed. "Well, I can tell in three ways. One, you look like you have a suntan, two, you have a Southern accent, and three, the girls from Wisconsin aren't as good looking as you are."

What a line that was!

"I don't know about being better looking than the girls in Wisconsin," Aries repeated laughing, "but I do have a tan. I was on vacation in Florida last month."

"Are you from Florida?"

"No, I'm not from Florida. I'm from Tennessee."

"Tennessee, huh? What brings you to Wisconsin?"

"What brings me to Wisconsin is business. I work in temperature control and I'm up here trying to figure out how to warm up

Wisconsin," she replied coyly.

This comment brought a hearty laugh from the guy.

"By the way, you didn't tell me your name. In fact, I didn't tell you mine, either. My name's Donald Hollis and yours?"

"My name is Mary."

"Well, Mary," he said, with a smile on his face. "It's nice to meet you. May I buy you a drink?"

Aries had been nursing her first drink along and she wasn't really interested in his offer but being polite, she thanked him. He raised his hand motioning to John, "One more beer Johnny and one more for the lady." John looked at her puzzled. She answered by shrugging her shoulders knowing he would understand.

Pretty soon, a heavy set fellow came in, all smiles, wearing a leather jacket over a turtle necked sweater. Speaking to the couple seated at the end of the bar, he took off his jacket, hung it on the hook and walked around behind the bar. That must be Charlie, John's manager. John had told her about him. Hopefully, he was there to relieve him so they could get out of there. She liked being near John better when they were tucked away somewhere in private booth having a drink, alone. He was so busy at his place of business that she couldn't even talk to him.

Charlie checked the cash in the register and started waiting on the customers. John headed for the telephone. He was probably calling his wife to ask her if she wanted him to bring anything home.

Off the phone, he slipped on his jacket and taking his time, he stopped by the cash register to talk to Charlie. Aries had gotten the signal that it was time to go so she donned the sweater that she had hung on the back of the bar stool.

"Going somewhere?" Donald Hollis asked.

"Yes, I have to go, now."

"Well, come back tomorrow if you're still in town. I'll be here and I'll save you a seat."

"I'll try but I may be leaving."

"So soon, what a pity! We could use more girls like you around here."

John had made his exit through the side door so Aries went out the other way. He was waiting at the curb with the car motor running. He tooted the horn and reached over to the passenger side to open the door for her.

"Gee whiz," said Aries upon seating herself. "That was a real experience in there. Who was that jerk who tried to flirt with me?"

"The fellow on your left?"

"Yes."

"Oh, that was Donald Hollis, he's a friend of mine. He's perfectly harmless, just friendly."

"Well, I wish he'd been friendly with someone else. He was very nosey and he almost bent my ear off."

Changing the subject, John said he wouldn't have time to stop at the hotel with her that evening. When he had called home, his wife told him that the meeting had broken up early and she had invited friends over for dinner.

"I promise to be there early in the morning so we can spend some time together before your plane leaves. Which flight are you taking?"

"I have reservations on the twelve forty-five flight."

"That will work out, perfectly. I'll be at your hotel at seven. We'll have time to make love one more time without rushing, Then, I'll run to the bank, drop off the money at the lounge and come right back and drive you to the airport. I'll call Charlie as soon as I get home and tell him to come in early tomorrow."

"Are you sure you have time? I don't want to cause any trouble."

"Trouble, it's no trouble. Honey, I'd do anything to get to spend a few more hours with you. You say and do such sweet things to me."

"It's only because I love you."

They made their way through the evening traffic and pulling up at the hotel they were greeted heartily by Riley, who was on duty. After six days, the bellhops were getting used to seeing them coming and going. Aries was sure Riley knew they were having an affair but being a good employee he heard, saw and said nothing.

Back in her room, Aries changed clothes and slipped into one of her flimsy night gowns. She sat down to write a "see you later" letter to John. She would pin on the door with roses attached. In the letter she reiterated how much she loved him and what a loss she'd suffer if they should ever part. She told him that though she must leave him, they wouldn't really be separated, that distance between them would make no matter, she still would feel him there beside her warm and beautiful.

Aries was getting to know him better now. She was beginning to see beyond his exterior and to communicate with his soul. His soul was truly beautiful.

Morning came along with the pain of the reality of having to leave John. Aries was always sad on the day of her departure for she knew that days and weeks would have to pass before she would see him again.

Traveling back and forth to the Madison, Wisconsin from Florida was expensive. Their long distance romance was a financially draining upon both of them. Aries didn't know how much longer she could afford it. It wasn't just the money involved. She lost customers, too, when she was out of town. But facing reality she loved John Roberts so much it didn't matter how much it cost to be with him. She would find a way.

Aries was up at the crack of dawn the next morning preparing for John's arrival. This would be their last morning together for a long time and she didn't want to waste a minute of it. She bathed, slipped on the flimsy gown and climbed back into bed to wait for him.

In bed she dozed, intermittently, between passionate thoughts of her love. Pretending he was in bed making love to her, she could feel his hard cock plunging into her moist hot vagina. Oh, how she loved making love to him. Just thinking about him made her so hot she could have cum without him but she dare not go that far. She would wait. It was hard to hold back an explosion that was ready to burst but she knew that before John finished with her she would be climaxing over and over again during their sweet interlude of togetherness.

She checked the time. John was probably in the elevator on his way up to her room. Touching her pussy, she felt it fiery hot and juicy, just the way he liked it. The tapping on the door came soon. There stood John. He was so gorgeous! Aries greeted him with warm hugs and kisses with an extra kiss for the tip of his nose still red and frost-bitten from the cold outside. Hanging his leather jacket in the closet by the door, John dropped his trousers, his silk bikini underwear and went into the bathroom. Coming out, he headed for the bed bare assed as a jaybird. As he lay down, Aries leaned over him and one by one started unbuttoning his shirt.

"Let's get this shirt off, too, honey," she told him softly. "I want to feel you all over." Removing the shirt, Aries lay down beside him.

"Hurry, let's pull the covers up and let me get you warm," she purred. "You're freezing, darling."

"The weather is really bad out there this morning," he said.

"I know but I've been keeping the bed warm for you."

John wasn't cold for long. Aries had a way of turning him on and making him as hot as a firecracker. Her magic made him moan and groan with delight. He had the same effect on her. There was definite chemistry between them. Their love making was supreme, absolutely undescribably delicious. It was more than just sex. Aries loved every part of him and John acted like the feeling was mutual.

Aries climaxed quickly. She removed his cock from her vagina, began licking his balls and going down on his throbbing erected penis. He loved it and she got a particular joy out of driving him crazy in bed. Ecstatic with pleasure, John was in absolute heaven. She had him by the balls, by the cock and at her mercy leaving him no choice but to erupt like a powerful volcano. His warm cum was shooting profusely into the cavity of her mouth flooding it. She swallowed it to keep from choking.

"Darling, darling, I love your cum. I love your cum in my mouth and in my pussy."

"You're so wonderful," he whispered. "Let me rest a little bit and then, I'm going to make love to you again. I love the way you make love to me."

Soon John was dozing, softly. After awhile he stirred from slumber and began caressing her. His penis was erected once more as hard as before.

"Get on top of me, honey, I want to fuck you for a long time."

Aries could hardly wait to feel his dynamite cock back inside of her vagina. She loved the sparks that flew when they touched flesh to flesh. She adored fucking him in any position. She mounted his frame

212

and started riding his cock. At first, she had pretty good control but soon his cock was controlling her and she was helpless. John Roberts was dissolving her and she was climaxing furiously. He kept fucking her and fucking her.

"Oh, you're killing me," she whined.

"I've just started," he told her smiling. "Turn your ass over, baby, because I'm going to fuck you." Flipping her ass over, he grabbed her buttocks up in his hands and commenced fucking her in rapid motion. Aries grasped his buttocks and raised her buttocks up to meet his hard cock. John stroked her with short brisk strokes until she begged him to slow down.

"Slow down, I can't breathe, slow down while I catch my breath."

"Come on, baby, get your ass up here, come on baby," He was excited. "Get your ass up here, I'm going to make you cum again." John slowed his stroking and he plunged his big cock deep inside of her vagina. She thought it was going all the way up into her stomach. Rubbing her quivering and electrified cunt up against his powerful, penis, it felt so good. Moments later, she wailed, "not again, goodness, I'm coming, again."

"Cum baby, cum baby," he chanted. "Cum baby and I'll cum with you." They were at the point of no return. Aries was exploding in orgasm like a stick of dynamite. John joined her jerking, shaking and shooting cum deep inside her vagina. Together, their climaxes were like a thundering earthquake.

"My goodness, this is better than dying and going to heaven," she exclaimed.

"It's terrific," sighed John as he rolled over taking her with him, his contented cock still inside of her. Glued together, they fell into a contented sweet slumber.

When Aries woke up it was late, too late to catch the twelve forty-five flight. She'd have take a later one. John was still asleep. He wouldn't have time to take her to the airport now because it was lunch hour at his place of business. Waking him up, Aries told him they'd overslept and she would have to catch the next plane.

"Don't worry about it, honey. I know you have to get to work. There's another flight at two and I can take a cab to the airport and catch that one."

"I'm sorry, gosh, I'm really sorry," he said. "I didn't mean to fall asleep but I was so content."

"It's alright darling. You were sleeping so peaceful I hated to wake you up when I did."

Jumping out of bed, John explained that he really had to get going. He hadn't been to the bank yet, and they were going to be in a mess down there without any cash.

"Mind if I take a quick shower?"

"Not at all, go right ahead."

While he was showering, Aries called the airport to make reservations for the two o'clock flight. Then she called the bellboy to come take her bags down to the lobby and to call her a taxi.

All dressed John gave her his usual tender farewell. "Write to me and I'll call you. I'm not so good at writing letters."

"When will I see you, again?"

"I'm not sure, I'll have to look at my calendar and see what my schedules like. Maybe you can come up the next time my wife goes out of town. I get nervous with the two of you in town, together. She's been talking about taking a trip to the islands. I told her I couldn't take off to go so she's thinking about going with a girlfriend. When she makes up her mind, I'll let you know."

"That would be great! Then can we go to dinner or go dancing?"

"We can do both and I can spend the night with you, too. I've got to run now, honey. Be good and I'll talk to you soon."

After John departed, Aries made a last minute check of the room to see if she had forgotten anything. The bellboy was knocking on her door ready to take her bags down to the curb. The cab would be there, shortly.

The trip back home was a sad one. As usual, the misery of missing John was already beginning to set in.

Back in Fort Lauderdale, the weeks passed, slowly. Aries could hardly wait until she could see him. The long distance phone calls between them helped but nothing could take the place of their being together "in the flesh."

John's wife postponed her trip to the islands and she was threatening to cancel out completely. John had tried to convince her to go but he wasn't successful because she didn't want to make the trip without him.

"Don't go with her," pleaded Aries. "I can't stand you taking vacations with your wife."

"I'll try not to go"

"You know, I'm jealous of your wife. I'm jealous of her because she has you all the time and I have only bits and pieces of you. It's bad enough knowing you're with her when you are at home but to take a vacation with her when you have nothing to do but make love, I don't like that idea at all."

"Don't get upset, you know my heart belongs to you. She may be my wife but you're the wife of my heart. I think of you all the time and when I make love to her, I pretend I am making love to you. She really has very little of me."

John's sweet speech had convinced her once more to be patient.

"I'm sorry. I didn't mean to complain but it's so hard for me being so far away from you. I know that though we're apart, we're together in spirit. I found you here yesterday. I was showing some condominiums and as I stood on the sidewalk outside the complex, I could feel your presence in the smooth soft sway of the leaves in the gentle wind. It was a strange but wonderful feeling. You are always with me. Forgive me for complaining. How could I ever doubt your love? Just try to get us together, physically, soon."

"I will. I'll try to get my wife to take a vacation without me and when she does, I'll call you to come up."

A few weeks went by and finally Aries received that long awaited call. Ava was going away on vacation leaving John alone and as free as a bird in Madison. They'd had a great big argument and in her anger she phoned her girlfriend and re-scheduled the trip to the islands.

"She's leaving tomorrow. I'm sorry to give you such short notice but can you fly up tomorrow afternoon?" John said.

"I'll be there with bells on," Aries told him happily. Pick me up at the airport at six. I believe Delta had a flight that can get me there by then. If there's any change I'll call you."

The next night, Aries was back in Madison. John had made dinner reservations for them at an excellent Polynesian restaurant. The meal was good but being in love, Aries had little appetite for anything except for John's loving. After dinner, they had a couple dances before going back to the Seron Hotel. John took her up to the room and went home to check on his children. He'd be back to spend the night when he was sure they all were in bed.

After he left, Aries readied herself for bed and sat down to write him another love letter. He loved her letters. The hour was late and she could feel the weariness creeping up on her. She curled up in bed and was almost asleep when she heard a tapping on the door. It was John all full of apologies for being gone so long. The kids had stayed up longer than usual. With Ava out of town they figured they could get away with burning the midnight oil and he couldn't get away without them suspecting something.

"It doesn't matter, at least, you're here now."

It was wonderful lying beside him that night. There had been few nights that they could sleep in each others arms. Sleeping together made her realize what she was really missing. Deep down inside, she wanted to be his wife. She had lied to him when she said she didn't want to marry him. She wanted to be Mrs. John Roberts, his wife, and to have his babies but she couldn't tell him. She feared that hearing this truth would frighten him away.

Aries wanted him to feel comfortable and secure in loving her. But how long could she keep on telling the man she loved to stay home with his wife and children? How long could she be "just the other woman?" How could she make such an emotional sacrifice without destroying herself? As she lay with him many deep thoughts were rambling through her head.

The next morning, Aries was still thinking about their situation. She was afraid to tell him how she felt for fear of losing him She would wait for him to make a decision. But why should he make any decision when he could have his cake and eat it, too?

Aries knew they were just borrowing time and someday, they would have to pay it back. She was thinking and thinking was danger-ous. It meant that she was contemplating making a move, right or wrong. Something would have to change in their relationship. She wouldn't mention it on this trip, she would consider the matter more before saying anything to him. This was a pleasure trip. Why spoil it? Serious talk could come later.

Aries spent most of her three day visit in Madison flat on her back. Their love making was exciting and tumultuous.

On the way to the airport for the trip home, he invited her to come back to Madison the week before Christmas. "We can celebrate our Christmas early since we won't be able to be together, then," he said.

Aries was thrilled with his invitation. "Wisconsin at Christmas! That will be wonderful. I love the snow. Sure, I'd love to come." Thinking of Christmas, she wished she could be with him on Christmas Eve but she knew this was out of the question. He had a wife and a family. When you're committed to a married man you take what you get and pretend to be happy with what you are getting. Certainly, anytime they had together was better than no time at all.

After returning to Florida, Aries began to make plans for the Christmas holidays. She had met Ellen Mann, an artist, who lived in the suburbs of Madison on one of her trips there. Ellen had invited her to visit her when she came back up. She would call her and see if the invitation was still good. If so she'd stay at the Seron Hotel until John went home after the employee party on Christmas Eve. Then, she'd visit Ellen for a couple of days.

If she went back to Florida she'd be spending the holiday alone. It was Greg's turn to have the children this year. This would be the her first Christmas without them but being divorced, she had to share them with their Father. They deserved to know both of their parents.

Aries told John she'd be there on December 19th. Plans made, she notified her office that she'd be spending Christmas in Wisconsin.

"You two must be getting serious," said Margie. "Why doesn't he divorce his wife and marry you?"

"He can't. They have children and he has an obligation to stay at home and be a father to them. I don't want him divorced. I like it the way it is. There are no strings attached and I can come and go as I please."

"Yeah, I'll bet you do. Marriage would probably ruin your relationship, anyway. That's what it did to mine. I really loved Hal but after we were married he became so insanely jealous of me that he drove me away from him. We had a stormy marriage. I tried to stay with him because we had a couple of kids but, finally, I couldn't take it anymore and I left."

"But what about David? You ask me why John doesn't marry me and I'll ask you the same question. Why doesn't David divorce his wife and marry you? The gals in the office tell me he's married and still living with his wife and that you two have been having an affair for years."

"That's true. I've been going with him eight years in January."

"What's your secret, Margie? How have you two managed this when his wife is right here in the same town?"

"Believe me, it hasn't been easy. He's married but he really has no relationship with his wife. They don't even sleep in the same bed, anymore. They stay together because of the children and as soon as his daughter graduates from high school, he's going to divorce her."

"Don't tell me he doesn't sleep with her. They all say that. Do you actually believe him when he tells you that?"

"Yes, yes, I believe him," said Margie emphatically." He loves me and he loves my body in bed. He knows he couldn't get any better sex than I give him, anywhere."

"Well, John Roberts loves me and he loves my body in bed but I know damned well he's making love to his wife, too. Their marriage wouldn't last if he didn't."

"David told me his wife doesn't like sex." Margie was trying to prove her point.

"That's a bunch of malarkey. All women like sex and any man who thinks they don't is an idiot. Sex is a biological necessity, just like the need for food and water. When you don't sleep at home it's for damned sure that you're sleeping somewhere with somebody. Enough for this conversation. If it makes you feel better just keep on believing him. I've got to get busy. I have lots to do to get ready for my trip."

December 19th arrived. Aries had no problem getting a reservation to Wisconsin, although all the flights were booked solid from

Wisconsin to Florida. Who would want to leave Florida's nice weather and go to Wisconsin in December in the snow? Most folks up there were trying to figure out a way to get out of that mess.

The weather didn't matter. Aries was going to the North Pole but, after all, wasn't that Santa Claus land? She remembered Christmas as a child in the snow in Tennessee. She was told that Santa Claus lived in the North Pole where he and Mrs. Santa spent all year long making toys to bring to the children at Christmas. On Christmas Eve she hung her stocking on the coat hook by the living room door and put milk and cookies out for Santa. If she was good and went to bed early, Santa would come on his sleigh to her house and leaving his reindeer tied up outside, he would climb down the chimney, fill her stocking with goodies and leave her presents..

Seeing snow at Christmas would be a delight. Seeing John Roberts and giving him his present would be a further joy. Aries hoped he would like her gift, a chain with a solid gold piece bearing their astro-logical signs. She had it especially, designed for him with the Lion pressed on top of the Ram The Lion was John, symbolically, and the Ram was Aries. If he wore it he would carry her with him always in the position she loved best, beneath him.

John was at the airport to meet her as planned. On the way to the hotel they chatted, shared thoughts with one another and caught up on the news. They had much loving to catch up on later, too. She was so happy to see him.

John had been terribly busy at work because it was the the holiday season. Everybody partied and celebrated more, then. There was only a week left before Christmas and, still, his Christmas shopping was incomplete. Aries agreed to help him with it. "Just give me a list and I'll do your shopping during the day while you're working."

"Gosh, Aries, I'd really appreciate it."

"Who do you need to buy for?"

"I've done some shopping but I have six presents to buy for the people at work, Charlie, Janie, Eddie, Cindy, Earl and Dawn. I promised Jodi I'd get her new ice skates --- and a camera for Johnny and my wife, I haven't gotten anything for Ava."

"Your wife, repeated Aries. You want me to buy a present for your

219

wife?"

"Would you?" he asked hesitantly. "I hate to ask you to do this but I've got to get her something and I don't know when I'm going to have time to do it."

"What do you want me to get her?"

"Luggage," he answered with a grin on his face. "I thought if I bought her luggage she might take the hint and leave town." Of course, he was joking.

"Well," laughed Aries, "if that's what you want me to get her, I will. I can't think of anything I'd rather she do than get out of town."

"She's really not a bad person, in fact, she's nice," he responded.

"That's wonderful. Maybe, I'll get to meet her, someday."

"I don't think you'd like that. She'd know immediately that there was something between us and she wouldn't treat you kindly. She'd probably scratch your eyes out."

"Well, I certainly don't want to meet her and I will take all precautions to avoid meeting her. I don't want her getting her claws into me. Let's don't talk about her anymore. I'll help you finish your Christmas shopping. I'll start tomorrow."

"That's my girl. You're a life saver."

The week went by quickly. The spirit of Christmas was everywhere. It was a beautiful sight! There were Christmas decorations everywhere and Christmas chimes played carols throughout the city. The strands of Christmas lights outside her hotel cast a pink glow on the glistening snow. People scampered back and forth in preparation. Christmas in the winter wonderland of Wisconsin was enthralling, so different from the tropical Christmas in Florida.

On the afternoon of Christmas Eve, John invited her to come to the employee party at the lounge. The invite was probably to thank her for buying all of their presents. When she arrived there no one seemed surprised at her appearance. The employees were like a family. They all were loyal to John and they all seemed to know that she was his woman.

After overhearing a few comments about Ava, Aries got the impression that they weren't too fond of her. Fortunately, Ava would not be attending the party. She, according to John, had too much to do at home.

Aries was glad to see some of John's world.

Donald Hollis was at the party. She'd met him once before and she had lied to him, telling him her name was Mary and that she was from Tennessee. The last part was true but she didn't live there anymore. John was introducing her to everybody as Aries Winston from Florida. She wondered what Donald Hollis would think.

During the party he came over and sat down beside her.

"Well, Hello Mary. It's nice to see you, again. You tried to fool us didn't you?"

"What do you mean? We folks up here in Wisconsin aren't so dumb. You didn't have to tell us anything. One look at John and one look at you and we all knew that you two had something special going. He's a great guy and we all love him. We wouldn't hurt him for anything. You can trust us. Any friend of John's is a friend of ours, so welcome. I won't ask you this time what brings you to Madison because I know, but I will ask you to go to dinner and to midnight mass with me this evening."

Aries was flabbergasted. Donald Hollis laughed and explained that since John had to be with his wife and family, he had asked him to take care of her.

"Well, it would have been nice of him if he had told me."

"He probably will tell you when he gets a chance. He was talking to me before you came and he told me he didn't want you to be alone."

"I appreciate your invitation but I'm really not going to be alone."

"Oh, stepping out on John," he commented jokingly.

"No, I'm spending the night with Ellen Mann in Woodbury and we're going out to dinner together."

Having no plans for the evening, Donald suggested joining them for dinner. "The three of us could have dinner and afterwards, I'll take you to St. Paul's Cathedral to midnight mass. John will be there with his crew."

This news made the story different. Aries took Donald's telephone number and promised to call him after she talked to Ellen and knew definitely what plans she had made.

As she spoke with him, her eyes followed John in the crowd. She watched him take his jacket off the hook on the side wall and walk toward her. "Young lady, are you about ready to go?"

"Just waiting for you. I'll get my coat on. See you later," she told Donald who had gotten up out of his seat to help her on with the coat. Waving goodbye, they made their exit out the side door.

Fresh snow was falling outside and John had to clean his windshield so he could see how to drive. The cold was so penetrating. Aries was freezing to death. She sat shivering with teeth chattering, waiting for the motor to get warmed up so they could feel some heat in the car.

"This is really like the North Pole. It's beautiful but I don't see how you stand it here."

"It's not so bad. We're used to it. I get tired of these long bitter cold winters though. I'd like to be in the sunshine, getting a tan in Florida where you are. Look at you, it's Christmas and you have a beautiful tan. What do you do stay on the beach all the time?"

"No, as a matter of fact, I hardly ever get to the beach. I get suntanned accidentally when I'm out working, showing property to my customers in the Florida sun. The weather has been nice down there but I stay so busy taking care of winter visitors that all I get to do is look at the ocean as I'm driving by it."

"You shouldn't work so hard, honey."

"That's what I keep telling myself."

Arriving back at the hotel, they went up to her room where they exchanged their Christmas gifts. John loved the his present.

"I shall wear it always," he told her.

"What if your wife sees it?"

"If she sees it I'll tell her that Charlie gave it to me."

"I hope she doesn't look at it too closely," Aries laughed, "because if she does she'll see a Leo on top of an Aries."

"That's just where I want to be," smiled John, "on top of you, darling. Come on, let's make love now. Let's make love and I'll give you your best Christmas present."

How she loved that man! It took no convincing to have herself stripped to the flesh and flat on her back in bed.

"I'm going to miss you this evening, John. I'm going to miss you, tonight and tomorrow, too. Think of me, darling, because I'll be thinking of you. It'll be a blue Christmas without you."

"Cheer up love, it's only for a little while." He tried to comfort her.

"I want you to be home with your children," said Aries. "After all, you're Santa Claus aren't you?"

"Yes, I am and speaking of that I'd better get on the road. I'm sure Ava will need some help tonight."

As he was preparing to leave Aries told him that Donald Hollis had invited her to go to dinner and to midnight mass with him.

"Why don't you go with him? He's a nice guy and he'll take good care of you for me."

"You don't mind?"

"No, I asked Donald to watch over you because I didn't want you to be alone."

"I'm spending the night with Ellen Mann, the artist I told you about. I'll ask her what she has planned. Maybe the three of us will go to dinner."

"If you come to Mass you'll get a chance to see my wife and the kids. We'll probably be sitting about ten rows back on the left side."

"All I need is to see your wife."

"Don't worry about it. If you sees you, she'll think you're Donald Hollis's date."

"I don't know if I'll be there or not. I'm Ellen's houseguest and it depends on what she wants to do."

"I've got to run now, honey. Be a good girl and have a Merry Christmas."

Aries called Ellen after John left to tell her about Donald Hollis's invitation. Ellen had planned dinner at home that night but she told Aries to go ahead out with him.

"No, no," she replied. "He invited us both and I'm not going alone with him. Come on Ellen, go with us. He's just a friend, not a boyfriend."

"Okay, you've twisted my leg, I'll go. Give him my address and tell him to be here at seven o'clock."

"Very well, I'll call him and then, I'll get a cab out to your house."

"You don't need to do that, I can drive into town and get you."

"Don't bother, the weather is too bad. I'd rather take a cab."

"Have it your own way."

Calling Donald, Aries told him that the date for dinner was on. They'd be ready at seven. He seemed pleased that they had decided to join him.

After dinner, Donald drove the girls back to Ellen's house. Ellen served coffee and showed them some of her art work. She wasn't bad as a artist but Aries didn't like her style.

Ellen declined the invitation to go to mass so Aries and Donald would go without her. It was almost time to head for the cathedral.

"Better take off those high heels and put your boots on," Donald cautioned. "It's sloshy and slippery out there." Aries went into the bedroom to change into her boots. After searching, she realized she had left them in her room at the hotel. Woefully, she had no choice but to wear her silver slippers.

The cathedral was beautifully decorated and the ceremony was quite impressive.

Aries was nervous knowing John and his family were there. She was glad they had chosen seats a couple of rows behind them. This way she could see them without them seeing her. Ava had brown hair a little longer than hers and it was darker, too. Aries couldn't get a good look at her face but from the back, she wasn't bad looking. John must have been jittery knowing that both she and Ava were in the same room.

Aries had called the children at Greg's house earlier that evening. She talked to Sara, her youngest. Sara resented her spending Christmas in Wisconsin, although they wouldn't have been together if she had been in Florida. Aries was sure Greg's bitch of a wife had been filling her children's heads with false rumors about her. Once she told Gregory that his Mother was dating a black football player. Aries told him she was incorrect and to prove it she showed him a picture of John.

"Look at him, he is as white as a sheet but don't tell her any better. Just let her keep on making a fool of herself."

Sara was visibly upset over the phone and Aries wasn't sure why.

She imagined that she wasn't too happy being where she was this Christmas.

"I love you, Sara. I love you and I miss you very much."

"You don't love me, Mom. If you loved me I wouldn't be here and you wouldn't be there. If you loved me you would have taken me to Wisconsin with you." "I love you very much but it was Daddy's turn to have you at Christmas. I promise to take you to Wisconsin with me, sometime."

"You never should have gotten divorced from Daddy," screeched Sara, "then we could have had Christmas with both of our parents. I want spend Christmas with both of you."

"Honey, I know you do but Daddy's married to someone else now and Christmas with both of us isn't possible. Have a good time at Daddy's and I'll see you in a few days. Don't cry, Sara. Mommy loves you and your Daddy loves you, too."

Christmas hadn't been the same for Aries and the children since her divorce from Greg. Becoming nostalgic, she remembered the good times at Christmas with Greg and the children. She recalled the bad times, too, like the last year of her their marriage after Greg discovered her affair with Bob Benton. Things weren't the same between them after that. Greg was hitting the bottle hard and he stayed drunk all during the holidays. He refused to get out of bed on Christmas morning to watch the children open their presents. Their last Christmas was a sad one and the horrible memory of it was one that Aries wanted to forget.

Ellen's next door neighbors had invited her for dinner on Christmas Day. When she told them she had a houseguest they insisted that she bring her along. The Huggendorf family welcomed Aries making her feel quite at home. After dinner, she thanked Ellen and the Huggendorfs and went back downtown to the hotel.

Drake Huggendorf, the husband, was really taken with Aries. So much that he called the next day inviting her out to lunch. She politely turned his invitation down flat. A relationship with one married man was enough.

Aries was reunited with John on the day after Christmas. Her time in Madison was running out. Soon, she would have to go back to Fort

Lauderdale and back to work.

A few weeks after her return to Florida, John called to say he was going on a trip to the Canary Islands with Ava.

"Why?" .

"I haven't taken her anywhere in a long time and she's picked out this place for a vacation. I wish she'd go alone but she won't go without me. I've been working hard and I'd like to get out of this cold weather, too. I haven't seen the sun in so long that my face is beginning to look as white as a ghost. I need a vacation badly, myself. I just wanted you to know where I was in case you called."

"Thanks for telling me. Don't worry, go on with her. I'll be there with you in spirit."

Continuing their conversation, Aries asked him where the Canary Islands was?

"It's on the southern tip of Africa."

"Gee, that's a long, long way. I don't like you going so far away from me."

"Don't worry, honey, I'll think of you everyday and I'll be back home before you know it. I'll give you a call when I get home."

While he was in the Canary Islands, Aries thought of him and imagined herself there with him, "out among the rocks," on the beach. She didn't know what the Islands were like but she imagined that there were rocks on the beach. She could actually see herself standing there with John amid huge, high mounds of rocks.

John called when he returned home.

"I'm so glad you're home," Aries told him gleefully. Did you find me there?"

"Yes, I found you."

"Where did you find me?" She hoped John's mind had been attune to hers. Without hesitating he said he had found her there, "out among the rocks." That was exactly where she'd been with him, mentally. Thousands of miles away, he had picked up her mental vibrations. Their thoughts had been on the same wave length. They could be together in the atmosphere without physically moving a muscle. This was a beautiful realization. Their spirits were attuned and they could join at will. She could send him a mental message and he would receive it and respond.

"Your magic travels far," John told her.

A few weeks later he called to say he was coming to Florida. Aries was elated to hear the news until he announced that Ava was coming with him. They were going to the west coast for a week with another couple.

"Since my wife will be with me, I can't get away to see you."

"I'm getting sick of you taking vacations with your wife. First, it was the Canary Islands and you've hardly been home and now, you're taking off with her again."

Aries was irritated.

"I'm sorry. These friends of ours have a place down there and they've invited us to be their guests. Our day will come but right now I have no choice. She's my wife, you know."

"Yes, I, above all people know that she's your wife," stormed Aries. "Please don't rub it in."

"You sound upset, honey."

"Well, I'm not too happy, I haven't seen you in almost three months and you keep running around everywhere with your wife. I love you and I miss you and I'm getting tired of pretending we're together. I want to touch you and be with you."

Trying to pacify her, John said, "Your birthday is coming up in April, isn't it?"

"You remember?"

"Yes, funny face." He laughed. Of course, I remember. Maybe, you can come up to Wisconsin, then."

"Yes, I guess I can come up there and sit in the hotel every night and wait for you to come back the next day," complained Aries, unhappily. "I'm getting tired of playing second fiddle." She didn't know what had gotten into her but she was letting him have it.

"I'll see if I can't get her to take the children and go visit her mother for Easter. Then maybe you and I can slip away somewhere for a couple days. I promise, I'll try. I really am doing the best I can. I have to make certain concessions to my wife if I intend to stay married to her."

After the trip to Florida, John called and invited her to come to

Madison Easter week. "Ava's not going to her Mother's but you can come up, anyway. We'll get to spend time together during the day while you're here."

Aries had been so starved for his loving that even under these terms and conditions she agreed to come. He had a wife and he was keeping her. What right did she have to complain about things he did with her? She had been letting her emotions get the best of her and she was sorry about that.

It was the Saturday before Easter and Aries had made plans to fly to Wisconsin the next day. She'd spent all week, in her free time, planning her wardrobe for the trip. She even got a new hairdo. She wanted to look her best when she saw John.

All day, she had been working on a contract for the sale of an apartment. The deal was almost complete but it had not gotten that way without much painstaking effort on her part. She had been going back and forth between the Seller and Buyer, getting initials on changes, checking inventory of the furnishings, etc. By the time she had the Seller's signature on the dotted line, the Buyer had gone out for the evening. He left a message that she could find him at the the piano bar in a local pub. She was leaving town, tomorrow, so she'd deliver the the contract to him there. She had to get the deal finished.

Aries didn't know when she delivered the contract that she'd meet a man who would become a part of her life in the future.

Arriving at the pub, the party was in full swing in the smoke-filled room. She was tired and just wanted to get her contract finished. Her client saw her as she entered and motioned for her to join him at the piano bar. He had saved her a seat.

A distinguished looking man with salt and pepper gray hair was sitting on his right. The man was accompanied by a heavy set blonde who, at first, Aries didn't recognize but later she remembered just when and where she had met her.

Sitting down , Aries handed the client the contract."I had a hard time getting the Seller to sign this. He feels that he has been reasonable and if the contract is not acceptable with these changes he wants to forget the deal."

"I'll initial it like this," said the Buyer. As he took out his pen to sign, Aries told him they would need witnesses to his signature. Turning to the gray-haired man, she asked if he and his friend would mind being witnesses. Laughing, they obliged. After the contract was signed, Aries placed it neatly in her briefcase and was preparing to leave.

"Don't leave now," said the Buyer. "You've got the contract signed. Relax and have a drink!"

"Don't mind if I do. It's been a very long day. I'll have a scotch and water, please."

Her client got involved in a conversation with the man he was with and the witnesses started talking to Aries. The woman looked familiar. "Don't I know you?" She asked the woman. "Didn't we meet a few weeks ago, one night, when I was working late at my office?"

"Oh, yes. You were at the typewriter typing and you let me read one of your poems."

"You were on the way to Mr. Howe's office. His front door was locked and I let you in through ours. I'm sorry but I don't remember your name."

"It's Carla and this is my friend, Stuart," she said pointing at her distinguished gray-haired companion. "He's a crazy friend and I wish you would take him. "Here take Stuart," she repeated.

This comment seemed strange but Carla was German and maybe, Aries didn't understand what she had meant.

Stuart joined in the conversation and soon, the three were talking like they weren't strangers anymore. Carla was drinking like a fish, getting drunker by the minute. Stuart slid his leg over toward Aries's leg under the piano bar counter. It was obvious that he was trying to get closer to her without Carla noticing him.

They invited her to go down the street to another place where there was music and dancing. Aries tried to politely beg off.

"Really, I'm too tired and I have to catch a plane to Wisconsin tomorrow. I would rather take a rain check."

Carla insisted. Finally, she gave in and agreed to join them. They piled into the little blue Austin Healy that Stuart was driving for the ride down the street to King Neptune. Carla was in the middle as they drove. The establishment was closed when they arrived so they turned around and headed back to the lounge where Aries had left her car.

"Just drop me off at my car," she insisted.

"Are you sure you want to go home?" asked Carla.

"I'm sure."

Carla started touching her and she was becoming very friendly.
Aries was beginning to wonder whether Carla liked Stuart or her.

"Spend the night with us," pleaded Carla. "I want you to stay with
me."

"Oh, no, I couldn't. I must go home now. It is very late and I have
a plane to catch tomorrow. I'm not even packed yet."

"Where did you say you were going?" asked Stuart.

"To Madison, Wisconsin."

"Why on God's earth are you going up there?"

"There's a guy up there that I like. I haven't seen him for awhile
and I'm looking forward to the trip. I really enjoy those Wisconsin
folks."

Carla acted disappointed when she refused to join them at her
apartment. Aries discovered later that Carla went both ways and to
boot, she was one of the town's high classed prostitutes. She was acting in that capacity the night she knocked on the office door. She'd
been called there by, Mr. Howe, the alcoholic building contractor who
shared office space with her broker.

Aries spent her birthday in Wisconsin and, as usual, she was
delighted to see John. Married he was but for five days he belonged to
her as often as possible. He didn't want to create any suspicion at
home but he was still announcing at the radio station so he could leave
home, very early, in the morning. This week, he recorded his shows
instead of being there live. Ava didn't know that he wasn't working.

John was very attracted to Aries. The chemistry between them was
great. It had been that way from the start. Theirs was one of those
once in a lifetime romances and sex between them was special.

It had been over three months since they had been together. Their
long distance love making sessions had been good but this week she'd
be making love to him in person.

John arrived at the hotel and came to her room.

Hi, honey. You are a sight for sore eyes. I want to make love to you," he whispered. "You don't know how often I've dreamed of this moment and here you are." John always knew the right thing thing to say. He was such a swooner.

Aries sat on the bed watching him as he unbuttoned the last button of his shirt. How she loved him! She even loved his clothes, the smell of them, the smell of him.

"Which side of the bed do you want?" she asked.

"It doesn't matter. I just want you, darling. I want to feel your warm, soft body."

In moments, they were blending together, body and soul and for awhile all of the outside world was forgotten. They belonged to each other. What ecstacy, what joy! Nobody could make her feel the way John Roberts did.

After making love Aries laid her head on his stomach and started licking it. Her tongue inched downward until her soft, moist lips were resting upon his hairy warm balls. Licking his asshole briefly, she slowly advanced her tongue to his left ball and began licking it finally, taking it in her mouth. Working her mouth up and down on the ball, she held his cock firmly in her hand. Then, she went down on his throbbing, pulsating cock still oozing with cum. She licked his cum with her tongue and swallowed it.

"I love your cum. I want to eat your cum. I'm in love with you, John."

After the tantalizing, he rolled her ass over and started fucking her again.

"I'm going to put my big hard cock inside of you, baby, and I'm going to fuck you and shoot hot cum inside of your pussy. I love to make love to you."

"Please, please fuck me, fuck me deep, she pleaded."

Obliging her, he thrust his hard cock into her begging pussy. She could feel the heat exuding from their bodies as he buried his penis deeper and deeper inside of her hungry vagina. Aries wailed, "I love you so much. This is so wonderful."

"Can you feel me baby? Can you feel my big cock?"

"Oh, yes, I love your sweet cock. Please fuck me deep. I want you deep inside of me. Oh, oh, I'm going to cum now," she cried.

"That's beautiful. I love it when you cum. Sweetheart, suck my balls some more. I know you love to suck my balls."

"Oh, yes, I love to suck your sweet balls. I love everything about you."

Flipping over, Aries began sucking and licking his organ. John was as hot as a firecracker. Suddenly, his body began to tremble and jerk and he was shooting fiery hot cum into her mouth. She drank his cum and kissed his lips. Contented and satisfied, John lay back on the pillow with eyes closed.

"I want to make mad love to you, again," he whispered.

They rested for awhile and later when the urge hit them, they began fucking passionately all over again.

"I'll never get enough of you. I want you, again," Aries confided.

"Take me, baby, take me, baby. I love making love to your sweet pussy."

"I love your cock in my pussy."

Fucking themselves into oblivion, Aries began to orgasm and John joined her with tumultuous jerking as he poured his hot cum into her appreciative vagina reducing her to nothing.

Moments later, he was out of bed telling her that he had to run. He had to be at the lounge before lunch hour started.

"Be a good girl today," he said smiling. "I'll stop over at five-thirty on my way home. I won't be able to stay long. though,because my wife has made plans for us to go to dinner tonight."

A look of disappointment appeared on Aries face. John picked it up, instantly. "Maybe I can arrange to stay in town late on Wednesday. You'll be here until Friday, won't you?"

"I guess so. I thought I'd get some rest, do a little shopping and play some tennis while I am here. I hate it that you always have to go home to your wife but at least I know where you are when you're with her. I don't mind you having a wife but please don't fall in love with anyone else. I love you, John."

"I love you, too. Now, have a good day and I'll see you this afternoon."

After he left Aries spent a few minutes trying to regain control of her sensibilities. How she loved him! He made absolute putty of her in bed. With all that fucking she was as limp as a dish rag.

She decided to go back to bed and take a nap. Shopping could wait until after lunch. Those hours in Wisconsin waiting for John were long ones and there was no point in rushing. Why had she had fallen in love with a man who lived so far away and why she had picked a married one?

Around five-thirty John called and asked her to meet him in the downstairs lobby. He was running late and would have time for only one drink.

"Okay, I'll be in the lobby waiting for you." She wouldn't tell him how she hated it when he was in such a damned hurry.

Over the drink, John asked what she would be doing that evening?

"Nothing, I'll just stay here, eat dinner in the dining room, watch television for awhile and go to bed early."

"I'm sorry I have to leave you, honey, but I'll be here early in the morning. Keep the bed warm for me. He was grinning. I've really got to go now," he said as he downed his gin and tonic.

"Do you mind if I stay here and finish my drink?"

"I'm sorry, I thought you were finished or I wouldn't have gotten up. I just get nervous when Ava has obligated me to go somewhere I didn't want to go in the first place."

"That's okay. Go on home. Your wife is waiting. I'll just sit here and watch the people for a few minutes."

John was gone, again, leaving Aries to her lonesome. She finished her drink went back to her room.

She poured a glass of wine and sat down at the desk to write down the thoughts of her heart. "Dear John, Don't ever leave me. As beautiful as this world is, I would not want to live in it if you were not within the atmosphere. If ever I become irritated or disagree with your decisions it is for my own selfish reasons. Being totally in love with you, I am inclined to be unhappy and bewildered when we are apart. Those times when we are able to meet for a few brief hours, I am filled with joy and sadness, simultaneously. I experience joy with the physical joining of our souls and sadness at knowing that all too soon, I must walk this world leaving you, losing you physically, again. Our spiritual togetherness is complete when body and soul we are joined as one. We are bound together in a sad but beautiful way that shall remain throughout life to into eternity, my love." Sealing the letter in an envelope, she laid it on the desk. Perhaps, she would give it to him tomorrow unless she changed her mind.

The night crept on and bedtime came early.

The next morning John arrived at his usual time and the love making was even better than it was the day before. Afterwards, they ordered coffee from room service and sat by the window sipping it.

During their conversation John mentioned that he didn't know what to do about his wife.

"What's the problem?" Aries asked.

"My wife gets mad at me every time you're in town."

"Why should she get mad at you when I'm here? She doesn't even know me."

"She says I don't make love to her enough."

"Why not?"

"I can't. Aside from the fact that I don't want to, I'm not able. After I make love to you I have nothing left."

Aries looked at him.

"What's wrong? Is she giving you a hard time?"

"Yes, she was a regular grouch last night when I got home. She ruined the dinner party by fussing at me all evening.

"I'm sorry but I don't like you making love to her, anyway. You really should make love to her sometimes. though, or else she'll think you're doing it somewhere else."

"I try but my wife and I can't communicate like you and I do."

"You poor thing. I'm sorry for you and I'm sorry for your children. I love you and I love them because they're a part of you. I wish I could have your baby," she blurted out. "I love you very much."

"Don't talk nonsense, Aries. A baby is all we need. Let's just keep it the way it is, uncomplicated. That way we can have each other for a long time."

"A long time, I want to love you forever and ever."

"You're just too much. You love me too much. I've never had anybody love me the way you do." He was smiling.

After the coffee, John left for the bank and Aries took pencil and pad out to write down her feelings for him. "Another day in Madison with you penetrating my body and soul. If only you knew the beauty that lies within our grasp. I couldn't find the depth in your eyes today but I caught the expression on your face. dear John, I love you."

The week went by and the day before her departure, she scribbled another note to her love. "I awoke early this morning in my usual state of mind, still loving you. Time flicks swiftly on and our moments remaining for this brief encounter are lessening. Today may be just another day for some but for me it's important. Tomorrow, I must leave you for an undetermined time. I cannot face this separation in a casual way, although we have parted in the same manner, many times, before. So much of me will remain with you and so much of you will depart with me. I love you. Neither time nor distance will change it. God bless you and keep you safe until we meet again."

The day of Aries's departure arrived. John put his sports show on tape that day so they would have a longer time, together.

"Don't cry, baby," he consoled her. "We'll be seeing each other very soon. I promise."

"I can't keep flying up here so much," she complained. Do you know that it costs us six hundred a month, without eating?"

"It's probably a luxury that neither of us can afford. I'll help you as much as I can," he offered.

"I know you will but it costs a lot for us to get to see each other for such a short period of time."

"Had you rather not come?"

"Oh, no, I want to come. I want to be with you. One hour with you is worth every penny it costs. I'm just worried because I don't know how long we can keep this up." Aries was crying.

"Dry your eyes, baby, and make love to me one more time." John tried to comfort her. Charlie's opening up for me this morning and after the loving, I'll drive you to the airport. Lie down, darling, I want to love you. I love that sweet body of yours. You make love to me beautiful. Even over the telephone, you make love to me beautiful. Your magic travels far. Lie down, darling, let me hold you in my arms."

As Aries undressed John marveled over her body. "Nobody would ever believe that you've had five children," he commented.

"The doctor who delivered them doesn't believe it, either. He said that I still seem like a virgin."

"You have such a tight sweet pussy. I love your tight pussy."

Removing his bikini undershorts, he was naked and gorgeous with everything in the right place, including his seven inch penis which was now pointing horizontally. What an absolute perfection of man, almost like Adam!

In bed he whispered sweet nothings in Aries ears. He was such a romanticist. "I want to fuck you, baby. I want to fuck you and lick your sweet pussy."

"I want to fuck you and suck your balls and kiss you all over," she responded gently.

Gazing at his stately frame sprawled on the bed, she could feel her pussy getting moister and moister. Her love juices were flowing. She could almost have an orgasm just looking at him.

After kissing and fondling, John offered her, her favorite, "his balls." "You want my balls, don't you? He asked ready to submit..

"Yes, yes, darling, I want your balls. I love you so much."

"You love me too much. Love me but don't love me too much. I don't want you to be hurt. I have very deep feelings for you, Aries, and I don't ever want you to be hurt. Put your mouth on my cock, and kiss it a little bit. I love to feel your sweet lips on my cock. Oh, oh, you're driving me crazy. What am I going to do with you?"

"Just love me, darling, just love me and enjoy it. Remember me and how this feels when I am gone."

"You love me so nice."

"I love you nice because you are nice," she sighed.

Soon the words between them were replaced by moans of ecstacy. They were consumed with passion and a burning desire to become one as they experienced one orgasm after the other.

After the loving, they were content and happy. Saturated with love, they fell into peaceful sleep in each others arms.

Awakening to the sound of the maid's knocking on the door, they realized they were going to have to rush like hell to catch the twelve-thirty flight. John agreed to take her luggage to the car while she checked out of the hotel. Dressing hurriedly, Aries took a last minute check for forgotten items and then, she headed for the elevator.

On the way to the airport they chatted.

"Sure hate to see you go."

I'll write to you, John, but I need to get back home to my job. Several of my clients called while I was here and one of them bought a house from somebody else because he thought I had moved. That cost me fifteen thousand dollars in commission. I'm not complaining though. A week with you was worth it."

The remainder of the ride was fairly quiet. They just held hands and watched the scenery. What more did they really have to say? It had all been said and done and now they were suffering from the pain of parting. Aries hated that ride to the airport. She hated leaving John Roberts so far away.

Arriving at the terminal, John gave her bags to the caddy at Northwest for checking. "I'll drop you here, honey. Your plane will probably be leaving before I have time to park. See you later."

Aries gave him a last embrace and four hurried kisses, one on each cheek, one on the forehead and one on the mouth. "Until the next time. Be good and promise you won't fall in love with anyone else."

"I promise."

As John waved and drove away Aries could hardly hold back the tears. Goodbye my love, she told him silently, "You are the Summer, Fall, Winter and Spring of all my eternity."

"Better hurry, ma'am," said the ticket agent. "You're just going to make it. You don't have time to select a seat. Hurry right on to boarding gate. They're boarding at Gate 60."

"Where's that?"

"Down the terminal and to the right," he pointed.

"Thanks," yelled Aries as she ran in the direction of the gate.

They were preparing to close the plane door when she arrived.

"Hey, wait for me," she shouted. The steward held the door and Aries ran in.

"That's calling it close," said the steward. "You almost got left behind."

"Well, I wouldn't have minded," she told him smiling.

237

"Just take any seat. You can get a seat assignment when we get to Cincinnati."

Plopping down in the first seat she saw available, Aries fastened her seat belt and sat back to catch her breath and relax. Damned that was quite a run! Closing her eyes, she rested for a few minutes in an attempt to regain her composure.

When her eyes opened, the plane was landing in Chicago. Stay on board, the voice on the loudspeaker told the passengers. No problem she thought as she closed her eyes again. The next stop would be Cincinnati and they'd have a thirty minute layover. That would give her time to go to the bathroom and get a seat.

As she disembarked from the plane in Cincinnati, she felt the gloom and the dreariness of the area. Aries had stopped there before, many times and still she wasn't fond of that red dirt place. She was glad she didn't have to spend any time there. She recognized the ticket agent at the arrival gate. He was the same agent who was there the last time she passed through.

"Hello," he said. "Passing through again or are you going to stay awhile with us this time?"

"No, just passing through. I hate this place. I wouldn't want to stay here. It's raining and muddy every time I come here."

"We have better weather most days. You folks must have brought the bad weather with you from Chicago."

Aries rushed to the bathroom, got her seat assignment and waited to reboard the plane.

Four hours later, she arrived in Fort Lauderdale tired and weary from the trip. The ride home had been a long one and already she was missing John terribly. It was that way every time she had to leave him. Why did she persist in torturing herself by loving a married man? Now, she was returning from her sojourn in paradise with nothing but fond bitter sweet memories.

The next evening after a hectic first day back at the office, Aries wrote in her diary: "A day without John. Feelings of numbness and restlessness penetrate my body. It is as if my total being is dangling in some sort of suspended state or separation, that I am helpless in my efforts to reunite myself. Flash backs of quiet moments when we were together at rest, the aftermath of a powerful climax in your arms, holding you tightly, hoping that moment would never end. Knowing that time would have to pass apart but ever steadfast in knowing that our love had deepened in its passing."

Aries was head over heels in love and as she wrote those words fate was about to wield her a fatal blow. After her April visit to Wisconsin, months went by with no word from John Roberts other than an occasional phone call to see how she was getting along. He continually postponed any plans she might have for visiting him in Madison. Aries couldn't understand what was wrong. Over and over she asked him, "What's the matter, John? Don't you love me anymore?"

"Yes, yes, I love you but I am trying to work things out with my wife. We haven't been getting along so well and your coming up here would only complicate things. We'll get together, Aries, but you've got to be patient while I work things out at home."

Maybe, he was serious but all of his reasons seemed like just excuses. John had to make a decision. He couldn't keep her dangling on a string like a puppet, forever.

A few weeks after their conversation Aries flew to Philadelphia where her son, Mark, was attending school. She had been called for a parent-teacher conference concerning his behavior. She had rather have been going on another matter but when you have five children, things happen.

On the plane she wrote, "dear, John, today I am flying to Philadelphia on business. It dissatisfies me to be headed in your direction without being able to continue on to Wisconsin but this is life. Days are passing and I feel that our time for being together is coming closer. Daily, you are in my thoughts. It is as though I were being punished in this life, having tasted a fruit oh so sweet that for the most part I must avoid. What a pity for I love you so!

June came and still there was no word from John. Finally, she received a call from him one afternoon at work. "Things are really bad here between my wife and I. She's talking about getting a divorce." He seemed to be pretty upset but promised to keep her posted. The news was surprising.

A few evenings later, Aries went back to the office after dinner to do some work. While there she wrote him a letter. " Dear John, You have been on my mind, constantly. You have monopolized my total being since the day we met and now, you tell me to stay here and do what I have to do. This is so funny I could cry. I cannot help your circumstance with your wife. God's plans are not always as we would like them to be but they usually turn out best for us. I will pray for you."

Apparently, her prayers helped because it wasn't long until John called. He and his wife had been to the priest and a marriage counselor and they had decided to give their marriage another try."

"I'm glad," said Aries upon hearing the news. "It's better to stay married when you have children. Children need to be with both of their parents, if possible."

The next week she called him at the lounge and Charlie informed her that he was out of town, in San Diego playing in a racquetball tournament.

"Well, tell him that I called, Charlie."

"I sure will. Say, when are you coming back up here to see us?"

"I don't know. I guess that will depend upon John."

Charlie laughed. "You know that guy's goofy over you, Aries, but he's got a problem, he's got a wife."

"How well do I know!"

Charlie said John would be in San Diego for a week. She didn't know where he was so she wrote him a letter. "Sweet John, Though distance separates us, I am powerless to erase your image from my mind. Your total being continues to penetrate my atmosphere. I called you this week only to find that you were away. I miss you terribly. Somebody somewhere loves you."

On Sunday, Aries took the day off from real estate. Most of day her thoughts were of John. She wrote these words, "I need you to see you soon, if only for an hour. If you care for me you will respond in some form or fashion. I stretch myself in all directions to be near you and to let you know that I love you. Even a warm, beautiful thought will suffice."

June in Fort Lauderdale was a boring month. The winter visitors had gone home leaving the city quiet and peaceful. Real estate was slow. It was always that way in that time of year. Business didn't pick up much until the week of the Fourth of July, when families with children came to make Fort Lauderdale their permanent home. They would buy in July or August so they could get settled before school started.

Aries sold real estate for one reason only, to make a living. She hated what being in the business had done to her. No longer could she appreciate a property for its beauty alone. Now, she had to view it for its highest and best use. She enjoyed the winter tourist season because she got acquainted with new people and she formed new friends. It was really dull in town after they went home. She usually used May and June to work on improving her own home as she had little time for this during the winter months. In June, she could spend some time at home and on weekends and take in some sun bathing on the beach.

Aries spent most of her free time with her children or her best friend, Margie. There wasn't a guy in Fort Lauderdale that either of them would give two cents for. Most of the locals were bums looking for rich women to support them. The permanent male residents of marrying age were rejects and divorcees from other states who had fled to Florida to keep from paying child support.

Aries was making plans to fly to New York the latter part of July. She had been working on a manuscript which was almost finished, and several New York publishers had agreed to take a look at it. Mia was accompanying her and she was excited because she'd never been to New York before. Aries needed a change so the trip was timely.

In the midst of making preparations for the journey, Aries, impulsively, called John to tell him she'd be in New York. She hoped he would invite her to fly on to Wisconsin. He was sorry but he wouldn't be in there. He was leaving for Canada to play in another tournament. He had some good news for her though. He would be flying to Fort Lauderdale to see her the next weekend.

Aries couldn't believe it. John was coming to see her!

"I'll call you when I get back from Canada and we'll make our plans," he said.

"Great!" She was excited and just the thought of being with him again started her juices flowing.

They left on a Saturday for New York. Mia was like a little girl at Christmas. She loved to travel and she loved taking vacations with her Mom.

"You'll buy me some shoes there, won't you, Mom?"

"Of course I will."

Mia really had a thing about shoes. No matter how many pairs she owned, according to her, she never had any. Aries didn't mind buying her shoes. She had such beautiful feet. In fact, inside and out, Mia was beautiful. She was kind, gentle, stately, feminine, uniquely attractive and intelligent. To Aries, Mia was like a beautiful, elegant Egyptian Princess.

On the way to New York, while Mia was dozing, Aries scrawled a letter to John that read, "I am in the clouds on my way to New York on a journey, hopefully, to get my works for the first time in print. I am a little nervous as this is a new experience for me. On the other hand I will be glad to turn this material over to a publisher as I have gone as far as I can on it without someone else's help.

Mia is accompanying me. She is excited about the trip and eager to see New York. I am eager, too, but mainly to get this task over and to return home and wait for your arrival next weekend.

I hope you did well in Canada. I would love to watch you play. That's one thing I have missed in our relationship, not getting to watch you win. I am proud of you but as you have said, 'there will be time for us.' I hope so. See you next weekend. I can hardly wait to be in your arms. I love you."

The trip to New York was a real experience. Aries and Mia spent their days walking from 3rd to 5th Avenue visiting the publishers. Aries only scored with one of the publishers but one was all it took. She signed a contract with them for the publication of her book.

Mia felt so proud of herself taking care of her Mom in New York. Later, she swore that Aries would have never made it out of the city alive if it hadn't been for her. Aries wore her diamonds and her mink stole, one evening, when they went to Chinatown for dinner. On the way back to the subway, two hoodlums were walking very close on their heels with sticks in their hands.

"Run Mom," warned Mia. "They're coming after us. Run as fast as you can." They started running. The guys were running after them. Finally, a man and a woman came out of a building onto the sidewalk ahead of them. They ran up to the couple and grabbed ahold of them. They were scared shitless. Apparently, the hoodlums were scared away when they realized they were going to have to tangle with four instead of two. The girls apologized to the couple and headed to the subway.

Mia blamed Aries for the incident.

"If you had dressed like a pauper, Mom, they wouldn't have been after us."

She was probably right. After that night they spent the rest of their evenings in the lounge of the Americana Hotel. It was a nice place and there was no point of being out on the streets of New York asking for trouble.

Aries bought Mia five pairs of shoes. Each time she bought a pair, Mia complained, later, that they hurt her feet so Aries would buy her another pair. She suspected that Mia's feet were hurting from just plain old walking between the publishing houses but if she wanted shoes, Aries wanted her to have them.

One evening while there, they met Jerry Weinstein, a former client and friend, at a restaurant for dinner. Jerry always was a barrel of fun and it was nice to see him in his own element.

After three days their business was finalized and they were ready to return home. Aries would await John's visit and Mia had to pack up and drive back to Oklahoma where she was enrolled in college.

On their last day in New York, Aries received a phone call from John. He had called Florida and the secretary at the office told him where she was staying. His wife's father was ill and she had to go to Nebraska to see him. John would have to cancel his Florida trip and stay in Wisconsin to mind the house and the children. "Since you're in New York, already, why don't you just fly up here for the weekend before going back?"

Aries certainly hadn't planned on this one but she agreed to go. "I'll change my reservations from Florida to Wisconsin and I'll call you when I arrive."

Breaking the news to Mia, Mia got a good laugh out of that one.

"Mom, I never know where you are going from one day to the next. I'll go home and hold the fort until you get there."

"Thanks honey. I really want to see him. I haven't seen him for a long time."

"Go ahead, Mom, just get home in time to give me some money before I leave for Oklahoma."

The weekend in Madison was short and sweet. John reiterated the problems that he'd been having with his wife and he said, "Things were better between them now."

While she was there she saw John's friend, Donald, one evening at O' Reilly's and they had a long conversation. Sympathetically, he confided, "We have no doubts that John's in love with you, Aries, but there is no way he can ever divorce his wife. There's too much money involved and he couldn't afford to divorce her."

"I don't want him to get divorced, I want him to stay with her and raise his children." Aries lied.

That weekend, John made beautiful love to her. He treated her like a queen but the one thing she wanted, he couldn't give her. He was committed to another woman. He would let this relationship go on forever but it would have to be under his terms, not hers. Sometimes, Aries thought she should give it up but she knew she never would unless something drastic happened between them.

The morning she left, she gave him a letter as she was leaving. It read, "Dear John, I am so very much in love with you that I can hardly stand myself for allowing this to happen. Although I appear confident and strong, I have placed myself in such an insecure position, which consequently is leading me to much suffering and pain. Away from you I hurt and close to you I hurt.

Feelings, involvement, that's the last thing I wanted. When I have learned the secret of not falling in love, I will have achieved a great feat. Loving you appears to be becoming an ill in my life. I would like to reject you but it is impossible for me to do so. I love every part of you. Being unable to blot you out of my physical and mental existence, totally aware that our spirits are entwined, I cannot abandon my love for you. Nothing beautiful ever comes to one without great sacrifice. I love you."

Aries returned to Fort Lauderdale, back to real estate and back to mooning over John Roberts. She couldn't concentrate on her work. Something was bothering her.

Finally, she decided that no matter what happened in John's marriage, she wasn't going to stay so far away from him. She didn't believe that absence made the heart grow fonder.

Real estate was at an all time low. She'd written more than three hundred thousand dollars worth of deals that month and all of them for one reason or the other had fallen through. She decided if she couldn't make some money she might as well just spend some. Disgusted with business, Aries was thinking about making a change. But what would she do and where would she go? Longing to see John again and feeling a strong need for physical intimacy with him, she decided to pay surprise visit to Madison. Where else?

Telling her boss she was taking a vacation, she packed her bags, put her car in the shop for a check-up and made final preparations for the trip. She had never driven farther than Tennessee before but being in no hurry, she could take her time and enjoy the sights on her way to the Mid-west.

John was really going to be surprised to see her. This would be the first time she'd been to Madison without an invitation. If she waited for him to call it might be another three months and in her present state of mind, she knew she'd go bananas.

She would use business as an excuse for appearing there. The real estate business takes you everywhere at one time or another. If he was busy when she arrived she had other friends there she could visit. At least, she'd be in the same town with him and that might help her, emotionally.

The trip to Wisconsin was a long, hard one. She had a close call when a transfer truck ran her off the road as she was driving through Chicago but finally she arrived in Madison. Pulling her car up to the Seron Hotel, she was greeted by Riley and the other bellboy.

"Welcome back, Miss Winston," they said. "We knew you'd be back to see us, again and Mr. John, we knows you'll be seeing him."

Aries smiled but made no comment.

"Go right on in. I'll park that nice Mercedes in the garage and bring you the ticket." Riley flashed his pearly white teeth and smiled.

At the desk, Aries asked the clerk if her same room was available.

"No, Miss Winston, it's taken now but we can give you a similar room on the fifth floor."

"That will be fine."

She could hardly wait to get to the room, shower and get some rest. She wouldn't call John until tomorrow. Worn ragged from driving, she needed time to rest up before surprising him.

The next morning she dialed his work number. John answered the phone.

"Hi, guess where I am?"

"You're in Fort Lauderdale."

"No, guess again."

"If you're not in Fort Lauderdale I don't know where you are. Where are you?"

"I'm here, I'm here. I'm here in Madison at the Seron."

"You're here," he repeated in surprise.

"Yes, I had to come up here on business. I have a customer who lives in the outskirts of Madison and he wants to trade his house for a house in Fort Lauderdale. He offered me five hundred dollars to come up here and appraise it so I couldn't turn that offer down."

"That's great but I wish I had known you were coming. I won't be able to see you much. I'm busy all day, today. In fact, I'm getting ready to leave now."

"Where are you going?"

"I have to go to Duncan, a little town about one hundred miles away and I won't be back until this evening. Then day after tomorrow, I'm taking off for San Diego for another racquetball tournament."

John's voice sounded irritated.

"What's wrong? Don't you want to see me?"

"Yes, I want to see you but you should have let me know you were coming. I can't change my plans now."

"I don't want you to change them. I just want to see you for a little while, that's all."

"Well, I'll come over to see you Wednesday morning. What's your room number?"

Looking at the number on the phone, she told him it was room 519.

"By the way, when you call the lounge don't ask to speak to me," he warned. "Ask for Charlie and let him give me the message. My wife drops in here, sometimes, and she answers the telephone."

"What's wrong, John? You sound upset."

"Nothing is wrong," he answered sharply. "I just don't like it when you come up here without asking me."

"I'm sorry. I wanted to see you so much that when I got this opportunity, I jumped at it. I didn't think you'd mind."

"I've got to go now. I'll call you before I come over Wednesday morning. Bye."

Hanging up the phone, Aries mentally retraced their conversation. She was hurt. By his tone of his voice, he was obviously irritated at her being there but she didn't know why. He couldn't see her today and the day after tomorrow he would be leaving for San Diego. If he loved her why couldn't he have invited her to go with him? She would ask him about that when she saw him.

By evening Aries was getting claustrophobia sitting in her hotel room. Since she had the car she decided to drive out to Tracy's, one of the "good places" in town. A client had highly recommended it. She hoped none of John's friends would see her there but if they did, so what? She was single. John Roberts had no strings on her. Before leaving the hotel, she called Tracy's to ask for directions. She had never driven in Madison before and she didn't know how to get around.

Tracy's had a nice atmosphere, the music was good and there were quite a few people there, especially lots of men, all dressed up in suits, white shirts and neckties.

Aries sat down at a small table in the center of the room. Her Scotch-Irish mother had taught her to always be a lady and to always act like a lady. She didn't think that sitting on a barstool unaccompanied by a gentleman would be ladylike. Many times, men told Aries she was a lady. She considered that to be a fine compliment and always replied, " My mother would appreciate that." Mama was dead and in heaven now but Aries knew she was still watching over her. In fact, she had a better view. Now, she could see everything and Aries didn't want to disappoint her.

Tonight, she was alone but she intended to make the best of it. She really needed some adult companionship after that long drive by her lonesome in the car. She'd had about all the solitude she could handle.

It was disheartening to arrive in Madison only to hear that John was too busy to see her. It was her own fault though. She should have given him some warning. What did she expect him to do, drop everything because she had unexpectedly arrived in town? Why not? That's exactly what she would have done for him.

When the barmaid came over Aries ordered a scotch and water with a twist of lemon. Tracy's was a nice place and strangely enough, she had learned about it in Fort Lauderdale. A client from Madison told her told her about it. "That's one of the best places in town. It's my regular hangout after work," he said. If this was true and if he was back in Madison, maybe she would run into him there.

During the evening, she met a man named Eric Hammer who asked if he could join her at her table. Having no one else to talk to, she agreed.

Aries told him she was in Madison on a business trip. John Roberts, she mentioned, was a casual acquaintance of hers. Eric said he knew John and upon hearing his name, he began to spiel out a wealth of information about him. Apparently, he disliked him. Aries had met some of John's friends but this was the first time she had run into one of his enemies. As she listened, she was convinced that Eric was talking about none other than "her John."

This guy told her things about John, his wife and his brother. Some of it she wished she hadn't heard. Hammer was a local resident. He had lived in Madison for years. Apparently, he had no business nor social connections with John but he knew a lot about his activities. That's what happens comes when you're a celebrity. Everybody knows your business. Who this fellow was wasn't important but the things that he was saying were real eye openers. He claimed John considered himself "God's gift to women." Aries agreed with him on that. He said John had friends but he also had some enemies.

"That guy has a blown up feeling of superiority and self-importance.

He's an ex-football star who can't face the fact that he's a has been. Folks around here like his brother but they're not too fond of him. He's too damned cocky."

Then, he started talking about John's personal life. "He's got a wife and a couple of kids but he thinks he's a casanova."

"Casanova," repeated Aries.

"Yeah, he's got a string of girl friends all over the country. He's got a wife in Madison and a girlfriend in Duncan."

"Duncan. Where's Duncan?" Aries was curious.

"Oh, Duncan's a fishing town about a hundred miles north of Madison. Silently, Aries recalled that Duncan was where he was going that day. Her ears perked up because it looked like this man was giving her some answers about what was really wrong with John. No wonder he had become upset when she inconveniently arrived in town. He had a rendezvous with another girlfriend that day.

"He sounds like a real "ladies man," replied Aries forcing a smile.

"Yeah, he thinks he's a ladies man alright. His wife is no prize but she sticks by him and takes care of his children while he's off with some woman or on jaunts to a racquetball tournaments."

"Well, with all the women he has which one is he in love with?"

"None of them, he just uses them to boast his ego. Roberts doesn't love anybody, except himself. The woman over in Duncan was his girlfriend in high school. She's married now to a school teacher but somehow she manages to make the trip to Madison every Tuesday. Supposedly, she comes over here to shop. They don't have many good stores in Duncan. She may take something back with her but while she's here, she's meeting him. Every Tuesday they're shacked up in some hotel downtown near his place of business. I hear he's got a girl-friend somewhere in Florida, too, who comes up here, sometimes. That guy really stays busy!"

Aries was thinking while Eric was talking. Today was Tuesday and John probably didn't even go to Duncan, he just wanted to clear away the day. He was probably with that woman in her same hotel in Madison.

Aries was destroyed.

"How do you know all these things?"

"I know the woman. I met her at a bar one Tuesday during the cocktail hour after Roberts had fucked her and left her to go home to his wife. She got drunk after he left and she spilled the beans. She told me all about her affair with him and their secret meetings on Tuesdays. She used to be in love with him way back when they were younger."

"What about now? Is she in love with him? Is he in love with her?"

"Who knows? Who knows who is in love with who? Who knows what love is anyway? Roberts goes around the country wooing women, fucking them, messing up their marriages and breaking their hearts but, in my opinion, that guy doesn't know how to love anybody. He's too hung up on loving himself."

That was enough. Aries couldn't take anymore. "I have to go home now," she said getting up from the table."

"Home? Why don't you come to my place, instead? A nice girl like you shouldn't be alone. I've got a great big bed big enough for both of us and I'd like for you to keep me company tonight."

"No thanks. I have to leave now." Aries looked at that overweight pig and wondered why he, without even knowing, had sat there and destroyed her faith in John Roberts.

On the way back to the hotel she kept chastising herself. How could she have been so gullible? How could she have believed she was the only one besides his wife? She might have known if he would play around on Ava with her, he would play around on her with someone else. Perhaps, this was her destiny, finding out.

 Pre-occupied with the gossip she had heard, Aries had driven her yellow mercedes back to the hotel without paying attention to the road signs. Parking in her space, she went up the parking garage elevator to the fifth floor.

It was a quirk of fate that had taken her to Tracy's. If she hadn't gone she wouldn't have met that man and she would have gone on in her dream world believing that aside from Ava, there was no one else in John's life but her. That's what he wanted her to believe.

She started putting two and two together. Today, she was sure he had been with the girl from Duncan. That's why his voice sounded different when she called and that's why he chastised her for coming up uninvited. She had, unfortunately, arrived in town on the wrong day. Tuesdays' apparently belonged to the other woman.

Aries wondered how long this affair had been going on between them. She tried to think back to the other visits she had made to Madison. When she was in town before, there were other Tuesdays' that John had been busy. Once he told her that he had to go to a meeting in Duncan. Another Tuesday, he told her he would be tied up with his accountant, all day. Little by little she began to fit the pieces of the puzzle together. He'd been meeting this woman from Duncan and fucking her on Tuesdays all along. And to think she had been fool enough to give him all of her love. Aries felt used and cheated. How could she trust him anymore? She knew he was fucking his wife, it was to be expected but she didn't believe she could take sharing him with another girlfriend.

When Aries saw John she confronted him about his involvement with this woman. He denied it vehemently and emphatically. After hearing his denial she told him she believed him but, deep inside, she knew Eric Hammer had no reason to make up a story like that. There must have been some truth to it. Cross examining him would be to no avail and their relationship would be marred if the subject wasn't dropped. He vowed that she was his only girlfriend so she would leave it at that.

The remainder of their brief time together was loving and, seemingly, perfect. Aries saw him off at the airport on Thursday when he flew to San Diego. Desperately in love with him, she begged him to let her accompany him.

"Not this time, honey. I'm playing in the tournament and then, I'm flying straight back. Maybe another time. Be good and go back to Florida. I'll call you next week."

Aries was at his mercy so after his departure she checked out of the hotel and went back to the airport to go home. On her return flight Aries wrote this note but never mailed it." Dear John, For more than a year now I have flown like a bird from place to place never resting in one spot for long.

I have been a torn and separated person never all together, except in my thoughts. It has been a most difficult time for me with my body being in one place and my soul longing to be in another.

If you can only grasp a small portion of the extreme love I hold for you, then you can understand my feelings. I am never really at home until I am softly caressed within your arms.

I want to settle but I cannot for I find that my nesting with you is of such a temporary basis. I must remain like a bird flying through the air, back and forth, seeking the sun, enduring the cold, never settling. I have set my sights upon a star but John I am so tired."

Back home, Aries knew things had to change between them. He had told her he was in love with her, that he had very deep feelings for her. Together, they were sexually dynamite. She never wanted their relationship to end but this long distance loving wasn't working. How could she expect to hold her man when there were so many miles between them? Absence never did make the heart grow fonder.

Giving the matter serious thought she came to a decision. She did not have to stay in Florida. Her children were grown up and all away in school. She could get her real estate license in Wisconsin. There was no reason why she couldn't sell the house and move lock, stock and barrel to Madison.

She would rent an apartment there, not near John's house, but in another area near the city. She needed to be close enough to see him on a regular basis. If they were careful his wife would never know.

When John called Aries told him she was considering a move to Madison. He laughed and said, "Awe, you don't want to move to Madison. That's too close to my wife. She would find out about us. You can move to Austin if you want to."

"Austin where's that?"

"That's about 100 miles south of Madison. It's probably too cold there. You'd better stay in Florida with your job and your children. It's nice there. If I didn't have this business up here I'd like to move there, myself."

"Then, why don't you sell the business and move here?"

"We'd never move to Fort Lauderdale. My wife doesn't like it there. She prefers the west coast."

"Well, even the west coast would be better than it is now. At least, we wouldn't be so far apart."

"We couldn't move anywhere until my wife's mother passes. She's very attached to her and she would never go that far away from her."

Aries could see that the conversation about change of residence was nothing more than talk. If anyone was going to make a move it would have to be her so she set about to do just that.

In August, she wrote John a letter that read, "Many decisions must be made in this life... indecision is very discomforting. We all try to make decisions that are best for the ultimate course of our lives. This is a difficult task for a person must live with a decision that he has made.

 I love you.The time has come that I must listen to my inner self and leave the warmth of the sun to seek the snow and the cold of winter. Welcome me to Madison."

Putting her house on the market, it quickly sold it. She had a sale to dispose of the furniture. The small things went right away but she couldn't bear to let her fine furniture go at garage sale prices so she rented a warehouse for storing it. Transferring her money out of the local banks, she deposited it in the Madison bank account she had opened on her last visit there.

The day before she was to leave Fort Lauderdale for Wisconsin, Aries past came back to haunt her. It had been eight years since Bob Benton had moved away taking everything he had with him, including her heart. She had been very much in love with him when she was married to Greg. Now he was in back in town and he wanted to see her. Aries recalled how wonderful making love to Bob had been. Of course, she would see him.

They met, one evening, at her mostly emptied house. They had dinner and afterward, they spent the night together in his hotel. Greg Winston wasn't there to shoot him this time and Lana was miles away. Tonight, they could make love without fear. After the love making, Aries felt strangely uncomfortable and restless. Bob could sense that something was bothering her.

"What's wrong?"

At first, she told him nothing was wrong but she never was a good at pretending. Sitting on the edge of his bed, she looked at him lying there in the nude. What a perfect specimen of humanity! He was perfect but it was he who had been responsible for her divorce. Aries wasn't blaming him because she loved him but during the years that followed, he hadn't been around to help her. Time had passed and things between them had changed. Reluctantly, she explained that they'd been apart for a long time and she had fallen in love with a real nice man who lived in Madison, Wisconsin. She was leaving Fort Lauderdale, tomorrow, to move there.

The passion she had before for Bob was gone. He went away hurt but it was better that he know the truth. Now there was nothing left to do but quit her job, pack her clothes and take off. She had written to the children of her anticipated move and told them she would notify them of her new address in Madison.

Going to her office she told her Broker that she was leaving.

"You can't leave. What will I tell your customers? Tell them to write me at PO Box 11665."

"Aries, you're crazy? Where are you going?"

"To Wisconsin," she answered smiling.

"Well, if you have to go, go, but just take a weeks vacation and come back."

"I won't be back. Take my desk and give it to someone else!"

"You must be losing your mind," complained her Broker. "What on earth are you doing?"

"I'm not doing anything, I'm merely taking a mental sabbatical."

Aries left her real estate office with little notice. She was headed to Wisconsin with full intentions of taking up permanent residency there.

John Roberts almost died when he realized that her talk about moving to Madison was now a reality. Afraid his wife would learn about their affair, he was now worried about saving his own skin. With Aries in town, Ava's chances of discovering her were greatly increased. He would have to take some drastic action to get her to change her mind about living in Madison.

Aries was there and she had no plans of going back to Florida. This news put John in a state of shock. Certainly, her being in Madison would complicate his life. He loved her but he wanted to love her on his own terms and conditions. Having her that close to Ava was not one of them. Putting his thinking cap on, he considered ways of persuading her to leave. He would refuse to see her if she stayed in Madison and maybe she'd go back home. At least, it was worth a try. He called her and in a serious voice he said he wanted to come over and talk to her.

"Sure, come on over, we'll talk."

John arrived at her hotel without delay. His behavior was grossly different. This time, he didn't drop his trousers as soon as he walked in the door. He seemed very upset.

"Sit down, Aries, I want to talk to you," he ordered.

"I'm sitting." Aries positioned herself in a chair by the window. John's speech began.

"I want you to go back home. I love you but I can't handle having you and my wife in the same town. It will be a disaster and if you insist upon staying, I'm not going to see you anymore. If you stay up here you'll have to make your own life without me. If you have come up here because of me, you might as well go back home because I'm married. I'm trying to make my marriage work but it will never happen with you here. If you love me you'll go back to Florida."

"I like it here," Aries argued. "It has nothing to do with you. I like this place and I like the people. My moving to Madison wasn't because of you, I wanted to move here because I like it. It's a free country, you know, and you can't tell me where to live."

"No, I can't tell you where to live, but I can tell you I won't see you or make love to you as long as you insist on staying here."

"Why not? Don't you love me anymore?"

"I've had very deep feelings for you, Aries, but they are beginning to change."

"Oh, and can you tell me why?"

"Yes, I started feeling differently about you when you came up here on your own without my inviting you."

"Well, that's your fault. If you had made arrangements for us to see each other more often, I wouldn't have come on my own."

"Don't you realize I have a wife to keep happy and a business to run. I can only spread myself so thin. I've had to practice racquetball and workout, too. I haven't had time for extra-curricula activities."

"Extra curricula activities." Aries raised her voice. "Now you're referring to me as an extra curricular activity. I thought I meant more to you than that."

"You do. I love you but you're ruining it for both of us. Go home and stay there until I have a chance to get away. Then, I'll take you somewhere nice and we'll do all the things you've wanted to do."

"Promises, promises. I'm here and you might as well get used to it because I'm not leaving."

"I've told you how its going to be if you stay here. Don't call me. Make a life of your own," he warned as he abruptly walked out slamming the door behind him.

Aries was crushed. How he could do this to her? It was hard to fight back the tears. All she had ever done was love him and this was the appreciation she got from him.

She would make a life of her own, she told herself with determination. She didn't want anybody else, she wanted him but she'd show him that he wasn't the only guy that she might appeal to. She'd dress up and go to his lounge and flirt with the guys. John Roberts wasn't the only fish in the sea.

Aries made her plans but all the while she was dying inside. John's rejection was killing her. After a couple of days in the hotel, she moved out into an unfurnished apartment in a nearby condominium. She wanted to stay close to him although he had vowed not to see her. Her living in Madison was no reason for him to reject her, she reasoned. Perhaps, this was just his initial reaction to the news she had given him. Maybe he'd get over the shock of her being there in a few days and things would be fine. It was his fear of his wife discovering them that made him nervous. Maybe she should have moved to Austin like he had suggested.

Aries spent the next few days trying to get settled in her new residence. The move was easy because she had no furniture! She had left everything behind so she was starting out from scratch in Madison. Furniture was expensive and at this point in her life, she didn't want any excess baggage to lug around. It was difficult enough just moving her clothes, her typewriter and her writing in and out of places. All she really needed was a bed, a table and some chairs. The rest could come later.

Aries called John to tell him where she had moved and to give him her telephone number. He took the information but he kept his promise not to see her. Days passed and although she missed his companionship, she was determined to stay in the city. He wasn't the only person she knew there. Her ex-tennis partner from Fort Lauderdale lived in the outskirts and John had introduced her to some of his friends. She would survive if she had to, without him.

Aries signed up in real estate school in preparation for obtaining her Wisconsin real estate license. Some evenings, she went to John's lounge and chatted with his friends after he had left for the day. She knew they'd tell him she'd been there. Hopefully, he would miss her and call.

Donald Hollis was single and unattached so he took her under his wing and offered to help her with furniture for her apartment. She accepted. He was a good friend of John's and that was all he could ever be to Aries, just a friend.

Once in awhile she called John begging him to come over and make love to her but he held hard fast to his decision.

"I won't see you as long as you persist on staying up here. I warned you that if you insisted upon living in Madison, you were on your own."

Most of their telephone conversations ended up in heated arguments. Aries hated his stubbornness.

One day she decided to call, Jeff Ross, a scout for the Snobirds and a friend of John's. She had met him once in Fort Lauderdale when the team was there for game against the Dolphins. That time, John hadn't come with the team. They hit it off great, so well, that if she hadn't been in love with John she would have gone for this guy. Jeff was available but she had met him too late. John Roberts had top priority in her life. She recalled the evening she spent with Jeff. They went out for dinner and dancing and they had lots of fun. He told her to call him if she ever came back to Wisconsin. Well, thanks to John, today was the day. She dialed the Snobird office number and he was there.

"Hi, do you remember me?"

"Well, Hello," said the voice on the other end of the line. "You aren't in Madison are you?" Jeff sounded surprised.

"Yes, I am."

"Well, lets get together for a cup of coffee, later today."

"Fine, that will be fine. Just tell me when and where."

Jeff hesitated a moment and continued. "I'll probably be buttoning things up here around three. Where are you staying? Why don't we just meet at your place?"

"My place, my place would be fine but I don't have any furniture yet."

"Furniture?"

"Yes, I live here now and temporarily, I've rented an unfurnished apartment at the Travell."

"Don't worry about furniture. I'll pick you up there, anyway. What's your apartment number."

"It's 716, but you'll have to call me from the entrance and I'll open the lobby door so you can get in. They've got security guards and locks and everything here. It isn't easy to get in without a key."

"I'll manage. I'm bigger than they are so I don't anticipate any problems. I'll see you around three-thirty. Thanks for calling me."

Hanging up the phone, Aries gazed around her sparsely decorated, practically empty apartment. Jeff's going to think I'm crazy living here with no furniture, she thought. Her total decor consisted of a cot, that Donald had brought over, a small table and two chairs in the kitchen. She would tell him she was camping out here, that she didn't want to buy furniture until she decided exactly where she wanted to live in the area.

That matter settled in her mind, Aries had another problem. What if John decided to come over, after all, and what if he bumped into Jeff in the building? They were the best of friends. John would never believe Jeff was just there for a cup of coffee, even though it was true. He would be very upset if he thought she was sleeping with Jeff. Well, she hadn't, yet, but if he kept playing these games with her it might come to that. She had to get sex somewhere and Jeff Ross was damned appealing to her.

The thought of meeting Jeff, a second time, excited Aries. He was a nice person with good looks and good manners. Maybe she should get to know him better. He was a widow and he needed a good woman

woman to love and take care of him. What if she fell in love with him and gave John up? That would be a real turn of the worm.

John didn't know that she knew Jeff. She'd never told him they had met. She was afraid he'd be jealous. Well, that was before. Now she'd call him and tell him she had coffee with Jeff Ross. She would tell him about meeting him in Fort Lauderdale before the Miami game. She'd explain that their meeting in Madison was accidental.

When Jeff arrived at her apartment he discovered she wasn't really set up for entertaining.

"You know I haven't even bought any coffee yet," she explained

"No problem," smiled Jeff, "I've had too much coffee today, anyway. Lets go out and have a couple of beers."

"Good idea." We don't have anywhere to sit here, anyway. I don't have any comfortable chairs."

"You're got a bed don't you?" Jeff was smiling as he looked toward the open door to the bedroom.

"Yeah, I've got a bed if you'd like to call it that. It's really a cot that one of John Robert's friends loaned me."

"Well, a bed's all you really need isn't it? I imagine you and John spend most of your your time there."

"Not really. John hasn't been in this apartment, yet, in fact, you're my very first guest."

"Well then, I'm honored. Get your things, sweetie, and let's bust out of here. They've got free hot snacks at Flanagan's and we'll be just in time." Hesitating a moment, he asked jokingly, if she had rather go to John's place?

"Oh no! I don't want to go there. He would flip if he saw us together. Let's go to Flanagan's, that will be fine."

"You didn't tell John that we met in Fort Lauderdale did you?" Aries asked with a puzzled look on her face.

"No, no I didn't tell him anything. Our relationship is a secret between us."

"Good, let's keep it that way." She was relieved.

"At Flanagan's Aries spilled her whole story out to Jeff, of how she had sold her house, put her furniture in storage and made the decision to come to Madison.

"I'm fancy free," she told him. "I can live anywhere I want to."
She confessed that John's attitude toward her moving here had been
something less than favorable.

"He doesn't want me this close to his wife."

"Can you blame him? That poor fellow must be a nervous wreck
with the two of you here. It's hard enough to keep one woman at a
time happy but with two it's virtually impossible. Actually, he's not
being fair to you and he's not being fair to his wife. Sooner or later a
man's having his cake and eating it too catches up with him."

"John won't even see me since I've moved up here. He says he
loves me but he won't have anything to do with me unless I go back
to Fort Lauderdale. I have made my mind up that I'm not going back.
Those long distance love affairs are for the birds."

"Well, welcome to Madison, Miss Winston," he said laughing.
Now that Roberts seems to be out of the picture, maybe ole Jeff will
stand a chance. You know I like you very much, Aries. Why don't you
get rid of this apartment? Nobody, lives downtown. Get something
out my way."

"Where do you live?"

"Oh, I have a nice town house in Westerville. It's a up and coming
area, close in, but just far enough away from the city."

"I'll ride out there one day and look at it," she promised.

After the beers Jeff drove her back to Travell.

"Would you like to come in?" Aries asked as they reached her
door.

"Yes, I need to use your phone to call my sitter and tell her that I'll
be a little late getting home."

"Sitter. Why do you have a sitter?"

"For my daughter. I have a little girl at home. She's nine years old.
My wife died two years ago and I hire a sitter to care for Cindy while
I work."

"Oh, I didn't know you had a child. That's too bad about your
wife."

"Everybody has their cross to bear. You've had your own haven't
you? Five kids to raise with no father around."

"I sure did and believe me it wasn't easy. Nothing that's worth it is ever easy."

"Where's the phone?" He asked changing the subject.

"It's on the wall in the kitchen."

As he made his call Aries sat on the window sill by the living room window surveying her new surroundings.

Finished with the call, Jeff joined her. "Everything's fine at home so there's no need for me to rush. Mind if I use your powder room?"

"Go ahead. It's in the bedroom. It's probably a mess but go ahead and use it. While you're there I think I'll ship into something more comfortable."

When Jeff came out, Aries had removed her brown slacks, blouse and white sweater, and she was standing in the bedroom clad in a blue silk outfit with a loose cut low necked blouse and tight pants that hugged her hips and buttocks.

"My, my, but don't you look sexy. Let me take a look at you." He closed the bathroom door. "Come here and let me look at you."

As she came closer Jeff reached out and took her in his arms. "Oh, you just look so beautiful, you're turning me on. You're making me want to make love to you."

Jeff lifted her face up began to kiss her, feverishly. Aries couldn't resist responding. His huge cock was getting very hard. She could feel it pressing against her body. Those silk pants she had on left very little to the imagination.

"Let's get these clothes off and try your new bed out." Breathing very hard, Jeff began to unzip her blouse. "Take it off, Aries, and show me your nice breasts."

Embarrassed to be undressing in front of him, she knew they both had reached the point of no return.

"The bed's too little for both of us," he commented.

"You're too big for the bed," she laughed. "You'll break it."

"If I break it I'll buy you another one." Jeff smiled standing there stark naked.

Surveying his muscular frame, naturally, her eyes fell upon his gigantic cock, totally erected and ready for action. "Oh gracious," exclaimed Aries. The bed's too little for you and you're too big for me. You'll kill me for sure. I know you'll kill me."

"Don't worry, sweetheart, I'll be gentle with you and it will fit you just fine. Come on, lie down, hon. I promise you the best fucking you've ever had. After me, you'll forget all about John Roberts."

John Roberts. Aries wished he hadn't mentioned his name. How could she have the audacity to fuck his friend? "I'm afraid to make love to you," she pleaded. "You'll tell John and you'll tell all the Snobird team and I'll be ruined. My reputation will be destroyed and John will never speak to me again."

"Don't be afraid, I promise I'll never tell anybody. This will be our secret and no one will ever know, I promise."

Aries sat down on the side of the bed with her firm tits standing at attention. Her her hard nipples were begging to be sucked. Jeff joined her at the bedside, lifted her legs up and placed her in the center of the bed. Then with his over sized cock sticking out like a pointer, he mounted her with his naked, hairy, strong muscular frame.

"Help me put him in. Take your hand and guide my cock into the mouth of your pussy. I'll be easy. Let's just get the tip in."

She reached her hand up and placed the head of his throbbing cock at the opening of her vagina.

"I did it. Oh, oh, you're so big," she moaned.

"Yes, baby, I'm so big and hard for you, just for you. You make me so hard. It's all just for you, baby. Careful now, I'm going to put it in a little deeper, open up a little now, baby, spread your pretty legs."

"I'll try but please, don't hurt me."

"I'm going to hurt you but I'll hurt you good. You'll love it."

Soon Aries found herself moaning and groaning with sighs of joy. Jeff's cock was deep inside of her vagina, giving her unbelievable thrills. He was right. She was getting one of the best fucks she had ever had in her life.

Jeff was enjoying the hell out of it, too. He was perspiring like a horse. When it was over, their bodies were drenched with perspiration.

"I'm coming, I'm coming, moaned Aries."

"Come on, honey, let go, let go. Pour that sweet love juice all over my cock."

She let go and Jeff was right behind her flooding her pussy with his wet, hot cum.

262

"Oh my, that was wonderful," murmured Aries. "Thank you, Jeff Ross."

"Thank you Miss Winston. I must have really needed that one. Now that didn't hurt you did it?"

"No, yes, it hurt me but it hurt me so good."

"We'll have to do that again, sweets. I'd better take a shower now and get home to Westerville."

"Now, now," repeated Aries. Lay with me a little bit, please."

"I can't hon, I've got a meeting tonight so I've to get on the road."

Jeff, got up and Aries lay there enjoying the beautiful aftermath. She dare not get up, yet, because she was still in the clouds. She would rest a few minutes until she regained her composure, until she got her equilibrium back.

Jeff had left the bathroom door open and with no shower curtain up, Aries had a perfect view of him showering and dressing. He was wearing a look of quiet contentment on his face.

Sitting up on the edge of the bed. she reached for a cigarette. Lighting it, she went to the closet, pulled out a night shirt and put it on.

When Jeff was ready to leave she walked him to the door.

"You're a good girl." He put his strong arm around her shoulders. "I'm going out of town tomorrow for a few days on a scouting trip but I'll call you for sure when I get back in town."

"Fine. I'll await your call but please do me a favor. If you see John Roberts, please don't tell him about today."

"Put your mind at ease. I promise never to tell."

"I'll tell him myself that I ran into you today at Flanagan's and we sat and talked and had a couple beers. I'll tell him you were nice but that's all I'm going to tell him. There's no reason to hurt him."

"I've got to go now, take it easy and stop worrying about Roberts. He's my friend but he's not worth your losing any sleep over. He's a married man, a very married man. He's the one that being unfair try-ing to hog up the single women for himself."

Aries laughed and saw him out the door.

With Jeff gone, it didn't take long for her guilt to start to set in. How could she have violated John Roberts? She loved him. No matter how he was behaving, she shouldn't have slept with Jeff. Aries spent the rest of the evening admonishing herself.

As the days passed Aries was consumed with sadness at John's continued refusal to see her.

One afternoon she stopped by his lounge. While she was there Donald Hollis came in. As they chatted over a couple of beers he told her that John was playing football that night with the local team. He asked if she'd like to go to the game with him and watch him play. Donald knew how much she loved John.

"I'm afraid he wouldn't like it," Aries replied.

"Like it, John loves his gang there cheering. Come on. Don't you want to watch him?"

"Of course, I do."

"Well meet me back here at seven o'clock," he instructed.

Aries went out for an early dinner and at seven, she arrived back at O'Reilly's. It was sprinkling rain a little and she wondered if the game would still be on.

Entering, she spied Donald sitting at a table with five other guys. Looking beyond him, she saw John hemmed in a booth between two women. It was surprising to find him there and not at the ball field. The game must have been called off.

She joined the party at Donald's table. From her seat, Aries had a perfect view of John in the booth across the room. The three were laughing and having a good time. He hadn't noticed that she was there. It was all she could endure seeing the woman who sat beside John, touch him and make eyes at him. Aries got up from the table and excusing herself, she put her coat on in preparation to flee. She fought hard to hold back the tears.

When she stood up to leave John caught sight of her and extricated himself from the women in the booth. She was getting out of there and getting out fast. John came running behind her.

"Wait, wait," he yelled. "You don't understand."

Aries heard him but ignoring him, she kept on walking as fast as her feet would carry her. He followed her out the side exit into the parking lot. As she fumbled for her car keys, he tried to explain that his sitting with the women in the booth meant nothing.

"Nothing," wailed Aries. "I saw that woman touching you and making eyes at you. You're not only running around on your wife, you're running around on me, too. I think I'll have coffee with your wife in the morning and tell her about it."

Aries was hysterical and in tears.

John was shouting and threatening her. "Get out of my town. If you call my wife I'll have the Irish mafia on you."

By now, Aries had found her car keys and was in her car. John was standing in front of it. "Get out of my way," she cried as she started the engine. "Get out of my way before I run over you, you infidel." He moved and allowed her to drive away.

This was their first real fight, the first time they had spoken harsh words and it was killing her inside. She loved him and this episode had totally devastated her.

Observing a marquis at a nearby hotel, she noticed that they were featuring a psychic named Mendel. She decided to stop there to see him. She hardly ever went to psychics and had little faith in them but tonight, she felt like she needed one.

Finally her turn with the psychic came and before the session was over, the topic of John Roberts came up.

"It's over," said Aries. "We had a fight tonight and it's all over."

"No," said the psychic. "It isn't over. It's just the beginning between you two. You'll see him again," advised Mendel. He was right.

The next morning John called and asked if he could come over She couldn't believe it. After days of refusing to see her he wanted to come over. "I'm sorry about last night. I love you and I didn't mean to hurt you," John professed.

"Of course, you can come over," Aries said. She'd been dying to be with him but she didn't know it would take a fight to bring them together.

Not long after his phone call, John was ringing her doorbell, all apologetic with a loving look in his eyes. They made love three times. After the loving they talked about their relationship and the problems in his marriage. Sympathetically, Aries told him she understood his situation. He asked her to go back to Florida for six months. During that time, he was going to try to keep his marriage together. After that, if it didn't work he'd throw in the towel and divorce his wife. Aries promised to give him that time without her physical presence complicating the issue. She would leave Madison in a few days. She loved him too much to see him unhappy.

The day of her departure came. The goodbyes had been said. As she walked away from John's place of business to her car she tried to feign some composure, although she felt more like flinging herself down in the snow and bawling her eyes out. She told herself, "Don't cry now. Walk away and don't look back. Be brave and hold back the tears. There will be much time for tears in remembering. Don't cry now, Aries." Over and over, these words kept running through her head as she walked away from John.

As she headed in another direction her body moved forward in a numblike way. It was as if she were dying and could not reverse her fate. Clutching the chocolate that Charlie had handed her, minutes ago, when she told him she was leaving, she felt the soft new snow melt as her feet pressed firmly into the pavement of the parking lot.

Part Fifteen

Entering the car, Aries drove slowly away from the place she wanted to be most, away from the city and the man she loved with all her heart.

Aries's head was filled with many thoughts. Were they destined to meet and sadly part in this life? Beside herself with emotion, she could do nothing but think of John. Neither of them had ever mentioned or accepted the possibility that they might never see each other again, that each time might be the last time. Neither of them had wanted to face that raw reality. The expectancy of meeting again, at some future undetermined time, always existed between them.

Aries knew their souls were bound together to eternity and yet, they seemed doomed to love each other without the constancy of physical intimacy. This intimacy had been so precious and exclusively theirs, those times they lost themselves in their paradise of peace and serenity away from all else in the world.

As Aries made her way out of the city, the snow fell covering her shiny yellow Mercedes. Her mind rambled on with thoughts of John until she felt that she would go insane. Paying little attention to direction, she moved aimlessly along in the four o'clock traffic. Where was she going? What highway should she take to get out of the city? It really didn't matter where she went or when she got there. She was lost and alone. She was leaving the man she loved in Wisconsin. She really didn't want to live in this world without him.

Why had she agreed that it would be better for both of them if she went away for six months? Why had she come to Wisconsin in the first place? The answer was simple. She had to come. Something inside of her kept hounding and knawing at her until she had no choice. She had to reunite her body and soul, once more. She had been miserable in Fort Lauderdale away from John and she was miserable in Madison knowing that he belonged to someone else.

In the beginning she thought that being the other woman would be enough but somehow things got tangled up and what started out to be just an affair turned into genuine love and caring. That hurt! Both she and John got hurt. They couldn't handle the situation and now a powder keg was about to explode...probably right in Aries face. She knew that someday it would come to this but she didn't want to face the reality. She wanted their dream to continue.

Aries wondered what highway would get her out of town and where was she headed. She had to decide where she was going before stopping to ask for directions. John had told her to go back to Florida and wait. She didn't want to go back there. It was hundreds of miles from Madison.

She told John that she might go to Oklahoma to visit her daughter, Mia, before returning to Florida. How far was Oklahoma? Maybe she would drive straight there. Mia had planned to come to Madison in a few days after she got over a bout with bronchial asthma. She would be surprised to see her. In fact, she would think she was nuts to leave Wisconsin, so suddenly.

She had to go somewhere. She couldn't continue to drive around
aimlessly with thoughts of John consuming and overwhelming her
sensibilities. She had to get him out of her mind. She had to go somewhere and start a new life without him. She would to go to Oklahoma.
Maybe there she could forget John Roberts.

The falling snow made the roads slippery. She looked at the fuel
gage. It was almost on empty. The last thing she wanted to do was to
run out of fuel in that foul weather. There was a truck stop up ahead.
She would stop there for fuel. Luckily, driving a diesel, she didn't
have to stop often in that rotten cold to fill her up.

While getting the diesel, she asked the attendant to check under the
hood. Everything was okay. With a long trip to make alone, she didn't
want any trouble on the road. Checking the atlas, Aries estimated the
mileage to St. Louis. Perhaps she would stay the night there.

Down the road Aries chastised herself for going to Madison in the
first place. She must have been insane running after a married man.
She had a good job in Florida with a long twenty year reputation for
honesty. She had abandoned her home, her job and her children for
John. She might have known that being Irish Catholic he'd never
leave his wife and children. She might have known that Ava would
win.

Aside from other things, there was too much money involved for
John to get divorced. No wonder after consulting a marriage counselor, a priest and an attorney, he decided it would be better to work
things out with his wife. To heck with love. What did that have to do
with it?

As she drove through Missouri, Aries remembered that she used to
have a girlfriend in Fort Lauderdale who came from there. She got
divorced and moved back. She wondered if she lived there now.
Missouri was such a barren state. It looked like all they had to do
there was milk cows and make love. Aries was hell bent on making it
to St. Louis that night but it looked so far away on the map. Trucking
along at seventy-five miles an hour, she wondered if the highway
patrol was out. She hadn't seen any of them, yet. Jeff was right when
he told her to leave John and to go back home. In a way she wished
she had met him first. He was such a nice fellow, she'd keep him as a

friend and try to forget John. But how could she forget him? Nobody ever loved her like he did. If she couldn't have John Roberts she would just become a nun.

The car was driving great and not one cop was in sight. It looked like she had clear sailing on the road. She had spoken too soon.One came one out of nowhere. She slowed down. She was traveling through some desolate areas. It was dark on the road so she stayed behind the big silver truck ahead of her.

It was in the middle of night when Aries hit the Saint Louis exit so she passed straight by and kept on driving. Mia had sounded real sick on the phone when she called. Maybe she needed her.

Driving through the night, Aries thought the road would never end. It was dawn when she reached the town of Wilburton, Oklahoma, a place no more than small hole in the road. She stopped to call Mia but was unable to find her listed in the telephone directory or in information. In her haste to leave Madison, Aries had left her address book in the apartment and she didn't know Mia's address.

Mia was enrolled in Oklahoma State College there. Going into the service station, Aries asked the attendant for directions to the college. He told her that the school was a couple miles down the road. Pointing south, he told her to take a right at the stop sign and head south.

Thanking him, she got back in the car and took off. She found the school alright but it was closed. It was Saturday and there wasn't a soul around. Now, she had a problem. She drove up and down the streets that bordered the school hoping that Mia lived on one of them. Why on earth had she come to Oklahoma without bringing the child's address?

Having no success on the streets, Aries headed back out to the main road. The only thing left to do was to keep looking for a little red volkswagen with Florida license plates and a luggage rack on top. Suddenly she remembered that Mia was sick when she called her. Perhaps she visited a doctor and gave her address there.

Going back to the service station, Aries asked how many doctors there were in town? The attendant said three. He told her that two of them were located up the road, this time he pointed north, and the other doctor had his office on Main Street beside the post office.

Thanking him, she went looking for the doctor's office. She hadn't been driving long until she spied a little red volkswagen with a luggage rack parked in front of a building. "At last, I've found her." Aries breathed a sigh of relief. Pulling in and parking beside the vehicle, she got out and looked at the license plate. Sure enough it was Mia's car! Only the Lord could have led her to Mia. This had to be a miracle.

Aries walked into the doctor's office and asked the receptionist out front if Mia Winston was there.

"Yes, she's in with the doctor, right now." Aries didn't bother to sit down. She headed for the examination room door leaving the receptionist wondering what was going on.

Flinging the door open, she found Mia lying on the examining table.

"Mia," Aries cried.

"Mom," Mia screamed excitedly. "I don't believe this. Doctor, I told you my mother would be here. I talked to her in Wisconsin day before yesterday and she didn't say a word about coming but I knew she'd come. She didn't even have my address and she found me."

The doctor was amazed and Mia was so happy.

"What's wrong with my daughter?" Aries inquired of the doctor.

"She's just suffered a miscarriage."

"A miscarriage. Mia you didn't tell me you were pregnant."

"No, but I told you I'd been bleeding with my period a lot."

"Is my daughter alright?"

"She's lost a lot of blood but with the proper food, rest, vitamins and blood builders, she'll be in fine shape, soon."

"It's a good thing I came. Mia, where on earth do you live? I went to the college and it was closed. I left your address in in my apartment in Madison."

"It wouldn't have helped you, any way, Mom, I've moved from where I used to live."

The doctor finished his examination. Aries paid the bill and followed Mia to the local pharmacy to get her prescriptions filled. Just like a Mom, Aries thought, always showing up in time to pay the bill.

While they waited at the pharmacy Aries asked her if she needed any food. "We might as well stop at the grocery store, too, while we're here."

Mia never was one to turn food down so she accepted the offer.

"Follow me, Mom, Mia told her as they left the grocery store. "Follow me to where I live."

"Who do you live with? Are you still living with the girl I met out here, last year?"

"No, she dropped out of school. She was very poor and couldn't afford to go. I'm living with Claus now, you've met him, remember? He's the German boy who lived at the motel in Oklahoma City where Mark and I stayed."

"Oh, yes. Is he the one who got you pregnant?"

"Well, what do you think? He's the boy I've been living with."

"Are you in love with him?"

I like him but I'm not sure that I'm in love with him."

They pulled up into Mia's driveway. She was living in a shack. Aries was appalled at her living circumstances. She couldn't believe the way those kids had been living. They had practically nothing. Aries read Claus the riot act about keeping her daughter in a dump like that. Although Claus appeared to be very nice, it was obvious that he was penniless. He had gotten her daughter pregnant out of wedlock, too.

Mia was on semester break from school. Aries told her she'd check into a hotel for the night but she would be back in the morning.

"When you leave here, where are you going, Mom? Back to Florida? You've seen Florida. Why don't you go to California and see how you like to there?"

Still distraught and upset at leaving John, Aries couldn't have cared less where she went.

"Okay, I'll go to California. Come with me," Aries begged.

"Mom, I can't go now. I can't just walk off and leave Claus."

"Go ahead to where you're going and then, call me. Tell me where you are and I'll fly out to join you. That way I'll have a couple of days to break the news to him."

Aries stopped by Mia's the next morning on her way out of town. She would go to Arizona and from there on to California. "I'll call you when I get to Phoenix and I'll wait there for you to join me, Mia."

Saying goodbye, she hit the road again, feeling better after having seen her daughter. She was glad that Mia was going to accompany her on her trip to no where. Aries hadn't mentioned her problems but right now, she really needed a friend.

The trip to Phoenix was an experience. Aries drove over the long miles through Texas and New Mexico toward Phoenix. The road through Texas was broad, wide and desolate. Another barren state like Missouri. She'd never seen so many wide open spaces.

New Mexico was different. It was past midnight when she arrived in a small Mexican town. Literally exhausted from the long drive, she needed was a good night's rest but where would she find it? The streets were thick with drunken Mexicans who appeared to be a rowdy bunch. All of the motels signs were shut off. The innkeepers had closed for the night.

Leary of stopping, Aries decided to drive on to Albuquerque. Later this proved to be an unwise decision because outside of town, she found herself on a narrow mountain road with cliffs overhanging. It really looked very dangerous. She was very tired, so tired that she could hardly hold her eyes open. As she drove, she kept fighting back sleep in an effort to stay awake.

There was no sign of civilization along the highway. Only dirt roads that led into the woods. She saw little evidence of habitation, except for signs of Indians. Although exhausted, she was afraid to stop the car and rest. She drove on hoping to get out of the mountains and away from the Indians. Nobody told her that the road to Phoenix would be like this. She had timed her travel wrong to end up in a God awful place like this in the middle of the night.

Aries felt herself falling asleep at the wheel. The car swerved toward the cliffs. It was only a miracle of fate that she regained consciousness in time to escape driving over the them. After this frightening close call she kept her eyes open and her mind on the driving until she hit Albuquerque.

Checking into the first decent motel, she collapsed and slept for hours. When she awakened she still felt like she had been run over by a truck. Another good night's rest and surely, she'd be back to normal. She had been pushing it too hard since leaving Wisconsin. She had traveled from Wisconsin to Oklahoma and to New Mexico in a matter of several days. What was she trying to do, kill herself? And if she died would John really care?

John's name kept racing through her mind. She had traveled as far away from him as mind and body could take her, only to arrive at her destination and find him by her side. He was still in her heart, her mind, her soul.

After a good rest she traveled on to Phoenix, Arizona and checked into a hotel there. That night, she called Mia's neighbors and left a message for Mia. Returning her call, Mia was happy to hear that she had arrived safely in Phoenix.

"It's a nice town. I think I'll stay on here for awhile before going on to California," Aries announced.

"I'm coming to join you, Mom. Call the airline and make me a reservation for tomorrow. I'll call you back to find out which flight I'm taking. You'll have to pay for my ticket though, I'm broke."

"I know. I'll prepay your ticket. You can pick it up at the airport."

"Thanks, Mom. I'll call you back in a little while."

Aries made Mia's reservation and she prepaid the ticket. It was waiting for her at the Continental ticket window. She was pleased that Mia was joining her. She needed this and Mia needed to spend some time with her Mother. She'd never taken a vacation alone with her daughter. Surely, this togetherness would give them a chance to become better acquainted. This responsibility would help her get John out of her mind, too, she prayed.

Aries picked Mia up at the airport the following afternoon. After spending one night cramped up in the motel, Mia begged Aries to find a bigger place so they could have more room. The next day they went apartment hunting. Hearing that the best place to live was Scottsdale, they went looking there.

They rented a furnished apartment for a month at the Greenwood Tennis Club. The courts looked great and while they were there she hoped Mia would get serious about her tennis. Her brothers had always over shadowed her in the game so consequently, she withdrew and decided not to take up the sport.

Soon after moving in the Greenwood complex, Mia signed up for tennis lessons. "I want to learn how, Mom," she said. "Then, maybe you'll play with me. When I was little you were always hitting with the boys." Mia took private tennis lessons and along with the lessons, she ended up getting a bonus. The pro, Dick Fisk, fell for her and when her lessons were over he kept on teaching her free! He kept Mia company day and night while they were there.

Aries met a friend at Greenwood, too, one night at a social gathering. Tim was a bright young fellow with fiery red hair. He was an avid tennis player and she had been looking for a singles opponent.

Tim was good on and off the court. He was a younger man but it didn't really matter. They enjoyed playing together, no strings attached, no romantic involvement, just good tennis and good clean sex. Aries needed both.

After a month in Arizona, Aries was getting itchy to move on. She had stayed at Greenwood long enough to win the championship match and to improve her tennis but there was nothing there that appealed to her. She told Mia she was getting tired of the weather in Phoenix and suggested that they give up the apartment and go somewhere else. Mia wanted to go to California but looking at the map, California would only put her farther away from John.

"What about Denver, Colorado?" she suggested.

"Oh, Denver sounds good. I've got a friend outside of Denver," Mia declared.

Fortunately, neither of them had developed any strong emotional ties in Phoenix so they could depart without being sad. They packed up and headed through the mountains of Falstaff on their way to Denver. Mia insisted upon driving so Aries took the passenger side. She needed some shut eye, anyway. She hadn't gotten much sleep the night before. She'd been too busy fucking Tim, goodbye. Mia had spent her last night with Dick, too.

It had been almost a month since Mia had joined her. They had been having fun playing tennis, eating in fancy restaurants and talking about the men they'd met.

On the trip to Denver, they'd been warned not to stop in the mountains outside of Falstaff. Sometimes, the Indians set up road blocks and forced people out of their cars and stole them.

Aries dreaded going through that Indian bit again. She warned Mia to stop at a service station to fuel up, change the oil and to make sure the car was okay so they could keep the doors locked and get past the Indians without stopping along the way.

Mia laughed and told her that she was funny.

It snowed all the way to Falstaff. The scenery was much more beautiful than it had been in Phoenix but Aries was eager to get out of the mountains.

Past Falstaff her Mercedes groaned painfully as they climbed hills upward to Colorado. Sometimes, Aries thought the car wasn't going to make it. It would have to be serviced when they reached Denver because something was wrong. Later, she took the car to a dealer and she learned that it needed some adjustment for the altitude.

"Your car, just like you, needs to be adjusted when you change altitude," said the mechanic.

Aries hadn't known that. Maybe she should have read her manual better. She'd never learn all she needed to know about that foreign car.

Outside Denver, they crossed over the painted dessert. It was getting on in the afternoon but Mia insisted on driving through it. "Oh, Mom, this is beautiful! You drive now and let me get out along the way and take pictures." Aries had never seen her so enthralled. She was like a little girl at Christmas.

The trip went slowly because every few miles Mia wanted to get out and snap another shot of that glorious natural scenery. After the painted desert came the snow capped mountains of Colorado. They were beautiful.

Mia was so excited and so thrilled at all of the beauty laid before her eyes. She had never seen anything like this before. Aries too, would never forget these sights but most of all she would remember the joy in Mia's eyes. This trip, Aries decided, was one of the nicest gifts that she could have given her daughter.

It was nightfall when they reached Denver. Aries had napped during the last few hours of the journey. Mia awakened her when they were coming into the city. "Wake up, Mom, wake up and look how beautiful it is here. Aries sat up in her seat and looking out she saw the snow covered mountains rising up all around them.

"My, what a beautiful place!"

"I told you, Mom. I told you it was beautiful."

It was getting dark so they started looking for a motel. The fuel gage was getting very low. They would need to stop for fuel. Denver was another big city and neither of them knew their way around.

Mia was driving again. "Just go down this street and look for a motel, Mia, or let's stop and ask somebody where we should stay." People gave them directions but they kept getting lost. It would have been nice if they had a city map. Finally, they spied a La Quinta Motel up on a hill.

"Let's stop here," said Mia.

Luckily, they were able to get a room there. After bringing their bags in, Mia went to ask the desk clerk about good places to eat. He suggested a restaurant about five miles away. The food was supposed to be good and they were having a big show that night. Some big movie star was entertaining there.

"Maybe, if you go early you'll be able to get a seat," said the clerk.

"Let's go," said Aries after hearing about it. "Let's bathe and get dressed up and go out for a night on the town."

It took them awhile to get ready because Mia couldn't for the life of her decide which outfit to wear. She kept trying on clothes, modeling in front of the mirror and then taking them off. By the time Aries convinced her that she looked absolutely smashing, the entire floor was strewn with clothing.

"Leave them there. We'll hang them up when we get back," said Aries. "We'd better get going now or else we'll never get into that place. We've still got to find it, you know, and at the rate we've been going since we hit this town, we may not make it."

Fortunately, there was still some light outside and they found the restaurant that had been recommended. Entering they learned that they were too late for the first show but if they wished to wait in the lounge, they could be seated for dinner and the second show.

"Let's stay. We don't know how to get anywhere else so we might as well stay here," Aries told Mia.

"I'm starving, Mom. I hope they have food at the bar or something. Sitting down at the upstairs bar, Mia was more interested in what she could find to nibble on than she was in having a drink. Pretzels was the only thing the bartender had to offer.

"Anything is better than nothing," said Mia thanking him.

It was several hours before the hostess paged them and took them to a table downstairs. The girls had partaken a several drinks at the bar and by then were feeling no pain. They had dinner late and they sipped on wine as they sat through the show. When Aries got up to walk out of there she could hardly make it.

"Those drinks really hit me, tonight. You'll have to drive us home, Mia, because I think I'm drunk."

"I'm drunk, too, but I guess you're the most drunk so I'll get us there."

The parking attendant brought their car and with Mama in the passenger side Mia drove away.

"I think the motel is this way," she said as she headed south.

Aries took her word for it because she couldn't remember the name of the place much less how to get there.

Mia drove for miles and couldn't find the hotel.

"Stop the car," said Aries. "I'm sick. I'm getting very sick. I've got to throw up."

Mia stopped the car to let her out. Vomiting her head off, she had never felt so sick in all her life. "I'm dying, Mia, Aries groaned. I can't even stand up. Do you think they poisoned us there? How much farther is it to the motel?"

"I don't know, Mom. I'm lost and I can't find it."

"Well, you'd better stop and ask somebody where we live." Aries moaned.

In sympathy Mia stopped the car so her Mom could get in the back seat and lay down. Lying on the floor board of the back seat, Aries passed out cold.

Mia stopped to get directions to their motel but nobody could help her much because she couldn't remember the address. Finally, a nice, courteous passerby checked the telephone directory for her and called all the La Quinta's to find out which one they were registered in. "You're staying at the north one," he told her. "Follow me and I'll lead you there."

Mia welcomed his offer because she was pretty well out of it her-self. As she followed the car ahead Mia noticed that the red fuel light flashing on the car. They had forgotten to get fuel. All they needed was to run out of diesel, now.

Pretty soon the fellow pulled up at the La Quinta. "I hope you have your room keys," he said.

"Mom's got them," answered Mia as she dug into Aries purse looking for them. Mia tried to wake her but she was out cold.

"Sir, I'm sorry to ask you but could you do me one more favor and help me get my Mom into the room? I can't budge her."
Together, they pulled Aries out of the car and helped her into the room where she collapsed.

Mia apologized and thanked him for helping.

"I don't know what's wrong with my mother," she told him very embarrassed. She's never done this before."

"It's the altitude. It'll do it to a newcomer every time," the man said in a friendly manner.

The good Samaratin left and Mia couldn't get to the john fast enough. She was vomiting now, too, and as sick as a dog.

It was two o'clock the next afternoon before either of them had the strength to crawl out of bed and open the drapes. Welcome to Denver! They had learned that alcohol and altitude didn't mix. Aries never did get used to it. Each time she tried to drink, she became violently ill.

On another night, they were escorted by two nice men from Denver to one of the finest restaurants in town. They had red wine before dinner. Aries liked her date and she wanted to impress him. Things were going great until her plate was placed before her. At that instant she began to feel ill. She knew she was going to vomit. Sitting on the inside of the booth, she couldn't make it out in time. She threw up all over the table. Mia went to the rest room with her to clean up and the waitress moved them to another table. Nobody was hungry after that. Her date comforted her during the evening but after that, she never heard from him again.

Soon after arriving in Denver, Aries rented an apartment. This time, they had to take one unfurnished. That evening they met, Huge

Horton, an executive in a life insurance company who upon hearing of their plight agreed to send them a bed, a table, two chairs, dishes and utensils. So they had the basics and, at least, they had a fireplace.

Mia had met a young man from Minneapolis and they were becoming quite cozy. It was funny how it all got started. They were listening to music at one of the night spots in town, one evening, when Aries struck up a conversation with this young fellow as she was returning from the restroom.

"Who's that lovely young lady sitting at your table?" He asked.

"That's my daughter."

"Well, she's lovely! I'd like to meet her. Perhaps you ladies would join us at our table. We're sitting over there, near you," he said pointing. There's my friend waiting for me."

"Well, we might join you. I'll ask my daughter." Back at the table Aries told Mia about the young man who wanted to meet her. He's sitting over there with another guy. Mia looked over and as she did, she caught the smile of the fellow who wanted to meet her.

"He's cute," she remarked.

"They'll be over here in a minute to ask us to join them," Aries warned. The guys came over and invited the them to sit at their table. As the evening grew on the four became acquainted.

Mia explained how they were moving out of their hotel to an unfurnished apartment the next day. "My Mom's crazy. She rented an unfurnished apartment when all we have with us is two forks two knives, two spoons and two glasses. I guess we'll be sleeping on the floor. Mom really does weird things. She has an apartment in Wisconsin, an apartment in Fort Lauderdale, one in Scottsdale and she doesn't live in any of them. She keeps traveling over the country trying to decide where she wants to be.

"Well, Denver's a nice place," said Hugh. "Why don't you young ladies just stay here? I can help you out with some of furniture. I've got a bed, a table, some chairs and things I'm not using. Give me your address. I'll send them over in a truck tomorrow."

"That's really nice offer but we can't take your furniture. I'll buy it from you," said Aries. She was amazed at this stranger's generosity

"No, replied her dark-haired friend. It's a loaner from me to you.

Welcome to Denver!"

Mia's friend's name was Bruce Bower. They were getting along fine. Aries was glad she had met someone decent.

When they were ready to leave the guys insisted upon meeting them at their hotel for a nightcap. The girls were foot loose and fancy free so why not? Maybe, they would try to sleep with them but that wouldn't be a bad idea. They looked like nice, clean men. Sex was probably what they both needed.

The fellows ended up spending the night with them. There was only one double bed in the room so Aries and Huge slept on the bedsprings and they gave Mia and Bruce the mattress.

Somehow they managed to rig up a blanket as a curtain between them for privacy. Mother and daughter had never slept in a room together with men before. It wasn't so bad in the dark. In fact, it was an experience for Aries to learn that her daughter loved sex just like she did. That damned box spring that she and Hugh slept on was very uncomfortable but he didn't complain.

The next morning when Aries awoke, Hugh was getting dressed. Being a big wheel at the insurance company he had to show up at the office. Bruce needed to get up, too, so jerking the blanket down Aries decided to shock him.

"Young man," she exclaimed in a dead serious voice.

"What are you doing in bed with my daughter?"

As Aries lorded above him Bruce looked up from his mattress bed on the floor. Laughing, he told Aries she was just the kind of mother-in-law he'd like to have.

Mia and Aries never talked about what happened that evening but, after that, mother and daughter were a lot closer. From then on Mia told her everything.

They dated Hugh and Bruce while they were in Denver. Bruce was single and available. Mia had fun with him, skiing and going different places. Aries suspected that Hugh had a wife at home because his habits of coming and going were somewhat like John's had been. His status mattered little to her because she had no intentions of becoming attached to him. One broken heart was enough for her.

She hadn't contacted John since leaving Wisconsin. She'd called Jeff from Scottsdale because she knew he would be worried about her. She told him not to tell John where she was and she knew he wouldn't. John wouldn't be asking him about her because he had no idea that they were acquainted with each other..

Aries couldn't help wondering if John had tried to reach her in Fort Lauderdale. Nobody there knew where she was, except Margie, and she had her word of honor that she wouldn't reveal it to anyone.

Aries hadn't worked for four months. Nothing seemed to matter now. She would have to go back to work, someday, but she still had money from the sale of the house and frankly, her mind was still on a mental sabbatical.

After being in Denver for three weeks Huge convinced her to try her hand at the insurance business. He even offered her a job in his company. She went there twice and took a bunch of tests. Passing with flying colors, she was due to start the new job after Thanksgiving.

On Thanksgiving day, Aries cooked a turkey although nobody was coming for dinner. That evening after Mia was in bed asleep Aries stood in front of the bay window of her apartment looking out over the lights of Denver. She was pensive.

"What am I doing here, thousands miles from home in this strange city?" Thinking the situation over, she decided against taking the job with the insurance company and furthermore she decided against staying in Denver. Why don't I go home where I belong? She asked herself. People know me there and I've got a good reputation in the real estate business. As Aries asked the questions she answered them. It was in the wee hours of the morning but she couldn't sleep. She was busy making decisions.

Part Sixteen

Before dawn her mind was made up. She was going back home to Florida. Why plant a new tree when the roots of the one she had already planted were so strong? Why not nurture it? She would go back to her job, her home and her friends. She was without John but she had her children. That was a lot to be thankful for.

When Mia awoke Aries gave her the news. "We're leaving. We're leaving today. I'll take you back to Oklahoma to get your car and then, I'm going back to Florida."

"Mom, we can't leave yet," Mia complained. "I've got to find Bruce and tell him goodbye. And what about Hugh Horton's furniture, what are we going to do with it?"

"I'll call him and tell him to come pick it up."

Mia got dressed and taking the car, she went to tell Bruce goodbye. While she was gone Aries packed up their things. She decided against calling Huge. He expected her to come to work at his office. Being a chicken, she wrote him a resignation letter mentioning the furniture on a footnote.

It was late afternoon before Mia returned to the apartment. Aries imagined that her parting with Bruce had been "such sweet sorrow."

Finally they had everything loaded in the car. It was packed to the hilt. Aries got behind the wheel to take the first turn at driving.

"Wait a minute Mom we forgot something," said Mia.

"What did we forget?

We forgot the turkey, our Thanksgiving turkey."

"Well, go back in and get it. I don't know where were going to put it though."

Mia brought the turkey from the refrigerator. They put it on the console in the front seat beside them so they could pick on it on their way to Oklahoma. As the trip progressed they wished they had left the turkey in Denver. It was greasy and smelling up the car.

Arriving in Oklahoma, Aries dropped Mia off to pick up her car and then they drove to her girl friend's house. She was a pretty thing but she was so poor. She lived in no more than a shack on the side of the road. Feeling that the girl was poverty stricken, Aries told Mia to give her what was left of the turkey.

Mia decided to stay in Oklahoma for a few days before returning to Fort Lauderdale. Aries wanted to continue on.

"Stay tonight in Oklahoma, Mom," begged Mia with warmth and affection.

"No, honey, I've got a long drive ahead of me and I'd better get on the road."

"I'll be home in a week or so," Mia said hugging her.

"I love you, Mom."

"I love you too, little girl," said Aries as she stroked the falling tresses of Mia's strawberry blonde hair. "I love you, honey." She kissed her goodbye.

Leaving both Mia and the turkey in Oklahoma, Aries set out on the long drive from Denver to Florida. She'd have lots of time to think and plan over those miles of solitude and aloneness.

Before moving to Wisconsin she had sold her house in Fort Lauderdale. She was going back and for the first time in her life she didn't have a home to go to. Gregory had graduated from college, Mia was in Oklahoma with friends, Mark and Ralph were residing with their father and Sara was away in private school. During the past few months the only person she had to take care of was herself. Before that she always had a houseful of children.

She called Margie when she arrived in to Fort Lauderdale seeking her hospitality for a few days until she could rent an apartment. She didn't want to buy anything until she'd had a chance to make some money and survey the current market. She wouldn't go back to her old real estate office, mainly, because she didn't take too well to a woman being her boss.

Before leaving Fort. Lauderdale she was involved in commercial real estate. She had accumulated files on commercial properties that she discarded the night before she left for Wisconsin. She should have stored those files because many of those properties were still available and she'd have to gather the information all over again.

After thinking it over carefully Aries decided to seek employment with a well known commercial real estate firm, R. J. Sampson & Associates. The company had been in business there for thirty years and all of the agents, mostly men, were experienced. She could get the training she needed there.

Margie was glad to see her and though she had out of town guests, she welcomed her to stay there.

Several days later Aries became an associate at R. J. Sampson's. It was a good feeling to have a desk and an office to report to once more. Real estate was her profession and it was time she got back to it. Things would be different now that she wouldn't be waiting for John's calls or planning another trip to the Midwest. She could get down to the serious business of selling. Mentally, she set her goal of making One Million Dollars, a virtual impossibility but it gave her incentive to make sales.

Her next task was to find a place to live. Margie told her about the apartment units for sale at Coral Ridge Country Club. There were a couple of units for rent there so she rented one of them. The apartment was spacious and nice. Most of the residents were older but it didn't matter, she'd be busy working. She wouldn't be socializing with "those folks." She hoped they wouldn't raise their eyebrows when she had gentlemen callers.

It was almost Christmas. The children would be having Christmas with their father again, except for Mia. She had re-entered college in Oklahoma and was having Christmas there with friends. Aries had mentally accepted the fact that she would celebrate Christmas alone. It would be another sad time without the children and without John.

One evening during the holidays she and her girlfriend, Judith, went to the Hover House for a drink. As they sat in the lounge Aries noticed a tall, lean and lanky fellow sitting at the bar. At first, he talked to Judith.

She was a red-haired Scarlet O'Hara type, fairly attractive, but excessive drinking and over-eating had rendered her somewhat obese. She was very self conscious about her weight but she never seemed to do anything about it.

For awhile, Aries listened to their conversation. The guy was a German optical salesman. Having worked for an eye doctor in college, she knew a little bit about the optical field. Having her limited knowledge of his profession, she entered into the conversation. After her intervening, the two began a chat that continued although Judith was sitting between them.

Aries didn't mean to crowd Judith out but she was enjoying talking with him. Finally, Judith had enough of their heads leaning over her.

Left out of the conversation, she excused herself to go to the powder room. While she was gone Aries slid over into her seat.

"What was your name?"

"It's Mike, Mike Weindorf."

"Oh, that's a German name. What are you doing out so near Christmas? Don't you have a wife and family at home?"

"Well, as a matter of fact I do but I'm all alone tonight. That's why I stopped off here. I have a wife but no children. She's out of town visiting relatives up north."

Aries got along well with Mike and when she decided to leave he followed her into the parking lot.

"Where are you going?" He called as she headed for her car..

"Home."

"Don't leave yet."

"It's late," answered Aries as she unlocked her car door. "I didn't mean to stay as long as I did."

"Well, let me go with you. It's lonesome at home alone, let me come to your place. We still have lots to talk about."

Aries didn't know why but she said okay. Following her to her apartment, she told him where to park his car.

Inside the apartment Mike wasted no time. Taking her into his arms he wrapped his lanky frame around her. "Let's go to bed, honey," He suggested.

"I can't, I can't. I don't even know you."

"What difference does it make? We've got chemistry together."

Aries knew he was right because she had felt that funny feeling when he kissed her.

"But you're married," she complained."

"So I am but tonight I'm yours. Let's make the best of it."

"But, I'm in love," she protested. "I'm in love with someone."

"So you're in love. Where is the lucky guy?"

"He's far away. He's married and I don't get to see him too often."

"Well, somebody needs to take care of his honey in his absence and I'm here to do just that." He smiled down at her as she stood a foot beneath him.

Aries had gotten herself into this mess. She had allowed him to come home with her. The evening was late. She was alone, too, so why not let him keep her company?

"Come on," she said taking him by the hand. "Come on, you win. Let's go to bed."

That night and the morning that followed was an experience she'd never forget. They made love not once, not twice, not three times but before Mike staggered out at noon the next day, they had made love at least a dozen times.

Mike was fantastic in bed. He told her that she had to be the best lay south of the Mason-Dixon line. Still flat on her back she vowed that she was the best north and south of the Mason Dixon line. He surely was a surprise package. What a solid twelve hours of absolutely great sex! It didn't matter anymore that he had a wife or that she was in love with John Roberts. This was a beautiful sojourn for both of them.

Still lying in bed Aries cuddled next to him. "Gracious, what are you trying to do?" Give me Christmas early?"

"I came here to give you a Merry Christmas," he said laughing. "How do you like your Merry Christmas?"

"I love it, I love it! I just can't seem to get enough of you."

"Baby, you make such great love to me. I'm going to have to see you again but now I'd better get home. My wife's gone but I've got to be there when her mother comes over to check on me."

"Yes, you do have to get out of here. I love it but I'm about to holler uncle. I need to get some rest. Why don't we call times? How long is your wife going to be away?"

"She'll be gone for a week."

"Well, would you like to come over and watch the Super Bowl play offs, Saturday? Gloria, a friend of mine, is having a party. It'll be fun."

"Sounds great! I'll call you after I get rested up."

Super Bowl Saturday came and Mike called but only to tell her that he didn't think he could make it. He would have to catch her later. Aries was disappointed but, after all, he was a married man.

A few months later Mike called her. He was going to the West Coast on business and wondered if she would like to meet him in Naples for dinner and for the night. Of course her reply was in the affirmative. She hadn't forgotten how delicious he had been in the sack.

They had a good reunion at one of Mike's special places. In bed, once more sex was excellent but Aries was determined not become emotionally involved with him. She was still terribly in love with John Roberts. Nothing was going to change that. Mike meant no more to her than a friendly port in a storm.

The next morning she thanked him for everything telling him she'd look forward to the "next time." Mike explained that his wife kept pretty close tabs on him, he couldn't get away often but when he did he would be sure to give her a call.

Aries knew he loved her in bed. He was a such a damned good fuck but she wasn't going to lose her head over it. One head lost over one married man was quite enough.

After their meeting in Naples Aries's life was consumed with real estate, except for tennis games and dates with clients and friends. She was living the hectic life of a single woman, loving them all but in love with none of them.

Finally Mike called. He wanted to come over that night. He would bring some champagne and they'd celebrate. Aries remembered what happened at their first meeting at Christmas and a repeat performance in Naples. It had been a while. Now, he was coming back to give her another Christmas in July! Indeed, this was a pleasant surprise!

Expecting him at eight that evening, she prepared a few tidbits and placed fresh daisies on the table. She knew it would be a delightful evening. It always was with Mike. He truly had a way of satisfying a woman.

Their third meeting lasted through the night until dawn. Mike fucked the hell out of her. After that session Aries never heard from him again. Maybe he died, moved or maybe he couldn't find her. She had changed her telephone number to an unlisted one but he knew where she lived. She wondered what happened to him.

Being single had its disadvantages but lack of sex wasn't one of them. She never had to do without it. A good portion of the married males in town were out chasing women and Aries managed to get her fair share of sex.

Tennis turned out to be a good sport. The courts were great hunting grounds for snaring guys who were out for exercise as well as extra circular activities. Tennis has a tendency to make a sexy man sexier and sometimes, gaping at mini skirted female tennis players with asses twisting was almost more than a normal man could stand.

As Aries thought of Jay Thomas, a tennis player she knew, she remembered her love affair with Bob Benton, another tennis player. The affair between them wrecked her happy home and eventually caused her divorce. After that she stayed off the tennis court for almost two years. Time heals all or does it?

She met Jay Thomas on the courts. He was a fair player but he was interested in more than tennis. Not long after they met, he was curious about where she lived and he was inviting himself over for a drink. Soon, they were in the sack together. Of course this was in the afternoon, after work, when his wife thought he was playing tennis with the guys.

Jay had brown hair and piercing black eyes that smiled. He was anything but tall, dark and handsome but he was trim, wiry and good in bed   Aries felt a little guilty about seeing him as she was seeing another fellow in town. Fortunately, his visits were brief as he always had to hurry home to his wife. Aries liked this arrangement. It left her free to spend some evenings with Dodge Doolittle, her new "special friend." What a nice warm, soft body he had!

One rainy afternoon she and Jay were fucking in the king sized bed in her shade drawn, darkened bedroom when there was an unexpected knock on the door. Aries grabbed her shorts and top as Jay scrambled into his trousers. They were out of breath and perspiring profusely.

Aries yelled, "Wait just a minute. With quick thinking she told Jay to get in the closet and stay there until she saw who was at the door."

Leaving Jay in hiding in the closet, she hurried to open the door. There stood Dodge and a friend of his.

"Hi, sweets. We thought we'd stop by and have a beer with you. You do have some beer, don't you?"

"I don't know," said Aries, still holding on to the door knob. "I'll have to check the refrigerator."

Dodge walked into the apartment bringing his friend, whom she had never met with him.

"Come on in the kitchen, fellows. Dodge, please see if I have any beer. If not you guys will have to go back out and get some. Excuse me a minute, I'll be right back."

Aries went back into the bedroom. Opening the closet door, she saw Jay still there crouched behind the row of dresses."

"My other friend is here and if he sees you I'm in trouble. You'll have to get out of here."

What else could Jay do but comply with her request? Tying his tennis shoes, he stumbled to his feet. "But how am I going to get out of here? It's hot as hell in this closet."

"There's a door behind these boxes that goes out into the hallway." Aries pointed to the door. Jay reached down to move the heavy boxes that blocked it.

"I've got to get back in there. Please leave quietly and close the door behind you."

"Okay," he said blushing. "I just hope I can get out of here without anybody seeing me with this big hard on," he grunted.

"Just keep your hands in your pockets and hold it down." Looking at him, she couldn't help but giggle until she almost peed in her pants. His cock was protruding and bulging terrible in those tight tennis shorts.

"Sorry baby, that we couldn't finish what we had started," Jay lamented.

"Me, too. You were fucking me great but we'll have to save it for later. Now for God's sakes, get out of here."

Closing the closet door behind her, Aries ran back into the kitchen where Dodge and Rick were making themselves at home, drinking beer and engaging in boys talk.

"Where in the hell have you been, Aries?" Dodge looked at her suspiciously.

"I'm not coming over to see you anymore if you are going to disappear as soon as I get here."

"I'm sorry. I was in the middle of something in the bedroom I had to finish."

"Yeah, I'll bet you had some guy in the bedroom that you had to let out through the closet."

"You've got to be kidding."

She had forgotten Dodge was familiar with her closet door getaway. In fact, she had let him out that way once when her daughter arrived home from college, unexpectedly.

"Get your beautiful ass over here; I want Rick to see what a gorgeous butt you have. I brought him over here with me and I told him you loved to fuck and that you would fuck us both."

Aries really had the hots for Dodge. She wasn't crazy about his big mouth but her body loved his in bed.

"No, I couldn't do that."

"Do you like to fuck me?"

"Sure, I love it."

"Well, if you want to keep on fucking me, then you'll fuck my friend too," he jested.

It was obvious that neither Dodge nor Rick were feeling any pain. They had been to the Knight's luncheon that afternoon. After the Knight's parties none of the wives saw their husbands until the next day. Dodge usually ended up at her house. He had better be kidding about her fucking his friend because she didn't like this idea at all. That wasn't fair.

"I'll call Margie to come over," she suggested. "She'll like Rick."

"What does Margie look like? Maybe I'll fuck her too," Dodge teased.

"Over my dead body you will. If she fucks you, I'll claw her eyes out. Your body belongs to me."

At this point, Rick decided to go out for more beer.

After he left Dodge wanted to get the show on the road. He had to be home by midnight. Those were orders from headquarters.

Beverly, his wife, was a very attractive brunette with penetrating dark brown eyes and smooth olive skin. A bit on the heavy side, she stood a whole head taller than Dodge. She was very jealous of Aries. Woman's intuition, she guessed. Bev looked daggers at her every time she saw her. Maybe, it was because she and Dodge were too obvious in public.

Even with his wife around, Dodge was always friendly with all of the girls, except Aries. Perhaps, it was his guilty conscience that caused him to ignore her. That made them both stick out like sore thumbs. Everybody knew they had a thing going, everybody, except his wife.

Luckily, Rick never came back and they spent the afternoon in bed, as usual, communicating the way they knew best, from the waist down.

Part Seventeen

As the weeks went by Aries was busy listing and showing property, trying to sell real estate but never knowing where her next dollar was coming from.

One Sunday, she advertised a home that she had listed in Lake Estates. That evening, at seven-thirty, a Mr Burns called on the ad. He wanted to see the house, right away. Aries called the owner, arranged it and called the prospect back. She gave him the address and told him to meet her at the property.

Before she could get out of her apartment the telephone rang, again. The caller was Stuart Arson, the lawyer, she'd met the week before at the local pub.

"Hello, this is Stuart Arson. Do you remember me?"

"Sure, I remember you. You're Carla's friend."

Stuart laughed. "Well, she's a friend but she's just a friend. I was wondering if I could come over to see you, tonight?"

"Oh, I was just on my way out the door to show a house."

"At this hour of the evening?" His voice sounded astonished.

"Unfortunately, yes. That's the kind of business I'm in. It's a lot like being a country doctor. You never know what time of the day or night they're going to call you."

"Could I come along?"

"I'm sure you don't want to go with me to show a house. You'd be bored to tears."

"I don't know about that." He seemed persistent.

"Give me the address where you're going and I'll stop by there in a few minutes."

"Well, okay, if you insist. I'll be at 4500 S.E. 35th Street. It's a white house with blue trim and it's on a culdesac. I'm driving a yellow mercedes so if you see my car parked outside you'll know I'm still there."

Aries arrived at the house and at about the same time Mr. Burns drove up with his short pimpled faced daughter.

After talking to him she learned that he owned a home on the west side of the city that he was interested in trading for a house on deep water. Well, wouldn't everybody? After inspecting the property he told Aries to draw up an offer to trade. She advised him that the Seller may not be receptive to trading. It was a new listing and there was a lot of activity on it. Furthermore, his house wasn't in the best location to induce the Seller to trade.

As they re-entered the house from the backyard where they'd been talking, the owner invited them to join her for a cocktail. Aries waited for Mr. Burns to respond. He took her up on the invitation. They were sitting in the living room having drinks and discussing the home when the front door bell rang. Polly went to the door. The visitor was Stuart Arson inquiring if Aries was there.

"Yes, she is. Would you like to come in?"

Stuart joined them. Aries thought it was a little odd for a guy she'd never been out with to meet her at a client's house. Fort Lauderdale was a strange city and not much anybody did there surprised her.

After finishing his drink Mr. Burns made an appointment to come to her office at nine o'clock the next morning to discuss the house matter further. Thanking Polly for showing the house on such short notice, Aries led Stuart back to her apartment where they sat down to get better acquainted.

"Where is your girlfriend, Carla?" she inquired.

"She's at home, I suppose," replied Stuart blushing. "You must have known the night we met that we were destined to meet again."

"I didn't know if I would see you again or not but now that you're here, tell me about yourself."

Then the long story began.

"Where do you hail from? I can tell by your accent that you aren't from Florida."

"No, I'm from the Midwest."

"Whatever brought you to Florida? Aries asked out of curiosity.

"That's a story in itself. I met this woman, Carla, at an attorney's convention. I fell instantly in love with her and left my job and my wife to follow her to Florida. Here I am. I'm separated from my wife. I've taken a new job here and I'm having problems with my girlfriend. I love her dearly but she drinks too much. When I saw you I knew we would have to meet again."

"Really. That's quite a story! What about your wife? Where is she now and what does she think of all of this?"

"Naturally, she doesn't like it." Stuart appeared perplexed as he spoke. "But there's not much that she can do about it. I'm not going back to her. She bores me."

"Did you tell her that you were leaving her for another woman?"

"No, I lied. I packed up my things and told her I was going to visit my brother in Texas but instead of going there, I came straight to Florida. I thought Carla would let me move in with her but when I got here, she declined. I've been staying in a hotel near her apartment for the last four months waiting for her to come to her senses. My wife has been threatening to come to Florida to find out what's going on but I don't think she will. She's a good woman but I left because I didn't love her."

"Why did you marry her if you didn't love her?" Aries had a look of puzzling dismay on her face.

"That was a a a mistake! I met her one night when I was drunk and I asked her to marry me. She accepted my proposal and we tied the knot before I sobered up."

"Was she your first wife?"

"No, she was my second wife. I was married to a girl named Dorothy for twenty years and we had four children."

"Hum, and what happened in that marriage?"

"I divorced her because I came home one day and caught her in bed with another man, right in my own house"

"My, my. How could she have done such a thing to you? With four children, too, that's too bad. It's a shame you couldn't have forgiven her."

"Forgive her. I forgave her with a shotgun. I got that bastard up out of my bed and told him to get out of my house and to take that hussey with him. It's just as well that I divorced her because I was getting tired of her anyway."

"Oh."

"I realized afterward that it was my fault. She was sleeping with another man because I didn't give her as much sex as she needed."

"Didn't you like sex with your wife?"

"Yes, when we were first married she was good in bed but after the children came, I got tired of her and having sex with her was more like a chore than a pleasure. I waited a year after divorcing Dorothy to even go out with a woman and then, I went out and got drunk and wound with up my second wife, Lisa. She's as dumb as an ox but I have stuck with her for eight years because I figured she didn't have sense enough to make it on her own."

Stuart was telling her his life's story. He spoke about growing up with a domineering mother and an alcoholic father. He spoke of the various jobs he had before he went into service. Later, he entered law school, became a lawyer and finally, a Judge in Kansas. In spite of all of his accomplishments Stuart had been unhappy and depressed all of his life. That is, until he met Carla and fell head over heels in love with her.

Aries listened to his sad story and sympathized with him. If he was so much in love with Carla, why was he here with her? Pretty soon, she was to find out.

"Can I stay here with you, tonight?"

"With me? We hardly know each other."

"I'm not asking you to make love to me, we don't have to do any-thing. I just want to be close to you."

"What will your girlfriend think about this?"

"She doesn't have to know. Please may I stay with you?"

Stuart begged so pathetically that Aries didn't have the heart to turn him down.

"Alright. You can spend the night if you want to but you will have to go home early in the morning because I have to go to work. I have an appointment at nine a.m."

"I promise."

The evening was late and Aries was exhausted. She prepared for bed and Stuart climbed in and lay beside her. Not long afterward he started caressing her and whispering sweet nothings in her ears. She was a little sexy but she really hadn't planned this night with Stuart.

"I know you're tired but please just let me put him in a little bit before we go to sleep," he begged.

"Now you promised to be good."

"I'm trying to be good," Stuart answered giggling, "but you're very hard to resist. I've wanted to make love to you since the first time I laid eyes on you. You must have known that first night when my leg kept getting close to yours as we sat at the piano bar."

"Yes, I noticed. You were embarrassing me. What would Carla have thought if she had seen you trying to play leggies with me?"

"She was too drunk to notice anything. Carla told you to take me, that night, and I was never so embarrassed in my life. Here I am, Aries, Carla told you to take me. Here I am. I am yours to take. Take me, please."

With those words Stuart awkwardly plunged his erected cock into her waiting vagina. After a couple of thrusts, he exploded overwhelmingly inside of her. It might have been good but he came so fast she didn't have time to tell. His excitement had been at the optimum. Stuart fell asleep and Aries lay there wondering what to think of that whole damned evening.

The next morning Stuart awakened like an adoring puppy dog. Aries served him coffee and orange juice and told him he had to leave because she had an appointment at the office.

"I'll take you to lunch," he offered.

"Aren't you working?"

"Not today. I've got a few days off and if you don't mind I'll just stay at your apartment this morning and stop by your office at noon. Maybe there's something I can help you with there."

That's just what Aries needed. Her own personal lawyer at the office. What would the other associates think of her bringing a boyfriend to work? Knowing her they wouldn't be surprised.

In the days that followed, Stuart became her constant companion leaving her side only when he had to go to work. By now, he was professing his love for her but she was trying to ignore the whole thing.

"I like you, Stuart, but I'm in love with a man in Wisconsin."

"I'm here to make you forget about the man in Wisconsin. I don't want to hear about that guy, anymore." Stuart's dander got up when ever she had mentioned John Roberts.

"Well, I don't want to hear about Carla either and you have talked about her, constantly."

"That's fair. I won't mention her if you won't mention him."

"That's a deal."

Aries was fond of Stuart in a peculiar way but she was beginning to wonder about his choice of friends.

One afternoon he invited her to accompany him on a sailing trip that he had planned with his attorney friend, Martin. When they arrived at his place, they found him sitting on the patio stoned half out of his mind. Aries asked Stuart what was wrong with him?

"Oh, he's just high on Perkodan."

"What on earth is that? Do you mean to tell me that this guy is a practicing attorney? How could he possibly hold down a job?"

Aries was shocked and astounded at what she saw. Stuart laughed telling her that Martin was one of the smartest attorneys he knew. "That guy is practically a genius," he remarked.

"He may be smart but he's not acting smart if he's taking drugs."

Aries was appalled by everything that was going on that afternoon. When they went inside, they found everybody sitting around smoking pot. They passed around the reefer offering them a hit. Aries turned it down but Stuart, gayly, joined the crowd. She wanted to go home. Stuart Arson had brought her to the wrong kind of party!

"What kind of square did you bring down here?" yelled some guy on the other side of the room.

Aries answered that question. "Square? I don't need to smoke pot. I don't smoke pot."

"Oh, come on, you'll like it, the guy retorted. Take a few puffs and then you won't be such a bore."

Stuart joined his friends in trying to convince her to take a puff off the joint. She refused, adamantly. Stuart finally gave up because he knew he wasn't about to change her mind.

The party got merrier and eventually, some of the guests disappeared into the bedroom. Stuart was trying to behave himself but it wasn't easy. After smoking that pot he was beginning to think Aries was a bore, too.

"What kind of party have you brought me to? You don't think I'm going on a sailboat ride in the ocean with this bunch, do you?" Aries said in an irritated tone of voice.

"Aw, knock it off, Aries. Martin could sail that vessel with a blind-fold on. We belong to the same sailing club and he's an expert sailor."

"And what about that child?" Aries looked at a little boy about two years old. The high as a kite guests were now passing the child around like a beachball.

"Oh, they take him sailing all the time. His grandfather's a sailor and it's in his blood. That kid loves to sail. Just wait and see."

"Well, I think this is all disgraceful and I wish you would take me home."

Soon the group had begun to reassemble and they headed for the dock where the sailboat was moored. It was getting dark.

"Isn't it too rough for going out in the ocean?" Aries complained.

"Oh, no, it's a great night," said Martin who now was coming out of his perkodan fantasy world. "Hey, Stuart, where did you find this one? Sure hope she doesn't ruin our party."

"I'm a good sailor," Aries assured him. "I've even raced in sailboats. You don't have to worry about me but I do think it's too rough for the child."

Motoring the boat from the port, they set out to sea. The weather was damned wicked and the boat was overloaded with drugged up passengers. Aries was uneasy but Stuart advised her to keep quiet and not to interfere with the captain. She vowed this would be the last time she'd go sailing with that bunch. In her opinion, Stuart had some crummy friends. That Martin was a real loser! Acceptance of Stuart's pot smoking would take some adjustment in her thinking as she had never before been exposed to such.

One evening after dinner, they discussed pot smoking. Aries told Stuart that she definitely was not going to tolerate any pot smokers in her house. She disapproved of it and she disapproved of his pot smoking friends, too. Stuart became angry and left abruptly. Weeks later, he called saying he was sorry he had become upset the last time he saw her. He missed her and he wanted to see her again.

"Let's have dinner tonight at the Raindancer and talk things over," he suggested. Aries reluctantly agreed to meet him.

"You'll find me at Jerald's at six-thirty. Everybody at the office will be going over there for a drink after work," she said.

At six o'clock sharp, Stuart came sauntering into Jerald's. Aries was sitting with the gang from her office. Stuart joined them and Aries introduced him to her friends.

"This is Stuart Arson. He's a former Judge from Kansas."

"Hello Judge," said Dodge, who was beginning to feel no pain. He must have been there since lunchtime.

The group invited them to join them next door at the Raindancer for dinner. Ben, Peggy, Dodge and his wife were all going.

"Let's go with them," said Aries. Ben's an architect and Dodge is a building contractor. Let's have dinner with them, they're my friends." Stuart agreed although he would rather they be alone. He had something on his mind but it could wait until after dinner.

Aries relished the idea of being near Dodge. Since returning from Colorado, she had become intimate with him. Although he was married, they had a special affection for one another. Dodge's body next to hers was like the missing piece of a puzzle.

Bev looked daggers at Aries at dinner. She probably resented the warm glances and smiles that Dodge was casting in her direction. If he hadn't had so much to drink he would have acted more properly.

Before the dinner was over Stuart was becoming annoyed with the attention Dodge was giving her, also. He was seated on her right at the table and Dodge had taken a seat on her left across from his wife. During the meal Dodge kept rubbing his upper leg up against hers. This touching was getting both of them sexed up but any thoughts they might have about making love would have to be forgotten.

There would be another time and another more suitable place.

After dinner Stuart and Aries went back to her apartment to talk. Stuart wanted to talk about why he had barged out of her place weeks before. He was upset about her unfair feelings about pot smokers and long haired hippies. He was sorry for his sudden departure and he wanted to renew their friendship.

"What's going on in your life, Stuart? Are you still separated from your wife?"

"Yes, I'm still separated. She followed me to Florida after all, but she's living alone on the west side of town."

" What about Carla?"

"I still have this thing for Carla but that isn't working out either. I just can't seem to work things out with her."

"What about you, Aries?"

"Me. The same old thing. I'm still in love with the fellow in Wisconsin. I have plans to fly there in a few days."

Stuart got this funny look on his face when he heard this news.

"When are you going to give that guy up?" He seemed agitated. "He's a married man and he probably intends to stay that way. Aries, I have become very fond of you. If we could spend some time together we might come to like it."

"I like you fine but John Roberts still has a big place in my heart and I'm not ready to give him up. I might as well be honest with you. You've already have a problem with two women, you don't need a third one."

"I think I've fallen in love with you," Stuart professed.

"That's ridiculous! Don't even say that. Let's just stay friends."

Stuart wanted to stay the night but Aries turned him down.

"No, not tonight. My daughter, Sara, is home for two weeks. She's out visiting with friends, right now. I picked her up at the airport this afternoon. Sara got suspended from private school because they caught her boyfriend in her room after bed check. He's from Panama and he's suspended, too. He's supposedly staying with friends here but I suspect they are planning to get together. She's only sixteen and too young to get involved like this. Maybe you could help me talk to her."

"Sure, I'll talk to her but when the love bug hits, it just has to run its course."

As Stuart was leaving, he asked, "By the way, who's watching Sara while you're in Wisconsin?"

"Nobody. Sara's old enough to watch herself but I hope she doesn't have that boy in this apartment while I'm gone."

"Relax, I'll stop in and check on her once in awhile."

"Fine, you do that. I'll tell her you're a Judge and that you're in charge of supervising her while I'm out of town. That should dissuade her from having Jorge spending the night here."

The day before leaving, Aries told Sara she had arranged for Stuart Arson, a Judge, to come by and check on her while she was away.

"I don't need him to check on me," she complained.

"Well, I'll feel better about leaving you if you have someone to call if you need help. She gave Sara Stuart's office telephone number and told her to call him if she had any problems. "He's a Judge and he's got four children of his own," Aries reminded her.

Aries hated leaving Sara but her plans were made before she was suspended. It had been awhile since she had seen John and surely she could manage alone for a few days. She gave Sara the keys to her Mercedes and that made things better alright.

"Just leave me the Mercedes and some money to spend, Mom, and I'll be fine, said Sara. Can Jorge come over to visit me while you're out of town?"

"I'd rather he wouldn't. What would people think of you having company here when your Mother's away? That boy had better get on a plane and go back to his family in Panama. His parents are going to kill him when they find out he's been suspended from school."

"He hasn't told them yet and there's no point in him spending money to go home for two weeks. It costs too much. He can stay in a hotel here cheaper. Mom, when you see him, please be nice to him."

"I'll be nice to him but I'm not pleased about some Chinaman chasing my daughter."

"Jorge is a very nice boy," Sara argued, "and he's not a Chinaman, he's Chinese."

"What's the difference? He's a Chinese Chinaman."

Sara didn't want to hear anymore. She was very touchy about the subject of Jorge. Seeing her reactions, Aries canceled any further speeches. Maybe Stuart would give those two kids some good advice.

The trip to Wisconsin was a good one. John was glad to see her after all of those months of separation. Nothing had really changed between them. His status was still married and Aries was still his love coming back for more of the same. As usual, seeing John was worth the trip. She would always love him no matter how much distance was placed between them and no matter how infrequently she saw him.

On this visit she had the feeling that many months would pass before she would see him again. She didn't know why. John was the same beautiful lover he had been before but somehow, something was different. Aries believed the difference was in her own heart. She loved him but ever since the night the stranger clued her in that he had a girlfriend in Duncan, she hadn't felt quite the same about him. He denied it all saying it was an untruthful rumor. The subject had been dropped but her trust in him had lessened.

During their months of separation, Aries had admonished herself for falling in love with a married man. There was no future in their relationship. She was tired of being the other woman in his life and she was tired of hurting every time she had to leave him. Twas' as if she were a glutton for heartache.

The days in Wisconsin passed quickly and soon she was saying another tearful "see you later."

When she arrived back home Sara told her the Judge had been over and one evening she and Jorge had dinner with him. "He was real nice to me, Mom. One day he gave me twenty dollars to spend. He must have missed you a lot. He called everyday asking if I had heard from you and wanting to know when you were coming home. How was Wisconsin and how was that football player you went up there to see?"

"Wisconsin was beautiful and my friend was beautiful, too. I had a really good time."

Stuart called the night she arrived home. They met for dinner and afterwards they had a long talk about Sara, Jorge and the events that had occurred while she was away.

"They're in love," Stuart declared. "I had dinner with them one

301

evening and they told me they wanted to get married."

"Well, I hope you told them how foolish that would be. They're both too young to marry and besides, I don't want my daughter marrying a Chinaman."

"I tried to tell them they were making a mistake but they seemed pretty determined and I don't know if they listened to me or not. I even told them they couldn't get married in the state of Florida without parental consent. Then that daughter of yours asked me which states would allow them to get married without consent. She's a smart little lady. She told me I was a Judge and I should know. I agreed to research it for her."

"Heavens, it sounds to me like you're trying to help them instead of stopping them," Aries protested.

Stuart laughed and told her not to worry about it. It would all come out in the wash.

The next day Aries asked Sara to invite Jorge for dinner.

"He'd like that Mom. He wants to get to know you."

After dinner Aries had a talk with them about their education and about them talking to Stuart about getting married. Jorge spoke up and told her it was true. They were in love and they wanted to marry.

"Marry," laughed Aries. "You are both just children. You haven't finished high school and you still have to go to college."

"We're both graduating from high school in June, Mom. Jorge wants to get married this summer after graduation. Then we can go to college together."

"You're both too young. If you do something foolish like getting married you will never finish college."

"Think about it, Mrs. Winston," Jorge pleaded "I love Sara and she loves me."

"I don't want to hear anymore about it. Sara has her education to finish and if you still love each other after that, you will have my blessings. Sara, don't let your father hear you talk this way or he'll never send you to school. You two have already gotten yourselves into enough trouble by getting suspended. You should concentrate on your studies and forget this talk of getting married. Marriage is for adults."

"Well, thanks a lot," said Sara. "Now she's calling us children.

Come on Jorge, let's get out of here. There's no point in talking to her, she will never give us her permission."

The subject was temporarily dropped. A week later Sara went back to school and Aries got back into the swing of real estate.

Part Seventeen

One Sunday Aries's friend, Frannie, mentioned a house that was just listed for sale on the beach side. "It's really priced right," she said as they were driving home from church.

"Let's ride by and take a look at it," suggested Aries. Frannie drove her to the house. It was vacant and on a lockbox. They went inside to look around. The layout was good. The part Aries liked best was the grounds. There was a large oak tree in the front yard and a huge sea grape tree stood firm and staunch in the backyard. After viewing the trees little else about the house mattered. She fell in love with the trees! That day she put a contract in on the property. The Seller countered her offer but finally, they came to terms on the price and Aries, unexpectedly, had bought another house.

She spent the summer decorating her new home. The yard was almost perfect but the house was sorely in need of tender loving care. She was adept at revamping houses and making them look warm and inviting. She was going to need a sledge hammer with this one, however, because changes needed to be made in several areas. First, she knocked down the old fashioned white brick planter in the living room. It was ugly and it dated the house. The wall between the dining room and the kitchen was the next to go.

As the decorating and remodeling progressed Aries realized it would take hours and thousands of dollars to make the house look right. Luckily, she had purchased it at the fair price. In her opinion, she had gotten one of the last good buys in the beach area. Prices on houses were rapidly rising and she could see the day that one would have to pay over one hundred thousand to get a "handyman's special" in that area.

Aries planned to fix this house up and keep it but being in the real estate business it was hard to resist the temptation to sell. There's always another one, the agents reason.

Twenty-five thousand dollars later, the renovation of the house was completed. The drab house she had purchased was lovely and if she put it on the market it would bring at least one hundred forty thousand dollars. That would be a good profit because she had paid only sixty thousand.

In the romance department there was nobody Aries loved except John but she hadn't seen him since April. Other males she associated with were no more than a diversion. The winter visitors had gone home and the local yokels were for the birds, save Dodge. At least, she could depend on him for quality sex. Lately, Dodge had done a lot to service her sexual needs. They had become "good buddies" and when she needed a warm and tender body she usually sought his. Dodge wasn't unhappy with his wife, in fact, he liked her a lot but there was enough of him to share and he enjoyed sharing it. His friends nicknamed him "Studley." Aries enjoyed him for the sexual satisfaction he gave her. He deserved an Emmy Award for a great job of accomplishing this.

Dodge stayed out on Friday nights until dawn. This made his wife as mad as as an old wet hen but this didn't stop him from following his itinerary. He belonged to Aries on Friday and she had grown to love and expect it. Every Friday was "Thank God it's fucking time." Sometimes, they jumped the gun and celebrated Friday on Wednesday afternoon, too. That was an extra bonus!

Aries looked forward to her time with Dodge. He gave her some dynamite, good loving. Their bodies were a natural blend and they made sweet music together until he turned into a pumpkin again and had to go home. She didn't love him. Love was what she had for John but with him being so far removed Dodge had entered the picture.

Margie disapproved of their relationship. She told Aries if Bev found out she would tear her eyeballs out. Who was Margie to be talking like that? Wasn't she the pot calling the kettle black? What about the affair she'd been having with a married man for eight years now?

"Dodge Doolittle's not good enough for you," Margie said.
"Why are fooling around with him?"

"Why do you think? He's good in bed! What do you want me to do waste away and shrivel up like a prune? John Roberts is a long way away. Do you think I can survive without sex?"

Margie was fighting a losing battle on this issue. They had conversations about sex before and she knew that sex to Aries was like playing tennis, she never would get enough of it.

For some reason, Margie always took it upon herself to be her mentor. Aries complained about her being too bossy but she said she was telling her these things for her own good. Sometimes, she wondered.

Aries never intended to become attached to Dodge but intimacy between two people has a way of leading to attachment. She was beginning to want him on days that didn't belong to her. This wasn't part of their original game plan. With her pleading Dodge began taking her with him on out of town business trips. They flew to the mountains of Tennessee, to the Bahama Islands and other places. He laughed about how they had fooled everybody and had gotten out of town without anybody suspecting anything. Aries laughed, too, but she felt somewhat guilty.

On one of their jaunts, Dodge put a contract to purchase in on a mountain house. "This will be a nice place for us to go," he said. "When I get back to Fort Lauderdale I'll get a couple of my buddies to buy and interest in it." Aries thought buying the mountain house was a neat idea.

Not long after, Dodge moved his contractor's office into the same building where her real estate office was situated. This wasn't such a good move. Bev was his secretary and pretty soon, she was hearing bits and pieces about what was going on around there. Aries never knew whether somebody spilled the beans or if she put the puzzle together herself but one day, Bev called her. Irate and raving, she accused Aries of sleeping with her husband. Aries remained silent throughout her outburst. Irritated, Bev warned her to keep her hands off of her husband and slammed down the receiver. She must have given Dodge the same speech because the next time she saw him, he was aloof and he seemed to be on his guard.

A few days later they met and discussed the fact that they'd been caught. Dodge didn't know how she'd found out but in the light of the situation, they decided to cool it for awhile. Bev suspended Dodge's Friday privileges and she started accompanying him when he went out of town. Everywhere she saw him, his wife was clinging onto him like a vine. Dodge was obviously back in his cage.

Their affair was halted in late fall, September tenth to be exact. The timing couldn't have been better because Mia was coming home from college in Oklahoma and Dodge's running around the house bare naked wouldn't have worked so well. He was such an exhibitionist. He enjoyed showing his body off.

Aries was happy to see Mia when she returned home. She was so beautiful and such a precious soul. Mia said she was just home for a visit, that her brain needed a rest from school.

"What are you majoring in now?" Aries inquired.

"Horticulture," she answered smiling.

"Well, that's a switch isn't it? The last time I talked to you, you were studying to be a dancing teacher."

"I've changed my mind."

That was no surprise. Mia was in the habit of changing her mind and being indecisive about things.

"What about that boy you were dating, when I was there? Are you still seeing him?"

"You mean Claus? Yes, I've still been dating him. In fact, he has asked me to marry him. He'll be graduating from college this year and he's going to be a forester."

"Are you in love with him?"

"I don't know, Mom. I guess I love him but I'm not ready to get married yet. I'll probably end up marrying him, someday. Claus is a really nice person and he's very intelligent. He reads all the time."

"That sounds pretty dull to me. You have to watch out for those book worms. Sometimes, they are living in a world of fantasy. They are passive people."

After several weeks Aries knew she wouldn't have to worry about Mia's going back to Claus. She had started dating a young fellow named Mike Jonas. Mike had dark curly hair, an infectious smile and he was always laughing. The twosome hit it off right away. He was a commercial artist and all Mia talked about was how well he could draw and paint. She had known him when she was in college in Gainsville but then, he was dating her roommate.

"I didn't pay much attention to him, Mom, but I feel different about him now," Mia confided.

Mia's affections were put to a test that fall. She received a phone call from Claus. He invited her to come to Oklahoma to accompany him on a mountain climbing trip. When Mia told her they had been scaling rocky mountain cliffs Aries was frightened for her safety.

"Don't you dare do that again," she warned. It's too dangerous. "You might fall and kill yourself."

Mia laughed and said they tied ropes to one another to break their falls and that the sport was fun. She displayed her mountain climbing boots proudly, further making her Mom uneasy.

Claus offered to send Mia a ticket for the trip to Oklahoma. She told him she would let him know if she could come. She wrestled with her emotions for a couple of days trying to decide whether she should go with Claus or stay in Fort Lauderdale with Mike, who had become her constant companion. Finally, she announced that she wasn't going to Oklahoma. Soon after, Mia and Mike started living together.

Aries's life those days was devoted to real estate and writing. She had completed and published one book of poetry and she was working on another.

Still consumed with sadness over John, Aries had nothing but her precious memories of the moments they had shared together. He had a life of his own and apparently, she was not a part of it. She missed John but she had conditioned herself, mentally, to stay away from him as long as she could bear it. Frankly, she couldn't afford a trip to Wisconsin, anyway, because after buying and remodeling the house her savings were at rock bottom.

Part Eighteen

As she sat at her desk in early October, Aries thought it was just another work filled day in her heart broken, dreary life. Little did she know that something would happen to change her humdrum world of boredom and nothingness. With no crystal ball, she couldn't foresee the accident that was going to occur that evening and the events that would follow. Fate had planned for her to meet another man from the state of Wisconsin. With this soul she would experience a deep love relationship, the most emotionally intense of her life.

That evening fate took charge of Aries life. She was enroute back to Fort Lauderdale from Hollywood where she had accompanied one of her co-workers, Jeannie, on a listing appointment. On the way home, they decided to stop off for a happy hour drink. The long hard day was over and they could relax and socialize a bit.

After the drinks, the girls headed home in separate directions. It had started raining and the continuing downpour made driving pretty hazardous. As Aries was approaching her exit from the interstate high-way the car ahead of her, driven by an elderly couple, stopped dead still. She had no choice but to slam into its rear. This made the evening a total disaster. They didn't get the listing and to make things worse she had collided with another car damaging the front of hers.

Fortunately, no one was injured in the accident but her car had to be towed in for repair. The highway patrolman who came to the scene gave her a ticket. Since she was devoid now of transportation he took her in his patrol car to the nearest Holiday Inn and dropped her off so she could get to a telephone.

Thanking the him for the ride, Aries took her briefcase, (the one with the Snobird team emblem engraved boldly on the front), and headed for the outside patio bar. She was visibly traumatized and shaken up because of the accident. She needed to calm down and regain her composure before calling Mia for a ride home.

Mentally, she began to recap the events of the evening. For a time, she was lost in thought. The waiter came up and she ordered a glass of water. Feeling sorry for herself, she rubbed her hands through her rain soaked hair. She'd been drenched in the rain for at least an hour on the highway and she was sure she looked a sight.

The fellow sitting on her right spied the emblem on her briefcase. He said, "Oh, the Wisconsin Snobirds."

"Oh, yes," she replied. "I love Wisconsin but I don't get up there much anymore."

"You don't! Well, if you won't come to Wisconsin tonight Wisconsin has come to you. Would you like a drink?"

"Oh, no. I'm drinking water. I just wrecked my car and I don't think I need anything to drink."

"Why not?" He laughed. "You're not driving! How are you going to get home?"

"I'm going to call my daughter as soon as I calm down and tell her that I've smashed the car. I really hate to bother her at this hour."

"Then don't. My brother and I will give you a ride home. My name's David Sanders and this is my brother, Tom. We're here from Madison on a business trip. We will be glad to take you home. Come on, have a drink and we'll talk."

"Very well. I'll have a Scotch and water. Thank you."

After an hour of talking and sipping they gave Aries a ride home. Thanking them for the lift and handing them her card, she promised to take them out for dinner if they came back to Fort Lauderdale again.

Those guys were perfect gentlemen. Aries was glad they didn't try to make passes at her that night because she was definitely not in the mood. She'd probably seen the last of those friendly fellows.

About a week later a call came in for her at the office. She was out showing property at the time so Grace took the message and gave it her when she came in. "Some guy from Wisconsin is in town looking for you. He wants you to call him back before five," Grace reported.

Aries remembered the name, David Sanders. He was one of the fellows who gave her a ride home the night of the accident. Back at her desk, she dialed the number on the slip. A switchboard operator answered the phone and connected her with his room.

"Hi, girl with the yellow Mercedes. Do you remember me?"

"Oh sure, sure I do. You and your brother were kind enough to give me a ride home the night I wrecked my car."

Aries wasn't certain which one of the brothers she was conversing with because she hadn't separated them as individuals in her mind at their first meeting. It didn't matter though. They were both so nice.

"How about having dinner with me tonight?" He asked.

"I'd love to but I have two clients from Canada in town and I have already promised to have dinner with them this evening."

"Bring them along."

"Really."

"Sure, the more the merrier. Where shall I pick you up?"

"I'm supposed to meet my clients at the Galt Mile for cocktails and we had planned to eat at the Down Under. Is the Galt okay?"

Sure, but you'll have to tell me how to get there from Pier 66."

"That's easy. Just follow A1A. The Galt Mile Hotel is on the right, direct oceanfront, just past the stoplight. I'll meet you in the Rathskeller Bar at seven o'clock."

"Great! It will be nice to see you again. I'll see you there."

Saying goodbye, Aries picked up the phone to make another call. This call was necessary because aside from the couple from Canada, she had a date with Dick Mason. She canceled Dick out making the excuse that she had to entertain unexpected out of town clients who had arrived.

"I'm really sorry to call so late but this is how this darn real estate business is. You never know what is going to happen next."

That matter taken care of Aries packed up her briefcase and bid good-bye to the Grace who had overheard her little white lies on the telephone. Naturally, she had to comment. "Aries, you're just too much. Do you think Dick Mason really believed your story?" Her laughing brown eyes were sparkling as she spoke.

"Well, I don't care if he believes me or not. I didn't want to go out with him anyway. This other fellow is real nice and I want to get to know him better. It's five o'clock and I'm going home."

"Have fun! Tell us all about him on Monday. I sure hope your lover in Madison doesn't hear about this fellow. Wouldn't it be funny if they knew each other? You would really be in the stew."

"So what if he does did hear about it? He has a wife. What rights does he have on me, a single woman?"

"That's right, Aries," agreed Grace. "He can't have his cake and eat it, too."

Outside, Aries stepped into the green Mustang she had borrowed from Dick Mason while her car was in the shop. She hurried home to bathe and to decide to wear on her first date with David Sanders. I'll wear the white dress trimmed in yellow lace, she thought. I look good in that. He's never seen me looking good. After all, I was drenched with rain and I'd been bawling my head off the night we met. I'm sure my makeup was all disappeared. He won't know me tonight, all cleaned up.

Seven o'clock arrived all too soon and Aries, still not dressed was rushing to get out of the house. Luckily, she lived near the Galt so she was only twenty minutes late in arriving. Being prompt never had been one of her virtues.

As she walked into the lounge the waiter recognized her and gave her a message from her friends from Canada. They would be a little late. This was good news. This would give her time to get better acquainted with David Sanders. She hoped she could recognize him.

As she headed toward the bar a clean shaven fellow dressed in a dark brown coat, tan trousers and a printed cream colored shirt turned to her smiling.

"Aries Winston. Hello, there."

"Hi, David. Sorry, I'm late."

"That's okay. I haven't been here long. Where are your other guests?"

"Oh, they called and said they would be a little late."

"Fine. That will give us time to have one drink alone. My my, Aries, you really look great!"

"Thanks, I figured you wouldn't know me for I looked so bad the night we met."

"Oh, no. You looked fine. I called you when I came back to town didn't I?"

311

"Yes. Why?"

"I called you because I wanted to see you again. I decided that the first night I met you but I couldn't tell you because my brother was with me. I'm in town alone this time and I want to get to know you better."

The conversation was going fine when Aries guests arrived to join them. They left the Galt after the introductions and headed to the Down Under to dine.

The wait to be seated there was so long that, Janet Downs, the girl from Canada became ill and asked her husband to take her back to the hotel. Aries suspected the real reason for their sudden departure from the restaurant was because the cost of the meals was too expensive. The waiter brought a menu into the lounge where they were waiting and shortly thereafter, Janet wanted to go home.

What luck! Now the twosome could dine alone. Becoming fond of David, already Aries knew she'd rather not share his company with her clients. The restaurant had a beautiful waterfront, moonlit setting. They dined by candlelight with wine amid the sounds of strumming violins. The evening was perfect! They had become cozy companions by the time they are ready to leave the establishment.

After walking back to the Galt where they had left the car, Aries invited David home with her to read some of her poetry. Frequently, she entertained her guests with her writing. Arriving, they decided the poetry could wait until another evening. Tonight they had other more pressing things to consider.

Collapsing in her king sized bed, Aries motioned for David to join her. Lights out, all was well. He held her in his arms until they awoke the next morning. Sex with David was wonderful! Somehow it was different than she had experienced before.

Although she still proclaimed to be in love with John Roberts, her feelings were becoming somewhat mixed. Both men were from the same town, both were married and Aries adored both of them. But two lovers in the same town? What if they met each other and talked? Somehow she would have to keep them apart.

David made love to her with depth and emotion. She had known him for such a short while but Aries was beginning to think she was in love with him.

The next morning after making love David turned to look at the clock that sat face down on the right hand side of the bed. "Oh, goodness, look at the time. I am late for work. I was supposed to be on the job at six-thirty to get the men started. Look what you've done to me. I'm the boss, and I am not setting a good example for the guys."

"I'm sorry."

"That's okay this time but we can't let this happen again. Young lady, in the future we'll have to get up at five so I can make love to you and still be on the job on time. They're paying me a fortune for this work and I can't afford to goof off. I have a deadline to meet with the folks who employed me. Honey, I really have to run. I'll call you this afternoon. How about dinner tonight?"

"Sure. I'll be ready on time, this time."

"Tonight we'll sleep at my place. I don't want to be late for work tomorrow. This morning I've got to go all the way back to my hotel and change into my work clothes before reporting to the construction site." David hadn't talked much about his work but he was involved in steel somehow, in big construction.

Aries, too, needed to get out of bed and get dressed for work. Reaching for her green stripped lounging coat and throwing it on her nude body, she walked David to the door.

"How do I get out of here?" He asked.

"Just go up to A1A and head South. You'll run right into the Yankee Clipper."

"Thanks, hon, I'll call you."

David backed his car out of her driveway. Aries watched him until he was out of sight. She was comfortable and happy. She had no way of knowing that this second encounter with David Sanders was the beginning of a deep love affair, one which would penetrate her thoughts for years to come.

David's big project in Florida would last until Christmas. From their first date until the job was finished they were constant companions. At his invitation Aries vacated her home and moved into the hotel to stay with him. She remained with him until the fateful day of his final departure home to the Midwest.

Every day after work, she rushed to Room 102 at the Marina Motor Inn to wait for David to come home. Sometimes he would get there first and he was usually on the phone with his office in Madison when she arrived. His wife was the secretary there and apparently, she was chief in charge. He reported in to her daily. Aries hated this but Sally was his wife and although she and David were in love, she was still first lady in his life.

Aries adored David. Often she would sit on the floor at his feet while he talked to Sally on the phone. She hugged his strong muscular legs, kissed his dirty boots and ran her hands over his rough jeans across his penis until it became hard and bulging. Responding to her caresses, it was difficult for him to keep his thoughts. While conversing with Sally he squirmed in the chair delighting over his big erection. Aries moaned softly as passion and desire mounted within her being.

While David was still on the phone she carefully unzipped his faded jeans. Placing her hand inside she captured his swollen penis, and gently stroked it driving him wild. This action quickly shortened his conversation. Grasping his fully erected and pulsating penis, tightly, she curled her soft moist lips tightly around his throbbing organ. Cum began to ooze and trickle into her mouth. Loving him, she swallowed it. Clasping her lips around the shaft, she licked and sucked it harder and harder. David slumped in his chair, writhing with delight. With face flushed he bid Sally an abrupt so long.

Phone slammed down, they quickly unclad themselves and fell upon the bed. Their excitement was intense and the love making was ecstatic. One orgasm led to another as their passion rose higher and higher.

On many nights they never made it to dinner until very late for they couldn't resist the joys of loving making and being in each other's arms. Food could wait, they could live on love. David was enough for her appetizer, her main course and her desert.

As time passed Aries was absolutely elevated into the clouds by this man from Wisconsin who had so abruptly come into her life. Over and over, she professed her love for him. "I love you, David. I am in love with you. Oh, I love you David. You're a married man but it doesn't matter to me. You're my soul mate and I love you."

Thanksgiving came and David had to fly home for the holidays. After some discussion he decided to take Aries with him.

For almost two months they had made their home in a motel room. Aries had a house five miles away. She had invited David to stay there but he declined saying it would be better if they stayed at the motel. His wife had arranged for him to stay there and he didn't want to alarm her by moving, particularly into a private home.

After Thanksgiving the trip back to Florida was a good one. They snuggled together in the airplane seats, touching and making love as much as possible without being detected by the stewardess They were sexually aroused and David had a great big hard on when the plane landed. He wondered how he was going to get off without someone observing the huge bulge in his trousers.

"Walk with your brief case in front of you. Put your raincoat on or push it down," Aries laughed.

"I can't push it down, silly. I have no control over it."

"Oh!" Aries accepted his answer, somewhat puzzled. She didn't know much about those things.

Back at the motel they finished what they had started on the plane. They were so happy to be together and so much in love that sex between them was ethereal.

The next afternoon Aries asked David about his wife's reactions at Thanksgiving.

"Was she mad because you were late?"

"No madder than an old wet hen," he answered laughing.

"Did you make love to her when you were home?"

David paused for a second and looked the other way a moment before answering that question.

"The answer is no. No, I didn't make love to her."

"Well, why didn't you? She's you wife."

"I didn't want to make love to her. She's my wife alright, but she's more like a sister to me. I haven't made love to her in several years. She just doesn't turn me on."

"That's awful. I wouldn't want to be married to someone I didn't to make love to."

"Why do you two stay married?"

"Because I have an obligation. We have two daughters."

"Oh, so you stay with her because you have two children." Aries paused. "But they're almost grown and soon, they'll be leaving and you'll be left with just your wife. Then what will you do?"

"I don't know. I've been giving strong thought to just that. I've been thinking about changing some other things in my life, too."

"What things?"

"My business for one. I don't like the partnership arrangement that I have with my brother." David went on talking about his business arrangements with his brother. He said that he was doing all the work and splitting half of the profits with his brother, Tom, who according to David, contributed very little of his time and effort to the company.

"Well, if you don't like the situation my advice to you is to get out of it. I never liked partnerships anyway," replied Aries.

"My father used to run the company but he finally turned it over to my brother and I. He doesn't like the business nor does he know much about it."

"Buy him out or dissolve the partnership and start over on your own."

"That's not as easy as it sounds but its getting to the point that I'm going to have to do something. I'm going to have a serious talk with him when I go back to Madison."

"Please, don't talk about leaving."

"I will be leaving. I'm flying out on December 24th, for the Christmas holidays. We have a week off for Christmas and I have to go home."

"I know, I know but let's don't think about it until we have to. I can't stand the thought of being away from you."

Aries counted the days they would have left together. David would be leaving in three and a half weeks. At least he would be in Fort Lauderdale for the Christmas parties. The biggest one of all would be at Paul Sherwood's. The food was good, drinks were flowing and the guests always had fun. This year, she would be in the company of the man she loved.

They accepted invitations to several Christmas parties, including Paul's but later decided they'd rather spend their time together than to attend them. Often they were so wrapped up in making love that even dinner was put on the back burner.

On Saturday mornings they slept in. Weekdays, David had to go to work early so sleeping in on Saturday was a real treat. This particular morning, they were making love with Aries on the top and David on the bottom. Suddenly, she felt herself floating weightlessly as if she had been lifted from the bed into the clouds. The feeling was one of ecstasy for David was in the clouds with her, making love.

"David, do you feel funny?" She asked.

"Yes. I feel like I'm making love to you in the clouds. The feeling is so beautiful."

"The same thing is happening to me. It's unbelievable. I've never felt like this before. We aren't even on earth. What a cherishing experience!"

At breakfast they were still talking about what happened. The experience they had was very special, almost God given. Aries felt that surely a heavenly bond must exist between them. Their love was different.

Aries loved David so much that kneeling at his feet and kissing them with his dirty boots still on, was merely a token of her extreme devotion. She loved the smell of David, too, so she asked him to leave one of his dirty shirts in her closet so she could smell him when he was away.

The spirit of Christmas was all around. A week before Christmas Aries ordered a Christmas tree for David's motel room. It would be a surprise for him when he came home from work. Standing in a crystal vase on a pedestal, the small tree was decorated with little gold boxes tied with red ribbons. She brought a sterling silver ice bucket from home, filled it with ice and chilled a bottle of fine wine. Under the tree she laid one neatly wrapped present for David, a new shirt. This would be their first Christmas, perhaps the last they would celebrate together.

David came home that evening to find the decorated tree, the wine and his present on the table.

"What's all this? He asked smiling.

"It's Christmas! This is our tree, our first Christmas tree."

David hugged and kissed her. Tears were swelling up in his soft blue eyes and they rolled down his chubby cheeks. He was crying. Aries wiped his tears away with her kisses. Overcome with emotion, he took her in his arms.

"Nobody has ever done anything like this for me before."

That night and every night until the twenty-third when he left for Wisconsin, they celebrated Christmas.

Before leaving David told Aries that he could have gone out and bought her a very expensive Christmas gift but he wanted to give her a part of himself. Being inquisitive, she begged him to tell her what her present was.

"Just wait."

"I can't wait. Tell me now."

"No, it's my surprise for you. I'll bring it to your house before I leave."

After waiting patiently, four men and a truck came to deliver her gift. Aries stood in her doorway and watched them unload it. She had never received such a gift before. David had given her the results of his blood, sweat and tears. Her present was the gear to the bascule bridge that he had spent so many weeks removing and replacing. She was touched because she knew how much finishing the job and finishing it well had meant to him.

The day he left they exchanged their last gifts. Aries gave him a book entitled <u>Come Climb My Hill.</u> A verse from it read "because you have listened to the quietude of silence in the woodland paths, you are especially invited to come climb my hill." Inside, she had inscribed, "Someday when we have nothing else to do, we'll sit and read the verses in this book. They are as beautiful as you are."

David's other gift to her was his boots, the ones he had worn everyday, the boots she had kissed at night when he came home and one of his blue work shirts. Aries loved his gifts.. He had given her a precious part of himself.

Parting at Christmas was a sad occasion. The only consolation Aries had was the fact that he would return for a time after the New

Year.

David returned to Fort Lauderdale the day after New Year's. Her love was back and Aries was joyful at the sight of him. They were in love but Aries couldn't fault him for honoring his prior commitment.

They had another beautiful two weeks together before D-day arrived. David's work assignment was completed on schedule and there was no more work to be done. He had no more reason to remain there. His wife was calling. The time had come for him to pack up his gear, take his van and go home to Wisconsin.

Aries was sad beyond words.

"Don't leave me, don't leave me," she begged. "I love you, please stay."

"I can't darling. I would like to stay but I have to go back home and run my business."

"Please let me go with you. Let me ride with you as far as I can. At least, that will give us another couple days."

David looked at her. How could he turn her down? He loved her and it was hurting him to leave.

"Okay, but it won't be much fun riding in the van."

"I don't care. At least, I'll be close to you."

It was quite a trip. All of David's tools were rattling in the back of that silver van as they traveled over the miles from Florida to Wisconsin. It was the mid January and from Georgia on the weather was bad. The roads were slick, icy and dangerous. They moved along slowly but surely. The snow covered terrain was absolutely beautiful. Awed by the beauty that surrounded her, Aries took out her pencil and pad to wrote some poems capturing the beauty she beheld.

The weather worsened as they reached Wisconsin. It was freezing cold and snowing. Despite the hazardous weather conditions, they made it through the miles and miles of ice and snow.

It was cold outside and cold inside the van. No matter what she did Aries couldn't get warm. David stopped for fuel and to clean the ice off his windshield. She went inside the service station and held her frozen fingers over the stove trying to thaw them out. Back in the van, David told her to put her hands under his armpits as he drove.

"That's the way the Eskimos keep warm," he said.

It was almost dark and they nearing the town of Madison.

"We'll stop for the night in a hotel," David remarked.

Aries was happy to hear this news. Today was his birthday. He was a January baby, a Capricorn. They celebrated his birthday that night in a restaurant in the outskirts of Madison. It was deadly cold outside so back in the hotel, they ran a tub of hot water and got in together to thaw out. It was so relaxing and making love in the tub was good, too.

Early the next morning it was all over. David drove her into the city where she would check into the Summerton Hotel and spend the night before flying back home. She asked nothing else of him. She knew his wife was expecting him.

On the way to the hotel David said he was going to drive her by John Robert's former business location. John had called during Christmas and told her that his place of business, O'Reilly's Pub, had been destroyed by fire. It apparently had been arson and the fire burned three buildings in the block. Aries told David about the fire because he was from Madison but she never would have asked him to take her there.

"I'll drive you by Roberts place because I know if I don't, I know you'll go there anyway," he said with a sad look on his face. David must have known she still had tender feelings for John. They reached the site and as John had said, "it was a disaster."

Without stopping, David drove on to the hotel and parked the van out front. Aries knew it was time for him to go. He was exhausted from driving on the trip and he had to get home. He was overdue from Fort Lauderdale as it was and he would probably have some explaining to do. The van was at a dead standstill. She didn't want to leave him but fate had given her no choice. In tears, they said their farewell.

David's words would forever ring in her ears. "I love you, Aries. I know I will see you again but I don't know where or when."

Aries saw the expression of suffering on his face. She tried to watch him drive away but the her sight was blinded by her drowning tears. David was gone from her vision.

Heartbroken after their parting, Aries wondered how he felt living with his wife, Sally, now. Surely, his memories of their four months together would haunt him. Surely, he would miss her and want her.

She felt somewhat peculiar having two loves in the same city. David had known about John from the beginning but John was spared the real truth about her relationship with David. She merely told him she'd met someone else from Madison, a real nice person.

Trying to sort out her feelings for the two, she concluded that she was in love with both of them. Mentally, she recalled the things she liked about them. John had so many brownie points in his favor but if she were picking one of them for a husband, she would have chosen David because she felt that he would be more faithful.

In February, Aries was led back to Madison. She had affiliated with a firm that was preparing to publish a guide to rentals in Broward County and she was sent there to observe the operations of a similar company in Madison. She hoped to see both David and John while there. She would feel a little guilty about sleeping with John because of David but she wouldn't like to make a trip to Wisconsin without making love to him.

Checking in at the Summerton Hotel, she called David at his office. He couldn't talk but he took her telephone number and went to a pay phone to call her back.

"I'm tied up at the office," he said when she announced that she was in town. "I'm working on a project with my brother and at the end of the day, I have to go home with my wife. I'm sorry. I won't be able to see you on this trip."

Aries was deeply disappointed for she was dying to see him. She begged him to meet her but he vowed that it was impossible for him to get away. Sadly, she had to go back home without seeing David.

Things were different with John. He could hardly wait to see her.

"Finish your work at the Apartment Guide company and call me at the lounge when you get back. I'll come over to your hotel," he said sweetly.

It had been only six weeks since Aries had made the journey to Madison with David amid the snow and bitter cold of January. John had welcomed her, then, and again without an invitation she was back and he was glad. What had happened to make him change his tune? Maybe it was because he knew she had another friend in his city.

Aries didn't know his reasons but she was delighted.

The problem she had now was that of loving two men, both of whom were married. Her relationships with them were different. David loved her. He wanted to marry her and be with her but he had a prior obligation to fulfill. John just wanted her to be his lover. He wanted to have his cake and eat it, too. Aries wanted to marry David. She wanted to be his wife but the decision would have to be his.

The months she spent with him had been, perhaps, the happiest time in her life. Their parting had been traumatic not knowing where and when they would meet again. Aries remembered his words as they said farewell. "I know I will see you again but I don't know where or when it will be."

She promised to wait for him " I'll wait for you, I love you and I'll wait for you."

For years to come David's words would come back to taunt her. Now, Aries neither had David nor John. For all the love they had shared, she was left with nothing but a broken heart and a treasure chest crammed brimming full of sad but beautiful memories.

Falling in love with David hadn't lessened her warm feelings for John but loving him had made her content to leave him where he was, to let him live his life loving her from afar. Aries knew in her heart that she would never lose him in spirit. Knowing this, somehow, made their separation easier.

David was another matter. When they parted Aries was completely devastated and destroyed. Her heart ached as it had never ached before. Her love for him simply would not go away. She spent her days and nights in sadness, in misery. Their time together had been so supreme. She had a premonition that their separation wouldn't last, that eventually he would come back to her. But when? How long must she wait?

At night, Aries sat at her desk into the wee hours listening to music and writing odes of love. One evening, she wrote on her pad these words, " How long must we touch without touching? How long must our souls float aimlessly through the atmosphere? When will our scattered souls meet and vow that all of the world is a mere triviality, except our love?" David never got that verse but this was how she felt

322

about him.

Another night she wrote, " Sing to me, O' sing to me, my adoring wandering love. Sing to me, O' blessed love who left me yet walks here still. Sing to me, O' soul mate of mine and our song together shall become a sad duet." She was utterly consumed with sadness over her physical loss of David.

Part Nineteen

One evening, she was sitting alone in the quiet when the sound of the phone ringing startled her. It was almost eleven o'clock. Who would be calling at this late hour? The caller was Stuart Arson, the Judge who she hadn't heard from in six months. The last time they talked he was trying to work things out with his wife. Aries had heard that line before from John Roberts. If he was trying to work things out with his wife, why was he calling her?

Stuart was acting like it was old home week. "What have you been doing these days?"

"Nothing, absolutely nothing but working. "Where are you?" There were sounds of music playing in the background."

"I'm at home."

"At home? You're at home with your wife and you're calling me?"

"No, I'm at home without my wife and I'm calling you."

"Oh! Why are you calling me so late?"

"What time is it?"

"It's after eleven o'clock."

"I'm sorry, I didn't know what time it was."

"What's all that noise in the background?"

"It's the stereo. I've got out some of my favorite record albums and I'm playing them. I like the music loud."

"Oh! Where is your wife?"

"She's gone, she's gone to Nevada."

"For a visit?"

"No, she's gone for good. I finally got rid of the old bag. We've filed for divorce and she has taken her things and left."

This news didn't surprise Aries much because ever since she had known him Stuart had been going in and out of the house. When she first met him he was out on the town with that blonde prostitute, Carla. After that, he stayed at her house a couple of times. What wife would put up with a husband running around on her like that?

"Are you sure your wife's really gone?"

"Of course, I'm sure. Come on down here and I'll show you our petition for divorce. I filed it myself."

"Well, I hope you did it. You are a lawyer aren't you?"

"Yes, I'm a lawyer and I'm a damned good one. By the time I got through with Lisa, she was lucky to get out of here with the clothes on her back. Come on down, I don't want to spend the night, alone. Come on down and we'll take the boat out in the morning."

"I don't know about coming down there tonight. You live in the south end of town don't you? That's pretty far."

"It'll only take you twenty minutes. I live close to the interstate and my house is easy to find." Stuart begged so pitifully that finally Aries agreed to go.

"I'll come for a little while but I can't spend the night. I'm on the floor at the office tomorrow and I have to be at work at eight-thirty."

Getting in her car, she headed for Stuart's house. He had given her the address but she couldn't find it. Disgruntled at being lost, she turned around and went back home. She was getting ready for bed when the telephone rang. It was Stuart wondering what had happened to her.

"I went there and tried to find your street but I couldn't so I came back home. It's really late now, Stuart. Let's take a rain check on tonight." He was disappointed.

A few days later Stuart invited her for cocktails, after work. That night he related the events that had led up to his final separation. He said he came home one evening, sat down in his chair and told Lisa he wanted a divorce.

"I told her I'd been married to her for ten years and for ten years I had been bored." Ten years was enough.

Stuart was an intelligent man. Aries couldn't understand why he married an uneducated woman in the first place. He said he didn't really love Lisa. He was on the rebound from Dorothy, his first wife, when he met her one night in a bar. He got real drunk and they crossed the state lines and got married the same night. He had made a horrible mistake and he lived with that mistake for years. Either Stuart was too impulsive in his actions or there was more to this story than he was telling her.

As the conversation continued, Stuart said he wanted to put his house on the market for sale.

"Does our wife agree to this?"

"Yes, we've worked out a property settlement and part of the agreement requires us to place the house on the market, sell it and divide the proceeds. I'm looking for a good real estate agent," he said laughing.

"Well," answered Aries with a grin on her face, "you just happen to be talking to one, right now."

"If you can I'd like for you to come down to the house tomorrow afternoon around five and tell me what you think the house is worth."

"Sure, I believe I can be there at five."

Aries was surprised to hear about Stuart wanting to list his house. He was just a friend. She didn't know she was going to get a listing out of this relationship.

Arriving at his house the next day she was pleased with what she saw. It was a nice house on deep water and if he would price it right, it would sell fast. She gave him a list of comparable active listings in the neighborhood as well as homes sold in his area during the last year. She advised him about pricing the property, preparing it for sale, etc. Stuart reminded her that he was a lawyer and selling houses was not his business. He would leave those details up to her.

Gee, he's easy, she thought. It's nice when you get a client who doesn't overprice his property and who doesn't give you a lot of other hassles.

After listing the house, Stuart invited her to take a ride on his boat to the local raw bar and pub.

"That sounds like fun," Aries remarked.

"Well, come on, let's get on with this venture." Swinging his back

door open, Stuart led her through the yard and down to his private
dock where his twenty-four foot Sea Wind pride and joy was docked.

"Hop aboard," he motioned after climbing in.

"Ah, this is a nice boat you've got."

"I like it. I have a lot of fun with it. As she was getting in Aries
noticed the name Lisa painted on the stern.

"I see you've named the boat after your wife."

"Yeah, I guess I'll have to take it to the boatyard and get it painted
off."

Enroute to the pub, Stuart was driving the boat like a wild man! He
was singing, drinking and gunning the hell out of it. He was taking his
new found freedom like a kid out of school. Sometimes, Aries thought
he lived too dangerously.

She was really glad to get back to the dock that evening. Stuart had
downed at least a dozen beers at the pub and she wondered if he was
in condition to drive the boat home.

"Spend the night with me," he said when they got off the boat. It
was late and Aries had had a few beers, too, so she agreed to stay. She
felt somewhat strange sleeping in Stuart and Lisa's king sized bed that
night.

The next morning when she went into the bathroom she found
Lisa's bathrobe and underwear still hanging there. Stuart had gone to
the store for donuts and orange juice for breakfast.

Seeing Lisa's garments led Aries to conduct a further investigation.
Only Stuart's clothes were in the master bedroom closet but the closet
in the bedroom on the other side of the house was full of women's
apparel. Those clothes must have been Lisa's. Some of them were
brand new with tags still hanging on them. Her sewing machine and
sewing basket were still there. The kitchen cabinets were filled with
dishes, recipe books and things that a woman who was leaving would
take. Looking in the other closets, Aries found them full. Stuart's wife
had left her clothes, her makeup and most of her possessions. Aries
was confused. Why had she left her things behind?

Moments later, Aries heard Stuart pulling his Austin Healy up in
the driveway. She would ask him about this at breakfast.

When Stuart came into the house Aries was digging around in the cabinets looking for the coffee pot. "I can't find anything in your kitchen."

"Welcome to the club. I can't find anything either. Lisa was such a sloppy housekeeper."

"Well, I can vouch for that. This place is really a mess. She didn't work did she?"

"No, she stayed home all day. Most of her time was spent sitting in that chair," he said pointing to a worn green chair in the corner of the den, "reading romance magazines." She was so dumb that we couldn't hold an intelligent conversation together."

"Did only the two of you live here?"

"It was just the two of us, except when I couldn't stand it anymore and left home. Then there was just her here."

"It certainly looks like she could have found the time to clean up her house," Aries commented.

"She was slob, a fat slob. I guess I'll have to get someone in here to get this place in order."

"I'll help you but what about all of the things she's left? Are you sure she's gone? From the looks of her closet, her things are still here. Her bathrobe and underwear are still hanging in the master bedroom and there are clothes that haven't even been worn yet, hanging in the other bedroom closet."

"She's gone," Stuart assured her. "She took what she wanted and told me to throw the rest of the stuff away."

"My, that lady sure likes to waste money." Aries looked surprised.

"Don't worry about it. We'll pack them up and give them to the Salvation Army." Stuart laughed. "There are lots of needy people out there who would appreciate them."

Aries didn't stay long at Stuart's house because as soon as they'd finished breakfast he informed her that he had promised to take his secretary and some other people fishing that morning. "I'd invite you to come along but there isn't enough room in the boat."

"That's alright, I really have to get back home, anyway."

"I'll give you a call later on this evening when I get back."

On the way home Aries was glad there wasn't room for her in the boat. She didn't relish the idea of going out into the ocean in that small boat. She would much prefer spending the day at home. During David's stay in Fort Lauderdale, she hadn't spent much time there. She had missed sitting in the sun and enjoying the mammoth sea grape tree that grew in her backyard.

Today was Saturday. Today, she would sit in the yard and forget everything except the sounds of the birds chirping and and the peace of the silence. Today would be exclusively hers.

That afternoon Aries took her notebook out and opening it, her eyes fell upon a note she had written to David on her flight home from Wisconsin. It read, "Soon I hope you will be ready to return to my life again. You know, you never really left. Our days are being spent with the two of us being in other places, doing other things, trying to forget our love. I can still feel your coming and your going, your happiness and your sadness, along with mine. Today while flying in the clouds, I find you tenderly there. If you look you'll find that I am there, too, in the clouds waiting for the sun to show me the sight of you. My heart sends you its love." David would never read these beautiful thoughts unless he returned, someday.

Darkness was setting in and Stuart hadn't called. He probably got plastered on the fishing trip and he wouldn't be good company, anyway. As she busied herself with chores around the house, the phone rang. It was tardy Stuart. He was just down the street and wanted to know if it would be alright if he stopped by.

"Okay, but you can't stay long because I've had a long day," Aries announced.

A few minutes later Stuart arrived at her front door carrying a big red fire extinguisher. "Are there any fires around here?" He asked laughing. "I'm here to put them out." As Aries had predicted he was feeling no pain.

"Where did you get that?"

"A lawyer friend of mine, Russell, stole it from an apartment building down the street. He was drunk and he played a joke on me by putting it in my car."

"Some joke that was. Get that thing out of here before the police comes and arrests me."

"Relax, nobody is coming here. I watched as I came down the

street and nobody was near. Let me leave it here for now and later, I'll take it back to the building where he got it."

"Well, I certainly hope you do. I don't think that joke was very funny. Would you like another drink?"

"Don't mind if I do."

Aries fixed two drinks. "Let's take our drinks and sit outside in the yard. It's nice out there tonight."

In the yard, Stuart spied the hammock that hung between two lower branches of the sea grape tree.

"Let's sit there. I love hammocks. I haven't been in one for years."

"I'll try but I'm not sure I know how to get in it. The children put it up and I haven't tried it yet."

After missing several times Aries managed to get into the hammock with him. They lay there watching the stars and marveling at the moonlight. It was a beautiful night.

After awhile Stuart's tongue was loose and he revealed that his secretary was his date on the boating excursion that day. He said he had a thing going for her but it wasn't working out so well.

"Oh, so you mean I'm second choice?"

"Well, aren't I second choice, too?"

"Second choice to who?"

"To that guy in Wisconsin, the one you've been going up there to see, the one you told me you were in love with last year."

"Oh, you remember that?"

"Of course, I remember that. I could have been interested in you myself but you informed me that you were taken."

Aries told Stuart she wasn't seeing that guy much anymore. She hadn't seen him for awhile and she wouldn't be going to Wisconsin much anymore. Stuart asked how she felt about him.

"I like you, you're a good friend but let's just keep it that way just now. It wouldn't be right for either one of us to fall for each other on the rebound."

"Have it your way, young lady. Friendship it will be."

"That's the way I want it. We don't know each other well enough and besides, you're not divorced yet so let's don't start getting attached to each other."

"It's a deal."

Not long after Aries learned that Stuart was going into partnership with the law firm next door to her offices. How convenient! He would be convenient whenever she needed him for a legal matter. In the real estate business there was always a need for the advice of an attorney, especially a free and friendly one. This wasn't a a bad connection to have.

After Stuart made the transition Aries saw a lot more of him. He stopped by her office everyday after work. Usually they would go across the street to the local pub for drinks and day end chatter. It was nice having an escort but his constant companionship was tying her down and preventing her from being available to other men. Stuart came to her like a puppy on a leash but she didn't fancy having a puppy, right then.

Several weeks after Stuart joined Cohen's law firm, a contract came in on his house. They went through the usual counter offers and ultimately, a deal was made. The transaction would be closing in less than thirty days. Stuart would have to vacate the premises and turn them over to the new owner. Aries offered to help him clean the house out. She wondered what he was going to do with his furniture and his wife's possessions which were still there. She wished she hadn't been so quick to volunteer for the job. She was earning a commission on the deal but helping him move was beyond the call of duty.

On Saturday, Aries dressed in her jeans and reported for work at Stuart's house. What a disaster that place was! Aside from being dirty it was as cluttered as could be. Looking at the situation, she realized it would take the entire day and part of Sunday, to clear everything out.

"What will we do with all of this stuff?" She asked Stuart.

"Throw most of it away."

"Are you going to put your furniture in storage or have you rented an unfurnished apartment?"

"Neither. I noticed that you have an empty room and space in your garage. Since you're charging me a full commission, I wondered if you'd allow me to stack my stuff up at your house until I decide what to do with it. This move has come so sudden I haven't had time to do any planning."

Surprised at his request, she could see it now. Her extra bedroom piled high with Stuart Arson's junk.

"What about you? Where are you going to stay?"

"Bill Douglas, another lawyer in my firm, says I can bunk at his house until I get settled."

It seemed like Stuart had everything arranged in his mind. Aries didn't have the nerve to tell him he couldn't bring his things to her house on a temporary basis. After all, he'd been very nice to both she and Sara.

"Well then, it's all settled. You can store your furniture in the extra room at my house and I'll make space in the garage for the things that won't fit there."

"Thanks a lot. You're a jewel."

Aries had gotten herself into this mess. At least, all she was getting was his belongings. She was surprised that he didn't ask her if he could stay there, too. She couldn't have handled that. The pangs of heartache over David's leaving were too much on her mind.

After helping Stuart move his stuff she would make it clear to him, again, that they were just friends. He was to go his separate way and she would go in a different direction. The issue of their friendship and what relationship they really had came up a few evenings later. Although Aries was sleeping with Stuart on occasion, to her it was nothing meaningful, just a diversion from the hectic life of real estate. Stuart was talking about them "going steady" but she declined.

"No, I think it's better that we both date other people."

"Fine, if that's the way you want it."

"That's the way it has to be. I don't want to get serious with any-one. I've been hurt too many times."

Soon afterward, Stuart approached her about the possibilities of him taking a room at her house. He came up with some good reasons. It was crowded at his friend's house with his wife and two children. "If you'd rent me a room I'd be mighty appreciative. Your house is convenient to my office. My rent would help you with your mortgage payment. You're alone and you shouldn't be staying alone in the house."

What he was saying was true. She didn't like staying there alone.

There had been several nights that she had heard noises outside and had been frightened.

Aries promised to give his proposition some thought and to let him know the next day. Thinking it over she decided it wasn't the fear of getting too close to Stuart that was bothering her. She believed David Sanders loved her enough to come back to her, someday. In her heart she felt that sooner or later he would return. When he did she wanted to be free and unattached. Maybe she was just living on hopes and dreams, maybe her intuition was wrong. In the interim what would be the harm in renting to Stuart? He seemed to be a lost soul these days and he needed help.

The next day she told him he could take a room at her house.

"We'll still be just friends though," she advised. him. "We both can date other people."

"No problem," Stuart retorted. "In fact, I've got a date with my secretary, tomorrow night."

"That's great. I'm busy tomorrow night, too."

Stuart moved in the next afternoon. Since his furniture was stored in the extra bedroom Aries had no room left to give him, except Marks.

When Stuart moved in he stayed just long enough to hang his things in the closet. Then he said he would see her later.

On his way out Aries handed him a key to the house and reminded him that last one in turns out the light. "See you later," she said.

The next month Aries made a momentous decision in regard to her future career in real estate. For ages her clients had been bugging her to open her own office. She wasn't a broker yet but she knew one who was interested in opening an office. Jack Moreno had talked with her about establishing a partnership. He had the license so he would be the Broker and she would own and manage the company. She had the financial ability to fund the company. Mr. Sampson, her Broker, was surprised at her decision but he wished her well and offered her his assistance if needed.

"R.J, I really didn't want to leave you," Aries said. "If you had agreed to pay me seventy percent commission I would have never left your firm."

"I couldn't pay you seventy percent. Any real estate company that pays their employees seventy percent will go bankrupt. This company has been in business for thirty years and we're still in business. You have no idea of what the overhead in this office is like. It costs us ten thousand dollars a month to open the doors. That means that somebody in here has got to be out there selling a lot of real estate. Wait until you open your office, you'll see what I mean." She never forgot the advice that Roger Sampson had given her.

Aries told Stuart she was leaving Sampson's to open a company of her own and she asked him to draw up an agreement between her and Moreno, her partner to be. Stuart gave them a three o'clock appointment. In their discussion Stuart advised them to form a corporation. Aries asked about the cost of forming one.

Stuart smiled. "Well, for your partner the cost will be sixty dollars and for you it will be dinner this Friday night. Is that a deal?"

"It's a deal," she answered with a grin. "You're nice. Thank you."

The days that followed were extremely busy ones. Aries had no idea of how much work going into business for yourself entailed. There were the preliminary legal forms to fill out, licenses to change, dues and fees to pay, advertisements, office space to acquire, phones to install, etc., etc. She thought it would never end and frankly, she didn't know what she would have done without Stuart Arson's legal assistance.

Finally, the doors of Snow & Company, Inc. were open. Aries was so proud. Soon they were hiring new associates and listing property. Their signs were beginning to pop up over the city. Not many, yet, but enough for the other real estate companies to know they now had another competitor.

Those who knew Aries knew her company would bear watching for she was tenacious when it came to selling real estate. She had had good training in her field, first at B.K. Stein, Inc. and later at R.J. Sampson & Associates. They were real pros in the business and Aries had spent seven years picking the brains of the best of them. Yes, she was tenacious and dedicated to gaining a reputation as "one of the best."

The profession of real estate wasn't easy. It was one of the most difficult jobs that she had ever had but Aries loved the challenge.

In the days that followed, she came to realize she had undertaken a major project. No longer could she gather up her briefcase and walk out the door when she damned well pleased.

If Snow & Company was going to succeed she would have to devote long hard hours in accomplishing that goal. There were green associates to train and supervise, contracts to check, books to balance and a myriad of tasks to perform. Dealing with the public and advising them on how to invest their money was a huge responsibility. Stuart was still staying at her house and he didn't seem in a hurry to make other living arrangements. They saw less of each other during the day, now, because Aries had stopped going out to lunch and she didn't have time to go for cocktails after work. She was tied up at the office, sometimes, until ten o'clock at night.

When her day was over she was tired and usually, she went straight home. Nine times out of ten, Stuart would be there reading a book and waiting for her. Those nights at home with Stuart were spent in conversation over the happenings of the day, his and hers. After conversation and cocktails, it was bedtime. Stuart had his clothes in Mark's room but most of the time he had his body in hers. They were becoming accustomed to sharing the bed. Aries hadn't planned it this way but it was mighty damned convenient not to have to go looking for sex.

Stuart was as happy as a pig in heaven. He liked her warm body next o his in the night. Sex with him was nothing to brag about. Most of the time he had premature ejaculations or he wouldn't be able to get it up at all. Aries knew there was nothing wrong with her but Stuart's problems with sex baffled her a little. She'd never been around a man whose big cock wasn't standing right straight up, high and mighty.

She asked him what was wrong and he gave her the excuse that he was having problems because he felt like she was thinking of John Roberts when she was making love to him. His assumptions were incorrect. She hadn't been mentally fucking John or David. She wasn't about to place either one of them in bed with Stuart Arson. It would be an insult. Luckily, she hadn't told him about her affair with David or he would have accused her of thinking of him, too.

A month later, Stuart came home with the idea of their taking a vacation. "I need to get away from the pressures of my new office. That damned Cohen is a slave driver and he's shoving all of his nigger work in my in basket. I've been a lawyer for twenty years and I'm not interested in cleaning up his junk."

"Why don't you tell him? Tell him you're not going to handle those kind of cases. Tell him you want something more interesting," Aries replied to his comment.

Stuart threw his head back and roared in laughter. "Tell that prick, you can't tell him anything. He's the senior partner in the firm and he thinks he's God."

Aries knew Rob Cohen and he didn't appear to be an unreasonable man. "I'm sure if you talked to him he would understand and give you more challenging assignments."

"No, I'm just a peon to that young whipper snapper. He wouldn't hear a word that I said. He's got delusions of grandeur and no old gray haired fellow like me is going to convince him of anything."

Stuart's discontentment in his new law firm was probably due to his inability to adjust. He was used to calling his own shots and now, somebody else was the boss. He was apparently not adapting to being told what to do so well. His final divorce hearing was coming up soon. He hadn't talked much about it but maybe that was knawing at him, too. Perhaps he did need a vacation.

"About that vacation? Where would we go?" Aries asked.

"Well, I thought it might be nice to drive to Tennessee to visit your relatives and to spend a few days in the mountains."

When he said that she became more interested in taking a trip. It had been a long time since she'd been to Tennessee. After Pops and Mama died she hadn't had the heart to go back home. Three of her sisters still lived in the area, one of them in Mama's house.

Aries remembered the feeling she had gotten in her gut when she was there for Mama's funeral. After the services the family went back to the house. Aries slipped away from the rest to walk through Mama's thirteen rooms by herself. She could feel Pops and Mama everywhere. They were dead and gone and she'd never be able to hug and kiss them and tell them she loved them anymore. She had a big lump in her throat as she tried to hold back the tears. Without Mama and Pops there, home would never be the same.

Years had passed and Aries had not gone back. Maybe now, with Stuart, she would go there to visit her sisters and admire the violets that grew upon the backyard hill. Yes, she would go with him back to the small town of her beginning, Marksville, Tennessee.

Destination decided she asked Stuart when he planned to go.

"I thought we'd leave Friday after work."

"Friday. Today is Wednesday. That doesn't give us much time."

"Why do you need time?"

"I've got to make arrangements at the office. I just can't walk out and leave the associates."

"Call Moreno and tell him to watch over the business while you're on vacation. He's the Broker isn't he?" blared Stuart.

"Yes, yes, he's the Broker but it's my responsibility to oversee the company. I'm the General Manager. John Moreno doesn't even know what's going on. He calls in once in awhile but he's hardly ever there."

"Huh, letting you do all the dirty work and after you've done it he walks out with half the profit. That's about it."

"I thought he would spend more time there but he hasn't."

"Partnerships are never fair," proclaimed Stuart. "That's why I always advise my clients against them. Neither one of us have had a vacation and we deserve one. Call Moreno. Tell him you're leaving Friday and tell him to get his ass over to that office and take care of it."

Aries was pensive. Even if Moreno came, he still wouldn't be abreast of their procedures nor familiar with the files. She'd better ask Linda to pinch hit for her, too. Linda was one of her most devoted associates and she was there everyday. Maybe between Moreno and Linda the place would stay afloat in her absence.

"What about your job, Stuart? Who's going to service your clients while you are gone?"

"I'll ask Harvey to take them over. He knows more about law than the rest of them do around there."

"Is it alright with Rob Cohen for you to take time off so soon after coming with his firm?"

"I'm not going to ask him. I'm going to tell him I have had an emergency and I have to be out of town for ten days."

"Ten days. Is that how long we'll be gone?"

"Yes, I figure we'll need ten days, more or less. I don't want to rush up there and rush right back. If we take ten days we can travel leisurely and take our time."

Stuart had it all planned. The only thing left for her to do was to notify the office and get packed.

"Which car should we drive?" Aries asked.

"I'll do the driving and we'll go in my car."

Aries looked out the window at Stuart's old blue Austin Healy parked in the driveway.

"Do you think that car will make it?" She inquired laughing.

Stuart grinned and vowed that old Bessy had been faithful to him. "She got me all the way here from Kansas."

Aries listened to his speech but she'd been in that car and she thought it had seen its day. "I know you love old Bessie but in my opinion you really need a new car. Why don't you trade that thing in?"

Stuart took her advice. On the afternoon of their departure he called from the Austin Healy dealership. "Come on over here, I want you to see something."

Giving Linda her last minute instructions, Aries headed for the dealership to meet him. When she arrived he was like a kid out of school.

"Come on, Aries, I want to show you something."

"What have you done?"

Just what you suggested. I have traded old Bessie in for a newer model. Look, they're bringing it out now."

Aries opened her eyes wide in time to see a spanking brand new tan Austin Healy rolling in their direction. Stuart had traded old Bessie in. The trip would be certainly be more enjoyable traveling in a new car.

"Congratulations! Now your clients will think you are a successful attorney," Aries proclaimed.

Stuart looked at her and said, "Maybe so but it's not the kind of car you drive that makes a man a success. It's the brains he has up here." He pointed to his head. "Have you ever noticed how large my head is?"

She glanced at his head covered with a wavy mass of silken salt and pepper gray hair. "Yes, now that I look at it, you do have a big head. In more ways than one your head is very big," she teased.

After the salesman turned the new car over to them Stuart told Aries to meet him back at the house.

On the drive home, she decided to stop by the office one more time to remind Linda about tomorrow's appointment with Mr. Fisk. Stuart was eager to get on the road but if she hurried she could stop there without his knowing.

The phone was ringing when she entered the office. Aries answered it. Margie was calling to see how things were going with her new company.

"Fine, but I don't have time to talk to you. I'm in a real hurry."

"What do you mean, you creep? Why don't you have time to talk to your best friend?" Margie blared.

"I'm leaving on vacation in a few minutes. I have to hurry because Stuart is on his way to meet me now."

"Where are you going and when will you be back? I never get to see you anymore?"

"We're going to Tennessee, for ten days, to see my sisters. While I'm gone, I'd appreciate it if you would help Linda if she runs into any problems over here."

"Sure, just tell her to call me. Have fun and be sure to get in touch with me when you get home. We need to go out for a drink without Stuart so we can talk. I need to get caught up on all the trouble you've gotten yourself into when I haven't been around."

"Trouble, what do you mean?"

"I know you, Aries. When I don't hear from you, you're usually out getting yourself in trouble with another man. You've gotten pretty thick with Stuart Arson, so thick that you're taking a vacation with him. From what I can see he's not your type. Knowing you, you'll probably end up marrying him and be miserable."

"Don't worry about that, we're just friends. I have no intentions of marrying him or anybody else. I'm in love with David Sanders. Margie, I see Stuart pulling up at my office and I've got to get off of this telephone. See you."

Stuart parked his car by the curb in front of the office and came in. "Huh, I caught you, Aries. I thought you were going to meet me at the house."

"I was but I had to stop by here for a minute. After I got here that damned telephone rang and I made the mistake of answering it."

"Are you ready?"

"Yes, I'm ready. Go on to the house and I'll be right there."

As Stuart walked out the door toward his car, another car was backing out of the parking space on the other side of the street. The driver wasn't looking and he backed his car right smack dab into Stuart's brand new Volkswagon. What luck! Hardly out of the store and the car had a fender bender.

"The landlord's going to have to do something about the parking around here," Aries declared as she followed him out to inspect the damages. "The parking is too damned tight."

Stuart took the dent well. He took the driver's name and address and told him he would contact him when he returned from his vacation. The dent was minor and it would be alright to wait to have it fixed, Stuart said. Aries was sorry his car got messed up. If she had gone home like she was supposed to, it wouldn't have been parked there. Maybe, he would park in a safer place the next time.

They went to the house. Stuart loaded their luggage in the car and they were ready to roll. They were getting a very late start but it didn't matter because they didn't have to be anywhere at any particular time.

On the road, Stuart was testing out his new car. It drove like a dream and he really was proud of it. They traveled to Jacksonville and there, Stuart decided to call it a day. They would get an early start the next morning.

Traveling through Georgia was a drag but finally they hit the Tennessee. Discussing their itinerary, they decided to spend a few days motoring through the mountains before surprising her sisters.

They planned to visit Angie, Fannie and Gwen, one by one.

The mountains were beautiful and Aries was delighted to learn that she didn't get bit car sick anymore. She had been plagued with that ailment in her younger years.

They checked into a motel in a quaint mountain town, then set out to check out their surroundings. Finding a country style restaurant down the road, they'd have dinner there. Darkness came early in the hills and the eating establishments closed up early, too.

As they entered, the restaurant, the aroma of Tennessee country ham was drifting from the kitchen. That was one of Aries favorites . She hadn't had any for years and definitely, she would order that. Being from Kansas, Stuart didn't know much about good Tennessee cooking. He chose mountain trout and it was delicious, too. They topped the meal off with two big pieces of pie, pecan and apple. Bellies full, they'd had a meal fit for a king. If she kept eating like that, Aries vowed she'd be as fat as a pig.

"There's something in the air up here that makes you hungry," she commented.

"There sure is. That's why all the people we see are so fat. All they do is cook and eat." Stuart replied.

In the days that followed Aries did her share of pigging it down. That mountain climate wetted her appetite.

Stuart was having a great time. He was enjoying having her away from the telephone and all to himself. In some ways he was like a spoiled child. They wandered leisurely from one mountain town to another visiting antique and curio places. Aries loved antiques. She wanted to buy some and take them back to Florida but Stuart wouldn't hear of it.

"What do you think this car is, a truck?"

"No, I know it's a car but look at that old table over there. It's just like the one Mama left Angie when she died. I'd love to have it."

Stuart protested. "We don't have room to lug that table around. You can find another one like it, another time."

"Okay, but if you don't want me to buy things, stop taking me in these places."

At night after dinner they would talk for hours about every subject under the sun. Stuart was an avid conversationalist but Aries didn't understand some of the big words he used. She was forever asking him what different words meant. "Where did you learn all those words and why don't you speak in a language people can comprehend? I'm above average but I don't understand a lot of those words."

Stuart laughed saying "those words" were normal vocabulary for him. He learned them in college when he was in law school.

"Well, I went to college, too, and I was Phi Beta Kappa but they didn't teach me any words like that. Those words must be peculiar to lawyers."

"I wish you'd refer to me as an attorney. The word lawyer is so commonplace."

"What's the difference between attorney and lawyer? I thought both words meant the same."

"Country folks call us lawyers and city folks call us attorneys-at-law. Most lawyers prefer to be known as attorneys-at-law, it's more professional. You'd rather be called a REALTOR-ASSOCIATE than a real estate agent hadn't you?"

"I don't care what they call me as long as they call me," she chuckled.

Aries enjoyed Stuart's head a lot. He was an interesting person to converse with and he seemed to have more knowledge than she did about any subject they discussed, except real estate. He was a bust there.

Stuart was a bust in bed, too. After the talking ended they had little left to do except to lay in bed and hold each other until slumber took them.

When she had her fill of Stuart's mouth, Aries wandered outside to observe the wonders of nature. A mountain stream ran behind the motel and she walked there and gazed at the pebbles in the rippling stream of cool, clear mountain water.

It rained a lot while they were in the mountains and the rain made everything seem dreary. Consumed in silent tears of loneliness in those hills, Aries missed David and wondered what he was doing now. When will he ever come back to me? She asked herself secretly.

One evening when Stuart was sleeping she pulled out pad and pen

and wrote David a letter which she would tuck away in her treasure
chest. "O', to be with you for just one brief hour. I long to touch you
and hold you once more. This day shall not pass without my pouring
all the love that has crowded my humble heart upon this printed page.
I love you. Though days have passed since I have had the sight of
you, the interval of space and time has made no matter. I cherish our
beautiful memories from the first smile, the first touch, the first
moment of true caring. My soul reaches out across the distance to
touch you, to love you, to be near you. The silent voice within my
soul calls out to yours and I know you hear."

What was she doing there with a man she didn't love? Stuart's
companionship would never soothe her sorrow. Nothing could comfort
her, nothing but the return of her love.

Aries wanted to get out of those mountains. She was tiring of
Stuart's speeches and their constant togetherness. Maybe things would
be better when they got to her sisters. Then he would have someone
else to talk to and give her a break.

A visit with her sisters was long overdue and although they walked
in without an invitation, they were welcomed.

Gwen entertained them royally with her good cooking and her
homemade pound cake. Fannie cared little for cooking but she took
them to dinner at the local country club. Being a retired Army officer's
wife, entertaining this way was more her style. Angie was out of town.
Her flock of grown up children were there watching the house and
taking care of their babies while she was gone. Aries was sorry she
missed her but you never could tell where Angie and Bradley would
be. They were rich and always traveling.

Fannie was her least favorite sister. She was always fussing about
one thing or the other. It was a pity she had taken over Mama's house.
Since then none of the sisters, except Angie and Jamie, felt comfortable about going back there.

Fannie was ugly and mean to Aries and Gwen. She was jealous of
them because when Uncle Ross died he left them some of his land and
he didn't leave her any. She shouldn't have blamed them for what
Uncle Ross did. They didn't know what was in his will and besides,
he could leave his land to anybody he wanted to. It was none of

Fannies's business.

To even up the score, Fannie moved into Mama's house and after Mama died she never left. One might say that ostensibly, she had taken over the farm. Aries was opposed to the sisters allowing Fannie and her retired Colonel husband to remain there rent free. She made Mama miserable lording over her and on her death bed forced her to change her will. She took possession of all Mama's furniture and everything. She acted like she owned the place when she knew damned well that her rightful share of Mama's house was only one-fifth. The rest of it belonged to the other four girls.

Aries had a run in with Fannie the last time she saw her. Hopefully, this time, with Stuart along Fannie would consider him company and behave herself. If there was trouble Fannie would be the one to make it because Aries intended to kill her with kindness while she was there. Mama never wanted her girls to quarrel. She wanted them to get along. No matter what nasty comments Fannie dished out, Aries was determined to maintain her cool. It seemed like Fannie just thrived on getting her goat.

Dinner at the club was tasty. Fannie was queen of the show introducing her friends to her "little sister" and showing off like a big shot to all the towns people. She took Stuart under her wing and strutted him on her arm around to all the tables. Looking like a million dollars, he was all decked out in his blue serge suit. Fannie was intent on those folks knowing that the Able family hobnobbed with doctors and lawyers, too.

Aries didn't blame her for showing Stuart off and for getting back at those people. After all, some of them had looked down on the Able family because Pops was a farmer and he walked around town in his farming clothes. Mama tried to make him dress up for those city folks but he paid her no attention. "I'm not dressing up to go to the feed store," he told her.

On Saturday afternoon, Pops would take a shower, shave and get dressed in his Sunday suit for his trip to the cafe downtown. He drank beer there with the other men on Saturday afternoon. The rest of the week, even on Sunday, Pops wore his gray work clothes.

"A man's not judged by the clothes on his back," Pops told Mama.

"He's judged by how well his soul is dressed." Mama couldn't argue with that statement. She knew he was right.

Fannie invited them to spend the night. Aries told Stuart that she wanted to sleep in Mama's house. Stuart would have preferred staying in a motel but to please her he agreed.

Fannie gave them Mama's room and everything seemed to be fine. The next morning, Aries went into the kitchen to see if she could help fix breakfast. While she was in the kitchen Fannie went into the room where they had slept the night before. Stuart was in the bathroom shaving. Fannie came back into the kitchen yelling at Aries.

"You're the same lazy girl you used to be. You come up here from Florida and spend the night at somebody's house and you don't even have the manners to make your own bed. Who do you think I am your chambermaid?"

"I'm sorry. I was going to make the bed up after breakfast."

"Well," replied Fannie smirking, "you should have made your bed before you left your room. I have trouble with arthritis and it hurts my back to make beds."

"I didn't expect you to make my bed. I've only been out of it a few minutes and I was going to straighten the room up after we finished dressing."

"You're a slob and you're lazy, you always have been," Fannie shouted.

Stuart was in the bathroom on the other side of the kitchen and he was hearing all of this. What Stuart heard he apparently didn't like because he came storming out of the bathroom with the towel in his hand and, verbally, tore into Fannie like a lion.

"I won't tolerate your talking to your sister like that. The nerve of you humiliating her because the bed hasn't been made. Thank you for your lack of hospitality. We leaving here. Aries, get your things, we're leaving here right now."

Aries knew that Stuart meant what he was saying. He was red-faced, boiling mad and ready to explode. They gathered up their things and without saying good-bye, they drove away.

"We'll check into a motel and then we'll go to your sister, Gwen's, house for while," Stuart said. "I wasn't about to let you stay there and put up with that hussey's verbal abuse."

"I warned you how she was. We're just lucky we made it through dinner last night without her attacking me about something."

"Well, she's not going to attack you with me around." Stuart spoke emphatically.

After checking into the only motel in town they drove over to Gwen's house. Gwen was cut from a different mold than Fannie and they would feel more comfortable there. Aries told Gwen about what happened before breakfast at Fannie's. That didn't surprise her, at all.

"That's nothing. You should see how she treats me, my husband and my children. I end up in tears every time I go up there. She starts out being nice to you, then, she turns into an entirely different person-ality, one that's not very nice.'

"It's a shame, it's a shame that none of us can go home anymore in peace," Aries remarked.

"The only one she's nice to is Angie," Gwen went on. "She's rude to Jamie, too."

"Really. I thought she got along okay with her."

"She's on and off with her. Fannie's still mad at her for eating her ice cream cone when she was a child."

Aries didn't know what Fannie's problem was but she wished she wouldn't take her hostilities on her. All she had wanted to do was to go home again and browse around to refresh her memories of her childhood years there. She would always have ill feelings toward Fannie for depriving her of that nostalgia.

The next morning they left Gwen's and headed back to Florida. Since they had a couple days of their vacation left, they would travel, leisurely. Aries had heard the potential for real estate business was good around Melbourne and New Smyrna Beach. She wanted to stop there and take a look. Stuart was in no hurry to get back to his job, in fact, he dreaded it so he didn't mind tarrying.

South Florida was getting so congested and infiltrated with South Americans and New York Jews. Once peaceful Fort Lauderdale was quickly becoming a little Miami and Aries was looking, in the future, to escape the madhouse of South Florida.

They arrived in New Smyrna Beach and liked it. It was beautiful virgin territory ready to be tapped. The town was quaint and the beaches still were protected by massive clusters of palmettos bushes. The beachside was dotted with simple wood frame cottages.

As they drove along the coastline, they decided to stop, get some chicken and have a picnic on the beach.

Sitting on the beach, Aries had a good feeling inside. "I like this place," she said. "I like this place very much, so much that I've got a notion to go back to Fort Lauderdale, rent out the house, pack up my things and move here."

Stuart thought she was just talking but she meant every word she was saying.

"But what about your company?"

"My company can go where I go."

"You've barely gotten started in Fort Lauderdale."

"So what, if I'm good there, I'll be good anywhere else I go."

Aries recalled her real estate experience in Wisconsin. As a new-comer she hung her tag with a commercial real estate company and soon, she listed a property on Highway 90 for a million dollars. Everybody wondered why Mr. Dill, the richest man in town, would give the listing to a virtual stranger to the area. Aries knew why. She got it because she was good.

"In six months," she told Stuart, "Snow & Company can be one of the largest real estate companies in this town. Let's buy a newspaper. I want to check on apartments for rent. I want to talk to a REALTOR here about finding a space for a real estate office in the beach area."

"You're really serious about moving to New Smyrna aren't you?"

"Yes, I'm serious and when I make up my mind to do something, it doesn't take me long to do it."

"Impulsive, huh?"

"Call it what you like. I'm impulsive but I know this is a good area. I have wanted to get out of the rat race of Fort Lauderdale for years and I believe now is the time for me to make a move.

Aries was dead serious about making the move. Her friends and business associates were surprised when they heard she planned to leave town. She had resided in Fort Lauderdale for twenty-eight years.

Margie hated to see her go but she couldn't talk her out of it.

"You'll be back. Go ahead up there and get it out of your system. I'll hold the fort here until you return."

"Don't keep your fingers crossed waiting for to me."

Nothing had been said about Stuart's going with her. She expected him to find another place to live and stay in Fort Lauderdale. He had a new job with a well known law firm and if he wanted to he could make a fortune there.

Aries rented her house out for six months. The week before she was due to leave, Stuart made a shocking decision. He was going to quit Cohen's law firm and accompany her to New Smyrna Beach. He wasn't happy working with Rob Cohen so he would open up a private law practice there. "If you're going to be a pioneer I might as well be one, too," he said.

Aries warned him that she didn't want to be responsible for his leaving Fort Lauderdale. "You like this place and you have a good opportunity here. I can't see any reason for you to give that up."

Stuart insisted that he was planning to leave the firm, anyway, because he and Cohen just couldn't see eye to eye. There was nothing she could do to change his mind.

Aries had a week to finalize things in her Fort Lauderdale office before leaving. She discussed her business with Stuart and he advised her to buy Moreno's shares out so she would own the company. After negotiating with him Moreno settled for a thousand dollars for his shares and one-half of the net profit from the deals yet to close. He would transfer his listings to his other company. All of the details were worked out. Most of the money that had been invested was hers so Moreno had made a profit rather than a loss.

Aries was at the office, alone, late one day when the telephone rang. The caller was David Sanders. It had been almost four months since she'd talked to him and his call certainly took her by surprise.

"Where are you?" she cried. "Are you here?"

"No, I'm in my office in Wisconsin. Everyone has gone for the day and I'm here alone."

"So am I."

"Good, now we can talk."

During their conversation Aries professed her deep love for him and told him how she was suffering because they were apart. His words would forever ring in her ears. He said that after he got home he decided he couldn't keep on seeing her being married to another woman. He felt an obligation to his wife and children but he loved her and he couldn't handle the situation.

"I've received an offer to work in Saudi, Arabia for five years and I'm thinking seriously about taking it," he revealed.

"Oh, please, please. Please don't go to Saudi, Arabia. Then, I'll never get to see you." Aries was sobbing over the telephone.

"Don't tell me not to go because if you do I will."

He wanted her to know he loved her and missed her but that he could make no plans to be with her.

"I'll probably take that job in Saudi. When I get back you will probably have half of the state of Florida sold."

"Please, please don't leave. Please let me know before you do anything drastic like that."

Aries was so upset with David's news that she forgot to tell him she was moving her real estate office to New Smyrna Beach. When she got settled there she would let him know where she was, somehow. She had told him she'd opened her own company.

After hanging up the phone she tried to retrace their conversation. She'd been so flustered when they were talking. What did he say? He wouldn't see her because he was married. He still loved her but he couldn't handle things and he was threatening to go to Saudi Arabia for five years.

Visibly shaken, she dreaded going home and facing Stuart in this condition. She couldn't tell him that David had called. He was jealous of her as it was and there was no point in throwing her lover in his face.

When she arrived home Stuart had some news for her. His final divorce hearing had been rescheduled for the next day and if things went according to plan he would be a free man.

"Will your wife be at the hearing?"

"No, no, she'll stay in Nevada. She won't be there. We've already settled everything. The hearing is merely a formality. Her appearance won't be necessary. Bill Douglas is going in with me as a witness to my six months residency in Florida and as soon as the Judge signs the papers, I'll be as free as a bird."

"If that's what you want let me offer my congratulations."

"Well, I certainly want to get this thing over with. There's no point in staying married to a woman I don't love."

"You're right about that," she responded thinking of David Sanders.

"By the way, you had a call from a man a few minutes ago. I told him you were probably at the office," Stuart said with a suspicious look on his face.

"Who called?" She asked curiously.

"I don't know. Probably that dude from Wisconsin. It sounded like a long distance call."

Oh dear, she hoped the caller wasn't David. He didn't have the new office number so maybe he called the house before he called the office, she told herself silently.

"Who did you tell the caller you were?"

"Don't worry. I'm smart enough not to get you in trouble with your men. I told him I was an associate of yours, that I had just stopped by your house to pick up some information on a property. I gave him your office number while I was at it."

"Well, thank you. I don't know who called. I've been at the office all afternoon and I've received no long distance calls."

"Maybe, I was mistaken, then."

That night, Aries received another phone call and this time, the caller was John Roberts. She was sitting in the living room talking to Stuart when the call came in. She cupped her hand over the receiver and asked Stuart to leave the room so she could have some privacy. He obliged but he had a funny look on his face when he got up out of the chair to leave.

Aries couldn't believe she was hearing from both John and David in the same day. John was calling just to see how she was and what was going on in her life these days. She didn't mention Stuart but she told him that she was renting house out and moving to New Smyrna Beach to open a real estate company there. They chatted for a long time. The conversation on her side was somewhat stilted because

349

Stuart had left the bedroom door open and she assumed he was eaves-
dropping on them.

After hanging up the phone she called Stuart to come back in.

"Thanks a hell of a lot," he yelled as he was coming down the hallway. "I suppose you're going to tell me that wasn't a long distance
call, either." He remarked cattily.

"As a matter of fact it was. It was John Roberts calling from
Wisconsin."

"I hope you told him you are going steady and not to call here anymore."

"I certainly didn't. I told him no such thing. He's is a friend of
mine and he can call here anytime he wants."

"If that's the case you won't mind if Carla calls me."

Stuart knew he was hitting a sore spot when he made this remark.
Aries was jealous of Carla because she knew Stuart had been in love
with her and for all she knew he still was.

"Sure, let her call. I don't own you but remember, you're still a
married man."

"Only until tomorrow, dear."

Stuart was further infuriated when John Roberts called back a few
nights later. This time he was calling to warn Aries she could expect a
phone call from his wife, Ava, and that she might say some things
about her that he didn't mean..

"Why? Why would Ava call me? What are you talking about"

John explained that Ava had discovered their affair as a result of
the fire that destroyed his business. His private office had been
enclosed in steel and it survived the fire. Ava trampled through the
charred, smoke damaged building into his office where she pulled up
the bulging carpet and found evidence of Aries.

"She found the nude pictures, love letters, your books, gifts and all
of the things that you had given me through the years. Things that I
have cherished."

Aries understood that statement because once she had asked John
what he did with all the things she gave him. He said he kept them
under the carpet in his office---that he was never going to throw away
a thing that she gave him. "His stash was so thick under the carpet,"

he said, "that he could hardly walk on it."

Aries knew where John kept her but she never expected Ava to find her. Fate must have planned it way.

John didn't tell her what Ava might say that he didn't mean but Aries found out the following day. She received a call from Ava that afternoon at her office. Ava let into her with both barrels loaded. She yelled at Aries and accused her of blackmailing John with the nude pictures of them together. She said that Aries had forced him to have sex with her for five years. Right! John Roberts sure had come up with a stupid, false excuse for his actions.

Aries was taken aback in disbelief when she heard that one. Impulsively, her response was, "Listen, lady, how dare you call me and accuse me of that. I wouldn't harm a hair on John Robert's head."

Upon hearing this statement Ava went into another screaming rage. "Do you want him? Do you want him?" If she had read her books and letters to John she would have known that answer.

"No, I don't want him," Aries was quick to reply. That was a big lie. She would always want John Roberts, she was in love with him but for his protection she would try to soothe Ava.

Ava's call was a real shocker. What would happen to John as a result of Ava's discovering their affair? Ava would either divorce him or never let him out of her sight, again. Aries expected the latter to occur.

Aries took the next day off from work to finish packing for the move to New Smyrna Beach. Linda had volunteered to come over and help. Stuart was moving his furniture to storage because the tenant would need the extra bedroom. She had rented the house furnished so all she had to do was to get her personal belongings out.

Stuart gave up his position in Cohen's law firm. He was making the move with her. They'd been living together for three and a half months now, with few problems. In a way it would be nice to have a lawyer around to solve her legal problems.

Around five o'clock Stuart came home. Bouncing in the front door he grabbed Aries up, feet off the floor, and started kissing her. "I love you and now I'm free and I can ask you." Stuart proclaimed.

"Ask me what?"

"Ask you to marry me." Stuart smiled and continued sheepishly.. "Will you marry me?"

Shocked, Aries could have dropped her teeth. She didn't know what to say. When he turned her loose she stood back and looked at him. My! My! He was serious, he really meant it.

She had to drum up an answer. "Stuart, I like you a lot and I think you're great but marry you--- Don't you think this is rather sudden?"

"No, I think my timing is perfect. We're going to a new town, new jobs and we might as well start out with a new life, together."

"It all sounds good but I think we should just keep on living together for awhile. I can't, I can't get married now. I've got a new office to open and associates to hire. You'll be busy, too. Let's keep marriage on the back burner for now."

Stuart was disappointed with her answer but if that was the way she wanted it he would table the matter for awhile.

A few days later, they headed for New Smyrna Beach. On the way out of town Aries asked Stuart about Rob Cohen's reaction when he gave his notice.

"What notice?" He asked laughing. "That bird will get my notice when the next dummy he hires gets to the bottom of my in basket. That's where my letter of resignation is, on the bottom of all of the other trash he piled up on me."

Stuart's way of leaving wasn't very professional. If he ever needed a letter of recommendation he certainly wouldn't get it from the Rob Cohen's law firm. It was Stuart's business but she would have handled things differently. In her opinion, it was better not to burn bridges behind you for you may need to walk over them again.

Life in New Smyrna was a new experience. People were different there. The local residents known as "rednecks" didn't take to well to "city slickers" coming in and trying to take over their town.

After being there for awhile she met a broker who had moved there from Fort Lauderdale about five years before. Still, they had not accepted him in their narrow-minded local Board of Realtors. They tried to blackball Aries but with all of their searching they couldn't find any reason to keep her out. They prevented her from joining the Board from June to November, pretending to be investigating her.

The real estate folks in town didn't like the competition t her firm was giving them and they showed it by being rather uncooperative. Nevertheless, Aries held her ground firmly. She was a competitor and she was there to stay.

She published an Apartment Guide for the area. They desperately needed one there. She had established the first one in Broward County, previously. The publication was distributed free and the only real estate advertisement in the book was that of Snow & Company. Even the post office allowed her to leave copies for distribution on their mail counter.

Within several months, Snow & Company had ten associates, a secretary and a bookkeeper. Business was good. Finally, Aries took the broker's test, passed it and became the Broker. She was proud of her accomplishments.

Stuart had opened his law office a couple of doors down from her office in the same strip center. It wasn't easy for him to get his law practice established. Aries blamed it on the fact that he sat there and read novels when he didn't have anything else to do. He could have drummed up more business if he had been out getting acquainted with the towns people.

She hadn't realized it but Stuart was somewhat of a loner. He lacked motivation, drive and ambition. The better acquainted she got with him, the more she learned about him. He was a passive person who seemed to dwell more in passive activities, like reading, than being active in the real world. The good thing about this passivity was that when he was reading, he wasn't arguing with her.

They had rented a furnished apartment at a reasonable price on the beach. It was there that Stuart found his greatest pleasure and there that Aries found her greatest sadness. During the week she was so busy at the office that she rarely had time to sit alone and think. On weekends and in the evenings, she would sit on the beach and watch the waves wash onto shore. It was there that she found David in her moments of silence. She wrote in her diary one day.

"Your footprints are in the sand. Your name is written upon the crest of the rushing waves that roll onto the shore, coming to wash away the traces of your path. O' my love, I can hear your call. I can see your footprints etched clearly in the firm white sand and I run quickly to place my footprints next to yours."

It was a sad summer for Aries. Stuart was her constant companion but his company could not extinguish the fire that burned in her heart for David. Nothing could cure the pain she carried within, nothing except his return. She had mailed a brochure about New Smyrna Beach to his office. Enclosed was an accompanying promotional letter which bore her signature at the bottom as broker.

Maybe, he had tried to call her in Fort Lauderdale. Her telephone number there had been disconnected. She had the calls referred for awhile but eventually stopped the service because the phone company was charging her an additional fee. Perhaps he left a message at R.J. Sampsom's and the secretary hadn't given it to her.

Three months passed and Aries heard nothing from David. Maybe, he didn't get her letter. Maybe, his wife opened the mail and thinking it was an advertisement, discarded it. What if he had gone to Saudi Arabia, after all? Aries searched for an answer but she couldn't find one.

One day she even went to a psychic. The psychic saw him but she told Aries she didn't see him with a wife.

"Well, he's got one."

"I can't see her but I can tell you that this man will be coming back to you."

Aries hoped and prayed that the psychic was right. Stuart kept on begging her to marry him but hoping for David's return, she put him off. "Let's wait awhile," was her answer.

"Wait, all I have been doing is waiting," Stuart complained. "What are we waiting for?" Aries dared not tell him she was waiting for David Saunders to clear up his life and come back to her.

Summer was over and fall was in the air. Stuart was constantly pressuring her to make a decision. His mother was coming to visit and it would be ideal if they could be married while she was there. His brother could come to the wedding, also, because his mother was to visit him in Georgia, first, and he planned to fly her in his private plane to visit Stuart.

"Let's plan the wedding for the end of October so my family can attend. Mother would like that." Stuart pleaded.

Aries was about to give up hope of David's ever returning for despite her prayers, she hadn't heard a word from him. Still, something bothered her. What if she married Stuart and what if David came back, later? What would she do then? If David called she wouldn't tell him about the marriage. She knew what she would do. She would leave Stuart and flee swiftly to his side.

Stuart wasn't going to be put off much longer. He wanted her answer and he wanted it in time to tell his family about the wedding before they came. Margie was right. She had gotten herself in another mess. She never should have let Stuart move in with her and she shouldn't have allowed him to move to New Smyrna. She was glad Margie wasn't there to chastise her.

Aside being in love with another man, she faced with another problem. Stuart had a virtual inability to maintain an erection. Whenever they attempted sex, his penis hung there about two inches long and as soft as it could be.

Aries wondered what was wrong with him. When questioned he made make all kind of excuses from John Roberts to the fact that she was postponing their marriage. He would be alright after the wedding but her delaying things was causing him extreme anxiety. Stuart went to the doctor and came home with a prescription for tranquilizers. Then, it was the medicine that prevented him from getting a hard on.

With all of the good sex she'd had in her life, why was she even considering marriage to man who was apparently impotent? Annoyed and frustrated with the situation, she threatened to to pack up and leave.

"I can't live like this," she told Stuart.

The very mention of her leaving put him on the edge of violence and he scared the shit out of her. "It's all your fault," he stormed. "If you would marry me, everything would be alright. Everything would be fine. Your procrastination is driving me crazy. What is it with you? Do you have another man?" Stuart came at her like he was going to hit her but he backed away before he wielded a blow. After his outburst he acted hurt, very hurt, and made her feel terrible.

"Marry me, marry me," Stuart cried. If you loved me, you would marry me."

Marry him thought Aries. If I had any sense I would get the hell out of his sight. She couldn't believe a grown up man was behaving like this. They had a way of making up after their stormy bouts and continuing for another day. Surely, tomorrow things would be better.

One night in one of their discussions, Stuart drew up an agreement which he asked her to sign. The agreement was to the effect that she would never leave him. What made him think such an agreement would be binding and valid? She signed it just to please him.

The time was nearing for Stuart's Mother to arrive and no date had been set for their wedding. "Let's set the date, Aries. That way my brother can be my best man and his wife can be your maid of honor. Mother is eighty years old and she would be thrilled if she could attend our wedding. You know, I'm the apple of her eye."

Aries had never met Stuart's folks but she had heard a lot about them. He was from a well educated upper class family. His father had been involved with International Harvester or some kind of heavy machinery equipment company.

Finally, Aries succumbed to Stuart's pleading and agreed to set the date. She was good at making mistakes but this was probably the biggest fopaw she had made in her life.

Stuart called his Mother to break the news. They would be married on July 19th, the weekend she and his brother planned to visit. Aries talked briefly with her on the phone. She told Aries that Stuart was a wonderful, thoughtful son.

Stuart took charge of making all the arrangements for the wedding. All Aries had to do was to pick out her dress.

The next day, Aries had second thoughts about agreeing to marry Stuart. She must have been crazy. They hadn't been getting along well, at all. They fought half of the time. Did she expect things would be better if they were married? Stuart said they would. Maybe he was right.

The days went by and soon, the big day day arrived. It was her wedding day and still, she hadn't planned her dress. The wedding was scheduled for five-thirty in the afternoon. At lunchtime, Aries asked Polly to take her calls for the rest of the afternoon. Going to the local department store, she purchased a simple cream and peach two pieced outfit. Under normal circumstances, she wouldn't have been caught dead that garb but in New Smyrna Beach, it didn't matter. They rarely dressed up there.

None of their children were attending her wedding. Aries's kids were busy and Stuart's were all out of state. After the ceremony they would travel to Tampa. Sara arranged a wedding supper for them at a fine restaurant. Stuart's family would vacation at the beach in their apartment while they were away.

Aries finished shopping at three but she still had to go home, hem her dress and get dressed for the wedding. If she didn't hurry she was going to be late but that would be par for the course.

It took a little rushing but she arrived almost in time. Everybody was there waiting for her to appear. Stuart introduced her to the preacher and shortly thereafter, the ceremony began. It didn't take long for her to ruin her life and become Mrs. Stuart Arson.

After the vows were spoken, Stuart's brother set about to a round of picture taking. Punch was served and the wedding cake cut. Aries hadn't invited anyone from the office. She told them it was strictly a family affair.

When the wedding was over Aries excused herself to call in to the office for her messages. "There was nothing important," Polly said. "Some man came in to see you but I told him that you were quite busy this afternoon, getting married."

"Really, who was he?"

"He didn't leave his name. He was a good looking man and he got a real funny look on his face when I told him about your wedding."

"Hum, thought Aries. I wonder who that was. I've got to go now, Polly, but the next time someone comes in, be sure to get their name and telephone number."

A few days after her marriage, Aries happened to be in Sanford. Harry, a friend of David's lived there. Maybe he had heard from David so she would give him a ring. Going to a pay phone she dropped her money in and dialed his number. A woman answered.

"May I please speak to Harry?"

"Just a minute. I'll get him."

When Harry came to the phone, Aries identified herself as a friend of David's who was just passing through.

"Have you heard from him?"

"Yes, as a matter of fact I have. He just left. He was in my office two days ago but he's gone back to Wisconsin. He seemed upset about something and he said he couldn't stay, he had to get back home."

Aries hung up the phone. Now the picture was very clear. The man who came into her office on her wedding day was David Saunders. Polly told him she was busy getting married. David had come back after her but he had been too late. The psychic was right. What would she do now? David had returned and he had been given the untimely news of her marriage, simultaneously, with his arrival. He must have been devastated.

Aries was crushed. Why couldn't she have believed the words of the psychic and why couldn't she have been more patient and waited for him. She told him she would wait and she had broken her promise. What had she done to David? She must call him and tell him she had made a grave error and that it was he she loved, not Stuart Arson. She prayed that David would forgive her.

Before her marriage she had made an entry in her diary that read, "I have gone to live with an understanding companion who will try to soothe my shattered heart and comfort me in my sorrow. I shall plod through my wilderness as you plod through yours and await the mending of our hearts and the eternal joining of our souls, o'soul mate of mine.

In her writing, she was giving up hope of seeing David Saunders. again in this life. She was telling him she loved him but she needed a companion in his absence. She had to get in touch with him and explain what happened and why. Consumed with deep sorrow, she knew that David was hurt, so very hurt. A a bride of only two days, she had to find a time away from Stuart to call him, in private. Stuart Arson would kill her if he got wind of her calling another man.

Aries waited until the time was right. One day Stuart went to Daytona Beach to a court hearing and she was at home alone. She dialed David's number reversing the charges to her office phone. A female voice answered. This frightened her a little but she couldn't worry about that now. When David came on the line Aries asked him who answered the phone?

"That was my daughter."

Realizing the caller was Aries, he excused himself to close his office door and came back to the phone.

"Why are you calling?"

"I'm calling because I want to talk to you. I love you and I need to talk to you."

David's words to her were brief and definite sounding. " I don't want to talk to you."

"Why not?" She pleaded.

"Because I choose not to." He clicked the telephone receiver down.

Aries called him right back but his daughter told the operator that he was in conference. She would take a message but Aries left none. Hanging up the phone, Aries was engulfed in sadness. She went out to the beach and sitting in the sands of loneliness with tears streaming down the page she wrote, "The sound of constant wind, the flow of tears down palored cheeks; for naught."

For days, Aries called David, person to person. He took the calls but when he heard her voice, he hung up the receiver. She got the message. He was hurt, very hurt and he never intended to speak to her again. She had lost him. Wracking her brain, she tried to figure out how to dissolve the stone wall of silence that her marriage had caused David to construct between them. She would never get over his silence and in her heart she vowed that someday, somehow she would experience a happy reunion with her wandering soul mate.

Otherwise, she had a new company to build and a new marriage to consider. She would give the marriage a try but her heart was broken. If only she hadn't married Stuart Arson, if only she had waited for David to return. Mama had told her never to cry over spilled milk but deep inside she was crying.

Being a new bride, she should have been happy but she wasn't. Her marriage to Stuart was nothing but turmoil. Things didn't get any better in sexual department after their marriage and it became clearly evident that he was suffering from impotency. A real problem existed.

Frustrated about his condition, Stuart exhibited explosive behavior, at times. Aries was caught in a bad situation. She felt sorry for him but not half as sorry as she did for herself for having to survive without sex. Whoever said that women can do without it was a liar. Sex is a biological necessity for people.

The situation wasn't improving so Aries begged Stuart to make an appointment with a doctor, a preacher, a sex therapist or anybody who might be able to help him get over his problem.

"You can help me," he argued. "This is not my problem. It's our problem. There's no point in my going to see anybody unless you go, too."

"Fine, I'll go with you. I'll do anything to get this matter resolved."

She was glad he had agreed to bring a third party into the issue. She needed somebody's help. They decided to see a preacher about the problems in their marriage.

There were more problems than one, of course, because when the cock doesn't work in a relationship, there's not much else that works well either. In any relationship that survives you need head, heart, hand and ass. If any of these are lacking, then eventually the relationship will disintegrate. A person's needs are important and when they are consistently not met, WATCH OUT!

Before going to the preacher for counseling, Aries searched for clues that might assist him in his understanding of their situation. She remembered the conversation she'd had with Stuart's mother in their apartment after the wedding on the day she was leaving.

"Stuart told me that he didn't like sex," his mother related.

Aries wished he had said that to her before they were married. If she had known, she wouldn't have married him and she wouldn't be faced with all of this impotency shit.

Maybe he liked men instead of women. The idea of Stuart's being queer had crossed her mind a couple of times, particularly, the Sunday afternoon after their wedding when he was trying his best to perform. Finally, Aries got on top and fucked him the best she could with her imagination. His penis was soft and mushy but she could feel the head of it in the opening of her vagina. Anything at that point was better than nothing. She was trying to have an orgasm by rubbing her clitoris against his hairy personals. Stuart was on the bottom and getting very excited, wiggling and giggling. He was acting like a silly girl, not a man. This was disgusting. She was used to being the fuckee not the fuckor.

Stuart's violent behavior was becoming very tiresome. His days with her were numbered if this was the kind of relationship they were going to have. She hoped the preacher could shed some light on the situation. During the visit, the preacher talked about love and sex in a marriage. He told them they would need to come back for further counseling sessions.

Aries felt better when she left. At least, she had had a sounding board. Stuart left in worse shape than he was when he came. He was furious with the preacher and after they left he told her they wouldn't go back to see that phony.

"Didn't you see him eyeing you and mentally undressing you while we were talking?"

"No, I didn't see him do anything wrong."

"Well, I did," shouted Stuart. "He was undressing you right there in front of me. He wanted to fuck you himself."

"Stuart, you're talking ridiculous." Aries was dismayed. "That preacher had no intentions towards me. The poor man was only trying to help us." Unable to convince him of the preacher's innocence, Aries just shook her head. Stuart declared emphatically that he was finished talking to that man.

"Fine, we'll look in the phone book and find someone else who specializes in marital sex counseling." Stuart was ready to forget the whole thing but she was determined not to let this sleeping dog lie.

The next week they went to a female sex counselor. After the conference the woman gave them a book to take home and read. Part of the program she wanted them to follow was to be intimate, to lie in bed and touch without going all the way. She suggested they heat some baby oil and rub each other down with it. "You touch him for fifteen minutes anywhere you want to and then let him touch you for fifteen minutes," the therapist told them. "Do this for seven days but don't attempt sex."

To please Stuart, Aries agreed to try the program, though all she

361

needed was another week with no sex. That hot oil was nice, it turned her on but she hated the idea of touching and feeling with nothing ever happening. The treatment didn't help Stuart much, anyway. His cock just laid there all soft and mushy. Aries was humiliated.

Finally, the seven days was over and Stuart tried to fuck her. The only way he could get his penis into her vagina was to cram it there and after that, she still had to use her imagination to achieve an orgasm. This program wasn't working and Aries was becoming more disgusted day by day. Stuart would lie beside her masturbating while he twiddled her nipple with his left hand. The situation was so down right sickening, it made her want to vomit.

After Thanksgiving, Stuart decided to give up his law practice in New Smyrna Beach and return to Fort Lauderdale. He would go back to the firm he was affiliated with before he had gone with Cohen. Aries, secretly pleased, didn't try to sway him from leaving. She understood why he wanted to go back. He didn't have much of a law practice there and he was running low on funds to support his office. Due to his financial condition, she had been delving into her own kitty to pay the rent and the utilities for their apartment. He needed to do something to increase his earnings.

Stuart's returning to his old job would mean that her business would be two hundred fifty miles away from his. She'd spent the last six months getting started there and she wasn't about to throw in the towel and start all over. Aries encouraged him to go back to Fort Lauderdale. He could live in the house (the tenants lease was about to expire) and she'd keep the apartment there and come home on week-ends.

Stuart pitched a fit about going back without her.

Aries objected vehemently. "What did you expect me to do, give up my business? I've worked too hard and I'm not closing my office now."

"It's not going to work with you here and me there," he warned adamantly.

Aries listened to his objections but finally got him to agree to try it. What a relief it would be with two hundred fifty miles distance between them. With him out of her hair she could devote more time to her business and maybe, if she was lucky, get some decent sex, too.

Stuart departed for Fort Lauderdale and moved back into the house, as planned. Aries thought this arrangement would be a good one but she was wrong. Weekdays were peaceful and calm but on weekends he made her miserable by arguing and complaining about her never being there. He continually badgered her and accused her of sleeping with other men in his absence. What he didn't know was that she hadn't but it definitely was on her agenda. She would rectify this matter the first chance she had.

That opportunity came a few weeks later. She met a friendly real estate broker there who was happy to service her needs. Aries never developed an attachment for him but his night time visits to her beach-front apartment certainly took the lid off and made her sleep better.

Stuart never let up complaining and his constant storming at her long distance only served to aggravate her. She was glad she was away from him. Finally, he demanded that she close her office and move back to Fort Lauderdale. He didn't trust her out of his sight. "Our marriage won't last with you there and me by myself here," he stated.

"Hey, you're the one who wanted to move back."

The discussions continued until finally, Stuart won. She agreed to give up the apartment on the beach and move back to Fort Lauderdale. The real estate office in New Smyrna would remain open, though. She would get Ned Driscoll to manage the office and she'd commute about three times a week to check on things.

Stuart disagreed with this plan. "You can't run a company that far away. You ought to just close the damned thing."

"Let me try it," she insisted. The subject was dropped and Stuart seemed temporarily pacified knowing that, at least, she would be sleeping with him again.

Commuting three times a week over five hundred miles a day proved to be a real drag. To get there by ten a.m. she had to leave home at five o'clock in the morning. The drive back at five p.m. put her back in Fort lauderdale at ten o'clock at night or later. The driving was excessive and she was literally burning the rubber off her tires.

For awhile, she tried flying but the cost was prohibitive and it necessitated her renting a car for transportation after she got there. As much as she hated to admit it, she couldn't run a company that far away. Stuart was right.

Aries had a decision to make. Either she would have to divorce Stuart and stay in New Smyrna Beach with her business or she would have to close it. Traveling was becoming too much of a hassle. Stuart objected to her real estate business. He was making good money in his law practice and he wanted her to close the office, stay home and not work anymore. Since her break up with Greg Winston, Aries hadn't seen the day she didn't have to work. If he was serious she'd love to take him up on that offer.

Closing the New Smyrna Beach office and saying good bye to her faithful employees was a task she didn't relish. Snow & Company closed and it was a sad day for everybody, except Stuart.

That year, they were in Fort Lauderdale for Christmas. It was an unhappy one. Coming back to Stuart on a full time basis didn't solve their problems and Aries was beginning to doubt if anything could. He was such an obnoxious, overbearing, insecure disaster of a man. On Christmas Day, he stayed in bed most of the day, moping and reluctant to join in the festivities. When he did come out he had a long sour look on his puss. His company was boring and he was no fun to be around. Aries wished he could be more pleasant.

Stuart ruined her New Year's, too. They had been invited to a gala affair at R. J. Sampson's house. He got real drunk at the party and on the way home, he accused Aries of flirting with men. He commenced slapping and beating her about the face and head. They weren't far from home when this happened. At a stop light she flung the car door open on the passenger side, made her escape and started running away from him. Stuart he halted the car, jumped out, and ran after her. He grabbed her and snatched the gold necklace off of her neck.

Terrified, Aries screamed for help. The sound of her screams prompted him to hurry back to the car. He took off in the direction of home. A police car approached and Aries flagged it down. The officer drove her home. He rang the front doorbell and Stuart answered the door in his blue robe. He appeared as calm as a cucumber in the officer's presence. When confronted, he told the officer they had an argued and Aries jumped out of the car. He denied hitting her and he denied tearing her necklace off.

"My wife is imagining things, officer, and if she's hurt she must have done it herself."

Aries face was scratched and bleeding where he had attacked her. "Officer, he's telling a lie. He's lying about everything. Do you think I would want to hurt myself and do you think I'd be on the streets at this hour if I hadn't had to flee from his violence?"

Stuart just stood there laughing. The officer asked her what she wanted to do.

"I won't stay here with him. Let me get some things and ask him," she said pointing to Stuart, "to give me my car keys. I'll spend the night with a friend."

The officer waited while Aries gathered up some clothing. Then, he escorted her out of the house and waited in the yard until she was safely out of the driveway. He told her she could come down to the station the next morning and file a complaint against her husband. She advised the officer she intended to do that.

She drove to Margie's house. She hated waking her at one-thirty in the morning but it was better than staying at home with a maniac. At least, she'd be safe there. Margie was shocked when she saw her standing at the door with her face all scratched up. "Come in," she said standing back from the doorway. "What on earth has happened to you? You look like you've been in a lion's den."

"I have." Aries was crying. "Stuart attacked me like an angry lion on the way home from R J Sampson's party. He started slapping me and beating me in the car while he was driving over the Intracoastal bridge. I jumped out when he stopped the car at the stop light but he caught up with me. He grabbed me, tore my gold necklaces off and took my car and drove away."

"What was wrong with him?"

"He was drunk and insanely jealous. He accused me of flirting with men at the party."

"Well, knowing you, you probably were but that's no excuse for that creep to lay a hand on you. That guy must be nuts and if he comes here I'll shoot his eyeballs out." Margie wasn't serious. She had a gun and she knew how to shoot it but she wasn't about to shoot anybody. If Stuart came over there she would use that soft, sweet touch on him.

The next day Aries waited until Stuart's car was gone before she went home. As she was entering the house the telephone was ringing. Answering, Stuart was calling.

"What do you want?" asked Aries sharply.

"I know you're upset and you have a right to be. I was totally out of line last night. I'm sorry, I'm really sorry. I was drunk out of my mind and I don't know what came over me."

"You can't handle your liquor and when a person can't handle it, he shouldn't drink."

"You're right. I'll stop drinking."

"You're going to have to do something because I'm not going to live with you like this."

Stuart kept his word about quitting and for the next few weeks he stayed off the sauce. He started taking Lithium. Aries asked him why? He said the doctor prescribed it to keep him calm when he was going through his divorce. He had stopped taking it but since he wasn't drinking, he thought he needed to get back on it for awhile

"Besides," he said laughing, "I've been yelling at my boss at the office, recently, and he suggested I might need something to calm my nerves."

When Aries got to work she called a pharmacist and asked about the drug, Lithium.

"It's a drug they use for chemical imbalance in the brain. It's normally used in the treatment of manic depression," the pharmacist said.

"Manic depression. What does that mean?"

"It's a form of mental illness. Perhaps you should consult your husband's doctor about his."

"I will. Thank you."

Aries was beginning to fit some pieces of Stuart's puzzle together. She recalled a conversation she had with him not long after they met. Stuart had this funny look on his face and Aries had asked him what was wrong?

"I'm depressed. Sometimes, I get depressed," was his answer.

Aries hadn't thought much about it at the time. Why should she? Everybody gets depressed now and then. What Stuart had neglected to tell her was that he was a manic depressive. Stuart's doctor didn't return her call so Aries called Tom, an internist friend, to ask about manic depression.

"My goodness, didn't you know the guy was manic depressive before you married him?" Tom inquired.

"No, I didn't. He told me he got depressed, sometimes, but I didn't find out about his illness until he brought home a bottle of Lithium."

"Well, you'd better read up on that subject so you'll know what you're dealing with. For God's sake, keep him on the Lithium and don't let him drink liquor. Manic depression can be controlled with medication but without it, you'll have real problems with him."

This was all she needed to hear. Stuart's impotency was bad enough but now, she had to face another reality. The man she had married was suffering from a mental illness.

After talking to Tom she confronted Stuart asking him if he had ever been diagnosed as a manic depressive. He said, "yes." When he was in the service some doctor gave him that diagnosis. He went on to say he only suffered minimally from the illness. Minimally, hell. When this guy went off his pills and on the booze he had the potential of becoming dangerously violent. Stuart liked himself much better manic and out of control. These were his high periods and during these times, Aries had to take drastic actions to assure her own safety from the insanities of her husband.

She had learned not to expect sex from Stuart. If she needed sex, she certainly wouldn't look for it at home. The plan for her not to work anymore turned out to be a farce, too. If she lived on what Stuart made, she'd be wearing rags and eating beans.

Seeing the handwriting on the wall, Aries took up office space, beach side, and for the third time, re-opened Snow & Company. Oddly, starting over again was becoming old hat to her. Luckily, she had stored the office furniture and equipment so re-opening, this time was less of a hassle.

On St. Patrick's Day, Margie invited Aries to go out with her. "Leave that jerk at home so we can have some fun," she said.

Stuart had rightfully gained the reputation in town of being a party bore. Often Aries went out without him on the pretense that she was going to a business meeting. Frequently, the meeting place got changed to another location and she conveniently forgot to notify Stuart so she could relax without his barging in and embarrassing her. He behaved so badly in the presence of others that Aries avoided his accompanying her, socially. Stuart complained bitterly about always being left at home.

Aries accepted Margie's invitation. She loved the Irish and before Stuart, she had always dressed up "wearing the green" and gone out to celebrate. Her Mama was half Irish and she was proud to be part Irish, too. Certainly, she wasn't about to take a damned dull Frenchman to an Irish party. Her sisters, Angie and Jamie, were in town so Aries would invite him to have dinner with them. Afterward, she'd send him home with the excuse that she wanted to spend some time with her sisters. He'll buy that, she reasoned. Aries told Jamie the plan and she agreed to go along with the plot.

"Poor Stuart, I feel sorry for him. It's a shame he cuts up so badly that nobody wants to be around him. He just puts such a damper on things. He'd kill you if he knew what your plans really were tonight," she chuckled.

"What he doesn't know won't hurt him," Aries assured her. She felt bad about leaving him at home on St. Patrick's day, too, but she was damned annoyed at the dull existence she led with him.

Escaping from Stuart after dinner, Aries met Margie at the Irish Inn and what an evening that turned out to be! All night, they moved from party to party hoping to meet somebody interesting. Around midnight, they stopped by the Sandbar for one last drink before going home. Two fellows sat down at the bar beside them. Suddenly, one of them reached across in front of Margie and took Aries's hand. There was an instant passion between them. Chemistry was flying. It was love, instant love for the night.

The fellow was Hank Cox, a local attorney. Aries didn't tell him she was married to one. At that moment, all they wanted was to make love. Hank went out to the lobby and checked into the hotel. Margie and her new bearded friend were still talking at the bar. Aries told

Margie she was leaving, that she was in love, tonight. She would catch up with her in the morning. It was a lucky for Margie that they had taken two cars!

Barely in the room Hank told Aries he wanted her and he wanted her, badly. Happy St. Patrick's day! He was obviously younger than she was but age didn't matter. In bed their bodies blended perfectly. They made love over and over until dawn. What beautiful passion, such warmth and feeling! Everything about him felt and tasted good. Both fully satiated, Hank gave her one last hug and said he had to run or else he would have to appear in Court at eight a.m. in the same clothes he had worn yesterday.

"Stay here and get some more sleep, honey," he whispered.

"I believe I will." Quietly, he slipped out closing the door gently behind him.

Thank goodness Stuart had left for work when she arrived home. She knew he would be angry because she didn't come home. She'd tell him she sat up half the night talking to Jamie and falling asleep there. Jamie would vouch for her.

After that night Aries didn't hear from Hank for weeks. Then one day he called.

"Hi, sexy," he said cheerfully. "How's about taking off with me this weekend? My wife's going out of town and I thought we could slip away to Vero Beach on Saturday and spend a night or so."

"I'd love too."

"Great! I can't wait to get you in my arms again and to make love to you until I explode inside of your tight juicy pussy. I'll call you before we leave to confirm everything."

That week, Aries hinted to Stuart that she was thinking about taking a short vacation from the high pressured job that she lived and breathed.

Friday morning, Hank called. The plans were still on. "I'll meet you at your office on Saturday at two," he said.

Aries announced that she and Margie were going to Vero Beach on business on Saturday and they might stay overnight. "Maybe we'll just check in to a hotel to get some rest and get away from the real estate business for awhile," she said.

"That's perfectly ridiculous,"complained Stuart. "You can get some rest at home. You don't need to stay in a hotel where you can go to a bar, suck on whiskey and have men fondle you. You just want to get away from me."

He was right about that.

Unfortunately, Hank called back at lunchtime and cancelled. He had been called into a hearing on Monday and he wouldn't be able to get away, after all. Too bad! Stuart was happy when he heard her plans had changed.

Sleeping with Hank Cox reminded Aries of all the good sex she was missing and the sacrifices she was making by staying married to Stuart. It bothered her to walk under the guise of a marriage while actually she was in a marital bed without the amenities of marital sex. That night with Hank sparked her sexually again and made her more discontent with her situation. From now on she intended to find sex when she needed it. Stuart Arson didn't deserve her loyalty.

In April, Aries made an appointment with a psychic. Stuart accompanied her although he didn't believe in them. This didn't surprise her. He didn't believe in God either. Stuart was an Atheist. No wonder he was such a miserable creature. Aries efforts to help him along these lines were to no avail.

Arriving at the physic's place of business, the psychic left Stuart in the waiting room. She took her into her private reading room and commenced the session. Reverend Mizell, the psychic, was good. She had been written up in newspapers and even the police department solicited her help in solving crimes.

During the reading she told Aries she was sorry to tell her but she was going to have to divorce her husband. "He's not for you, honey," Mizell advised her.

"But I've only been married for a short time," Aries complained.

"I know but you must leave him. If you don't you everything you have will be devastated. Start taking your possessions out of the house and putting them in storage bit by bit so he won't notice it. Then, when he's not there take the big stuff and yourself and get away from him. Don't let him know where you are living. He's not the man for you. You've made a mistake and you have to rectify it."

Aries didn't need a psychic to tell her she had made a mistake. As much as she wished for her marriage to be a good one, it wasn't.

She asked Reverend Mizell about the possibilities of David Saunders coming back.

"You've passed that time and you can't go back. This news was no shock because he had not responded to her since her marriage to Stuart.

After Stuart went back to Fort Lauderdale, Aries heard a rumor that David was working on a bridge job in Jacksonville, Florida. She called the company he had been working for and they verified it. He had been working there but the job was completed. He'd flown back to Wisconsin for the weekend but he would be returning to pick up his van. It was still parked over near the loading dock.

Aries drove to the site in Jacksonville and she found David's silver van. She tied his boots securely to the door handle and slipped a note inside one of them. In the note, she professed her love for him and said she needed to see the man who had given her the boots. Aries hoped he would remember their deep love. David never responded. Losing him was one of the greatest sorrows in her life.

Aries hoped Stuart couldn't hear what Reverend Mizell was saying about him.

She asked if she saw her moving, anywhere. She couldn't see her moving out of Florida.

"You may a move to the Central Florida area, honey, but I don't see you moving out of state."

"What about John Roberts?"

"I see him in a uniform."

Well, the only uniform Aries could think of him ever wearing was his football uniform. To her knowledge he was never in the service.

"Have you ever though of what it would be like married to him?"

"Yes, as a matter of fact, I have and I'm afraid I wouldn't like it. He's too much of a ladies man."

"He's selfish, honey, and he has a lot of growing up to do. There's another man coming for you when you get your mess cleared up. I see a man about forty-nine years old graying at the temples. He wants to help you and to do nice things for you. He's your real mate but he won't come for you until you are out of this marriage. He works in or around an airport. I don't know whether he flies a plane or not but I do know he works very near an airport. You'll be living near the place where he works."

Aries wondered who the psychic was talking about. Session ended, Reverend Mizell escorted her into the waiting room where Stuart was waiting. Aries hoped the walls between those two rooms had been sound proof. The psychic apologized and told Stuart she wouldn't have time to give him a reading.

On the way home, Stuart inquired about what the psychic told her.

"Nothing, really, nothing that I didn't already know,"

"I don't believe in psychics, anyway," Stuart declared. It's a waste of money going to one."

"I guess you're right. I did it for fun but I won't go anymore."

Fortunately, the subject was dropped.

In mid-April, the situation with Stuart worsened. His outbursts of violence were frequent and unpredictable. Drinking usually trigged them. Aries pleaded with him to stop drinking. He would go on the wagon for a couple of days but then start right back drinking.

One Saturday afternoon, Bill Renault called. Bill, a new real estate licensee, was was interested in placing his license with Snow & Company. He wanted to set up an appoint for an interview. Stuart was watching television when the call came. Aries agreed to meet him at her office in fifteen minutes. He was a friend of her son, Gregory, and she had known him since he was a child..

Stuart overheard her conversation and when she hung up the phone, he jumped up off the couch and started yelling. "You're not going to that office this afternoon," he shouted in an upset tone of voice.

"Alright, I won't go," she replied not wanting to start an argument. "I'll stay here."

Getting his way, Stuart calmed down and sat back down on the couch.

Bill had called from his car phone and Aries didn't know how to get in touch with him to cancel the appointment. The office was closed so she couldn't leave a message for him there either. She was just flat standing him up.

Soon, a car pulled up in the driveway. Bill had found her house. Stuart answered the door and let him in.

It had been years since Aries had seen Bill. When he was a child he used to spend the night with Gregory and eat a dozen eggs for breakfast the next morning. It was nice to see him. He had grown up to be a fine young man..

They sat down at the kitchen table to chat. Stuart left his position on the sofa and joined them. Aries discussed the profession of real estate and related the policies, procedures, rules and commission split of Snow & Company. Later, Bill departed promising to be in her office on Monday morning to hang his tag.

After he left Aries went into the kitchen to finish preparing dinner. Tonight, she was making her specialties, southern fried chicken, and homemade sour cream fudge cake. The chicken was in the pan frying, the cake was baking in the oven. Aries stood at the stove stirring the hot fudge frosting for the cake.

Stuart came into the kitchen, poured himself a drink and went back into the living room. A few minutes later he came back for another drink. Aries made some comment about Bill coming to work at her office and Stuart exploded. He started accusing her of making eyes at Bill and hiring him because he was young and good looking. Such ridiculous accusations appalled her. She was like a Mother to that boy.

Stuart didn't stop with accusations. He went into a wild rage and picking up a heavy wooden chair from the table, he lunged it toward her. Aries ducked and he slammed the chair against the refrigerator making big dents in it's door. He had her blocked in the kitchen. Putting the chair down, he swung at her with his fist doubled up. She ducked and missed his blow. He swiped the hot pan of fried chicken and the boiling frosting from stove burners onto the floor. Luckily, Aries escaped being badly burned by the hot chicken grease and the frosting. Stuart cracked the chair over the kitchen table.

Seeing saw a hole for escape, Aries fled to neighbors house. No time to ring the bell, she ran through the front door. That maniac, she was sure, was right behind her. She ran past the living room into the bathroom, locked the door and started screaming. "Tricia, Tricia, call the police."

Tricia was outside on her patio entertaining guests but she heard her screams and came running. Trembling, terrified and embarrassed, Aries explained what had happened. She begged Tricia to call the police.

The police responded right away and the officer accompanied Aries home. Stuart came to the door and told him that everything was fine there. He didn't don't know what his wife was so upset about. The officer wanted to come in and look at the broken chair and the mess in the kitchen but Stuart advised him he was an attorney and that Statute such and such required a search warrant. The officer didn't press the issue.

He advised Aries not to stay there that night. "You should stay with a friend. Don't come back here. We've had reports on him before. If I were you I'd get rid of him. I can't believe he's a lawyer acting like that."

Once more, Aries stayed the night with Margie. She was becoming accustomed to having to flee for safety.

The next morning she went back home accompanied by her daughter, Mia. The sight was unbelievable. It was like the Vietnam War had gone through there. There were pieces of shattered glass strewn throughout, bashed in walls, broken furniture, a total path of destruction. All of her possessions had been destroyed. Stuart Arson had destroyed everything, except his possessions. The psychic had predicted this would happen. She had warned her to get her things out of her house or they would be devastated. She should have listened to the psychic. Her tears were flowing profusely for nothing could restore the possessions she had lost.

Stuart had made a fatal error this time. Aries went straight to an attorney to file for divorce. After that, she called a locksmith to change the locks on the doors. Lastly, she called Stuart at work to advise him she had filed for divorce and he would have to make other living arrangements.

A few days later Stuart appeared at the house accompanied by Martin, his perkodan taking attorney friend. He was there to retrieve his belongings. It was odd that all of her possessions were destroyed but his were still intact and untouched.

A few weeks later, Aries sold the house that she had put so much of her love and labor into making nice. She wasn't happy there, anymore, after the trauma Stuart had created within its walls. She'd miss the sea grape tree but the time had come for her to move, away from the house and away from the horrid memories of Stuart's violence. His mere presence there had left it tainted.

Aries showed the house to a prospective buyer, one day. The man must have had super sensory perceptions because he trembled when he was inside. Leaving, he told her he wouldn't be interested in that property because he could feel violence there. Aries didn't tell him but he had hit the nail on the head.

A short time later she bought an oceanfront villa in a private and secluded complex where, hopefully, she'd be safe from Stuart. For awhile the new residence was her secret but news travels and soon everybody, including Stuart, knew.

A few weeks later Aries had to make a trip up to north to transfer her son, Mark, from a school in Princeton, New Jersey to another one in Hartford Conn. She flew to Princeton, rented a car and drove to the hotel where she had reservations. The drive was a pleasant one. Princeton was a small, lazy town clothed in July green. It was peaceful and quiet. Checking into the hotel, she called Mark. He couldn't leave school until the next day so she would be left to her own devices that evening.

Aries looked forward to her out of town jaunts. She liked traveling into the world of the unknown. After freshening up from the trip she went to the lounge to listen to the music and have a couple drinks. Tomorrow, after Mark had been delivered to the new school safely, she would fly on to Baltimore to meet Keith Kiser, her old college love. He was expecting her. Theirs was one of these same time next year, once in awhile, relationships.

As Aries entered the lounge she looked down the row of barstools and summed up the crowd. There was a bald headed guy wearing a grey suit and a pair of horned rimmed glasses seated at the end of the bar. On his right, sat a dark haired young fellow casually dressed in a

Mover's Van tee shirt. The youth's deep brown eyes were drowsed from the beers he had obviously been drinking. As she took a seat on his left, Aries noticed a handsome fellow standing midway in the room. He sat down alone at a nearby table.

Aries commenced talking to the bald-headed man about writing and real estate investments. The man seated at the table could over-hear their conversation A few minutes later, he eased himself over to the bar, extended his hand and interrupted her as she spoke.

"My name is Timothy Holt. Would you mind sitting with me at my table for a moment? I heard you talking about Florida real estate and I control several major investments there. I'd like to chat with you and get your professional opinion on my portfolio."

Excusing herself from the conversation she was involved in, Aries moved over to his table. As they sipped on cocktails they talked about property and investments. It appeared that he was a man of means and he did have investments in Florida indeed. Deeply engrossed in con-versation and enjoying each other's company, the two hardly noticed that the lounge was closing. The bartender flicked the lights signaling it was time to go. The last of the patrons, they exited out into the lobby, still conversing.

"Where are you staying and how long will you be in Princeton?" Timothy Holt inquired.

"I'll just be here, tonight. I'm leaving early in the morning for Hartford with my son who's transferring to a school there.

"Come home with me. Come on, let's go to my house for a swim."

"Oh no, it's too late. I have to get up early in the morning and I don't want to go out, tonight."

"Come on. You can spend the night at my house."

"Oh, really! What about your wife?" She knew a good looking hunk like that had to have one.

"There is nothing to worry about. My wife's out of town for a week. No one is at home, except me."

"Really! Thanks for the invitation but I just paid fifty dollars for a room here and I'm going to sleep in it."

"Okay. Then, let's go swimming here."

"Well, that will be rather impossible." Aries laughed. "I didn't bring my bathing suit and besides I don't want to get wet at this hour. It is really late and I'm tired."

"May I stay with you?"

"Whatever you like, stay here if you like," Aries yawned. "Here's the key. Let's find the room."

Entering the room and feeling no pain, they undressed and fell upon the bed. Soon, they were contemplating making love.

"Wait a minute, I've got to go to the little girl's room," Aries announced drowsily. "Just stay like you are until I get back." Finished with tinkling and in bed, she was hot as a fire cracker. Timothy had a great big hard on. He stretched his arms out to enfold her warm, soft body. Quickly, they were entwined exchanging moist kisses and tender caresses. The urge within them was overwhelming. The passion between them was full blown and they were becoming more and more excited about making love. As Aries tucked her nude body close against his, she could hear each beat of his fast pounding heart.

"O' my God," Timothy sighed. Your nipples, let me suck them and play with them. I love the way they get hard and stand at attention." His hand moved downward from her breasts. He began to massage her clitoris and to finger fuck her hot juicy pussy. Placing her mouth on his erect cock, Aries went down on it causing him to groan in ecstasy. Using her moist tongue with surety, she licked his balls and tickled the head of his penis. Squeezing it tightly between her velvety lips, she took it deep into the cavity of her throat.

Suddenly, Timothy flipped her fiery body over, thrust his gigantic organ inside her vagina and began fucking her furiously. At his mercy, Aries lay moaning, groaning and declaring her love for his succulent body. They had simultaneous, powerful orgasms and quietly fell asleep in other's arms.

At six o'clock in the morning, Aries was awakened by the wake up call she had ordered upon checking in. At first, she was confused about where she was. Then, it dawned on her. She was in a motel in bed with a man she hardly knew and whose name she, momentarily, couldn't remember. Soon, she retrieved his name from the depths of her memory. Timothy Holt.

Aries rolled over, positioning her warm body next to his as he lay
sleeping. Her nearness aroused him from his slumber and a fresh
desire was created between them. Moaning and groaning sounds were
penetrating the room, once more.

"Fuck me deep and hard, Aries murmured. Oh, please, I love your
big cock inside of me."

"Honey, you make me feel so good, Timothy said softly. I love to
fuck you."

They clung together with every movemen in perfect harmony until
they melted and dissolved in climax.

Regaining her composure, Aries slipped out of the mustled bed and
into the bathroom. As she walked she could feel his warm slick cum
running down between her thighs. She was supposed to pick her son
up at seven-thirty. She wondered what time it was.

"Where is your watch? What time is it, Timothy?"

"It's over here on the table, murmured sleepyhead, Tim."

In the still dark room Aries moved her slender naked body over to
the table and fumbled for the watch. "Oh, dear, it's already seven-
thirty and I'm late. I've got to go."

Pulling himself up, Timothy asked if she knew how t o get on the
right road from there?

"No, but I'll find it. You stay here and sleep."

"No, I'll get up too, I have to catch the train to New York. Sweets,
I had a wonderful evening. I love your body and I am even more in
love with your mind. I've always wanted to meet a girl who had that
combination. You are a really super lady. Don't forget to give me your
address. Will you be back in Princeton, tonight?"

"No, I will be flying to Baltimore. Call me next week, I'll write
my address and phone number down for you. Hurry, Tim, if you're
going to direct me out of here, we must get started." Leaving the
room, they hugged goodbye and walked to ward their respective cars.

"Follow me. I will lead you to the highway," he directed. "I had a
super time."

"I loved it, too, Tim. See you."

Aries followed him down the road until he signaled for her to turn
left. Waving goodbye, she proceeded to Nassau Street where Mark

was patiently waiting for her to arrive. All set, they were off to
Hartford. Hopefully, they'd finish their business in time for her fly on
to Baltimore. She had promised Keith she'd be there by five and he'd
be leaving work early to pick her up at the airport

Mark was glad to see his Mom and he talked a mile a minute all
the way to Hartford. Aries was in no mood to carry on a conversation,
this morning, for she was exhausted from the evening of fucking.
Briefly, her thoughts took her back into the bedroom with Timothy. He
was really good in bed. She wondered if she would ever see him,
again. He told her that sex wasn't so wonderful "like us" when he
made love to his wife. He had made her feel "rather special."

It was a long day in Hartford and everything that could go wrong.
did. Realizing she would be unable to make the plane to Baltimore on
time, she phoned Keith. After she explained her situation and the bad
schedule of plane connections, he suggested they meet in Hartford that
evening, instead.

"That would work out great," she said.

They arranged to meet at the Holiday Inn at the airport.

"I can't wait to see you, sweetie," said Keith. "I have something
big and nice for you."

Aries knew what that was.

Keith was rather special to her because he had been her sweetheart
almost thirty years before, in college. She was in love with him but
due to a misunderstanding, they broke up and some months later she
married Greg.

After divorcing Greg she began to look for Keith. Through a friend
she heard that he was in the Navy and stationed in Hawaii. Rumor had
it that he had a wife and two children. This was a disappointment but
what could she expect. After all, he was a normal, healthy guy.

Although Aries learned about Keith's whereabouts, years passed
and she was never able to make contact with him. One day she was
sitting in a bank in Knoxville, Tennessee. The Vice-President came out
to greet her and he was none other than, Dewey Russell, a good friend
and fraternity brother of Keith's at the University of Tennessee.
During the conversation Aries inquired if he had heard from him.

"As a matter of fact, I have. In fact, I have a recent letter from him in my desk drawer," he said fumbling for the letter.

"Where is he living?" Aries asked eagerly.

"He's living in Baltimore, Maryland."

After all those years, almost thirty, she had found him. Dewey gave her Keith's address. When she got back to Florida she called the only Keith B. Kiser in the directory in Baltimore. Keith answered. Aries would have known that voice anywhere. They were ecstatic at hearing each other's voices, again. Wife or no wife they planned a reunion in Philadelphia, the next month. Aries counted the days with anticipation. She hadn't seen him since college.

On their meeting day Aries flew to Philadelphia, checked into a hotel and awaited Keith's arrival. Shortly thereafter, he called from the the downstairs lobby and minutes later, he was at her door. Aries was shocked when she saw him. He still looked the same, felt the same, tasted the same but he had lost his hair in the front. Thirty years before he wore a crew-cut! The bald head and the horned rimmed glasses were new but his body and his shoulders were still great! Keith had played right tackle on the University of Tennessee football team and he still looked like a football player.

They spent the day reminiscing about their college days, of being in love, and why they broke up and lost each other for so many years. Their reunion was touching.

After lunch at the Bookbinder, they drove back to the Latham Hotel where Keith insisted on escorting her to her room. Aries was nervous about being alone with him. She'd been so much in love with him in college but they never had sexual intercourse. Now, thirty years later, she knew that sex between them, this afternoon, was inevitable. She wondered what it would be like... Would he love her in bed? She had wanted to marry him and to be a virgin when they made love the first time. It was many years and five children, later.

In the room Keith wasted no time in carrying out his intention. Pulling her down on the bed, he began kissing and hugging her. "Oh, Aries, I'm so happy, I feel so excited with you. Let's take off our clothes and get between the sheets." He was acting like a giddy schoolboy.

With some effort Aries extricated herself with the excuse of having to go to the bathroom. She was shy about him seeing her in the nude. In college, she'd had a great figure but she wondered if Keith would find her body unattractive with age.

Overcoming all of her doubts and worries, she mustered the courage to join him in bed. He had a a monstrous hard on.and soon, she was smothered by his huge body on top of hers. The passion of the heated encounter was quickly tamed by simultaneous explosive orgasms, only to be followed by repeated love making. Aries was moaning and groaning so loudly she knew everybody on that floor must be hearing her. Keith's body was soaking wet with perspiration and his cock was so erected she thought it would never go down. Twas' as if they were trying to make up for the thirty years they had missed.

It was getting late and time for Keith to be returning to Baltimore. He was supposedly in Washington for an all day meeting but his wife would be wondering why he wasn't home. For sure, he wouldn't be any good to her when he got there for he had been well-fucked. Aries was exhausted. She fell asleep almost as soon as he left.

They made plans to meet the next month for two days in Washington when Keith attended a convention there. Aries looked forward to seeing him but she was uneasy about their becoming too involved. Her heart had changed and she wondered if she could love him as before. A lot of water had crossed over the dam since they were in college and it was almost impossible to go back.

Keith talked about divorcing his wife as soon as his two children finished college. He was hinting marriage. Did she really want to be tied down? Was Keith versatile enough for her? Had his Navy training and discipline made him too organized? Aries didn't like routine. She was a free soul and liked making her own decisions. She was uncomfortable at the thoughts of giving up her freedom but she'd keep him on her list until she made up her mind. A girl can never have too many lovers.

Keith met Aries in Hartford that evening. He looked great! After dinner they were off to bed for another round of love-making. It was good but Aries was still tired from her escapade in New Jersey. Timothy had beat him to the draw. Sex after dinner and sex before breakfast was the order for them.

They made plans to meet the next month in Fort Lauderdale. Keith planned to stay for two weeks as a test run to see if they liked living together. While there, he would explore the possibilities of a job transfer to that area. Maybe he would go into real estate or he would apply for a manager's job. Keith said he was great at organizing things. This was just what she didn't want to hear. She had led a disorganized life and she wasn't interested in someone trying to put some order into it after all these years. There he goes, she thought. It's that dam Navy discipline showing through.

Life with Stuart had been so hectic, it couldn't be worse with Keith. She had her hands full running her company and keeping things going with a husband who was constantly having emotional ups and downs, outbursts of violence, etc. That situation took all the strength she could muster up. Although she had filed for divorce, Stuart had disavowed their separation. He kept trying to reconcile with her. So as not to anger him, she tried to pacify him until the divorce was final.

Arriving home from the Princeton trip, Aries retrieved her car from the airport parking lot. There was a note on the windshield from Stuart asking her to call him upon her arrival. A woman answered when she called. He was at the store but she'd give him the message. Shortly thereafter, Stuart called saying he wanted to come to see her.

"Okay, okay, you can come over, tonight." Shit, she was worn out from the trip and to top it all, she had to be bugged by her deranged, estranged husband.

That evening, Stuart asked her to go to bed with him. In the sack, the same situation prevailed. His damned cock was as soft as mush.

"We'll try again in the morning," he said. Morning came and it still wouldn't work. So much for that. Maybe that plastic penis insert he'd been talking about was just the thing for him.

The next day, Stuart invited her to dinner. Reluctantly, she accepted but after a few dull and boring hours she left him at the restaurant. This really pissed him off.

In August, Aries went to court for her divorce hearing. Stuart had his defense all planned. He pleaded illness and he announced in court that he loved her. Rather than granting the divorce, the judge ordered Stuart to stay on his medication and to an inpatient treatment center for alcoholism. Stuart was an ex-judge himself and he must have been sleeping with that Judge. He had warned her if she tried to divorce him, he'd keep her in court for two years. She should have filed in another county where her husband didn't have an "in" at the court-house.

Stuart was as meek as a lamb in court and so apologetic for his past behavior. He promised the Judge to reimburse her for all the property he had destroyed and vowed he'd never hit her again. The Judge put it all in an order. Against her better judgment, Aries agreed to give the marriage another try.

Six weeks later, after his rehabilitation treatments, Stuart moved into her oceanfront villa. He had stopped drinking and things between them would be really different. The divorce suit was still filed and he knew that Aries could proceed if she chose. The lithium helped with his behavior but he was still impotent and socially, he was a bore. Married to him, Aries would have to find her sexual pleasures else-where.

In late September, she and Margie made plans to attend a mini real estate convention at the Posner Hotel in the exclusive Green Hills area. Rooms there were eighty- five dollars up so they would share a room and split the tab.

Plans all set, Margie stopped by the villa to warn Aries to be ready bright and early on Friday morning. "The meetings start at eight-thirty and we get a free brunch, so don't be late."

"Okay, okay. I promise to be ready. Shall we take both cars?"

"No, let's go together."

"Very well, we'll go together."

Waving Margie good bye, Aries turned from the breezeway and gazing at the ocean she day dreamed as she watched the sailboats and ships, slowly moving. Ah, she thought. It would be nice if I could just stay home and never go to work. It's so beautiful here. Look at those rich people out on the beach sun bathing in the middle of the week. Someday, some day, dreamed Aries, someday, I'll be in that position.

Entering her villa, she headed for the bathroom. She had an

appointment with Mr. Dunley at eleven o'clock so she would have to hurry and get to the office. With panties down and enjoying her pee, Aries thought how good it would be to get away, away from the office and away from her argumentative husband for a few days. He didn't want her to go to the convention but she didn't care. If he couldn't take care of his wife what she did was none of his business.

Off the pot, Aries was feeling sexy and masturbation seemed eminent . She had been so sexually deprived during her marriage that "fucking herself" had become pretty commonplace. Actually, she was beginning to like fondling her own body. Throwing herself upon her still unmade bed and lying face down, she pulled the covers up over her back. What would her fantasy be today? Today, she would fantasize that Stuart was having an affair with, Pat, one of her girls at her office.

Pat was a blue eyed blonde with a perfectly proportioned body, a real sex symbol. She had a flirtatious personality but not a brain in her head. Aries had to admit that she had one of the finest asses she had ever seen on a woman, excluding her own. She knew she wasn't lacking in that department. She was jealous of Pat because she had seen Stuart eyeing her and devouring her with his eyes gapping out as he followed her every move. They had tried to be inconspicuous but like any other wife she sensed the attraction between them. She knew that Stuart was dying to fuck her.

What an ideal fantasy to masturbate by! Today she would let them fuck. In her imagination she would put them in bed together. She would let him grab her ass and fondle her protruding nipples. She would let him enjoy the excitement of a secret affair in her fantasy. The thoughts of this turned Aries on!

She imagined that Stuart and Pat were meeting at their rendezvous at lunchtime. Aries lay there envisioning Pat dressed in tight fitting white pants and a flimsy scarlet red see-through blouse unbuttoned three buttons down. Pat tantalized Stuart by rubbing her protruding breasts up against him.

"Darling, I want you, Stuart whispered as he took her in his arms. You're driving me crazy. I miss you so much when I can't see you. Come here, you sexy little bitch."

"You're so sweet and such an angel," she cooed as she began to thrust her tongue into his mouth. As she mouth fucked him he drew her closer and closer rubbing his cock up against her cunt.

"Come on honey, let's lay down and talk this over. I've got to be back in the office by two so time's a wasting. I want to spend every second of the time we have, loving you."

Taking his hand, Pat led the way to the bedroom.

"I want to feel your beautiful body next to mine. I can hardly wait, let me undress you, darling,"

Stuart placed his hand inside her bra extricating one breast. Her firm tit stood up with it's nipple hard and erected. He encircled his tongue around the tip of her nipple. Taking it in his mouth, he sucked it until she screamed in pain and excitement. His cock was becoming ruthlessly hard, and he could feel it pulsating and throbbing inside his trousers. She squeezed it hard with her hand. "Unzip your pants, I want to kiss your cock and lick it all over," she cooed.

"Oh, yes, I love your warm sweet mouth on my cock."

Helping him get his trousers off, Pat placed her warm, moist lips on the head of his protruding shaft, licking it with her tongue as if it were the most delectable of treats.

"Oh, baby, he groaned. You make me feel so good. Let me take your panties off, I need to fuck you. I need to fuck you, now."

Shoving her gently back on the bed, Stuart unzipped her tight white slacks exposing her stomach and the pink lace bikini underwear she was wearing. He pulled the slacks down below her buttocks, put his hand inside her panties and began to massage her stomach. Snatching her panties down to her knees, he stuck two fingers in her pussy. "My but you're juicy, let me fuck you for a minute with my fingers." he said.

"Oh, fuck me, fuck me. I need your cock inside of me."

Obliging her, he laid his long slender body on top of hers and without delay penetrated her vagina.

"Oh, honey. This is so good," he uttered.

She lifted her ass up to meet his cock. He withdrew trying to hold back because he was about to explode and then it would be all over. "I can't wait long. Try to cum. I was too ready and I'm about to pop."

"Wait, wait! sighed Pat. I am going to come with you."

"Well, don't move. If you want me to hold it, don't move."

"I have to move. I can't cum unless I move. Think about something else. Try to divert yourself. Think of Aries and you'll hold off."

"I'm trying but it isn't working so well."

She was working her cunt on his cock like a suction cup, pressing, then releasing and driving him insane.

"Put your hands on my ass," she begged. "I love it when you grab my buttocks."

"I love to hold your ass but if I don't slow down, I'm going to cum."

Aries had a vivid imagination. She mentally had them in bed and she had them ready to reach simultaneous powerful orgasms. Fantasizing, she had created this passion scene for her own excitement. She was panting, wiggling her ass, finger fucking herself and rising to the point of violent explosion. In a mental trance, her hands on her ass became his hands on Pat's ass. Aries was out of the bed and Pat was in it fucking her husband. Whatever it took the end result was the same. Aries had a good orgasm and she was peacefully relieved. Falling into a sound sleep, she had forgotten about her appointment with Mr. Dunley.

Minutes later, she was awaken by the ringing of the telephone. Her secretary was calling. "Did you forget your appointment this morning? There's a Mr. Dunley here and he says he has an appointment with you."

"Oh, my goodness, give him a cup of coffee. I'll be right there."

Jumping out of bed, Aries ran to the bathroom to bathe before dressing. She hoped Mr. Dunley would wait.

Half an hour later, she arrived at the office. Mr. Dunley wasn't too happy but he was still there because she had something he couldn't get anywhere else.

She left work early that day to go shopping for a new dress and underwear for her trip. Those convention meetings would be dull but the evenings should be interesting. Upper classed people frequented the Posner and hopefully, she'd meet someone nice.

Aries spent half the night arguing with Stuart and explaining why it was necessary for her to attend the convention.

"Let me come up in the evening," he argued.

"Oh, no, I'll be sharing a room with Margie. We can't afford to have separate rooms and she would pitch a fit if you came. She's against my relationship with you, anyway."

"I don't like you traveling with that bitch but I know you're going regardless of what I think."

"Don't worry, I'll be good." As she said that Aries knew they would both be looking hard to see if they liked anybody there.

Friday arrived and Aries went to pick Margie up at her condo. Jumping out of the car and in her usual walking manner, almost a rushing gait, she went to the house phone.

"Come on, let's go, Margie."

"Come on up, I'm still combing my hair."

"You can do that in the car. Come on down stairs. I've got to drop a key off at the office on our way out of town, so come on."

"Don't tell me, Aries Winston, that you aren't ready. I knew you would foul me up."

"It will only take a minute. I won't go in. I'll blow the horn and the secretary can come out to get the key."

"Well, I hope so. If you go in that office we'll never get out of town."

Finally after loading Margie's three suitcases and hanging clothes bag, they were off. Margie had brought enough clothes to last her a month.

"Where do you think we are going with all that luggage, Margie?"

"I couldn't decide what to wear so I brought everything" she chuckled.

"Well, I hope you don't have to carry them in and out of the hotel."

"Are you kidding. I'm not lifting anything. There had better be a porter. Where's your stuff?"

I didn't bring much. I don't like anything I have so bringing nothing will give me a chance to buy some things in those nice shops around the hotel. I always do that."

They arrived at the Posner around lunchtime.

"Let's check in, first, get our name tags and then, let's sneak out to lunch," suggested Aries. "I'm starving."

"Good idea! They're showing movies this afternoon and we'll be able to get out easy if we sit near the back of the room," explained Margie. "Gosh, there are a lot of real estate people here. I hope the President of the Board doesn't see us "playing hookey."

They made their appearance, seeing several people they recognized. The the lights went out quickly and they were able to make their escape to the patio dining room. It was a real luxury to be sitting there drinking bloody Mary's and enjoying a leisurely lunch in the middle of the day. Usually, Aries went without lunch or gobbled down a fast food takeout while she was talking to clients on the phone.

Looking across the bricked courtyard from the restaurant, Aries surveyed her surroundings trying to see the tennis courts. She knew they had courts and she intended to play while she was there. She was considered a pretty good player, in fact, she'd been a first or second position player in local club tournaments.

Lunch was good but expensive.

"Don't worry about it, we won't eat dinner," said Margie.

When they got back to the meeting, the auditorium was packed with people. There was a guy on the podium giving a motivational speech. Aries already had so much motivation for selling that she scarcely had any free time for her own hobbies or activities. The speaker talked about his success, how he had won all those friends and influenced all those people making thousands of dollars.

"You can to it, too," he declared.

Yeah, thought Aries, he made that money by making speeches. He was a trainer not a salesman. When it came to selling, she was sure he was a loser. Real salesmen don't need that motivational shit. They just need time to work with their clients. Some real estate agents never make it because they spend too much time in classes and meetings and too little time showing property and selling.

The afternoon session came to an end at five o'clock. Afterwards there was the customary hand shaking parley around display tables filled with advertising and informational books about real estate. Some were on sale but others were free, including a few "goodies."

Sandra Shakey, the local convention coordinator, had passed the word that the booths would be closing at five-thirty and there was a free cocktail party in the East Garden.

"Are you ready to get out of here?" Aries asked Margie.

"Yes, let's stop by the party for a few minutes and then we'll go to the room and change clothes."

"That sounds good to me."

The cocktail party was a real drag. The main table was decorated nicely with a big frozen R made with ice but apparently the convention budget was tight so the R was decorated with carrots, broccoli and radishes rather than much preferred shrimp.

Aries spied her first real estate teacher there. She hugged him and and told him of her progress in real estate since then. He proclaimed to the bystanders that Aries had been one of those students who always had her hand up and he dubbed her a "precocious student."

"Can you believe I finally passed the Broker's test and and I have my own company?" Aries asked him smiling.

"Yes, I believe you could do anything you set you mind to, young lady, her gray haired teacher declared. It is so nice to see you, again."

By now, Margie was lost in the crowd. Excusing herself, Aries began to move through the group trying to retrieve her. She spied her talking to the President of the Board of Realtors so she went over to join them.

Aries liked Tom Talk. She had met him under social circumstances, several years prior to his being elected President when she and Mia were having lunch by the Intracoastal waterway one Saturday afternoon. The next day they were taking her first manuscript to New York in hopes of getting it published. It was in her briefcase by her side. They wound up in conversation with the group sitting at the table next to them. Tom Talk was in the group. Finally, Aries pulled the manuscript out and the group enjoyed reading it.

A year later, after the book was published Aries ran into Tom, again at a political dinner. He sat beside her that evening.

"Do you remember me?" she asked.

"I sure do and more particularly, I remember what you wrote. It has helped me a number of times since I became President of the

Board of Realtors."

"What on earth was it?"

Tom laughed and said, "I know it verbatim. There's no such thing as a problem. It is merely something that requires your attention." After reading that, every time I ran into a difficulty I thought of your saying and I handled things. It really works."

"Well, you're right. I did write that and I'm glad your application of it has helped you."

"Margie interrupted their conversation. "Are you ready to go?"

"Yes, I am. I was looking for you."

Excusing themselves, they departed the group and headed for the hotel lobby.

"Let's stop in the lounge for just one more drink before we go upstairs," Aries suggested.

"No, let's get dressed first If we stop now we'll end up in these clothes all evening."

"Okay, but let's hurry. I want to get back downstairs before the cocktail hour is over."

When they got to the room the message light was blinking.

"Hey, somebody is calling us," yelled Margie. Call the operator and get our messages. It is probably your weird husband calling you. I'll shower, first, then you can use it."

"Go ahead. I have to press my dress, anyway."

Lighting a cigarette, Aries sat down at the telephone and called the operator. The messages was for her from her secretary. A friend of hers, Brent O'Leary, from Ohio was in town. He wanted her to return his call. Aries dialed his number. Brent and his friend, Dwane, were in town and he wanted to come over to the hotel to see her around nine. Aries told him that she had a friend with her, a female friend, and she would have to clear it with her.

"Hold on a minute, let me ask her."

Going into the bathroom, Aries told Margie that her friend from Ohio was in town with another guy and they wanted to come over.

"What does the friend look like?"

"I don't know but Brent said he was nice and you'd like him."

"Tell him you'll call him back in an half an hour. I don't want to get stuck with a blind date. We might meet someone else we want to be with."

"Well, we've got nobody now and I like Brent."

"Tell him you'll call him back. I want to think about it."

Back on the phone, Aries told Brent that Margie was a little shy about going on a blind date. She'd have to call him back in a half hour.

Hanging up, Aries turned to find Margie out of the shower and pouring herself a glass of wine.

"I'll just stay in the room and go to bed this evening," Margie said. "You go ahead and go out with Brent by yourself. I'm not going out with a stranger."

"I'll do no such thing. Either we'll either both go or we'll tell them not to come."

"He's come all the way from Ohio to see you. You can't do him that way."

"Well, he should have let me know he was coming. He can't just barge in without notice. Please, Margie, let's just let them come over for awhile. If you don't like your guy, we'll send them away."

"Okay, call him."

Aries called Brent. They'd meet them in the hotel lounge at nine. In a way, she looked forward to seeing him. She enjoyed his bubbly personality and his incessant laughter. He was a tall, lean, lanky Irishman with blue eyes, and reddish brown hair. President of a big corporation up north, Brent was a good conversationalist, good dancer and tennis player. Another plus, he had money.

With all of these qualities, he seemed like a pretty good catch but Aries was sure there must be something wrong with him. On their second meeting, she found out what it was. He had a wife, probably a real good one. He was little different from the most of the men she knew. He wanted to have his cake and eat it, too.

Aries was just as clever as he was and she had the complete ability to love him and leave him to his wife with no obligation, no remorse, nor regrets. He was just a warm friendly lover for the night. She was a worldly woman and she knew for a fact that he was a better than a fair fuck.

Finally, the girls were dressed and hot to trot. Margie wore her long red jersey silk gown trimmed in black. Aries who had "nothing to wear," wore her slinky turquoise cocktail dress with low cut with ruffles trimmed in gold braid and a slit in the front mid-way to her upper calf. The dress clung to her and outlined the curves of everything she had. Her attire was seductive.

In the lounge, they sat down at a table for two near the bar. From their vantage point, they could see everybody who came in or out of the door way. They were sipping and talking.

"There are a lot of bodies in here. There are at least fifty people in this room and I don't see anybody," said Margie.

"I don't see anybody here either, we're just too particular. There are probably a lot of nice people here but we just don't see them."

A few minutes later, a tall and handsome gentleman entered the far side of the room. When Aries saw him something happened and instantly, she could feel her heart pounding.

Margie, look over there at that fellow. He's my type. Margie, that's my guy, I want to meet him."

The newcomer joined a group of men. He sat down and almost immediately, he glanced in Aries direction and smiled. She was embarrassed because she had just told Margie she liked him. Aries bowed her head trying not to notice his glance but the chemistry between them was too strong. Without an introduction they were drawn together like magnets. They were mysteriously connected and they both knew.

After exchanging glances, the stranger excused himself from his friends and walked across the room to their table. Standing beside Aries, he extended his hand.

"Hello," he said looking at her all flustered..

She could see the depth of his soul through his penetrating blue eyes.

"Hello, my name is Tim Tyler."

"Who?"

"Tim Tyler," he repeated. What's you name?"

"My name is Aries, Aries Winston."

"Well, Hello Aries Winston. I was just wondering if you were busy later this evening. I would like to get to know you."

Looking up at that gorgeous hunk of man, her heart was pounding with excitement. "I would like to get to know you, too, but I'm afraid that it will not be possible this evening. You see, we are expecting two gentlemen to arrive at any moment."

"Do you have a date with them?"

"Yes," she replied nodding her head.

"Well, tell them you can't go. I have a friend at the table over there and I will introduce him to your friend and we'll go out to dinner."

"I can't tell my date that. He has come all the way from Ohio to see me."

"Ohio. Where is he from in Ohio? I'm from Ohio. What's his name? I might know him."

"His name's Brian O'Leary. He's from Akron."

"Oh, I'm from Cleveland. That's in the other part of the state. I don't know him. Are you sure you can't cancel out and go with me instead?" Tim was insistent.

"Yes, I'm certain but I will give you my card and you can call me, tomorrow." Reaching into her purse, Aries pulled out her card and handed it to him. She hated turning him down because she had fallen instantly in love with this stranger who didn't seem strange to her, at all.

"I'll call you tomorrow around five. We'll be in meetings until then." Tim looked disappointed as he prepared to leave their table. Looking up, Aries saw Brian and his friend heading her way.

"Upps! Here comes my date!"

Blushing, Tim backed away and with a slight hand signal, waved her goodbye. At that moment Brian came bouncing, all six feet four of him, up to their table. Grabbing Aries out of her seat, he started hugging and kissing her like she was a long lost friend.

"Uh hum, I caught you," he jested. Who was that fellow looking so ardently at you when I walked into the room?"

"Oh, that was someone attending a meeting here. They're having several conventions at this hotel this weekend."

"I hope he wasn't trying to horn in on my best girl. Gosh, Aries, it's great to see you. You look really great!"

"So do you."

Aries turned and directed her attention to Margie who, by now, had taken the liberty of introducing herself to the fellow with Brian.

"You remember Margie, don't you?"

"Sure I do," said Brian, smiling. "How could I forget such an attractive, nice person as Margie? How are you, Margie?"

Margie answered gingerly, "I'm fine."

"I see you've already become acquainted with my friend, Dwane."

"Well," piped in Dwane, "if a fellow waited for you and your girl-friend to introduce him, he might have to wait a long while. You two have been so busy hugging and kissing, hello."

"Oh, excuse us, that's just the way we are. Aries is so cuddly that I just love to hug her. I just can't seem to get enough of it."

Sitting down, he motioned for the waitress. "Let's all have a drink to celebrate this meeting of ours."

"That's a good idea," said Aries reaching for her cigarettes. Brian was hovering all over her. She glanced across the room where Tim had rejoined his friends. The look on his face told her that he wasn't happy about the attention she was getting from Brent. Her heart sank when she saw him get up and leave the room with several fellows in his group. Now, she knew she would be miserable this evening with Brian. Tim had turned her head and heart, completely, but Brian was such a nice guy she dare not let him know.

After several drinks and a few dances the foursome made plans for dinner. "There's a good place a couple miles up the road from here," said Brian. I ate there the last time I was in town. They had a great menu."

"Oh, yes," said Margie. I have always wanted to eat there."

"Well then, let's give it a try. By the way, girls, grab your overnight bags because you're invited to be my guests in my new penthouse at the Bayou tonight."

"Guests at your place! We've just paid over eighty dollars for our room here," Aries exclaimed.

"Oh, no, we can't," protested Margie. We have to come back to the hotel. We have meetings that start at eight o'clock in the morning."

"Well, we'll work it all out," said Brian. Margie punched Aries who turned to see what she wanted. Margie gave her a look of disgust that told her she didn't particularly like the company and she certainly didn't approve of the arrangements those guys were making for them. Dinner was one thing. Margie could eat with anybody but who would want to spend the night with a fathead. The poor guy was nice but Margie would never sleep with a man who didn't keep his physical body in shape.

Arriving at the restaurant Margie wasted no time in excusing herself to go the powder room.

"Come with me, Aries."

"Okay."

"Here comes the waitress. What would you girls like to drink? Brian asked.

"Make it two scotches, we'll be right back," Aries replied.

In the powder room Margie let loose with full force. "I told you I didn't like blind dates. Now here I am with that creep and he thinks I am going with him to their apartment. When dinner is over you all can just take me home. The nerve of that guy thinking I would consider spending the night with him. What's more, he's probably married. Did you see his fat stomach? It's revolting just to look at it."

"Fine, you can go back to the hotel after dinner but don't hurt his feelings. Pretend you have developed a terrible headache. I don't know how I am going to get away from Brian. He expects me to spend the night with him. He will be disappointed if he doesn't get to make love to me. It's has been such a long time since I've had sex, I could use some. You know he isn't half bad in bed."

"Do what you like. You don't have to come back just because I do. He can give you a ride back there early in the morning. What's this wanting to have sex with Brian when you've just told me you're in love with Tim or Tom or whatever his name is?"

"I am in love with Tim. I can hardly wait to see him but tomorrow is tomorrow and tonight is tonight. It can't hurt anything to make Brian happy and it will help me, too. Sex is sex and there are all kinds of it. Sex for sex, sex without love, sex with love, sex, sex. Tonight, it will be just be sex for the pure enjoyment --- Brian and I enjoy each other. When we hit the sack together, it's fun. Just like when we're hugging and kissing, it's fun.

"Aries, you're really too much. He's married isn't he?"

"Yes. I told you he was married but what difference does that make? His wife is in Ohio and he's in Florida. I'm never going to cause him a problem. Why do you think he's so nice to her when he goes home? He's nice to her because he's sexually satisfied because I have fucked him to death. That's what makes him smile so much. Somebody is always fucking him. With his endowments he has no problem getting fucked and his pleasant Irish personality doesn't hurt him either. We'd better get back to the table. The ice will be melted in our drinks and the guys will think we've skipped out on them. Come on, Margie, let's go back to the table and please, be nice to your date for a little while longer. You can dump him later but let's eat first, I'm starving."

Back at the table the guys asked them if everything had come out alright.

"We thought you gals had gotten lost," Dwane said.

"Oh, no," responded Aries. "We had to wait in the powder room and you know how it is when a bunch of women get together, jabber-ing. We just couldn't get out of there."

"The waiter was here to take our order but we sent him back. I expect I had better get him over here as it's nearly closing time. Have you ladies decided what you'd like to have?" he inquired.

"I know what I want. I want Maine lobster," Margie said without even looking at the menu. She always ordered the most expensive item in the place when someone else was paying the tab.

"Lobster, you shall have," he said shaking his head positively. "And Miss Aries, what strikes your fancy?"

"Well, I had seafood last night so tonight I believe I'll have steak."

Aries, secretly excited over her new acquaintance, had suddenly lost interest in Brian. She just wanted to get this evening over with, get back to the hotel and find Tim. Brian sensed a sort of distance between them. Something was strangely different, something was wrong but he couldn't put his finger on it. Aries tried to irritate him, purposely, hoping he would take her back to the hotel but it didn't work.

After leaving the restaurant the guys insisted that they accompany them to the condo. Finally, to avoid hurting Brian's feelings, Aries agreed. Margie didn't have much choice in the matter. Ignoring her pleas that they take her home, Brian just laughed as he drove the car in a northerly direction toward the condo.

"You don't want to go home," chanted her fat date."

"Yes, I do, I want to go home," she screeched."

"Be nice, we'll go home in a little bit," Aries assured her.

"We'd better."

Inside the parking garage, the fellows removed their luggage from the trunk and escorted the girls inside.

"Who's apartment are we going to?" asked Aries in the elevator on the way up.

"Oh, it belongs to, Kermit Fields, a friend on mine back home. He comes down once in awhile to use it. He's looking to buy another condo on the water here so maybe you can sell him one," answered Brian.

"Maybe so. Put me in touch with him. I'll talk to him about it."

"They got off the elevator on the twelfth floor and went to number 1208.

"Here we are ladies, Home Sweet Home," Brian announced as he jiggled the key in the lock.

Margie tugged at Aries coattails signaling she wanted to talk to her. Aries turned and caught the angry expression on her face.

Inside, Brian put his luggage in the bedroom and headed for the kitchen to fix his guests a nightcap.

"Where's the bathroom?" asked Aries.

"Straight down the hall and to the left," said Dwane.

"Come on Margie, let's go."

" Margie abandoned her stiff position on the sofa, followed Aries into the bathroom, closed the door and locked it behind her.

"Let's get out of here. I'm not going to sleep with that fatso creep," Margie wailed.

"You don't have to. Just behave yourself for awhile and I'll insist that Brian drive us back to the hotel. I have decided I don't want to sleep with him either. I want to get back to the hotel and find Tim

Tyler. You know I'm in love with him."

"That's unbelievable. How could you be in love with someone you've just met?"

"Easy. I've been destined to meet him for fifteen years. The wedgie board spelled his name for me years ago, and I've been waiting to meet him. It was no surprise when he told me his name."

"That's eerie. You beat it all."

"We'd better get back in there."

"Yeah, let's get back in there and tell them to take us home."

When they emerged from the bathroom Brian was sprawled out on the bed wearing only his bikinis.

"Come here, you sweetheart," he called to Aries. "Come on in here, I've got something for you."

Margie was still standing in the hallway. "You can stay here if you want to but I'm ready to go home," she said vehemently.

Going into the bedroom and closing the door, Aries told Brian that Margie wasn't interested in her date and she wanted to go home.

"Aw, leave them alone, maybe they need to get better acquainted without us around."

"I don't think so. You don't know Margie. When she doesn't like someone she doesn't like them."

"Well, we'll take her home later. Right now, young lady, I want to make love to you."

Oh, shit, thought Aries. I've done it before so one more time won't matter. She undressed and lay her body down beside his lean and lanky frame. They started fucking and he was groaning and moaning with delight. She was getting fucked but this time she wasn't liking it because she wanted to be in bed with Tim Tyler, instead.

She could hear Margie and Dwane arguing in the other room. Brian's try at match making wasn't working out too well. Margie was pissed at this jerk trying to make out with her. For damned sure Margie wouldn't be speaking to her tomorrow.

Brian had fallen into a sound sleep and Aries tried to arouse him but it was to no avail. She'd let him rest awhile and then she'd wake him up and make him take them home. Aries fell asleep, too.

She woke up at seven a.m. Brian was in the kitchen making coffee.

Slipping her clothes on and going into the living room, she found Margie as mad as a hornet, still sitting on the sofa, fully clothed.

"Where's Dwane?"

Margie was stoned-faced and gave her no answer. Passing on into the kitchen, Aries told Brian they needed to get back to the hotel.

"I'll take you in a few minutes but first, let's wake Dwane up and have some breakfast."

"I'm not hungry. Wake him up and let's go."

Few words were spoken after that.

Dwane came out all hung over and wearing the look of a defeated man. He hadn't scored with Margie and disappointment was clearly etched upon his face. Finally, the guys were dressed and ready to go.

Enroute back to the hotel Margie told Aries that this was the last trip she would ever take with her. Eighty bucks for a room and they didn't even sleep in it.

"I'm sorry. "I didn't mean to stay but I fell asleep."

"You did it on purpose, you creep. I don't want to talk to you."

Margie would be okay after she sulked for awhile. They'd been friends for a long time and Aries knew the best thing to do now was to ignore her. She chatted with Brian until they pulled up at the hotel.

"Thanks for the evening," she told them. "Call me the next time you're in town."

Out of the car and into the hotel lobby, Aries raced to the room leaving Margie ten paces behind her. She was eager to see if she had a message from Tim Tyler. She did. Tim had called and left a message that he would call back at ten a.m. Thank goodness Aries thought, I haven't lost him yet.

Margie entered the room behind her and marched straight to the bathroom to put herself in order. She never went anywhere without spending two hours fixing her hair and putting her makeup on. Aries was a different breed, a natural girl. She'd quickly drag a brush through her hair and set about to plan her day.

The real estate meetings were still going on but she was bored to death yesterday so she would play hookey today. Perhaps, she'd play tennis if she could find a partner. Dressing for the game, she told Margie that she'd see her in a little while.

"Playing hookey, huh, wait till they catch you. See you in a couple hours.

Aries got into a game of singles and later, she was invited to play doubles. After tennis, she went with the group to the dining room for a late brunch. While sitting at the table, another couple came in and joined them.

During the conversation Aries learned that they wanted to buy real estate. She identified herself as a real estate agent but told them she was there on vacation.

"Well," said the man, "we wanted to go out and look at property this morning and we wonder if you'd like to show it to us?"

"Are you sure you want to buy now?"

"I brought an eight thousand dollar cashiers check with me to put down on a condo and I want somebody to show me something."

"Okay, if you're really ready to buy, I'll cancel my plans for the day and work with you."

Damnit, it wa s hard to resist a ready, willing and able buyer with cash in his hands.

"Let me go upstairs and change and I'll meet you in the hotel lobby at one o'clock."

Upstairs, she found Margie still primping and putting herself together. She, too, had decided to skip the morning meetings. Aries blurted out that she was going to show property.

"What? Going to show property. How could you, how dare you show property on our vacation?"

Aries tried to explain. "Margie, I met this man in the dining room this morning. He has an eight thousand dollar cashier's check with him and he wants to buy a condo. What do you want me to do, let him go to another REALTOR? Come on Margie, go with me. If you go with me this afternoon, I will give you half of the commission."

"We can't get away from this damned business no matter what we do," Margie complained. "I don't believe you, Aries, how could you?"

"He's going to buy a hundred thousand dollar condo, don't you like money?"

"I guess you're right, maybe we should go with him."

"Okay, let's get ready. I told him I'd meet him in the lobby at one o'clock. We can have fun when we get back."

"I certainly hope so because so far I haven't had any. Last night, you fixed me up with a creep and today, you are dragging me out to show real estate. You're unbelievable."

"Let's go, Margie. I promise tonight we will have a ball. Tonight, you'll meet somebody you like."

Dressed and in the lobby, they waited to meet the customer. He showed up with his wife and they took off to look at condo's in the Boca Raton area.

Knowing little about the condo market there, Aries contacted a real estate office in Boca for help. Taking the client to their office, the agent there suggested several buildings. After making the appointments to show, Aries and Margie carted them up and down the beach looking at condos. Before the day was over, the man put in contracts on two of them. It looked like he was going to buy one.

It was seven o'clock when they got back to the hotel and everybody was exhausted.

As soon as Aries got to her room, she called Tim but got no answer. She had missed him again. She guessed he had gone out."

"Let's go down to the lounge and have a drink," suggested Margie. "Then we can decide what to do this evening."

"Okay, but I've got to get dressed and I don't know what to wear."

"I'm wearing my green pantsuit."

"I guess I'll wear my green dress. Let me try it on and see if you like it."

She slipped the dress on. Margie took a look and said, "Are you sure you want to wear that tonight? It's really sexy."

"Why not? Start getting ready so we can go downstairs. Maybe we can meet someone before dinner and they can take us out. I hope Tim Tyler is in the bar. Can I have the tub, first?"

"Sure, I'm going to curl my hair."

Thirty minutes later, Aries was dressed and waiting for her roommate.

"What are you doing in there, Margie? Hurry, come on, we are going to miss everything."

"Keep your shirt on. "It takes me awhile to get ready."

"Well, it wouldn't take you so long, if you didn't wear all that makeup and eyebrow stuff."

"You'd look better if you wore it yourself."

"I don't know how to wear it and I'm afraid it would get in my eyes and make them bloodshot. Remember the time you dressed me up like Dolly Parton for Halloween. My husband snatched the wig off my head, called me a cheap whore and I had to go home from the party by myself. I don't think I look so bad like I am."

"Well you don't but you'd certainly look a lot better if you would try fixing yourself up, sometimes."

Looking at Margie making up, Aries asked if she'd put some of that stuff on her.

"Yeah, I can put it on you. Give me a couple more minutes." Finally, all dressed they went downstairs.

Aries was upset about not seeing Tim. They sat down at the bar and ordered a drink. No sooner than they'd been served, the couple they had shown condos to appeared in the doorway.

"Look who's coming in.," announced Aries.

"Don't look," said Margie. "Don't look at them, maybe they won't notice us."

No such luck, Mr Davis caught Aries's eye and headed straight toward them.

"Hello there." .

"Hi."

"What are you gals doing down here?"

"Oh, we're just relaxing."

"My wife and I are getting ready to go out to dinner. Would you like to join us?"

"No, we are planning on eating here at the hotel," answered Aries.

"Oh, come on, we know about a good Chinese place about ten miles down the road. Won't you join us?"

"Chinese, I don't think I like Chinese food."

"Oh, you'll like this Chinese food, it's the best you've ever put in your mouth. Come on, go with us," Mr. Davis insisted.

The girls looked at each other, hesitatingly. They'd been in their company all day and having dinner with them was the last thing they wanted to do. Feeling obligated to go, reluctantly, they agreed. They tried to finish their drinks.

"Bottoms up because my wife's hungry," prompted Mr. Davis.

"We're ready," said Margie. They paid the check and joined the Daviss'. Mr Davis drove them to the Chinese restaurant. Aries hated being there but after a couple of drinks she began to mellow. When the meal was served she had to admit it was the best food she'd ever put into her mouth.

After dinner, they returned to the hotel hoping to split but the Daviss' insisted on having a drink with them at the patio bar. The gals politely agreed. Why not? They had missed everything, tonight. What was there to do but have another drink and sack in?

As they sat at the patio bar with their customers, sounds of music floated from the dance floor inside. All of a sudden Tim walked up. It was eleven o'clock. He sat down beside Aries. As he moved closer, she again felt a strong, strong chemistry between them.

"Where have you been?" he asked inquisitively.

"Where have I been? I've been out showing condos all day and we went to dinner with our clients. I'd like you to meet Mr. and Mrs. Davis."

"Mr. and Mrs. Davis, meet Tim Tyler."

"Hello. So this is why Aries wanted to rush back," said Mr. Davis.

"Well," laughed Aries, "he's one of the reasons."

"It's nice to meet you."

Pretty soon, Tim whispered in Aries ear. "Let's get out of here."

"Suits me but where?"

"Oh, we'll find a place, just say goodnight to your girlfriend and let's go."

"I can't, I can't just leave her here. We have to introduce her to somebody."

"I have a couple of friends sitting over at another table, I'll go over and ask Jens to join us," Tim suggested.

"Good!"

Excusing himself, he went over to the table where his friends were sitting. In a few minutes he brought Jens back and introduced him to the group. Dark haired with flashing brown eyes, Jens was a good looking devil. Surely, Margie would go for him.

"Join us for a drink," invited Tim. Jens sat down. Thank goo.'ness, their clients decided to tuck it in for the night.

Left at the table, the four began to talk. Jens hit it off well with Margie and Aries was glad that, at last, she'd met somebody she liked.

Again, Tim whispered to Aries, "Let's get out of here. I need to talk to you." Getting up, they told Margie and Jens good night and they left.

"Where are we going?" Aries asked.

"I don't know but we can't stay here. Let's go check into a hotel. Have you got a car?"

"Yes, I have a Mercedes out in the parking lot."

"Let's take it because I'm sharing a car with another guy."

They drove the car across the Intracoastal bridge to U.S. Highway 1 where Tim checked into a hotel.

No sooner than they entered the room, they hit the sack. What an absolutely beautiful night! They made love into the wee hours of morning.

Finally, it was time to leave. Tim had to chair a meeting at eight o'clock that morning. They went out to get into the car and it wouldn't start. The battery was dead because they had left the lights on all night. Tim caught a cab to the meeting. He promised to call later. Aries called AAA and waited for them to start her car. What a night! Tim Tyler was an absolute dream. She knew she had to see him again.

That morning, the girls took the clients out to look at more condos. As the day progressed, they became involved in negotiations on another contract for Mr. Davis, and consequently, they didn't get back to the hotel until after ten p.m. Tim, apparently, had gone out to dinner with the guys in his party. The girls dined at a restaurant downtown. The evening ended with no signs of him.

The next morning they checked out of the hotel and went home. Aries felt sad because she'd found someone she really liked and she had been unavailable. When she retrieved her messages, she realized that Tim had been calling and calling every hour on the hour all day. She had missed him completely. His convention was over and he'd be returning to Ohio. She wondered if she would ever see him again.

A few weeks later Tim called. "Hey honey, I am sorry I missed you my last day in Florida. I have a meeting scheduled in in Atlanta next month. Would you would like to join me there?"

What beautiful music to Aries ears! "Oh, I'd love to. Just tell me when and where."

"Well, it's the fifteenth in the Peachtree Square Plaza. Catch a plane to Atlanta and I'll meet you at the hotel around seven p.m. for dinner. Go to the hotel and ask for my room."

"Fine, I will see you there. I'm glad you called. I thought I'd never see you again."

"No such luck. See you later, sweets."

Aries was pleased about the "invite" to Atlanta. Tim Tyler was an ex-pro football player, vice-president of a large well known company, and a well-liked man with an important job. With all the women he could have chosen to be his companion, he had picked her. She knew he liked her. He enjoyed her personality and he loved her in bed. He had a wife and children at home but he was willing to share a part of himself with her.

Lost in day dreams of Tim, Aries sat at her desk mentally mapping her plans for the trip. Pushing the intercom button, she asked Sandra, her secretary, to come in for a minute. She bounced in with pencil and paper in hand, her long straight hair flopping at her waistline.

Sandra was a real cutie. She was as efficient as hell but stupid when she had decisions to make in her personal life.

Aries sat poised behind her desk. "Have a seat, Sandra." I want to go over a few things with you. Would you like a cup of coffee?"

"No, I just had a coke."

Lighting a cigarette, Aries told her she would be taking a couple days off the week of the 15th. She was going to Atlanta on business.

"I'll be depending upon you to keep this ship afloat until I return."

"No problem, you need time off. I'll take care of everything."

"I'll call in for messages daily and I'll be just as close as the telephone," she assured Sandra.

The telephone rang. Stuart was on the line.

"Hi. What's up, Stuart?"

"Not much. I just wondered if I could come over tonight. I'll stop at the store and bring hamburger for dinner."

"I don't know. I've really got a lot of work to do," answered Aries.

"I won't bother you," he replied sheepishly. After dinner, I'll sit down and read a book."

"Okay, you win but don't come before eight-thirty. I'm working at the office late, tonight."

Damit! Aries had given in to his pleading. She could visualize another wasted evening with her dull-faced estranged husband. Stuart's behavior was so erratic and his propensity to violence so great that she had to handle him with kid gloves. Aries had lost all respect for him. He was just a bad penny in her life. Their divorce should have been final months before but with his power, influence and legal connections, divorcing him had not been easy.

Tonight, she'd tell him she was taking a trip to Atlanta on real estate business. Of course he would object bitterly but his complaints didn't phase her anymore. Fate had introduced her to Tim Tyler and this new association had given her shattered life a new meaning.

Soon Atlanta day came. Aries caught an early plane up so she would have time to do some shopping before meeting Tim. New duds always made her feel better, especially when she was going to be in the company of a man who really counted. Tim Tyler was just that. He was "a special someone."

Upon arriving in Atlanta, Aries took a cab to the hotel and shortly thereafter, she hurried to the nearest shopping center. She ended up in an upscale shop where after going through everything on the racks, she found a dynamite black designer original outfit from Italy. It was sleeveless, definitely sharp and very expensive, costing four hundred dollars.

Aries asked the clerk about shoes and accessories.

"Don't buy them here," the clerk advised. "Their prices are too high. If you'd like I'll go with you to another store during my lunch break and help you find just the right shoes."

Aries was amazed at the clerk's offer but not knowing her way around Atlanta, she accepted.

"I'll buy you lunch."

"That's a deal, I'll be ready just as soon as my relief comes."

They had lunch in the patio of Peachtree Square Gertie, the clerk, confided that she was having a hard time financially. She had split with her husband and was raising a child alone. Aries was familiar with the girl's story. She had been through the same shit but in her case she was the breadwinner for five while her ex-husband, Greg, was out fucking a real bitch for her money.

Greg told her before their divorce that he'd never marry again. This was a crock of bull. The nerd was married exactly three months after the divorce to that rich hussey, Isabel Finn. Ironically, Aries had played bridge with her, several times. Isabel was married to a lawyer, then, and they lived a few streets over. Aries didn't know how she got connected with Greg. She assumed that either she was his client in the stock market or he met her in the psychiatric hospital when he was having another one of his breakdowns.

Rumor had it that Isabel was a real nut, the type who had wild temper outbursts, threw dishes or anything within her grasp at people when she was raging. Aries knew none of this for a fact but she knew that even before her divorce, this hussy was fucking her husband.

After their marriage Aries was able to put two and two together and decipher Greg's tales about "this woman" he made out with on her living room sofa while her children were sleeping. This woman who shaved her cunt and loved it when he licked her was none other than Isabel, the whore, who snatched him up as her own just as soon as the courts made him available. What Isabel didn't know was that she wasn't getting such a prize.

With Gertie's help, Aries found accessories and a pair of black shoes to go with the black outfit. Thanking her, she took her purchases and went back to the hotel. Tim was still at his meeting so this gave her time to get organized.

Tiring of waiting in the room, at six o'clock she went down to the lounge leaving Tim a note inviting him to join her there. Sitting alone at a table, she took her legal pad out to do some writing. She fancied herself as a writer, a damned good one, although, the world didn't know it yet. The entertainment started and a few people were dancing. Not long after, she was interrupted by a tall, dark haired man who came up to her table.

"Pardon me, but my curiosity is getting the best of me. I've been sitting here watching you. What on earth are you writing so arduously? I was beginning to think you were writing a book," the man said politely.

"That's exactly right. I am writing a book." Aries smiled shyly.

"How interesting! Do you mind if I join you? I would like to hear more about this book."

"I'm sorry. I'm afraid you can't join me. I'm waiting for a friend. The book I'm writing if you're interested is a book about people, just people, everyday people like you and I.

"My, you must be smart young lady."

Putting the legal pad in her purse, she would save the writing for another time. Still standing there, the man asked her to dance.

"I can't. My friend will be here soon,"

"Come on, just one dance before he gets here," he begged with twinkling eyes.

"Well, alright, just one."

They introduced themselves on the dance floor. He seemed like a nice person but there was little time to get acquainted. Tim would be arriving at any moment. The tune ended and before she could get off the floor, they started playing a jitterbug. Fast dancing was one of her weaknesses. She dearly loved it. Pulling her back onto the floor, Avery Benson was getting into the swing of things.

"Let's try one more," he chanted. "Boy, you're really good."

Aries was a good dancer and she felt good, too. There were a few couples on the floor but she and her partner were stealing the scene. She looked toward the doorway and there stood Tim, perhaps, in shock.

"There's my friend! I knew I shouldn't have danced with you."

"Well, just tell him I twisted your arm. I wish you didn't have to go with him," said Avery sighing.

"I do and I must go to him now. Thank you for the dance."

"Wait, I'll take you back to your table."

Tim saw Aries returning to her seat and came up to join her.

"Well, hello. Having fun without me?" he kidded smiling.

"No, no, I was just waiting for you and this fellow asked me to dance."

"Oh! I'm sorry I'm late but let's pay your check and get out of here. I have a nice restaurant picked out for dinner with candlelight and atmosphere."

"That sounds good but I need to change clothes, first. It will only take me a few minutes."

"Fine, let's go to the room."

Elated at seeing each other again, they chatted all the way to the elevator. Upstairs, Tim poured drinks while Aries slipped into her new black outfit.

"How do I look?"

"Wonderful honey, you look great!"

"I went shopping this afternoon and bought this. It's some kind of Italian original."

"I like it a lot but I like what's in it better. Let's go to dinner now. It's been awhile since I've seen you and I want to catch up on your latest happenings."

"Suits me." Aries gathered up her evening bag from the dresser.

The restaurant was top quality and dinner was delicious. Tim was very eager to get the niceties over with and get back to the hotel. He had some serious fucking in mind. Aries, as expected, was somewhat nervous and shy about this for, after all, they had been together only once before.

Back at the hotel, they stopped in the lounge for a couple dances. They had arrived just in time to catch a few tunes before the trio went on intermission. When the music stopped Tim asked the waiter for his check.

"Let's go to the room, honey, I've got a big day tomorrow and we'd better call it a day."

Aries wasn't about to disagree. Tim was a big man. In college, he was a football player for University of Tennessee and her five feet two inches was like a whiff of air beneath his sturdy frame.

"I'm ready," she said. "Let's go."

Back in the room, they readied themselves for bed. Aries took the legal pad from her purse and laid it on the table.

"What's that?"

"Oh, it's something that I was writing while I was waiting for you. It's the story of Tim ."

"Of me? What do you mean?"

"Well, while I was waiting for you I decided to write about our meeting, my feelings for you, our feelings about each other, etc."

"Oh, baby, you'll have to tear that up. I don't want you to write a story about me."

"But its beautiful," she protested.

"It may be but our story is one I don't want put down on paper. My wife may read it and recognize me. I've got two children and I'm not known to play around. What we have been to each other must be kept very discreetly. Read me the story, honey. I want to hear it but when you are finished, promise me you will destroy it."

They sat up in bed while she read the story to him.

"And you feel that way about me?" Tim asked when she finished reading. He was touched.

"Yes, Tim, that's exactly the way I feel about you. I think you're a dynamite, super person."

"I feel the same about you, Aries, but that will always have to be our secret. We'll meet and I'll make love to you as often as we can but we must never let our affair be public knowledge. You know, I have a house in Vero Beach. My wife and I go there several times a year. I usually go down during the week and she comes down on the week-end after the kids get out of school. I'll give you a ring the next time I get a chance to come down and we can make our plans to meet."

"Please call me when you come down."

"But what about your husband?"

"Forget him, I'm trying to divorce him. We're separated. I'm just waiting for the final hearing. We don't live together."

"Oh, I'm sorry."

"There's nothing to be sorry about. I shouldn't have married him in the first place."

The hour was late. They had talked long enough and it was time to turn in.

"Times awasting, honey. I want to feel myself inside of you. I'm pretty crazy about you, you know, you really turn me on," Tim said.

Aries slipped her gown off and slid in bed beneath the sheets. As Tim took her in his arms she could feel the strength of his muscular frame. Rolling over on top of her, he was ready to plunge his big hard penis into her hungry awaiting vagina.

Their love making was a breathtaking, thrilling experience. Though she felt helpless beneath him, she loved it. He was so powerful, so strong and so much in control of the sex act. Aries's only choice was that of surrendering herself completely to him. He fucked her hard and fast, continually pounding her insides with his steel like penis until she thought there would be nothing left of her.

"Cum baby, cum baby," he murmured. He was sweating profusely. They were becoming very excited and neither of them could last much longer. They exploded in powerful orgasms, together.

"Oh, darling, please keep fucking me," squealed Aries. "Fuck me some more because I think I'm going to cum again."

"Wait a couple minutes, baby, and I'll give it to you. You really want me don't you?"

"I love you, I mean I love making love to you, Tim."

"Get on top of me. Ride it, baby. Show me how you love to fuck me."

Rolling over, she tucked her hands under his ass and began to lift her hips up and down, forward and backwards working his cock over royally.

"Do you like this, honey?"

"I love it, baby. You really know how to make a guy feel good."

"Help me a little," she murmured softly "Help me, I'm about to cum"

Tim put his hands on her buttocks and began stroking her vagina with his powerful cock. They reached a second climax and with his dripping penis still inside of her, they fell into soft sweet slumber.

The next morning, Tim went back to his meeting. He promised to come back to the hotel at eleven and and they would go to the airport. Fortunately, they had arranged their schedules so only one trip to the airport was needed. The hours had gone by swiftly and there was little time left for togetherness.

At the airport they kissed in the car as they prepared to head in separate directions. Tim turned to wave goodbye and said, "I'll look forward to seeing you soon."

That was the last time she saw him. About a year later he called. She asked him where he'd been and he said he had been ill. This news was shocking because he had looked so healthy.

"What was wrong?"

"Cancer. They operated on me for lung cancer."

"My, goodness, I hope you are alright." This news almost made her tremble inside. It was so unexpected.

"I feel much better now. I've been visiting relatives in Clearwater and I thought I'd come by on my way back home and spend a few hours with you."

Aries really wanted to see him.

"When will you be here?"

"In a few hours.".

"I'll be in my office, I'll wait for you. Call me when you get here."

Aries waited but Tim never called, never came and she never knew why.

Some months later, out of curiosity, she called him at his place of business in Ohio. The person who answered said he wasn't there anymore. Poor Tim must have died at a young age. Aries would miss him. He was a wonderful person.

Life in the villa away from Stuart could have been pleasant but Aries was still bombarded by his constant telephone calls pleading for reconciliation. "Drop your suit for divorce," he begged.

Aries refused to withdraw her petition but finally she agreed to put the matter temporarily on hold. Giving in to Stuart's desires and her failure to proceed with court action against him proved to be a big error. In the ensuing months her sympathy for Stuart did nothing but place her back in a vulnerable position. Although she had serious doubts about their ability to work the marriage out, she had allowed Stuart to move his belongings into her villa.

Not long after their reunion, the boredom and misery set in once more. Aries was unhappy with Stuart and her unhappiness was clearly evidenced by the unsmiling, worried face she wore.

"Margie said, "Look at yourself in the mirror and see how life with

Stuart Arson is aging you. You used to laugh. Just look at yourself now. Look what is happening to you."

Aries looked in the mirror, one day, and noted the drawn lines in her face that spelled sadness. Her friend was right. Stuart Arson's depression, his way of dealing with her and life itself had taken its toll on her. Things between them would never be any different. She should leave him but he was a hard man to leave. Although he had committed dastardly acts against her she tried to block them from her memory and to forgive him because of his apparent illness. In some ways Stuart behaved like a child. When he was good he was very good and when he was bad he was very naughty. Aries had come to accept that fact.

With Stuart Arson in her life Aries took on all the sexless days and nights that came from living with him. She wouldn't complain about lack of sex anymore because she was convinced he was impotent. He was incapable of being her lover, except in verbal expression and those times were rare. Stuart's intimacy with her consisted of a pat on arm and his broken record of "I love you." Other times, when he was frustrated and angry his tune changed to "Fuck you." Aries hated hearing those filthy words come out of his mouth.

Trying to tolerate the situation as best she could, she usually spent her evenings, at home, sitting beside him, quiet mouthed, stitching on her quilting while he stayed glued to television.

Days were different. She was away from his misery at her office and when she was dying for sex she knew a few studs in that town who were happy to accommodate her.

Living with Stuart was like being on a roller coaster, going up and coming down. Aries had to keep her running shoes on and her skates handy. She never knew when he would explode sending her fleeing to safety.

Stuart's docile behavior at the villa was short lived. Despite her warnings, he was continually raising his voice disturbing the residents. When he moved in he was taking his Lithium and he was sober but that didn't last long. Soon he stopped the Lithium and he was drinking like a fish. Living with him was definitely precarious when he was off medication and on the sauce.

Stuart's doom came to him one morning at the villa. Locking Aries in the bedroom, he stripped her clothing off and forced her to the floor. Then, he beat and kicked her about the chest and head until she thought he was going to kill her. Sobbing and crying, she pleaded with him to stop hurting her. Finally his raging ceased and he pulled her up and made her hug him, kiss him and tell him she loved him. Dressing, he went to work as if nothing had happened.

It was hard for her to believe that a man who acted like that could handle a law practice. Lawyers were supposed to represent justice and he was committing all sorts of injustices against her. Stuart said when he was a Judge in Kansas he put six hundred people in prison. He believed in punishment and he bragged about putting all of those criminals away. Too bad somebody couldn't do something about him.

Aries bathed and checked the bruises and cuts Stuart had inflicted upon her face, arms and chest. She didn't feel well, at all. She was experiencing sharp pains in her chest. Frightened, she went to the hospital emergency room to be checked. After making an examination the doctor admitted her. The diagnosis was an injured chest wall and a jammed hand. Hospitalized for three days, she notified the office she'd be away for a couple days but she was ashamed to tell them where she was and why.

Upon her release, she told Stuart that he had to leave.

"I'm not going anywhere," he declared. "You just try throwing me out."

His actions left her no choice but to call her attorney, reactivate the suit for divorce and place a restraining order against him. Her attorney cautioned her to follow through with the divorce, this time, and to stop falling for Stuart's tricks. "He's trying to avoid paying the money the court will order him to pay," he advised.

Stuart did nothing about leaving the villa so Aries went out and rented an apartment for him, packed his belongings and delivered them there. Afterwards she called his office, told him he had moved and gave him the address of his new place. Stuart received the restraining order that day so he knew she was serious.

Next, she changed the locks on her doors. Still in shock over Stuart's bizarre behavior she called a psychiatrist to discuss it. The doctor warned her never to tell him she was leaving him. "If you're going to do it, do it but don't tell him. With his illness, the thought of your leaving terrifies him and for God's sake don't ever mention another man to him." Dealing with Stuart was a delicate situation and apparently, it required special handling.

After moving into his apartment he called Aries begging her to postpone the divorce and to take him back. He'd stop drinking and get back on his medication. She had heard the same story a dozen times before. Stuart had caused his own exile.

After three years of a marriage filled with conflict, impotency, and violence, the final divorce hearing was scheduled. Margie went to Court with her as a witness. After the hearing Aries asked the Judge if she was divorced, yet?

The Judge answered, "No, not until I sign the final papers."

Stuart had sat mute during the entire hearing. He never uttered a sound. Mia was waiting outside the courtroom to join Margie and Aries for a champagne celebration of her freedom.

Days went by and her final divorce papers never arrived. Asking her attorney where the papers were, he told her that Judges were slow. Perhaps, but Aries imagined Stuart had something to do with the delay.

Several weeks later, Aries was invaded by relatives, two sisters and a brother-in-law, desiring a bucketful of good old Florida sunshine. Angie and Stanley, the married ones, always begged off after dinner but Jamie and Aries went out in the evening gathering whatever excitement and entertainment they could find. Jamie wa.s fifteen years older than Aries but when it came to men they had similar interests. They loved them.

It was Saint Patrick's Day again, so the girls went out to the Irish Inn to celebrate. Jamie loved to dance and she loved Irishmen. Being there made her nostalgic for her old love, Tom, now deceased. Aries had met him once.

"I miss old Tom. I loved him. He was good to me," Jamie said with a sad look on her face.

As they chatted Aries admitted she had an affinity for the Irish, too. "I'm going to Ireland in September and I'm going to make love to every Irishman I can find," she said jokingly.

As she spoke, she was thinking of her own Irish love, John Roberts. She'd been to Sweden the summer before and on the way home, she saw an Irishman at the Gatwick airport in London who looked so much like John that she mentally devoured him. When Aries saw him she wondered if all the men in Ireland favored John. If so she was going there. She'd like nothing better than having a whole country full of men like John Roberts unless they wanted to throw in a few Swedes, like David Saunders.

Thinking of John, she drifted into her own little world of absolute optimum satisfaction, the one she had experienced when they were making love. How she loved to suck his balls, kiss his sweet cock, touch him and love him all over. No one had ever been able to dissolve her and reduce her to nothing the way he did. Because of him Aries had a warm spot in her heart for Irishmen.

The girls wore green that night. almost everybody there wore varying shades of green, except for one woman who had the audacity to appear wearing a flaming red dress. This was a severe error on her part because before the evening was over the ladies verbally tore her into shreds in the rest room. Aries was going to the pottie when a big blonde who was four sheets in the wind yelled at the woman dressed in red. "Hey, what kind of traitor are you to come out on a night like this dressed in red? Get out of here. You are a disgrace to the Irish. You're not allowed at this party."

"I'm Irish," replied the woman.

"Oh no you're not," piped in Aries from the pottie stall. "No self-respecting lassie would dishonor her homeland by wearing red to a Saint Patrick's Day party." Not wanting to continue, Aries made a quick exodus back into the song singing merry crowd.

On the way back to her table she was shoved into a fellow in the people packed room. Leaning against him, she could feel the strength of his strong legs and thighs. Impulsively, her hand touched his thigh to test his muscularity. "Oh, my, what strong muscles you have!" Aries said to the stranger.

"What a way to introduce yourself, young lady!"

"Let me feel your legs, too." He smiled. "My name's Earl. Do you mind if I stand with you?"

By now, there was standing room only. Everybody was squashed together like sardines. Aries told him she was trying to make her way back to her table over by the piano bar. "My sister's waiting for me and I have to get back there."

Earl offered to help her get through the crowd and putting his hand out in front of him, somehow, he cleared the way. Jamie laughed as she returned with a male.

The room was filled with the sounds of harmonizing to "My Wild Irish Rose." The crowd was singing so loudly there was no point in trying to introduce Earl to Jamie, then.

He sat down at their table. Aries hoped he didn't plan to sit with them all evening because there were lots of good looking men there that she wanted to meet.

The dancing began and Earl asked if she'd like to dance.

"I don't like that tune." That was her stock excuse when she didn't want to dance with a fellow.

"Meet Jamie, my sister. Jamie, this is Earl." Jamie greeted him and asked where she had found that nice fellow?

"I found him on the floor on the way back to our table."

Earl laughed and told Jamie that Aries was out there trying to feel his legs. Jamie looked at her and chuckled. "Shame on you, Aries."

During the conversation, Aries bragged about Jamie's being was an excellent dancer. "Dance with her, Earl. She's won dancing contests everywhere." This was true. Jamie took up dancing after she moved to Florida from Tennessee and it became one of her favorite pastimes. Now, she was entering dance competitions all over the country.

Jamie was married to Claude Banner for thirty-eight years. They had eight children. Claude had taken a fancy for the widow next door and Jamie found out about it. That was the beginning of their end. Distraught, she packed up her things and moved to Florida. After their divorce Claude married the other woman. Not long afterward, he contracted a fatal illness and died. It's was a shame that Claude and Jamie gave up all those years of loving over something foolish.

Earl took her suggestion and asked Jamie to dance. Aries watched them. On the dance floor he was either clumsy or he'd had too much to drink. He was stepping all over her sister's feet. Back at the table, he thanked Jamie for the dance and excused himself to go to the head.

"Save my seat," he said upon leaving.

While he was gone Jamie asked where he had come from.

"I met him in the middle of the room and he followed me to the table. I don't want to be with him all night."

At that moment Aries spied Margie and beckoned her to come over and join them. Making her way through the crowd, she plopped herself down in a chair. Margie was a well groomed, approaching middle-aged Elizabeth Taylor type of individual. She was always well dressed and she looked good, although Aries thought she'd look better if she wore her hair a little shorter and didn't wear so much make up.

Earl came back to the table. They ordered another round of drinks. Earl, being a gentleman, paid the check. Aries introduced Margie to him. Bored and seeking excitement, Aries had a hankering to move about on her own in the room.

Earl asked her for the next dance and not to be rude, she accepted.

On the dance floor, Aries caught the eye of the Brian O'Leary, the guy from Ohio. She had met him there on Saint Patrick's Day, last year, and as they parted they made a date for the "same time next year." Brian had caught her eye, too, but momentarily they both were tied up with somebody else. He was dancing with a voluptuous blonde. Maybe she was his wife so Aries would wait for him to approach her.

The music continued and they were still dancing. Aries became more attentive to Earl hoping it might make Brian jealous. If that blonde woman he was dancing with wasn't his wife then she had full intentions of deposing her.

After the dance Earl escorted her back to the table and taking Jamie's hand, he escorted her back out onto the dance floor for a repeat performance.

"Margie, look over there! Guess who's here this year!"

Margie looked but she didn't see Brian. "Who, who's here?"

"Brian O'Leary, remember him?"

"Oh good gracious. I remember him and I sure hope that creep Dwane isn't with him."

"I haven't seen Dwane but Brian made a date with me for Saint Patty's day last year. He didn't call me but he's here."

After Brian and that blonde broad finished the dance, they were sitting at the bar laughing and talking.

"I wonder if the woman with him is his wife," Aries commented.

"Probably so. That's probably why he's staying away from you."

"Well, if she is she certainly doesn't look like his type."

Earl and Jamie came back from the dance floor. Seeing Brian had caused Aries to lose interest in the conversation at her table. She wouldn't be satisfied until she got his complete attention. Right then, he wasn't giving her any. Had he forgotten they had a date?

When Aries turned her head in his direction. Brian was making overtures to his blonde friend. Then, he left the bar and headed her way.

"Here he comes," Aries whispered to Margie.

Arriving at the table he gave everybody a hearty warm Irish hello. "What a pleasant surprise this is!" He said jovially.

Aries made the introductions but since the seats were filled she couldn't invite him to join them.

"May I have this dance, Aries?"

"Certainly."

On the dance floor, Brian started hugging, squeezing her and flooding her lips with warm juicy kisses. "I'm so glad to see you. I just love to kiss you, you taste and feel so good."

He was such an amorous bastard. Aries was glad to see him, too, but not that glad.

Brian said he tried to call her at least three times before he left Ohio but was unable to reach her. "I came on anyway because I knew you'd be here."

"I knew you'd be here, too. That's why I told my sister we had to come here tonight."

Earl was watching the two of them smiling, hugging, kissing and body dancing.

Brian was tall, better than six feet two and Aries was so short beside him. He was definitely Irish with his flashing blue eyes and reddish brown hair.

When Earl saw them on the dance floor he asked the girls what the hell was going on? "Does she know him?"

Margie told Earl in a kind and apologetic way that Brian was a friend whom Aries had known before. Jamie giggled and said, "She must know him."

"Well, I hope so because that guy's acting like he is trying to rape her on the dance floor."

After a few dances Aries told Brian she had to go back to her table and spend some time with her sister. They made plans to meet later that night after she took Jamie home.

When Aries got back to her table Earl grabbed her and pulled her down on his lap.

"Hey," he whispered, "I can take care of you."

Aries apologized to him for abandoning him. She said an old friend from Ohio was in town.

"I promised him, one year ago, I would meet him here tonight."

"That's alright, I understand but I'll be calling you later. That bozo is from out of town and he'll fly away. He won't be here long." Earl had a big grin on his face. I can wait. When he leaves you'll be left with just Earl, the pearl. I'll have no problem taking care of you. You know, my wife died in December and I didn't get to use it much those last few years but since then I've tried it on about three women and it seemed to work alright. If you 're a good girl I'll let you test it out." He was laughing.

"Well, I'm separated and almost divorced from a lawyer who neglected me for three years and I might take you up on that offer, sometime. Didn't you say you lived just down the street from me? I wonder if you would consider giving my sister a ride home tonight."

"Sure, I'll take her home and I'll show her where I live on the way."

"You're a peach, Earl. Thanks!"

The next week, Earl invited her out but she turned him down. She wasn't sure she liked him. Persistent, he wouldn't take no for an answer, he kept on calling.

One afternoon, Margie was in her office and she told her that Earl had been asking her out.

"Why don't you go?"

"I don't think I would like him."

"Well you'd better go. I know some people who know him and they say he's a very nice, well thought of guy. He's also an eligible man. If you're going to get mixed up with anybody Earl's a good pick. You can't judge a book by its cover. He must like you, give him a chance."

After Margie left Aries wondered if he'd call again. She'd turned him down three times and usually, three strikes you're out.

A few days later, Earl called and to his surprise Aries agreed to have dinner with him. After dinner, he took her by his house to meet his daughter who was of college age. Margie was right about him. He was very nice, not good looking but terribly attractive, soul wise.

They dated a lot in the ensuing weeks. His affidavit on the first night of their meeting was a truthful one. Earl, the pearl, was an absolute "sleeper." He was super dynamite in bed. Aries loved fucking him but neither of them were about to take their relationship for anymore than the friendship it was. Earl was a her "fucking friend," just someone to keep her warm in the night.

Before summer was over Stuart was offered an opportunity to buy into a good law practice in Tampa. He asked Aries for her advice and she told him she couldn't help him make that decision.

"Ride with me there for the interview," he begged.

Finally she agreed. They made it to Tampa over and back in the same day. After consulting with the Senior partner of the law firm and looking over the books, Stuart announced that he would give him his decision in a week.

Enroute back to Fort Lauderdale, Aries encouraged him to go ahead and buy into the firm. She didn't tell him but she wanted his ass out of Fort Lauderdale. He accepted the offer and the good news was that he'd be leaving town to set up residence in Tampa in two weeks. The bad news was that two of her children, both Ralph and Mia lived there.

Ralph was caretaking a farmhouse she owned there. Stuart, a sponger, asked if he could stay on the farm temporarily with Ralph and Katie, his girlfriend, until he was settled in his new practice.

Being a softie, Katie said okay. She'd call Ralph and let him know.

"Now remember, Stuart, this arrangement is only temporary. Once you've settled, you'll have to find a place of your own," Aries warned.

Stuart agreed but in late fall he was still living there, rent free. Aries had gotten to know his ways, pretty well, and she knew he wouldn't take a place of his own unless somebody did it for him.

She decided to drive to Tampa one Friday after work. She tried to call and tell them she was coming but getting no answer, she hit the road. Her visit would be a surprise.

Ralph and Katie were there when she arrived but Stuart hadn't come home yet.

"He stays out very late at night," Katie said. "He's been drinking and he's had all kinds of women trapseing in and out in the middle of the night."

Aries clued them in that she was there to move him out.

Stuart was still out at bedtime so Aries assuming he had a key, locked the doors. At seven o'clock the next morning, he came crawling in through the living room window. No key, after all? When he saw her sitting there on the sofa he was like a cat that swallowed the canary. The look on his face was priceless.

"Well, good morning, Mr. Arson."

Stuart responded by asking where the hell she came from?

"Fort Lauderdale, of course."

He looked like the devil and his red eyes were a giveaway that he'd been partying until the wee hours. Going into the kitchen to make the coffee, Aries asked him if he'd like a cup before he left.

"Before I leave? Where do you think I'm going?" Stuart chuckled with a puzzled look on his face.

"You're going to find yourself another place to live, today. I've rented this house for eight hundred dollars a month. I knew you could not afford that kind of rent so when I got an offer, I couldn't turn it down."

"What about Ralph and Katie? Where are they going to live?"

"Ralph's bought a trailer and they're going to move into it."

Stuart didn't like the news he was hearing but since he was living there "gratis," he had little choice in the matter.

"You're in real estate. Can you find me an apartment?"

"I don't know the area but I'll get a newspaper and if you'll tell me the good areas, I'll make the calls for you."

Aries spent the rest of the day making phone calls and driving around with Stuart looking at apartments. He was angry with her for renting the house out and for showing up in Tampa and interrupting his playtime. Extremely hostile and upset, he cursed and drove like a maniac. His behavior made her eager to get him a place and get him out of her farmhouse! He was such an unpleasant person!

Before the day ended they rented an apartment. Going back to the farm, they started packing his belongings. As Aries was stacking his books in a box his check book fell out. Being curious, she flipped through it and saw that months before, he had written a number of one hundred dollar checks to Carla, the high classed prostitute he had known. When confronted Stuart said he hadn't seen her for several years. He denied the whole Carla bit but Aries knew the facts. He had lied to her. You can't change the spots on a leopard.

"Get out of my house and get out of my life," she told him angrily. You're a liar and I can't stand liars."

A short time later Stuart tucked his tail and drove his Austin Healy down the long dirt driveway, away from Aries and away from the farm.

Ralph came in after he left and scolded Aries for allowing him to stay there in the first place. "This place was peaceful before he came, Mom. Why did you just let him move in on us?"

"I'm sorry. I was just trying to do him a favor."

"Well if you're divorcing him, you shouldn't help him. When are you getting rid of him? I wish you'd hurry up and get divorced."

"I'm trying. I asked my lawyer about it and he said the judge had postponed the final hearing."

"Why?" Ralph asked in astonishment.

"You know Stuart's a lawyer and an ex-judge. My attorney says he probably has an "in" with the judge and he keeps having him put the case on the bottom of the pile. It's what some folks call 'sleeping with the Judge,' getting him to do what you want him to do. Those dam Judges stick together like glue. Our divorce has been going on for almost two years and nothing has been resolved yet."

Katie had come into the room. Overhearing the conversation, she suggested that Stuart was delaying the divorce deliberately hoping something would happen to her and he would get all of her money. Aries laughed telling her there was no such chance.

With Stuart gone the remainder of the weekend was peaceful and quiet. Aries took the children out for dinner on Saturday for a treat before returning to Fort Lauderdale to the "salt mines."

A few weeks later Aries was surprised to receive an offer from a lucrative real estate firm in Tampa for the merger of her company with theirs. They would retain two offices, Snow & Company in Fort Lauderdale and Crescent Company in Tampa.

The Broker invited her to visit his company in Tampa to inspect the books and familiarize herself with the company's operations. He would do the same with hers. The offer sounded interesting but she she would have to do some thorough investigating before making a decision.

In October, she hired John O'Donald to manage her company while she was in Tampa checking out Crescent Company. While there she would stay at the farmhouse with Ralph and Katie. How ironic that she was being called to the same town where Stuart Arson was practicing law! That was the part she didn't like about it. There was a good side though. Ralph and Mia were there and she had missed her children. They all, one by one, had left Fort Lauderdale.

At Crescent Company Aries was introduced to the staff and the employees. They all suspected that she was there on a special mission.

One day she was having lunch with Hamid, the Broker, when Stuart walked into the same restaurant. Seeing her with another man, he became livid with anger. Furious, he came over to their table and called her a whore and a bunch of other unkind words. He made a royal ass of himself leaving Aries to explain things to Hamid. She hadn't mentioned her personal life but now, he knew that her estranged husband was a lawyer in Tampa. Aries was embarrassed by Stuart's outburst but Hamid was understanding about the unfortunate incident.

That evening, Shasta, Hamid's sister, invited her to go to the

Manford Hotel for the cocktail hour. After that traumatic run in with Stuart, Aries needed a "relaxer" so she accepted the invite.

Shasta was a dark-haired, attractive Iranian girl, not too bright in real estate but a good conversationalist. She was an agent at Crescent and Aries could learn about the inside operations of their company from another point of view rather than relying on what she heard strictly from the horse's mouth.

"I'll meet you there at five," Shasta said. "Do you know how to get there?"

"No, but I have a map and I'll find it."

"Just turn off on Pringle and take a left on Ryan."

"Will do!"

As planned the girls met in the hotel bar and after ordering drinks they became engrossed in talk about real estate. Busy conversing, Aries hardly noticed the tall, attractive man who sat down beside her. Suddenly, he interjected himself in their conversation. He, too, was in real estate. Taking a good look at him, he was a great big "hunk"of a fellow. Aries looked down to see his shoe size and sure enough, his feet matched the rest of him, BIG. She had heard you could detect the size of a man's penis by his shoe size. From then on she began to notice men's feet and after testing it a couple times she believed that tale.

"What's your name?" The fellow inquired.

"My name's Aries Winston. What's yours?"

"I'm Jake Andrews. Nice to meet you. You ladies seem to be quite preoccupied. You must have a lot to talk about."

We do, but I'm glad you interrupted us. We've talked business long enough"

"The music's nice here. Would you like to dance?"

"I'd love to."

She turned to Shasta and excusing herself, she was off to the dance floor with her new found friend.

The rest of the evening was delightful. Sometimes getting acquainted can be exciting. Compliments were flowing from both sides. Jake and Aries wanted to get to know each other better. There is absolutely no substitution for that undescribable chemistry that exudes without warning between two people.

Jake held Aries, tightly, as they danced and she felt good with his strong frame wrapped around her. Tonight, she needed someone to hug her and to make her feel wanted and beautiful. Jake was doing just that. Aries told him she was separated from her husband and he said that he had a very nice wife but at that moment, neither of their marital statuses mattered. They were thoroughly enjoying each other.

"My wife's working late, tonight. She's a switchboard operator. She knew I had an evening appointment but she won't expect me to be this late."

"Well, why don't you hurry home?"

"I'll have to go soon but first, I need to talk to you some more. Where are you staying?"

"Oh, the secretary got me a room at some hotel south of town. Almost everything was booked up on account of the General Motors convention. I have the address written down on a piece of paper in my purse."

"Let me see it and I will tell you how to get there, in fact, I will lead you to your hotel on my way home."

"Oh, no, I'll find it."

"You've had plenty to drink and I want to make sure you arrive where you're going safely. Come on, let's get out of here. Where did you park your car?"

"It's out front."

"Mine is in the parking garage, I'll go get it and meet you in front of the hotel."

"Okay, but I need to go to the bathroom before I leave."

"That's just like a woman," he responded laughing. "I'll see you outside."

Arriving at the hotel, Jake waited while Aries checked in. He told her it was unsafe for a woman to be wandering around alone at night. He seemed like such a gentlemen.

"Give me your key and I'll help you find your room," he offered.

"Fine, but you can't stay."

Jake Andrews had a smiling humorous personality. As he opened the door Aries observed him. He bore a strange resemblance to Keith

Kiser, her college love. Jake's build was like Keith's. He had those broad shoulders and that "hunk of man" look. Maybe, she would let him come in for just a few minutes.

Inside her room, the inevitable happened. In her state of mind she felt that she needed and deserved a good fuck. She had met Jake by accident that day. How it happened really didn't matter. Aries needed somebody warm, kind and gentle. Jake seemed to fit that bill. In bed the rest of him matched his shoe size. This was particular delight. She'd met him by chance but after the loving, she was sure she'd see him again and again.

After completing her investigation Aries decided not to affiliate with Crescent Company but to set up a branch office of Snow & Company in Tampa. She'd promote John O'Donald to manager of the Fort Lauderdale office and she'd come to Tampa herself and get the new office started.

John O'Donald accepted the position and Aries relocated in Tampa. She knew some people there, the folks at Crescent Company, Jake, a couple lawyers and her children. Socially, she knew nobody.

Being good in the real estate business, she had no fear of her new venture in Central Florida. As soon as she got established and found her way around, she'd definitely be a threat to the rest of them. She loved competition.

Aries had her hands full opening the branch in Tampa, getting organized, hiring associates and soliciting new business. Stuart had gotten wind of her being in the area and since her company telephone number was listed, he had that, too. On occasion he called to bug her but she was determined to avoid physical contact with him.

One day she went to Stuart's office to get his signature on some legal documents. Still her legal husband, this visit was necessary. The meeting at his office was disastrous. Stuart was in a very antagonistic mood. Getting up from his desk, he started pushing her and shoving her. Everybody must have heard him, including his law partners in the adjoining rooms and the clients and secretaries in the reception area. He created a real scene. One of the partners had to come in and call him off. Attorney or not, she was going to have him arrested if he ever laid a hand on her again.

Feeling pretty miserable after that disastrous bout, Aries closed her office early that afternoon. On the way home she stopped by the Melchor Hotel for a drink. A landmark in the area, the hotel was very old and quaint in appearance. Even the entertainment and the waiters dress was in keeping with forty years earlier.

As Aries entered the bar she spied two old ladies all decked out in their ruffles and feathers. She had seen them once before when she had been there. The Melchor must have been one of their regular hangouts. Walking around the bar as she frequently did, she assessed the group that was assembled for the cocktail hour. Unimpressed by any of them, she took a seat at the end of the counter. The bartender came over to take her order. It was rather stuffy in there so she removed the beige ultrasuede coat she was wearing and placing it neatly on the back of her seat. As she reached for the nut mix the woman sitting next to her turned and spoke to her.

"Hello, I'm Mary Tyler. What brings you here?"

"I was just in the neighborhood and I thought I would stop off here for a drink before going home."

"What do you do? Do you work in this area?"

Goodness, this damn broad was certainly nosy. All she wanted to do was to have a peaceful drink and she was being interrogated by this silly woman. Trying to be polite, Aries answered her question and proceeded to stuff her mouth full of nut mix. She would finish this drink and get out of there. Leaving her seat, she headed in the direction of the bathroom. The woman next to her yelled.

"Hey, don't leave now. I want you to meet my girlfriend. Here she comes now."

"I'll be back," Aries nodded. Feeling safer in the bathroom, she took a much needed piss. The entertainer entered the stall next to hers. Aries asked her about the places in town where a person could go for entertainment.

"Depends upon what you want to do."

"I just want to relax and enjoy some quiet music."

"Oh, then you might try the Sandhills or Hughies. I hear that they have good 50's music there. Are you new in the area?"

"Yes!".

Then, stop by the hostess desk on your way out and ask her to give you directions."

"Thanks a lot."

Leaving the rest room, Aries went to the hostess desk and got directions to the other two places. When she got back to her seat the ladies next to her were deeply engaged in conversation.

"Oh, I though you were leaving," said Mary. " I saw you standing at the hostess desk."

"She was just giving me some directions."

"Don't leave. Stay here for awhile and talk to us."

"Sorry girls, but I really do have to go now." Aries motioned for the bartender. "May I have my check?" Charging her drink on her faithful American Express, she bid the duo goodbye and made her exit. What a dull half hour!

Finding her car in the parking lot, Aries headed in the direction of I-75 toward Sandhills. The place was five miles down the road so she tuned the radio in to her favorite hilly-billy station. They were playing "On The Road Again." This song had become a favorite of hers because its words seemed to fit her current lifestyle. She was always on the road again.

Arriving at Sandhills, she found a space in the parking lot. She could hear loud music floating from inside into the atmosphere. Following its sound, she entered through the rear. Not liking what she saw, she turned around and went back to the car. The Sandhills seemed like a real rabble-rousing place. She would go on to Hughie's. After two losers this evening she was almost afraid to try a third time. Hughie's was nearby so within minutes she was there.

Another guest joined her at the entry way.

"Come on in, young lady. This place has a really good band. Perhaps, you will save me a dance or two, later. The house was packed and there were only two seats left at the bar. The man who greeted her took one and she took the other. Twas' just her luck. Everybody would think he was her escort and he wasn't her type. Politely, he asked her to dance and she accepted his invitation. After the dance, they sipped on their drinks while chatting. Three men were seated on her right, talking business. As they spoke she caught the eye of the short, athletic looking fellow in the center. His icy blue eyes pierced the pits of her warm brown ones. His laugh was infectious and his flashing smile penetrated the room. She could tell he was the boss and a ladies man.

The conversation came to a sudden halt.

Looking Aries's way he said. "Hello. Who are you?"

"My name's Aries."

"What brings you here this evening?"

"I was on my way home. I didn't plan to come here. It was an accident."

"I don't believe it. I wasn't supposed to be here either. Some uncontrollable urge suddenly brought me here. My name's Bill and I'd like to get know you better. I have to entertain some salesmen for awhile but will you wait for me?"

Aries shook her head affirmatively.

When the evening ended Bill Everhard accompanied her home. They hit it off well. He was a tiger in bed!

A few days after their first roll in the hay, he invited her to spend a weekend at the beach. She got only one glimpse of the ocean while they were there. The rest of the time was spent in bed making love, except for eating. Bill had quite a hearty appetite for sex and in that department he was just her kind of man.

Several days after the beach trip he invited her to stay with him and his kids at his house. Taking him up on his offer, Aries stayed there from October to December. This was a first for her. Before when she had lived with men, they stayed at her house, rent free.

Aries commuted back and forth between Tampa and Fort Lauderdale after opening the Tampa branch office. Her office manager was on a good salary and at first, he did a good job. However, with her out of the picture he began neglecting the office and working on his own deals. He got 75% on his own sales so naturally he would concentrate them. She had made the mistake of allowing the manager to compete with the salesman.

During the Christmas holidays Aries went to Fort Lauderdale to straighten out the office. A few weeks later, Bill left his job in the car business and came to Fort Lauderdale to help with her now struggling real estate company. There were a lot of question in her mind about what Bill's real motives were.

"I can make things pop in this company for you," he said. "Give me a few days and I'll have the Snow & Company's telephone ringing off the hook. Your salesman have been ripping you off, baby, and I am going to straighten their asses out. That John who works here, I want you to set up a meeting with me and him, just me and him. I am going to put him on the money, you'll have no more problems with him."

"Oh, please, don't say anything to make him mad. He is a good producer and he'll quit."

"Let me handle this, baby. I'm just going to talk to him man to man."

"He won't pay any attention to you as an outsider."

"Tell him that I'm buying the company.

"He'll never believe that."

"He will if he sees a contract for purchase. I'll buy the company. Notify them all, including your accountant that Bill Everhard is taking over and I don't want any interference from you either, baby. There can only be one boss."

"I'll keep my mouth shut. I really do need help. I can't handle any of them, not even the secretary. She does what she pleases, regardless of what I say."

"You're talking about Cindy, she's some cute dish. I'll have no problems with her. Give me a couple hours alone with her and she'll be eating out of my hands."

"Oh, really, she's too young for you. I don't mean it that way. I love you but I have a knack at handling people. I will just tell her how good she looks and thank her for the fine job she's doing at the front desk and she will bust her tail to please me."

Aries went along with Bill's plan of posing as the new owner of Snow & Company. After two weeks, Aries began to realize that he was a real con artist. His feigned takeover of her company was becoming a horrible nightmare.

He had her lease a new truck for the company. Why did the company need one? Wasn't her own car sufficient?

"Babes, you can use both of them. We'll put Snow & Company all over the side of the truck and that will be good advertising."

Well, Snow & Company never saw that truck except for glimpses of it passing down the street past the office. Aries had plunked down cash for the down payment, the insurance and she was paying for the gas, gas, and more gas.

After arriving in Fort Lauderdale Bill's children joined him at her villa. They were nice kids but six people in a one bedroom apartment was a little much. Aries told him that he'd have to rent a place because children were not allowed in permanent residency there. It was evident that he didn't have the money to rent anything.

Rules were so strict at her complex. One day, the manager approached her with a written complaint about one of her guests using the laundry.

"You can't do anything around here," she argued.

"You're right. The rules around here don't even permit sex. If you're planning on screwing, you'd better get a motel."

It was hectic having four kids in the villa. Bill promised to do something about it and he did. He sent the younger two, Gini and Aaron, to Grandma's in New York for Christmas. This helped some but still they were left with Tom, a handsome blue eyed blonde, hyperactive and oversexed for his tender age of fifteen and Rob who emptied the truck's gas tank at the tune of $1.39 per gallon (at her expense) on a daily basis.

You name it, Aries had it! It was like a three ring circus. There were kids all over the office, long distance calls being put on her phone, groceries and more groceries, clothing and entertainment costs for the kids and for Bill. She was working herself silly and her money was running out like water running out of a spigot.

Bill's newspapers ads caused the office phone to ring off the hook, as predicted, but Christmas was coming and all of the employees were out shopping. There was insufficient help to handle the calls so very few sales were made.

Stuck in the office, Aries had to send the the children to do the Christmas shopping. When she wasn't talking on the phone she was digging in her purse and handing out credit cards or signing checks.

Finally, Christmas came and at last she had a day off.

Christmas eve was spent grocery shopping and preparing food for the big feast the next day. Bill's estranged wife called and after that call, he spent the next day moping. When asked what was wrong, he got no sensible answer.

New Year's came and after taking Aries for a new two hundred dollar suit for the occasion, they joined clients and friends at Yesterday's for the celebration. She had to pick up the tab there, too.

"Pay it," he told her smiling. "You can write it off as a company expense."

Company expense, hell! Bill Everhard was a real user but what else could she expect from a car salesman. He thought he had a golden cock but he was about to get a rude awakening. She wasn't buying his merchandise anymore. He had met his waterloo and it was all over but the shouting.

One day he wanted to go to Tampa on business. Accommodating him, she gave him a lift in her truck. When they arrived she dumped him out and told him to "get lost." He could find a house and come back to Lauderdale to pick up his children. She'd had enough of his penniless pockets and promises he couldn't fulfill. "So long," she said. With these words she put the truck in gear and went on trucking down the highway. She would stay tonight at the farmhouse and tomorrow, she'd return to Fort Lauderdale to pick up the pieces of her office and her life.

Aries's escapade with Everhard had been so costly that she was now facing a financial dilemma. She would have to either close one or both of her offices or declare bankruptcy. Facing reality, her trust in the wrong people had caused her defeat. What she did in business herself she could count on and control but with too many hands in the pie, the whole damned pie was ruined.

She stopped by Howard Johnson's for a cocktail before going to the farmhouse. Throwing Bill out had been an unpleasant task and it left her feeling somewhat disheveled. As she sat at a table, alone, she felt a tap on her shoulder. Stuart Arson, of all people, was standing over her looking as meek as a lamb.

"Hello, Aries. Could I join you?"

Her resistance was low and Stuart seemed to be in a friendly mood so she allowed him to take a seat. Their meeting was a good one. Stuart's behavior was impeccable.

"I'm on a new medication and it's working. I've stopped drinking (he was drinking ginger ale) and I'm not impotent anymore," he announced happily. He was regretful of all his past behavior, he loved her and he wanted to make all of his wrong doings up to her. "Spend the night with me and you'll see."

Stuart had a way with her when he had his good side on and being a wandering soul again, she let him accompany her to the farmhouse. Ralph and Katie were very surprised when they saw them together. They thought the nightmare was over.

Stuart wanted them to get back together. Aries promised to give his proposal her serious consideration. She'd let him know but before she made a decision, she'd have to go back to Fort Lauderdale and to straighten out the affairs at Snow & Company.

"You ought to close that office," he advised. "You cannot control a business when you have to be in two places. John O'Donald will rob you blind in your absence. You'll never make any money if you're not there. Business is booming in Tampa. I expect to make two hundred thousand dollars this year. If you'll give up that business, I'll give you half of everything I make."

If only what he was saying could be true. After thirteen years she tiring of the hassles of real estate.

"Close both of your offices. Go to work for someone else and let them have all the headaches of running a company."

Aries promised to give him an answer soon. Her company was struggling but still, she dreaded the thoughts of its closing. She had spent four years nurturing it.

Offering her Lauderdale company for sale, she got some inquires from Northern sources. Potential buyers wanted her to stay with the company and this was unacceptable because she was trying to make the move to Tampa. Finally, she made a deal with Marvin Prance and Company. She transferred her clients and her listings to Margie, who worked there. Her clients would be in competent hands with her and Marvin Prance had a good reputation. The sales people, including her manager, could decide where they wanted to go. Marvin Prance agreed to pay her a referral fee on all business generated by Snow & Company's prior efforts.

The company calls were forwarded to Prances's office and the office equipment was put in storage. The company's transition was accomplished in about a week. It was sad to see Snow & Company devoured and swallowed up by the tycoons of Marvin Prance. Aries felt like she had been to a funeral when she stacked away the last Snow & Company sign. "You're dead little Snow & Company," she said as she looked at the logo admiring it.

She closed her Tampa office and as part of the agreement with Marvin Prance, she placed her license as a Broker-Salesman with their Tampa office. Now a simple salesman, the President's gavel along with the corporate seal had been removed from her desk.

Disheartened at the events of the past few months, Aries told Stuart she'd give their marriage one last try. In Mid January he moved into the farmhouse. When this happened Ralph and Katie moved out into the backyard in a trailer. They didn't want to be in hearing distance of Stuart's roars.

"He's promised to be different now," Aries advised them. Ralph looked at her in disbelief and Katie said she didn't think he would ever change. Ralph told Katie it was none of her business but he warned Aries not to disturb him when Stuart went on one of his bad rampages.

The first couple weeks Stuart was dull but quiet. He was still impotent. Luckily, when Aries got desperate Jake Andrews was around. Those out of town real estate conventions and meetings were her sexual salvation.

Working as a salesman, Aries was relieved not having salespeople to supervise. Still, she was called to Marvin Prance's in Lauderdale occasionally to handle problems with her listings and sales. Prance gave her a private office on these visits and it was nice sleeping with Earl, the pearl. A mighty fine stud, he was always pleased to have her company.

During the winter months and on into Spring, Aries plodded along with Stuart. He quit his medication saying it wasn't working and she caught him emptying the scotch bottles in his stomach and filling them up with water. Women were calling the house for him, common waitresses and the like. He had taken up the habit of stopping off at a "rough country bar" after work and he had picked up a bunch of rift raft for friends.

One of his best buddies, Eddie, was a hopeless drunk. He lived inside the alcohol bottle trying to look out. Stuart represented him in a manslaughter case. In his drunken trance he had struck and killed a twelve year old boy on a bicycle. Eddie was guilty as charged but Stuart's cunningness got him off with only a six months jail sentence. Then, he'd be back on the streets to kill somebody else. Stuart was only thinking of the money and the notoriety he'd get as a result of his courtroom victory. "Every drug dealer and criminal in town will be calling me now," he said.

Disgusted with his actions, Aries caught a plane to Fort Lauderdale for the weekend. When she returned she found evidences of a woman having been there. There was lipstick and makeup that didn't belong to her in the bathroom and she found a ladies bra and undies in the laundry. Stuart was messing around on her but his days of coming back to her bed were numbered.

Aries attended a real estate conference in St. Petersburg in May. Jamie lived there so she invited her to come back to Tampa with her after the convention on Friday.

She shared a room with Jake at the conference hotel. He kiddingly claimed that the only reason he was sharing was because his wife wanted him to have a roommate so his monthly business expenses would be cheaper.

"I'm glad she doesn't know your roommate is me," Aries remarked.

The two day escape ended swiftly. Aries spent the last morning fucking Jake "so long until the next time." That guy had a powerful hammer.

Stuart was angry when she got home but he tried to control his temper in front of Jamie. The liquor cabinet door was ajar and Aries discovered that the Scotch bottle had, once more, been emptied and filled with water. Her curiosity was getting the best of her. "Why do you keep drinking the scotch and filling the bottle back up with water, Stuart? Don't you think I can tell the difference?"

Denying the act, he said Ralph must have done it. Aries talked to Katie, privately. "He's drinking again," Katie told her. "Ralph doesn't drink liquor and he hasn't been in the house all week. Stuart's been drinking the scotch. He had some black haired woman here the other afternoon. He said his secretary came to get some typing but she stayed until the wee hours."

There was no point in even mentioning this to Stuart. He was a bald faced liar and he didn't know the meaning of the word "truth."

Stuart stayed up that night pretending to read a book after the girls went to bed. Aries was sleeping soundly when at about three-thirty a.m. he came roaring into the room shouting filthy words, abruptly awakening her.

"Please, please be quiet, Stuart, you're going to wake Jamie up. We've got a houseguest, you know."

Stuart paid no attention to her. He was very drunk. He cursed her for going to bed and not staying up to talk with him.

"I was tired and you seemed to be content reading your novel. Please come to bed and let me get back to sleep."

Stuart was on a trip of his own. He continued to badger her. Grabbing ahold of the mattress, he picked it up with her on it and flung it across the room.

The ruckus woke Jamie up. She walked down the hall toward the bathroom. Stuart's filthy mouth was still going. Aries snatched up her clothes and headed for the bathroom, too. "Get your suitcase," she whispered to Jamie. He's at it again and we're leaving. I'll meet you in the yard at the car. Jamie knew how to follow instructions well.

When Stuart turned his back to go into the other room Aries grabbed her purse and ran out of the house. Jamie was there as she'd been told and they jumped into the car and took off.

"Where are we going?" Jamie asked.

"I thought we'd take a ride to Fort Lauderdale and spend the weekend in the villa so we could get some peace."

Jamie didn't blame her for leaving the way Stuart was acting but she feared he'd be angry when he discovered they were gone.

"Don't worry about it," Aries advised.

On Saturday, Aries called home. Stuart was furious that she had eluded him. Two hundred fifty miles away, she was safe and she could say what she wanted to say. "I'm not going to live with you anymore," she told him over the wire. " It's over. Start packing your things. You have to leave and you'd better be out of there when I get back home tomorrow."

The next day, Aries took Jamie back to St. Petersburg before going back home. Stuart was sitting on the couch in the living room when she arrived at the farmhouse.

"Are you packed yet?" She asked coldly as she entered the room.

"No, but it won't take me long."

Aries sat down to talk to him explaining that their life together had been too traumatic and she didn't intend to live in constant fear of having to flee from her own house.

"Are you sure that's the way you want it? Are you sure you want me to go?"

"Yes, yes, I've thought it over and I'm sure. I'm not going to change my mind and ask you to stay."

"I've thought it over, too and I'm not going to put up with a wife running off and leaving me. If you really mean it, I'll leave forever. I'll go back to Kansas and live."

Aries felt sorry for him. She knew if she told him she loved him and wanted him to stay he would. He hadn't packed anything. She couldn't let her pity for him sway her rational mind. She would hold firm to her decision.

Getting up from the sofa, she went out to the porch and emptied the contents of the boxes she had brought home from the villa. Pointing to them, she asked Stuart if he wanted her to help him pack.

"No, I'll do it myself, I don't need any assistance." He must have taken double tranquilizers that day because to her surprise he remained amazingly calm.

It was late when he finished loading up his car. "Can I stay with you one more night?" He pleaded pitifully.

One more night you may stay, provided you'll be nice. Stuart held her in his arms all night. He even tried to make love to her as best as he could.

The next morning, Aries told him goodbye and watched by the doorway as he motored his blue Austin Healy down the long narrow driveway, away from the farm and away from her. A tear fell upon her check. Parting was such sweet sorrow. Standing there, a smile came to her lips as she noticed the rose bush at her feet. Deep down inside she knew her life, just like the rose, was just beginning to bloom.

Part Twenty

At last the storm was over. Stuart's departure from Aries life had been as sudden as his entry. More than four years had passed since the fateful night Stuart had called inviting her to come over, telling her that his wife had gone.

Sitting sat at his desk in the farmhouse, she retraced the events of yesterday, trying to remember the good about him as the horrible past kept creeping in to haunt her. If she should start to regret telling him to leave, she would jolt her memory to remember all the terrible acts he committed against her.

The storm was over leaving only traces of it's devastation in the calm that now prevailed. Stuart's desk had been cleared away. There was no evidence of his ever having been there before but for a brown telephone and some scattered files he had neglected to remove.

Is this real or am I dreaming? Aries asked herself as she sat in silence. Did he just pretend to be leaving? Will he come storming back during the night when all is still and burst in like a wild man and attack me? Surely, this time he was gone. He had taken his clothes and everything he could carry. His Austin Healy was loaded down with his belongings. The stuff that wouldn't fit in had been left sitting outside by his office door. Aries wondered why he had left his dress suits and his law diploma. Those things should have been important to him. Strange, too, he never cleaned up or changed clothes before he left. He claimed he was heading west to Kansas, yet, he had left in his garden clothes.

439

When he arrived safely at his destination Stuart promised to let her know. She'd breathe easier knowing he was out of Florida. He had friends in Kansas who could help him get started again. If worse came to worse he could always call his Mother, the lush, and she'd run to his aid.

Aries shook her head. Why should she be worrying about him? Stuart Arson had made his own bed and he would have to lie in it. He would have to learn the hard way that he couldn't go around lying, cheating and abusing people without suffering the consequences of his acts. Stuart never learned from his mistakes. He kept making the same errors over and over. His inability to assimilate was a definite sign of mental illness. Thank goodness, she was finally free of him.

For several hours Aries sat alone in the room thinking about the conversation they had the day before his departure. Maybe she should have handled it another way but how? Nothing she had done before had worked. Leaving him or getting him to leave had never been an easy task.

Aries had escaped from the prison of his insanities but still she could feel the weight of the chains that had bound her. Out of her cage of misery she was like a baby bird eager to flutter far but at first, she would flutter with caution.

Finally, she sauntered down the long pine paneled hallway past the door to her bedroom into the kitchen. She could see the dogs, Stormy and Lady playing together out by the garden. Those darn dogs were going to ruin that garden yet, she pondered. Stringing it off hadn't done a bit of good. She wished Ralph would get rid of them.

Stormy would probably miss Stuart when she realized he wouldn't be coming home. He was her friend. Stormy was a pit bull and nobody with any sense messed around with her, nobody except Stuart. They were two of a kind because both of them were likely to wield a surprise attack on a person. Aries stayed out of Stormy's way. It was too bad she hadn't realized in time that Stuart's bite could be equally as devastating.

Opening the refrigerator door, she found that it contained very little food. That's Stuart, she thought. He didn't bother to buy anything while she was away. Tomorrow she'd clean it out and buy some food.

Reaching into a covered bowl, she plucked a radish that they had grown themselves. Popping it in her mouth, she headed back down the hall. The house was strangely quiet but Aries could feel an unsettled air about its atmosphere. Twas' as if it was suffering yet from Stuart's thundering roar.

"Don't worry house, everything's alright," she told it as she gently rubbed her hands across the planks that flanked the brown hall walls. She was sure that house had a personality. The house and the yard, too, had sensed the tension that had prevailed. Things would be better now with Stuart gone. In a little while things would brighten up again.

At first, it was hard to adjust to the new strange silence around the house. Ralph and Katie were away for a couple days. As Aries moved about the house she was alone with her solitude and sounds of nothing save the creaking of the floor planks and the occasional sounds of the barking dogs. Life with Stuart had been a nightmare she wished she could erase from her memory, but it was too soon. It would take time for her scars to heal.

That weekend, to kill the time, Aries invited her friend, Noel, from Fort Lauderdale to come for a visit. Noel was panting for an intimate relationship with her but all he could ever be to her was just a friend. On Sunday afternoon, he went home leaving Aries to her own devices.

When Ralph and Katie returned from their trip, they received the news of Stuart's leaving. They were glad he was gone because he had caused too much commotion around there.

Aries told Katie she should have seen him leaving. "That Austin Healy was filled to the brim. The only stuff he left was his suits and his law diploma."

" I wonder why he didn't take them," said Katie puzzled.

"They wouldn't fit. There wasn't room in the car. He tried to take his suits but there wasn't enough room so he had to take them out."

"But he'll need his suits." Katie stated somewhat puzzled

"Maybe he's going to buy himself a new wardrobe. Half of his clothes were too big for him anyway." Aries suggested.

"I sure hope he doesn't come back," said Katie apprehensively, "maybe he left those things on purpose so he would have an excuse to come back."

"I don't think he'll be back. He promised to call me when he got to Kansas. When he does I'll try to find out where he's calling from." Aries knew the kids wouldn't rest easy until they knew for a certainty that Stuart was really gone.

"I wouldn't be surprised if he's still in town," said Katie. "He told so many lies that nobody could ever believe a word that came out of his mouth."

"He was good about that, alright."

A few days later Stuart called. He said he was in Topeka, Kansas and instructed her to forward his mail there in care of general delivery. The mail he was referring to was probably his final divorce papers. He would want to know when he became free and available. Stuart Arson wasn't about to spend a night without a woman. Aries had seen him in action. If she wasn't with him he'd pick up any stray cat for the night.

Aries felt very sorry for any woman who hooked up with him because the relationship sooner or later would lead to fucking misery.

Unable to determine whether the call was long distance or not, after he hung up Aries called his lawyer friend in Topeka to inquire if they had heard from him. They hadn't.

Before leaving Stuart mentioned that he might go back there to his old job but then he had talked about a lot of things. Once, he told her he might give up practicing law and go into another profession. He had been an attorney for twenty years. Surely he wouldn't throw all that education down the drain.

During the call Stuart dwelled on the fact that she had forced him to leave and had cold heartedly sent him away. He was angry and apparently, he was feeling sorry for himself. As usual, he had to have the last word and as usual, his last word was nasty. When she told him she had to hang up, he yelled "fuck you" and clicked the receiver down loudly. Aries was glad he wasn't in slugging range. With this sort of behavior she would consider herself lucky to be rid of him.

For awhile, everybody worried about Stuart's reappearing. Katie told Aries that a Mercedes had pulled up into the yard, one evening when she was out. The man driving had gray hair and he wore glasses. She could have sworn it was Stuart but what was he doing in that car? Later, Mia called to say her husband had passed a county car driving down Highway 17. The driver looked just like Stuart. He turned around and tried to follow the car but he lost him. Aries heard all kind of rumors, but none of them panned out. She told everybody to forget about wondering where Stuart Arson was and relax. "He's probably in Arizona with his Mother and we've e heard the last of him," she said.

Aries was ready to get down to some serious business. She had been lax with real estate before Stuart left because he kept her in such a turmoil. Now she could work her prospects without having to worry about his jealousy. She cherished her new found freedom to conduct her business without his constant complaining and interference. Even the air smelled better now that he was gone. There was only one thing lacking in her life, a man, and hopefully, she could solve that problem.

Parting with Stuart was different than parting with Greg had been years before. This time she was able to greet old loneliness as a friend knowing he would only be there for awhile. In Stuart's case loneliness would be the lesser of the two evils.

Maybe now, she'd take up tennis again. She loved the sport and she'd been pretty good at it. She had played with Stuart but he was a beginner and that didn't help her game much. Being jealous, he resented her playing with other male players who were on her level or better.

As Aries sat at her desk in the office at Marvin Prance & Company, she scanned the latest company Newsletter. She noted that the Meadowbrook Central Area Convention was to be held at Indian Rock Beach on June 19th. As one of the competition events a tennis tournament was on the agenda. She'd go to the convention and play in the tournament Tearing off the green application blank, Aries filled it out, wrote a check for the fee and put it in the secretary's mailbox.

A few days later, talk began around the office about convention weekend.

"Hey, Aries, are you going to Indian Rock Beach?" asked Craig.

"I guess so, I've signed up for it."

Aries always got a kick out of joking with Craig. He was blonde with flashing blue eyes and he stood a full six feet four inches tall. She was only five feet two and when she stood in front of him her head barely reached the top of his rib cage. Aries knew the tennis players in the office were but none of them had ever seen her play.

"Are you playing in the tournament?" Craig asked smiling.

"Yes, I'm playing and I intend to win it."

"No chance," teased Craig. "I'm playing and so is Vic. You can't win against old pros like us."

Vic, who was sitting at the desk across the room, heard that one. He raised his eyes away from the newspaper he was reading and entered into the conversation. Blushing, he pulled out a cigarette and lit it. Throwing his head back and laughing, he told Aries she would be playing against the "big boys" in this tournament.

"You can't beat us."

"Wanna bet! I can beat all of you."

As Aries made the comment she looked up at Craig and figured he might be a real threat because of his height. On the other hand, she had known real tall tennis players who were awkward on the court. Gazing at Vic, she could just visualize him out there. He was so damned fat she wouldn't waste her time worrying about him.

The guys told Aries they wouldn't bet with her because they didn't want to steal her money. Time would tell who the winner was but it was fun getting psyched up for the big match.

A number of associates signed up for the convention and plans were made to travel in a group on the company bus. Aries wasn't much for group traveling so she declined telling them that she'd meet them there.

Excited about the trip, she needed to go shopping for a tennis outfit to wear in the tournament and something sexy for the evening. She'd stop by Gibson's at lunchtime. She was on the floor that afternoon but if she left early she'd be back in time.

Mattie Sue called her on the intercom and asked her to go across the street for lunch.

"Sweetie, I can't. In the first place, I hate the food at that place and in the second place, I'm not hungry. I'm on a diet and I need to go shopping for a new dress. Wanna come?"

"Oh, no I can't. I have an appointment at one-thirty and I've got to get back here.

"Oh, well, we'll have to take a rain check on lunch this time."

Aries really loved Mattie Sue. She was a top quality person, one of the nicest girls in the office. In Aries opinion, she suffered from only two things, lack of self-confidence and lack of sex. Married for thirty years to a really nice guy, apparently she had become too wrapped up in her children and her husband had become too unwrapped with her in bed.

Mattie Sue impressed Aries as a woman who was bored with her marriage, frustrated with her life and as a woman who needed a good fuck. She enjoyed hearing Aries tales of adventure and she told her that she should stay single because she had it made. Aries could have told her the grass always looks greener on the other side but sometimes, it's merely an optical illusion.

Not long after Stuart left, Ralph came home one day announcing that he'd found a place where his Mom would really love to live. Why did Ralph think she'd like to move? She had a nice place on the farm. She imagined Katie was behind some of this talk. Maybe she wanted Ralph to talk her into moving out of the farmhouse so she could move back in..

"I found this beautiful place," Ralph went on. "I saw the red rooftops as I was driving down the Interstate and I took the exit to see what was over there. It was a private club, Mom, with guards wearing red coats on horses at the gate. It was just your style!"

"Well, I'll ride by and look at this complex when I get a chance."

Several days later, Aries was in the area Ralph had mentioned and she went by the complex. The girl in the sales office showed her the models. Ralph was right! This place was just her style, particularly since she was living alone and getting ready to be single. They had tennis courts, a lakefront pool and all the amenities. The sales agent said that a lot of executive men resided there. Aries was in a hurry that day but she took a brochure home with her.

A few days later, she leased an apartment there, on a month to month basis, until she could decide whether or not she wanted to buy. Ralph and Katie moved back into the big farmhouse. Katie felt like a real queen. Aries hoped they'd weed the garden and take care of the tomatoes. Maybe she would move back there someday if she ever found a proper man. For now, she'd make a fresh new start away from the unhappy memories she had there with Stuart.

Aries moved into her new apartment. It was definitely in a singles complex, beautiful and strategically located near her office. With only three days left before the convention she was at home preparing for the trip, one evening. Fixing a scotch and water, she turned on her favorite country music station and headed for the the the ironing board in the bedroom.

The bed was still unmade showing signs of last night's activity. It had really been nice of Sam to stop in. He was much too young for her but in her present state she wasn't about to turn all that excess energy down. Soon she would find a steady fucking mate but being devoid of one presently, she appreciated everything Sam had to give her. He was passionate and a wild one! He was an Aries and Aries doesn't have the sign of the Ram for nothing.

The ringing of the telephone interrupted her thought. Jamie was calling to find out how she'd been and to tell her that she and her girl-friend might come over that weekend for a short visit.

"Come on, I'd love to have you. Come on but we might end up in Indian Rock Beach."

Aries knew damned well if Jamie came she would end up in Indian Rock Beach. That's where she was going on Saturday morning and if Jamie came to Tampa that's where she was going, too. This wouldn't phase her though, for travel was her middle name.

"What's going on in Indian Rock Beach?" Jamie inquired half chuckling.

"Oh, they're having a real estate convention there. We'll have a ball!"

"Maybe they won't want Sadie and I there," she interjected.

" Nonsense, wherever I go, you are welcome. It's free and you can be my guests."

On Friday afternoon Jamie arrived with her girlfriend and enough luggage to stay a month. Jamie always traveled like that and after she reached her destination, she would swear she had nothing fit to wear.

Aries hadn't been around Sadie long until she knew that this woman's mouth was apt to drive her crazy. She didn't see how Jamie could stand going anywhere with her.

The next day the three took off for Indian Rock Beach.

It took Sadie two hours to get dressed for dinner that night so Aries and Jamie went ahead of her and chatted in the lounge while they waited. There weren't many convention goers there because most of the group would be arriving by bus, the next day.

At the table in the lounge, after dinner, Aries realized she was traveling in the wrong company to pick up a man. Her sister was older and the guys thought that she was with her Mother.

The next day the action started. The convention was in full force. After the luncheon they went to another boring meeting. Aries wanted to leave but she didn't dare because her boss was there giving her the eye every once in awhile.

Craig approached her during break suggesting that they sneak away from the meeting and hit a few tennis balls to warm up for the tournament. What Craig really wanted was to find out was what her game was like in advance.

"I'd love to but Sandra will kill us."

"Aw, come on, she'll never miss us."

"She'll miss me," retorted Aries. "She looks my way every few minutes just checking to make sure that I'm still there."

"Don't worry about it, she's probably as bored with the program as the rest of us are."

Aries couldn't turn Craig's invitation down. She'd much rather be on the court than in that meeting.

"Who in the hell planned this afternoons activities anyway?" She asked.

"Who knows. Let's get out of here while the breaks still going on. I'll met you on the court."

As they were preparing to walk away, Warner Works, the corporate head of Marvin Prance & Company came up. He had this suspicious looking grim on this face. Aries figured that he had overheard their conversation about playing hookey.

"Going to play tennis?" Warner asked.

"Shit, she was caught. He must have heard them talking.

"Well," stammered Aries, "why do you ask?"

"I thought, if you were I'd come out and watch you." He smiled to

447

her surprise.

"Oh, as a matter of fact Craig and I are planning to go out and hit a few balls. We're coming back to the meeting though. We've already heard what they're talking about and we thought we could miss some of it."

"You'd better get out there before Sandra sees you," he cautioned. "See you on the court!"

Aries didn't know whether or not she wanted the big boss out there watching her play. He might make her nervous and she was already getting worried about how well Craig played.

When she arrived Craig was on the court waiting for her. They commenced hitting and pretty soon, Warner came out bringing another company big wheel with him. They stood talking on the sidelines as they watched them.

Craig played well. There was nothing she could do to keep him from returning the ball. Too bad she had opened her big mouth at the office about winning the tournament.

After hitting awhile they played a set of singles and frankly, Craig beat her socks off. She was embarrassed at her performance on the court. Her game was really off. Tomorrow was another day and there was nothing that made her play better the next time than losing the time before. Craig thought he had his victory against her in the bag and she was sure he would tell Vic that he had beaten her.

On the way off the court, Aries asked a fellow who was hitting well if he would hit with her at six o'clock the next morning.

"I need to warm up for the tournament tomorrow," she said.

Aries thought he was probably kidding when he said, "Yes."

Warner caught up with her on her way back in the hotel and asked what she was doing for dinner that night? She told him that her sister and her friend were with her but they hadn't made any plans.

"Well, I was wondering if you'd tell your sister you've got plans and have dinner with me?"

Aries looked at the gold wedding band on his finger. She didn't have to look because she'd seen his wife come in the office to visit him once.

"You're married."

"I'm not married, tonight," he replied in a sexy voice.

"Who else is going?"

"I don't know yet but your boss and her husband will probably be in the group."

Gracious, what would the boss think of her boss asking her to be his guest at dinner? Aries thought. That damned company must finally be gaining some respect for her caliber of work. It was about time they recognized that she wasn't a peon. Of course, she would hobnob with the big shots that evening. She thanked him for the invitation and they made plans to meet in the hotel lobby at seven.

Racing back to her room she found Jamie and Sadie there, resting.

"Sorry to disturb you. I've got to hurry up and change clothes and get back to that darn meeting."

Putting on the same clothes she'd taken off, Aries was out of the room and heading down the lobby to the meeting room. Arriving she opened the wide brown doors, carefully, trying not to disturb the speaker nor to draw attraction to her entry. Taking a seat she directed her attention to the skit that was being conducted on the podium.

As she watched the performers she wiped perspiration from her dripping brow. She had really worked up a sweat on the court in that hot sun. Everybody else was sitting there looking crisp and cool in the air conditioning. Aries's hair was all wet. She hoped Sandra didn't look at her now.

The meeting was over at five and the group disbanded and scattered in different directions. Aries went back to the room to see what her guests were doing and to start selecting her outfit for dinner. The girls were there, cooling it.

"Why aren't you out on the beach getting some sun?" Aries asked.

"It's too hot out there for me," Sadie replied and Jamie's feet were hurting from dancing, last night.

"Would you believe that I've been invited out by the corporate head of Marvin Prance & Company for dinner tonight?" Aries blared out excitedly.

"You beat all," replied Jamie chuckling. "You might know she'd go for the top."

"Actually, I'm honored to have been invited. I'll be hobnobbing with management and all the big wigs. I don't know why they invited me unless they have me under consideration for a promotion. Warner Works asked me to be his guest and I accepted. Maybe at dinner I'll find out what's going on in that company."

"Well, behave yourself and please, don't tell them how to run the company," cautioned Jamie. She knew Aries was good at doing that.

She met Warner in the lobby, as planned, and shortly thereafter they were joined by Sandra and her husband, Clint.

"We'll be riding with them," Warner told her.

This surprised Aries because Sandra had acted so high and mighty in the office. It could be that Sandra had invited Warner to ride in her car not knowing that she was his dinner companion. This promised to be an interesting evening.

The attendant brought Clint's car and they were off. Driving about ten miles out of the city, they ended up at an upscale restaurant where they had reservations.

The Marvin Prance party was served in a private room upstairs. The decor was impressive. The food as well as the service was superb. The evening was filled with laughter interspersed with business talk and compliments. Their were twelve people in the party, some of them were managers of other branches of the company.

Dick, a red haired man with flashing blue eyes sat across the table from Aries. She knew instantly that he must belong to Carol French, the head secretary in the corporate office. Aries had met her before and she was a well-bred, likeable person. Dicks eyes fell upon Aries and he didn't take them off of her all night. He kept talking to her and completely ignoring his wife. Warner couldn't get a word in edgewise. Embarrassed at the attention he was giving her in front of everybody, she tried to avoid him.

After dinner the party disbanded and Clint drove them back to the hotel. Aries noticed at dinner that Sandra seemed to have a fancy for Warner Works, herself. Right in front of her husband, she kept talking to him, rubbing up next to him and touching him. Her approaches to Warner were obvious and in poor taste considering the position she held with the company. Maybe that's how she got that job in the first place.

Back at the hotel, Warner told Aries he had to spend a few minutes talking to Mark Thomas, a branch manager. Mark was in the lobby waiting for him.

"I'll come to your room in twenty minutes," he said.

"Come to my room! You can't! My sister's there with her friend. There are three of us in the room and we're really crowded with all their clothes and stuff."

"No problem," replied Warner smiling. "I'll just tap on your door and we'll take a bottle of wine and go out on the beach. Put your shorts on."

"Fine. I'll see you in a bit."

Jamie and Sadie were asleep when she came in. Aries turned the light on in the bathroom trying to change her clothes without waking them. They must not have scored that night or they'd still be upstairs dancing. Both were older and widows and as much as they liked the company of gentlemen, sometimes they had to settle for just keeping themselves amused. This never dampened Jamie's ambition of finding a decent man to keep her company in her old age. She'd told Aries about a couple of fellows that she'd met.

"I could have married either of them but they insisted on taking me to bed and I just couldn't bring myself to do it," Jamie said.

Aries laughed. "Why not? You might have liked it."

Soon Warner was tapping on the door. Aries made her escape, luckily without arousing the gals.

Warner had changed clothes, too. He had on plaid shorts and he was barefooted. The wine was wrapped in a blanket that he had swiped from his closet.

"It's a good thing you thought of the blanket or else we'd get sand all over us," Aries remarked.

She loved sitting on the beach in the sand and tonight was ideal for it. The moon was full and there were gentle breezes blowing. Finding a spot out among the rocks away from the crowd, they spread the blanket and took their positions.

Warner had thought of everything, including a corkscrew and two plastic cups. They were going to have a private party of their own. Now they could get better acquainted. There was little opportunity for that at dinner with all those people there, especially Dick French who had monopolized her attention. By the time the evening ended, Aries had decided he was an obnoxious bastard and she didn't see how Carol could stand living with him.

Warner and Aries chatted about the guests at dinner and company policy. Soon the small talk was over and Warner took up a more personal topic. "You know," he said, "I've had my eyes on you ever since you came to work with our company."

Well, no, she didn't know that. Warner was one of the first persons she'd met when she came to work there but she never envisioned he had eyes for her.

Warner told Aries that she was very appealing. "You exude sex," he said.

My, my, mused Aries. Warner Works has a yen for me. This was a surprise. He had done a superior job of hiding this in the office. It was a good thing because his domineering wife would have killed him if she had known.

Tonight, they were on the beach alone. Warner moved closer and put his arm around her. He asked if he could kiss her. Aries felt she should reject his advances because he was the corporate head of the company but his touch felt good and she responded.

His kiss was warm and gentle, at first, then it was sexy and very passionate. Warner began making moaning sounds and Aries knew where all of this was leading them. It wasn't long until they were declothed and embraced in the nude in each others arms. The wine and the moonlight was getting the best of them and they were ready to give each other the best that they had to give. Yes, Warner was very married at home but at this moment, he belonged to Aries.

With passion between them rising, sex between them was inevitable. She placed her hand on his pulsating erected cock. It was perfect and beautiful, such a big one for such a thin man. Mounting her, Warner's flesh was warm against her yearning body. She wanted him. She didn't care anymore who he was at the office. His body blended so perfectly with hers.

Aries pushed him away briefly, long enough to place her soft lips upon the head of his penis. Warner was gleeful. She licked its velvety head with her warm moist tongue, then took it deep inside of her mouth. Warner was so excited! He was about to cum without fucking her. Aries released her lips and he rolled her over, mounted her and inserting his throbbing penis into her vagina. Slowly but surely he penetrated her deeper and deeper. Making love to him was wonderful.

The first time was short and so sweet but Warner wasn't about to let go of her yet. A few minutes later, they were at it again. He had her ass high in the air, fucking the hell out of her. Aries squealed in delight. She absolutely adored fucking him. They made love, intermittently, until they could see the sun coming up. Then, they hurried to get off the beach before the early risers came and discovered them. All they needed was to be caught by some of the Marvin Prance folks. Warner walked her to her room. Kissing her gently, he told her that he would see her at the tournament. It was six o'clock a.m.

Aries had forgotten that this was her big day. She had made love all night and she was so sleepy she could hardly see straight. She was supposed to be on the court, right then, warming up. She wondered what her performance would be like now.

Entering the room, she found Sadie awake and in the bathroom. I'm caught this time, she told herself. Her bed was still made and Sadie would know she hadn't slept there. Of course, it was none of Sadie's business. She must have been young once.

Sadie greeted her and commented that she must have been at a real good party to be getting in so early in the morning.

"It was. We sat up and talked, all night."

"You must be exhausted."

"I am. I am," said Aries as she collapsed upon the bed. "Wake me up at seven-thirty, please, I have to be dressed and on the court for the tournament at eight."

"My, God," Sadie replied.

Aries was soon dead to the world.

At seven- thirty, Sadie woke her up.

"It's time to go. Get up and get dressed and get out there."

Bouncing out of bed, she hit the shower hoping it would wake her up. Jamie was arousing and Aries asked her to find the eye drops. Sadie was rummaging through her suitcase trying to decide what to wear that day. Aries didn't know how she was going to make it through the tournament but she had to try. She couldn't make a fool of herself out there, particularly, in front of Warner. He would be one of her biggest supporters. After all, she had been very nice to him.

Outside, Aries looked around to see if Warner was there. She knew that as corporate head he would be expected to show. Looking up, she saw him watching from the balcony outside of his room. She was relieved. She'd play better if he wasn't courtside.

The players arrived and minutes later, the match was in full swing. Aries couldn't think of any time she had been in worse condition on the court. She hated losing so she'd have to drum up the energy, somewhere, to take her opponent.

Craig and Vic were there, all smiles, just waiting to take the trophy and start kidding her. She couldn't let this happen. She had announced at the office that she would win the tournament and in keeping her promise she played her heart out.

Craig was in shock when he saw her score. Aries was winning the match with little effort. She couldn't believe she was playing so well. Maybe the Lord was swinging her racquet. She won! The trophy for the Meadowbrook Central Conference was hers. The crowd gathered for congratulations and celebration. Aries had done it and she was proud.

Tournament over, she could spend some time entertaining her guests. She would invite them to lunch and tonight, she hoped, would be a quiet one for she sorely needed to get some rest. My, but she had had such a wonderful time.

Arriving back in Orlando, Aries found a note posted on the front door of her apartment. Noel was in town.

"Damnit it!" Aries said to Jamie. Noel Johnson is up here from Fort Lauderdale.

"Who's he?"

"He's a friend of mine that I don't like too well. I certainly don't feel like entertaining him today. I told him to call me before coming," she complained.

"Well, be nice to him. He's driven all the way up here. The least you could do is be nice."

"I don't have to be anything to him. I'll introduce him to you and you be nice to him. You'll like him, Jamie. He looks a lot like Claude." Claude was Jamie's deceased husband and she heard that her ears perked up.

"I'm too old for him. If he likes you he won't be interested in me."

"He might, I've told him he should get acquainted with my sister."

Minutes later, Noel knocked on the door. Aries was exhausted from her trip and he was unwelcome this particular day. Barging in on somebody on a Sunday afternoon, uninvited, was entirely improper and Aries quickly let him know it. Furthermore, she instructed the guard not to let anymore guests in without calling her, first. Security at that complex was a joke. The barrier at the gate didn't work. Anybody could lift it and enter. The guards were slack, too, in performing their duties.

After telling Noel how she felt about him coming to visit without being invited, she reluctantly let him in. Her company was still there so one more for dinner wouldn't matter.

After dinner, Noel didn't want to leave. On the pretense of being too tired to drive, he begged Aries to let him stay overnight.

"I've only got one bed and my sister and her friend are sleeping there. As it is, I will be sleeping on the couch. We don't have any extra room."

"I can sleep anywhere."

Finally, Aries agreed to let him sleep in the den on the other sofa. That wasn't what he had in mind. He tried to convince her to take him on the living room couch with her. Having had her fill of great sex, she had no need whatsoever of his services. That horny little bastard would have to find some other woman to shove his eager cock into because it certainly wouldn't be her. His begging her to make love to him ruined her whole night's rest. The next morning, wearing the face of loser, Noel retreated. Aries prayed she wouldn't see him again for a long time.

Warner and Aries had really hit it off, sexually. Now that they were home they would have a problem seeing each other. Nights would probably be almost impossible unless his wife went to a meeting and daytime would be hectic with him being in charge of the corporate office. She didn't know when or where it would happen but she intended to make love to him more and more!

At the office Warner assumed that aloof boss attitude but when they were alone behind closed doors, they reminisced over the special evening they'd had and they talked about repeating it.

"We'll find a time, I want to make love to you," he told her in a sultry sexy voice.

Aries hadn't realized it before the convention but Warner Works really turned her on. Where on earth had he been hiding while Stuart Arson was still in town? If she had gotten friendlier with him sooner she wouldn't have spent all those months quilting while Stuart was reading books.

Aries devoted her days to real estate. As time went on it became obvious that she would probably have to wait for another out of town convention to have Warner again. His wife watched him like a hawk and she wasn't about to give him any rope. Aries couldn't blame her. If she had a husband so nice and so well endowed she'd stay close to him, too.

Aries chastised herself for always falling for married men. She had John Roberts portrait hanging on her bedroom wall, David Saunder's blue shirt was hanging in her closet and now, she had a yen for Warner Works. All she had was memories of her loves, memorable moments she'd had with someone else's husband.

She had never been fortunate enough to marry someone she truly loved. Her true loves were already married when she had found them. Aries didn't doubt that they loved her but she was always too late. She remembered the poem she had written to John once. It went this way. "I wish that I had known you when I was little. Then I would have had longer to love you. But the world was so big, it took me a long, long time to find you. And when I did so many spaces in your heart were already filled." This was so sad but so true. All of the men who Aries had loved deeply were already taken.

During the day she concentrated on her work and at night, she stayed at home and tried to do some serious writing. Being unable to find a man she was seriously interested in, Aries was preparing to seclude herself and accomplish something constructive as an author.

All of her intentions were commendable but her natural desire for sex kept diverting her mind from her work. It was lonesome alone in that apartment but she didn't want to interrupt Ralph and Katie's life by visiting them too often.

In need of companionship, she started visiting Lou and Ron. Yakking with them was better sometimes, than being alone.

One evening when she was there she told Ron she needed a new boyfriend. "Find me a good cowboy," she told him jokingly. Ron laughed and told her he would do what he could. A few days later, Lou called and invited her to dinner on Saturday evening.

"Ron's found someone for you." They had fixed her up with a blind date. Aries was leery of meeting someone this way.

"I'm not sure, Lou. What's he like? What if I don't like him?"

"Don't worry about it. I've met him and he's a nice fellow but if you don't like him you don't have to go out with him. Just come on out here for dinner and look him over. If you don't think you like him, after dinner, you can tell him you have to go home."

"Well, okay."

On Saturday night Aries showed up at Lou's house. She was late as usual but at least, she showed. It had taken a lot of courage for her to do that.

Steve Marshall, her blind date, was sitting at the table in the dining room talking to them when she arrived. After the introductions Aries took her seat at the table with them.

Steve was good looking and surprisingly, witty. He had dark, curly brown hair and a million dollars worth of talking, sexy blue eyes. They reminded her of Bob Benton's. She found it hard to resist his personality. Long before dinner was served, the two had established an eye contact that wouldn't stop. They were eager to get out of there and be alone.

Shortly after dinner they said farewell to Lou and Ron. Outside, they made plans for Steve to follow her to her apartment. Aries knew that sex between them was inevitable. Here I go again, she thought.

Making love to Steve wasn't like it had been with Warner but he wasn't available. This guy was single and available, too. In Warner's absence he made a hell of a good substitute. He was active, warm and alive in the sack.

Everybody had neglected to tell her how old he was, probably on purpose because she could sense that he was a lot younger than she was. In bed with him she felt like, "Hello, Mrs. Robinson."

Meeting Steve was timely though she knew their relationship could never become serious. He was just someone warm to cling to and he did a very good job of satisfying her sexual needs.

Steve was wild about Aries. He was the identical age of her oldest son, Gregory, but she learned that where sex is concerned age doesn't really matter.

Out of bed, however, it was another issue. Steve was a promising young engineer with a brilliant future ahead of him. Aries already had made her niche in life. She soon realized her lover was beneath her, both financially and intellectually. Flat on his back he was a comfort and a delight but out of bed she needed something more in a man. Realizing these facts and being aware of the extreme difference in their ages, Aries, mentally, refused to become serious about him.

Two months went by and Steve was falling in love with her. He wanted to move into her apartment but she turned him down. He was crushed when she declined his proposal but fate took over. He was transferred to Virginia without much notice. He cried when he gave Aries the news. She would miss him for awhile but his leaving was better for both of them. After he left he called often. Aries got his messages but she deliberately didn't return his calls. It was better that she fade away in Steve Marshall's memory.

In a way she breathed easier after Steve's transfer. She was able to concentrate on her work better knowing she didn't have someone waiting for her everyday.

The next few weeks were busy ones. She had purchased a condo in the complex where she was living and they were delivering it to her undecorated from the concrete floors up. She had to select carpet, tile, wallpaper and everything from scratch. Her work was cut out for her.

The day after the closing, she contracted a tile man to install grey brick flooring throughout. The wall papering she would do herself, on Saturdays and evenings after work. She selected a blue and white checked design for the kitchen. After hanging it, she didn't like it so she ripped it down and replaced it with a less disturbing pattern. Mia came over to inspect the apartment one day and she heartily approved of the wall paper selection. Too bad she couldn't have done it right, the first time.

Decorating the condo was a bigger job than she thought it would be but by the end of September, it was almost finished.

Aries was sitting at home one evening when Lou called.

"It's been a long time since we've seen you," Lou said. "In fact, I don't believe we've been together since Steve left. What have you been up to, Aries?"

"I've been busy trying to sell real estate and trying to get this damned wall papering done at night. You ought to see this place. It looks really nice. Why don't you and Ron come over here to see me, sometimes?"

"We will. I'm calling to invite you to join us at a country western party, Friday evening."

"That sounds good, I haven't been out in ages."

"Well, get your boots on and we'll see you up at Stacy's at eight-thirty."

"I'll be there. Thanks, Lou."

Aries was bored to death at the party. She didn't know anybody there except Lou and Ron and nobody she met there appealed to her. The band was playing loudly and couples began kicking and stomping on the dance floor to country music. Pretty soon, a cowboy from across the way headed in her direction. Lou and Ron had gone on the floor to dance. He came to her table and extending his hand said, " Come on, let's get out there and show them how to do it."

In an instant Aries was out there dancing with a partner who was holding her tighter than she thought he should. The band was playing a medley so she couldn't politely excuse herself until the music stopped. When the music stopped she excused herself and scurried back to her seat. She'd had enough of dancing with that guy. Unfortunately, he hadn't read her mind because when the band started up again, he was back.

"One more time," he said with a smile on his face.

"Go ahead, Aries," prompted Lou.

"Okay, just one more."

Aries was back on the floor with that tight hugging partner.

When the dance was over she refused the next one. She wanted to to home so she excused herself telling Lou and Ron that she had developed a bad headache. As she was leaving she thanked Lou for the invite and told her she'd call her next week.

Part Twenty-One

Nearing her complex, Aries decided to stop off at Harry Finn's for a nightcap before calling it an evening. Parking her car in the front, she walked in through main entrance and into the lounge. There she was greeted by a dark, handsome fellow who extended his hand and said, "How can I help you?"

Aries had just arrived and all the help she needed was to find a seat in that crowded place.

"I just got here and I'm looking for a seat."

"Here, take my seat," the dark-haired stranger offered.

Realizing there were no empty seats and not wanting to offend him, Aries thanked him and sat down in his seat.

"My name is Jim Winters. What's yours?"

"I'm Aries Able."

"May I buy you a drink? What will you have?"

"I'll have a scotch and water, thank you."

The music started and Jim asked her to dance. He was pleasant, laughing and he seemed like a happy person. On the dance floor he held her close like the cowboy had held her but this time, the feeling was different. Aries felt good in his arms.

As they danced they were interrupted by the man who was dancing next to them. It was Bill Everhard. She hadn't seen him since the day she had politely but firmly, threw his ass out of her truck. Bill was laughing at the outfit she had on. His partner, a blonde hussy, was dressed in some cheap slinky dress. Aries had on cowgirl boots and a plaid shirt with navy blue knee pants.

"What kind of crazy outfit have you got on?" Bill inquired.

"What's wrong with it?"

"You don't wear cowboy boots with silk stockings."

Jim was ignoring the whole conversation and enjoying his dancing. Aries apologized for the interruption telling him that he was an acquaintance of hers.

Back at the bar, he asked where she'd been in that cowgirl outfit.

"I've been to a country western party and some cowboy kept asking me to dance so I left. I know I'm not dressed right for this place but my stopping here was an accident."

"Where are you headed?"

"I'm on my way home and I just stopped by for a drink."

"Lucky for me! If you hadn't stopped here, I probably would never have met you."

As Aries conversed with Jim she could see Bill eyeing her from his table. She wouldn't have minded getting an update on his life but Jim was close by her side and now was not the time.

When she decided to go home Jim asked her where she lived.

"Oh, I live at Middletown Club. It's not far from here."

"Do you mind if I come with you for awhile? I live near there."

Aries had enjoyed his company. He seemed like an intelligent, interesting man.

"Sure, why not? Just follow me."

Outside, Jim cranked up his old white Mercedes and followed her home.

Once inside her condo, she mixed him a drink and they sat down on the sofa to continue the conversation they had started at Harry Finn's place. Aries told him that aside from real estate she was a writer. Jim appeared interested and he asked to see some of her work. She pointed to the published books of poetry she had written. While he was looking at the books, she went into the den and pulled out a manuscripts about real estate that she was working on at the time.

"I've got lots of unfinished manuscripts. I keep starting things and I never get finished." she revealed.

He started reading the first chapter. "This is very good, you should publish it," he declared.

"I intend to but it isn't finished yet."

"Well, what's keeping you?"

"Time and money."

"Procrastinating, that's what you've been doing."

It was getting very late. Aries's stomach was growling with hunger so she changed the subject. "Would you like something to eat?"

"Sure, I could stand a bite." What do you have?"

Following her into the kitchen he opened her refrigerator door. "You don't have any food in here. Are you sure you live here?"

"Yes, I live here but I don't do much cooking at home. I usually eat out. Would you like some scrambled eggs?"

"No, I'll just have a glass of milk."

After pouring him a glass of milk Aries devoured several peanut butter crackers and a glass of orange juice. It was two o'clock in the morning and she very was tired and ready for sleep.

Jim complained that he was too drunk to drive home and he asked if she would mind him sleeping on her sofa. She really didn't know him that well but she didn't want to be responsible for him having an accident on the way home, either.

Going into her bedroom closet, she reached for one of her country quilts and took it out into the living room. Jim was flaked out on the sofa so she spread the quilt over him, turned the lights down and went to bed.

Aries felt a little uneasy knowing there was a strange man sleeping in the next room on the sofa. Maybe she shouldn't have let him stay. It was gentlemanly of him, though, not to try to put the make on her the first time they'd met.

Awakening before dawn, she went into the living room. Jim was sleeping. Looking at him all curled up in an uncomfortable position on the sofa, Aries felt badly. Nudging his shoulder, she told him to come on and get in her bed. "You can sleep in my bed. You'll be more comfortable there. You can sleep in my bed with me but you must promise not to touch me." Promising to obey the rules, she led him into the bedroom and they went back to sleep.

When Aries awoke Jim was lying beside her, warm and appealing.

She glanced at the portrait of John Roberts that hung on the wall over her dresser. Then, she looked at Jim. They bore a strange resemblance. Was John Roberts coming back to her in another body? Aries could feel his body heat as she snuggled closer to him. He lay there keeping his promise not to touch her. She was getting turned on just with her toe touching his foot. She was beginning to desire him. Why had she warned him not to touch her?

Jim stood her sly advances as long as he could and then he turned over placing his nude body next to hers wrapping her in his arms. He kissed her with ardor and she responded. Moments later, they were making love. When he penetrated her Aries felt as she had never felt before. Jim Winters was certainly no stranger to her. She sensed that he was someone she'd been very much in love with before, perhaps in another life. She felt like they had belonged to each other and had been separated through no fault of their own. Now finally, they had been reunited.

Aries had found the man she loved, not for the first time but she had found the man she'd always loved and the man who had always loved her. It was the strangest feeling. When he made love to her it didn't seem like it was their first experience, they'd made love many times before, somewhere. Jim felt the same way she did. It was a happy reunion of "lover come back." Aries was sure that God had sent him to her, at last. That morning, when he left she knew she would miss him until he returned. She couldn't put her finger on her feelings but there was "something special" between them.

Jim promised to call and Aries would wait for that moment. After their meeting Aries never went out with anyone else. She had no desire for another man. All she cared about was when she was going to see her "one of magic," again.

Although he lived nearby, he never invited her to come to his house. They always met at her condo. Some nights, he told her he'd be out of town and wouldn't be able to see her. Aries asked him if he was single and he had answered, yes. Why then all this vanishing, periodically? Was he hiding a wife or he was a traveling salesman? Aries told him what she imagined and he just laughed.

"No, I don't have any wife. I used to have one but I've been divorced for twelve years."

"Twelve years," she exclaimed. "Why on earth have you stayed single for so long?"

"I never found anybody that I wanted to marry."

Perhaps not but in her mind twelve years was a long time for a man to be without a wife.

When she'd first met Jim, he said he was foot loose and fancy free, that nobody told him what to do. He came and went as he wanted. He boasted of his independence in his single state. He put Aries on the alert that he was tied down to no woman and that included her.

"That's fine with me. I just got free myself and I haven't had a chance yet to see what's in this town. She explained that she had lived with her husband until May of that year.

"You're still married?"

"What difference does it make? He's gone far away and he'll never be back. He's not bothering me, now, so why should I rush for a divorce? He's a lawyer, he's perfectly capable of divorcing us."

Her explanation didn't seem to satisfy him. He said that he was was uncomfortable dating her when she was still married.

"Do you see any husband around here?" Aries asked him chuckling?

"No, but I know you've still got one."

"Not I. I have divorced him in my mind and in my heart. All that's left to do is to get that piece of paper from the Judge."

"Well, what's holding you?"

"Nothing, I just figured that sooner or later he'd get the divorce himself and it would save me the time and the trouble. I have no plans to marry anyone so why do I need to be divorced?"

The conversation ended for the moment but that wasn't the end of the subject. Several weeks passed with them still dating but Jim was still clinging to his independence. He averaged seeing her about four nights a week but rarely on Friday. That was his night on the town.

On Friday mornings when he left he would say that he'd call. When? Friday night, Saturday morning, Sunday or when? Aries was quite fond of him but she wasn't going to sit home evenings and wait for his call. She told him just that. Jim wanted to continue seeing her.

"Well, just tell me which nights you want to see me. Then, the rest of my nights I'll be free to do what I please." She had put him on the spot asking him to pick his nights. He picked Monday, Wednesday and maybe Friday.

"No problem," replied Aries, "just as long as I know by five o'clock in the afternoon. Otherwise, I'll go ahead with plans of my own."

This arrangement lasted for about a week. Jim had apparently tried to call her a few times on nights that weren't his and sometimes, on Friday he'd called after five and got no answer. All of this freedom had been his idea but now he was reconsidering. Aries was playing his own game and playing it well. Some nights she went out with a girl-friend, deliberately, so she wouldn't be there when he called. Those nights out without him she was miserable but she wouldn't let him know. She wasn't interested in meeting other men. Missing Jim, she counted the hours until she would see him again.

Having second thoughts about his independence, soon Jim was seeing her on a constant basis. He was getting a major hold on her affections. Becoming romantically involved hadn't been as part of her plans. Her marriage to Stuart had been such a disaster that she had welcomed being alone and unattached. She had planned to become a recluse and write her books before she stumbled upon Jim Winters that fateful evening..

Now suddenly, Aries heart was telling her something different. They had become constant companions and their relationship was a well rounded one. Making love with him was wonderful but out of bed it was good, too. There was something dynamic and exciting about him. Aries refused to admit to the fact that she had fallen in love. It's too soon, she kept telling herself.

Jim had an uncanny way of reading her mind. Everything she thought he responded to even before she could voice what she was thinking. It was unreal. For instance, if she wished they could have dinner at Mario's, he would say, "Hey, how would you like to have dinner at Mario's?" How did he know she wanted to go there that evening? If she craved a banana and never mentioned it, Jim would bring home bananas. He could pick up her thoughts no matter what they were.

Although, it was nice to get her needs met without even asking, Jim's ability to read her mind was somewhat disturbing. This guy knows everything I think, she told herself. What if I think something that I don't want him to know? My brain is transparent to him. He sees everything that goes on in my head. That had never happened to her before. She asked him how he could always tell what she was thinking without her telling him. He smiled and he said he could read her "like a book."

Very well, thought Aries. I can't stop him from reading me like a book, but I can write the book that he reads!

One Sunday afternoon after a beautiful session of love making they were lying peacefully in bed when Jim initiated a conversation..

"I love you, Aries. I love you and I want to marry you. Will you marry me?"

Marriage! thought Aries. After Stuart that word scares me to death. She was quiet for a minute and then, she asked the question. "Why do we have to get married? Don't you like it this way? Don't you have fun with me now?"

"Yes, I have fun with you but I am not going to keep seeing you like this. Either you will get your divorce and marry me or I am going to start dating someone else." He spoke in a serious tone of voice. Apparently he had been giving the matter a lot of thought.

"I can't believe you would give up what we have together," she replied.

"I don't want to but I'm not going to keep on just dating you."

"Why not?"

"There's no future in it. Think it over and make up your mind what you want to do."

A few days passed. Aries hoped Jim would forget the conversation they had but no such luck. He wanted an answer and he wanted it, soon.

"What's the hurry?"

"We're wasting time. I will give you until Christmas to give me your answer and that's it," he said emphatically.

His pressing her for an answer made Aries a nervous wreck. She didn't want to spend a day or night without him but the marriage was a frightening undertaking after her marital experiences of the last four years. What if he made her miserable after she married him? Often men change after they get married. She wanted to be his lover always and husbands have a habit of having turning lovers into plain wives. Aries didn't want this to happen to them.

It was mid December and she was wrestling, mentally, with herself because Jim expected her answer by Christmas. If she didn't marry him she would never see him again. She would be unhappy with that alternative. If she did marry him would they be happy? That would be a chance she would have to take. And what about the children, hers and his? Between the two of them they had ten, all about the same ages. How would his children accept their father taking a wife after all these years? What would hers think about her marrying a man she'd known for only a few months? Aries had a decision to make and only ten days remained before D-day.

On December 18, she gave him her answer. "Yes, I love you and I will marry you. I don't know when though, I still have to go to back to Fort Lauderdale and get my divorce," she added.

"Do what you have to do but get it done" he replied.

"I promise to get a hearing date before Christmas. The divorce is already filed. All I have to do is to walk in on the Motion Calender."

Jim said he didn't know what any of that meant so he would leave it up to her.

On December 24, Aries went to court for a final dissolution of marriage. "Stuart Arson had vanished and she planned to be married again, very shortly," she told the Judge. Under these circumstances the Judge saw no reason to deny her request. The divorce was granted. and she was legally free.

Elated upon hearing the news, Jim wanted to set the wedding date.

"Not yet! Christmas is here and we'll be busy during the holidays. Let's wait until after the first of the year," Aries suggested.

The New Year rang in and along with the New Year came plans for a February wedding. Aries couldn't decide on a date so Jim, being the planner that he was, told her he would set the date. That evening he came home and announced that they would be married on February

2nd, Ground Hogs Day. That date was fine!

Aries loved Jim but still, she was somewhat apprehensive. She felt like she was being led to the slaughter. Should she really do it? Should she tie the knot again? The decision was made and despite her doubts and fears, there was no turning back.

They were married in the church and this time, Aries hoped it would be "happy ever after."

Since the marriage they have made a home of their own filled with understanding, devotion and love. As Aries looks back on it how could she ever have been afraid of marrying Jim? He was everything she had ever wanted in a man, a combination of John Roberts and David Saunders and yet, there was that special part of him that was "strictly his own." John Roberts portrait has been put away for Aries has no need for memories, anymore. She has married a man she truly loves and who truly loves her. He's a Libra and perfect for her, just like the astrology books say.

At last, the chapters in "Your Husband, My Lover" have come to an end and "happy ever after" now seems like a reality. She saw Margie recently and she spoke fondly of Jim as "My Husband, My Lover." As she talked her fawn-like brown eyes softened and she was smiling.

The End

Prologue

** After her marriage Aries wrote this letter to John Roberts:

Dear John, You know I have been wildly in love with you. I know you wonder where I am and what I'm doing these days. My love, I have met someone soft and beautiful, like you. Of course, no one could ever take your place but life offers us many substitutes for things we want but cannot have. I am as happy as I can be, away from you. With love, A

** Of David Saunders she wrote: "Sing to me, O'sing to me my lost and wandering love. Sing to me as I sing to you and, together, our song shall become a sad duet."

** Early in their marriage she wrote the following poem about Jim: "There are loves and loves and loves but my love is better. He senses my every need. He feels my thoughts without them ever being spoken. He knows what my soul requires. He gives me sunshine and roses in the warmth of his smile. He lets me breathe and he inhales my breathe. My love loves me. He sends me love in the dawn and love in the night, and morning glories, violets and sunflower seeds."

Footnote: Aries still stays in touch with John Roberts. The passion between them is still there. Nothing between them has changed. She has spoken with David Saunders but has never seen him again. Still, she feels a sadness at their parting. Their relationship lacks a closure. Stuart is now deceased. Aries was right about men changing after marriage. After fifteen years of marriage, Jim's her husband, not her lover. It's a sad thing when all that passion gets lost. Nothing lasts forever!